Miriam Kettlehak
6521 Ocala Ct
Dayton, OH 454

Straw Man

A Novel

by

David Kettlehake

Revised January, 2014

Cover design by Alex Saskalidis

187designz@gmail.com

Acknowledgements

Few writers work in a vacuum. To that end I'd like to thank all the wonderful people that helped me bring Straw Man to life. First and foremost is Leslie Smith, great friend and patient beta reader. She suffered through many iterations of the prologue and first several chapters while I muddled my way along at the start. Also key were my other beta readers who gave me much encouragement and direction: Heather, Kathy, Steve, and Lisa. Without their help I'm not sure Straw Man would have come to fruition.

I'd also like to thank my family, mainly my wife Lisa, who put up with the endless hours of my relentless typing on the back porch, and my daughter Nikki, who was more than instrumental in the initial uploads of the finished work to both Amazon and Barnes & Noble. And of course I can't forget my editor, Ike Watson, who truly helped clean and tidy the final manuscript.

Lastly, I would like to give a nod to Ohio University's student exchange program. Much of Straw Man's Mexican references and influence come directly from my six month stay in the wonderful city of Xalapa, Veracruz.

Well done, and you all have my gratitude and thanks.

Prologue

Rolland Schmidt was a good man at heart, but even good people make mistakes. Some mistakes are gone and forgotten in an instant, while others stick with you for life - no matter how short that life may be.

The early spring thunderstorm was ferocious and intense, the sky so dark the afternoon could've been mistaken for late dusk. Black, swollen clouds hugged the ground low enough to be snagged by the tallest trees in the forest, their contents spilling out in torrents as if gutted. As a kid Rolland's mom had called storms like these "gully-washers", and while he'd never really understood what she meant he would always nod his blond head and smile sweetly, his dimples clear. Now he got it. This was a damn gully washer for sure.

Soaking wet, terrified, Rolland tore through the woods at a full sprint, his arms outstretched and fingers splayed wide to protect his face and eyes. If a sapling or bush was small enough he ran right over it, anything larger than that he dodged around. He ducked under a low-hanging branch just as two gunshots roared behind him as loud as thunder – *boom! boom!* The first bullet smashed into the trunk of a towering oak on his left and blew off a chunk of raw wood bigger than his fist. The second slug went to the right where he heard it ripping harmlessly through the underbrush.

He pulled up short and stared at the wounded oak tree, his chest heaving, far too much white showing around the blue of his eyes. For Rolland this had just gotten very, very real. On the plus side he was pretty sure the two Mexicans were just shooting blindly, wildly, trying to frighten him into stopping and showing himself. *They need me. Even more they need what I've got*, he told himself. *They can't kill me.* He almost convinced himself it was true.

Then Rolland heard his two pursuers shouting somewhere close behind him, just beyond the tree line and back toward the house. With a muffled curse he took off in the opposite direction, heading deeper into the woods. In seconds he found himself in a clearing where a large sycamore had toppled over a few years before. He readied himself to hurdle the huge rotting trunk.

Boom!

The third bullet smacked into the back of his right thigh with a sound like a sharp handclap. The slug punched completely through his leg, the exit wound resembling an ugly, bloody mushroom. Rolland barked out an agonized cry and landed face-first onto the muddy, leaf-strewn forest floor. Rain pelted his quivering back as thunder rumbled overhead, the deep bass wave of sound shaking his guts like a speeding car on a highway rumble strip.

Son of a bitch! They shot me!

Rolland clutched his mangled thigh with both hands as dark red arterial blood began to well between his fingers. He rolled onto his back and threw an arm across his mouth to stifle the scream that was trying to claw its way into the humid, charged air. Fat drops of rain washed some of the dirt and blood from his face as he hugged himself tightly.

Then Rolland heard them again, but closer this time. *Shit! They're right on top of me!* Much as he desperately wanted to remain there curled in a fetal position he knew he had to move.

Biting back his cries he rolled clumsily onto his left knee. He tried to bring his wounded leg under him but the agony was so fierce he almost blacked out, his vision momentarily going dark at the edges. Odd sounds were pounding and echoing in his head, a *whoosh-whooshing* noise, like when he'd done whippets with his friend Otto at the Party Barn a few months back. He moaned, rocking back and forth on his hands and one knee like a toddler exploring the complex act of crawling for the first time.

"*¿Dónde está?*" he heard from behind him. It was a deep voice, loud and with a pissed-off edge, like its owner was yelling through clenched teeth. Then a second voice, higher pitched although still male, snapped impatiently, "*No sé. No puedo verlo!*"

Rolland translated without thinking. The first, deeper voice: "Where is he?" The reply: "I don't know. I can't see him!"

Desperation thrust him into reluctant action. He gritted his teeth so hard he thought he might shatter a molar, this secondary pain a welcome diversion from the agony coursing through his leg. He hauled himself to his feet using the decaying trunk of the sycamore for support. Once up he needed some time to snatch a few breaths before he could even consider moving. Gingerly he tried to walk but found he could only hobble forward a step or two, his wounded leg dragging behind him like a dead log. Had his pants not already been rain-soaked and filthy he might have noticed the huge bloodstain blossoming and spreading down his jeans like some deathly vine.

He steeled himself and tried again, but this time he reached down and manually lifted his leg, grabbing handfuls of denim and placing his foot forward. A minute of this and he'd made some limited progress and, even better, didn't hear his attackers any longer. *Oh, thank God.* So he'd either put some distance between them, which was unlikely, or they'd gone back to search his house. He was panting heavily now, sweating and gasping for air like he'd been dragging a car through the woods. Rolland knew he had to rest or he was going to collapse on the spot. He leaned heavily against a tree, a nauseous, sickening feeling stealing over him as shock and reality began to settle in.

Oh, shit, what the hell was I thinking?

As he stood there in the pouring rain clinging to a tree, his life coursing down his leg, an icy shroud settled over his soul. Filthy, trembling, and scared to death, he had a sudden urge to reach out and apologize to everyone he had screwed over in his lifetime, to do something, to somehow make amends. But as strong as it was even that urge paled in his need to talk to Marcus. He needed time to explain what he could to his older brother, to say he was sorry and to thank him for taking care of him over the years, for always being there. However, somewhere way in the back of his mind, drifting around the scary, black edges of realization, he was terrified he wouldn't get the chance. Right then he wanted nothing more than to sit down on the soaking wet forest floor, put his head in his hands, and cry.

Marcus, where the hell are you, man? I need you!

Instead he began to move through the woods again, his wounded leg a flesh and bone anchor threatening to tether him in place. He dredged up a childhood memory, something from the seventh or eighth grade, he thought. Marcus had taught him this trick when he was having a tough time running long distances in cross country, back when his mom was still alive and times were good. He'd said, "Just pick an object up ahead – a telephone pole, a mailbox, a parked car – and aim for it. Tell yourself, 'I'll keep running until I get there.' When you reach that goal, pick another one up ahead and run towards that. Before you know it the race is over and you're munching oranges and chugging Gatorade."

Rolland clumsily stumbled and elbowed his way through the thick forest and through the thickening fog in his mind. He picked out a sapling with tiny yellow flowers about twenty feet away, settled on that as his target and then moved out. He blinked once or twice and may have briefly lost consciousness en route, but suddenly, miraculously, he was there.

Hot damn, it worked.

He held on to the smooth wet bark for a minute, his breathing growing heavier and more labored. His fingers tingled like they were asleep and with a nasty start he realized his feet were cold and going numb. Rain pelted his back, big, fat drops that he could feel through his filthy shirt. Lightning illuminated the sky somewhere behind him like a monstrous flashbulb, and thunder rumbled deeply enough to vibrate his stomach again. *God is bowling.* Rolland wondered from what depths he had mined that particular childhood memory. His eyes were still wide with too much white showing but his pupils had contracted to mere pinpricks, little more than tiny black dots. Staring like a befuddled drunk through his dripping bangs he chose a birch tree about fifteen yards away and headed for it.

I never should have gotten messed up with this last business. His heart was heavy and thick in his chest, as solid as a cinder block, but he shoved back a sob because he knew if he started to cry he might never stop. *What the fuck was I thinking? I should've trusted my gut and run like hell, but I didn't. God I'm such a dumb ass.*

Suddenly there was the sound of barking coming from his house, the deep, throaty barks of a large dog that not even the pounding rain could drown out. *Sam!* He stopped and started to turn around but heard a loud *boom!* behind him, and a single short, sharp yelp of pain. His throat clenched and he stumbled, head down. He had to wrap his arms around a large oak to stay upright. A low, guttural moan escaped his lips as he pressed his face up against the wet bark of the tree, oblivious to scratches it left on his cheek. He knew at that moment that his pet and best friend was dead. He never should have left Sam there to guard the doghouse. *What the hell was I thinking?*

He concluded darkly that he wasn't thinking, that he never thought things through, never looked ahead to the potential impact of his decisions. His eyes squeezed shut and silent sobs finally began to wrack his body, heavy, jarring ones that sent jabs of pain shooting through his leg. He remained there unaware of the passing of time, despair hammering at his soul and threatening to cripple him worse than any gunshot could.

And then - *shit!* – the Mexicans were back in the woods. The rain had tapered off and he could hear branches and sticks breaking behind him, the sounds of men more accustomed to concrete and asphalt than trails and trees. Rolland knew with grim finality that there was nothing he could do to help his German shepherd. He mumbled a tearful farewell, "G'bye, Sam, I'm so sorry…" then sobbed again and tried to redouble his pace. If only his damn leg would cooperate! To compound his problems the storm was either ramping back up or his vision was getting darker; he didn't know which, and honestly was too scared to dwell on it. His right pant leg was completely black and sticky with blood, and he was too far gone to notice the thick, viscous warmth that had filled up his right boot as he stumbled along.

Dizzy and swaying, his normally broad shoulders slumped in pain and exhaustion, he took another step and nearly tumbled face first into a wide ditch filled with muddy, fast-flowing water. He stared at it dumbly for a few seconds with no more awareness than a cow gazing at a passing train until he realized it was the culvert next to his road. A very short distance away it dumped down an embankment and into the Stillwater River.

"The river," he mumbled, his tongue thick and strangely unwieldy, as if it were wrapped in heavy cotton. His words sounded odd to him and were little more than disconnected vowels and consonants. The steady rain streaming down his face masked his tears and sweat. "Can hide down…by the river… Hell yes…"

The yells behind him were getting closer and couldn't be more than fifty feet away. *Damn!* Their noisy progress and the rain made it impossible to make heads or tails of their conversation, but he didn't need to. He knew what they wanted, knew the two Mexicans wouldn't give up looking for him no matter what happened. They were both terrifying: the monstrous, soft-spoken one was bad enough, but it was the little one with the dead eyes that scared the shit out of him. He'd ended up on the wrong side of him before and knew what the insane little bastard was capable of. There was no way he could let those maniacs catch him. In a sudden, explosive burst of panic he dug in his pocket for his cell phone.

"911," he muttered. "Gotta...call 911." He fleetingly considered what he'd just said and repressed a manic giggle: he had never, ever wished for the cops before, but they might be the only ones who could save him now. For some reason a song chose that moment to push into his flickering consciousness, a hit from some late 70's or 80's rocker. Warren somebody. Zardoz? Zenon? Dammit, he'd always prided himself on being quite the music lover, so it annoyed the hell out of him that he couldn't dredge up the name. No, he wasn't just a music lover, he was a damn music aficionado. Yeah, that was him. So why couldn't he figure this out? One specific line from the song stuck in his mind and repeated itself like an annoying jingle:

Send lawyers, guns, and money – the shit has hit the fan.

Panicking, he groped in his pocket for his cell phone but his hands were heavy and freezing cold, as unwieldy as boxing gloves. He struggled and the little phone finally came out, as did some loose bills and a single credit card. The credit card spun in the air and stuck in the mud at his feet like a Japanese Shuriken throwing star. Rolland squinted and studied the phone, struggling to read it - but the rain and his muddled condition made it as slippery as a catfish and it popped out of his numb hands as if alive. He lunged for it, bobbling it comically, but he couldn't get handle on it and the little phone made a pitiful splash in the muddy water of the culvert and was gone.

"Oh, God, no..." he cried, his knees nearly buckling, staring stupidly at the spot where the phone had disappeared. He knew it was history and halfway to the river already. Snot ran freely from his nose and mingled with the rain.

Rolland's shoulders slumped further and his chin hit his chest. Huge drops of water dripped off his bangs and fell in slow motion, converging at a single spot between his muddy boots. He stood there for a moment, his breath coming in shallow, choppy gasps. His survival instinct flared and sputtered weakly, a once vibrant V8 engine now limping along on a single cylinder. Swaying, weaving, he looked up and stared slack-jawed at the flooded culvert. The stealthy gray chill had spread to the rest of his body and he was cold, so very, very cold. The song lyric ran through his head his again, but jumbled this time.

Send guns, and lawyers, and shit...

Slowly now, bouncing from tree to tree near the edge of the culvert, Rolland stumbled blindly along, no longer able to maintain a coherent destination or goal. Gravity had taken control and the slight slope of the ground was directing him toward the river. It took all his remaining willpower to simply remain upright even though several times he tripped and nearly face-planted. The temperature was in the upper 60s but he was freezing, his extremities heavy and bone-cold through and through. He was sweating and shivering at the same time and couldn't stop his teeth from chattering.

He heard a thunderous noise and dimly realized he had come to the top of the embankment. The water from the culvert was plummeting fifteen feet into the tremendously swollen Stillwater River. The river was usually thirty feet across and no more than ten feet deep, a serene, relaxing place for kids to hang out and fish during the warm summer months. But now it was twice that wide and much deeper, an ugly brown churning mess peppered with small whitecaps. The foamy torrent crashed and roiled angrily, flowing faster than he'd ever seen before. Branches and other debris spun madly in the rushing, agitated water that was flying by at a dizzying pace. Rolland just stood there, weaving, staring numbly at the river.

What the hell am I supposed to do? And why does my leg hurt so damn bad?

His last conscious thought was of his older brother, Marcus. Marcus had always been there to help before, with the cops, at school, and especially with their dad. Always with their dad. Sure, Marcus could save his ass again.

Send Marcus, guns, and money...

Rolland's final seconds ticked by before his knees buckled and he tumbled and rolled limply down the muddy hill, splashing into the river. The brown water grabbed him in its chill embrace and pulled him under, taking him without a sound.

Chapter 1

Marcus Schmidt stood in the open hatch of the little commuter jet at the Dayton International Airport and took a slow, deep breath. The light breeze blowing through the open hatch fluttered his short blond hair, hair that was almost white from so much California sunshine.

"Hmm, Ohio in May," he said to himself.

Marcus hadn't been back to the Midwest for years but he knew that Ohio had a certain, special smell in the spring. As the jet's engines spun to a halt and most of the exhaust blew away in the warm breeze, for a moment he truly believed he could catch the pungent whiff of freshly cut grass, the sweet fragrance of flowers, probably daffodils, as well as several cookouts happening somewhere well beyond the airport grounds. Then he took another deep breath through his nose and realized that in reality there was nothing there but the smell of sunbaked tarmac and spilled jet fuel.

Marcus heard a small cough behind him, no more than a polite throat clearing. He turned to see an attractive older lady, probably in her mid-70s, waiting patiently behind him. She raised her eyebrows and grinned gently, a small upturning of the corners of her carefully lipsticked mouth. "You're not scared of heights, are you, young man? Big fella like you?" she asked kindly, motioning toward the mobile stairway pushed up to the plane. She had to crane her neck up at an extreme angle just to make eye contact with him. She was short, certainly, but Marcus was over six feet, two inches tall.

"Oh, no," Marcus grinned. "I just haven't been back to Ohio for several years. I'd forgotten how nice it is in the spring." He saw the large carry-on bag she had. "Here, let me help you down the steps with that." He motioned for her to squeeze past with a gentlemanly sweep of his hand, then took her bag and met her at the bottom of the steps.

"Thank you, young man," she said sincerely. She wore a light blue print dress and had her gray hair up in a tidy bun. Unlike most of the passengers Marcus saw these days her generation still considered flying a special occasion, a cause for parading out their best. He was certain she had spent several hours preening prior to the flight, making sure her appearance was just so. His mother had been the same way.

Marcus smiled at her. "No problem, ma'am. If you like, I'd be happy to carry it to baggage claim for you."

She readily agreed. Before Marcus knew it he was being regaled with facts and observations about her life as they began the half-mile hike. Her name was Mary Lou and she was here visiting her grandchildren. She lived full time in Middleton, Wisconsin, just outside of Madison, where it was still "cold enough that Lake Mendota had just broken up last month, almost beating the old record of May 6th, set way back in 1857 – not that I was alive back then," she told him with a wry smile.

They crossed the tarmac and entered the sterile silver and blue atmosphere of Terminal B. They chatted amiably all the way to the baggage claim carousels, with Mary Lou sharing personal information freely, while Marcus talked quite a bit without actually saying much.

"So, young man, you're from California, you say? What do you do there?" Mary Lou asked kindly.

"I teach at San Diego State University, mainly Spanish," he replied. His full title was Dr. Marcus E. Schmidt, professor of Latin American Studies. He rarely used his title in school, and never outside of it. Only one person called him Dr.

Schmidt on a regular basis, a co-worker at the University, and that was a personal joke between them.

"Really, you don't say," she said earnestly. "That sounds fascinating, although you certainly don't look like you're from South of the border."

Marcus smiled. "No, ma'am, I suppose I don't. I just got interested in it when I was young, then decided to stick with it." He held back that he and Rolland had lived there for years when they were younger since that could've gotten more personal than he liked. And anyway, it was clear Mary Lou was quite comfortable leading the conversation.

"And you say you haven't been back here for a while. Visiting family?"

"Yes, I am," Marcus said. "My brother."

"Well that's nice. Spending time with family is important. Always remember that." She patted his arm in a motherly fashion.

"Yes, ma'am. Family is important," Marcus agreed. "Speaking of which, tell me more about those grandkids of yours."

That set her off again, proudly covering in great detail the minor exploits of her grandchildren, her kids, and her own life. She compared the Dayton Airport to the Dane County Airport in Madison, chatted about the weather, and generally seemed pleased to have someone to talk to. Mary Lou's amiable, homespun tales may have been as enjoyable as a toothache to some, but Marcus found them oddly pleasant, soothing, more like Novocain.

They arrived at the main baggage claim area and Marcus idly checked out his fellow passengers. Each one had a certain solid, Midwestern look about them, quite different from what he was used to in sunny San Diego. There were boots and button down flannel shirts in abundance, lots of non-designer jeans, not to mention ball caps of all kinds and colors, quite a few of them sporting baseball teams or John Deere logos. He spotted some ubiquitous salesmen with their ties loosened and their top buttons undone. Most had laptops open on their knees and cell phones permanently glued to their ears. Many of their wrinkle-resistant shirts had defied manufacturer guarantees and were in fact terribly wrinkled, one of the hazards of sitting in planes and uncomfortable airport chairs too long.

Standing quietly to one side was an Amish girl of about twenty-five, somewhat incongruous in her long cotton dress, the collar cinched tightly around her throat, her crisp white bonnet, her *kapp*, bright in the fluorescents. Marcus doubted she realized it but a single strand of auburn hair had worked its way free and was hanging in a loose ringlet down her left cheek. Out in California her presence would have been an oddity, but here in the Midwest no one paid any notice. One goal of the Amish was to be plain, and looking at her features he decided she could be considered plain by conventional standards. But peering more deeply he saw an attractive hardiness and resolve in her demeanor that he rarely noticed in today's women. She glanced his way and smiled primly. He smiled back.

The loudspeaker overhead intoned, "The current threat level, as determined by the office of Homeland Security, is yellow." No one seemed to notice or even care what the threat level was, but Marcus ran through them in his head. Green, blue, yellow, orange, and of course, red. A numbering system certainly would have been easier and more intuitive, he considered, but he had the current system memorized nonetheless. No one who knew him would have been surprised.

Just then the klaxon sounded and luggage began disgorging from the mouth of the conveyer belt. All the passengers surged closer en masse like cattle at a feeding trough, bumping and jostling shoulder to shoulder. They stared at each piece trundling by as if they only had a single chance to grab their bag before it disappeared forever into the mechanical maw at the opposite end. A dozen times or more Marcus saw someone pull off a black, innocuous-looking bag before sheepishly realizing it wasn't theirs and awkwardly replacing it on the line.

Marcus' own medium-sized black suitcase had a bright green ribbon tied around the handle for easy identification, and he plucked it up as it slid toward him.

He moved easily back through the crowd with his bag in tow, but as he did so he noticed Mary Lou craning her neck and peering nervously at the steady stream of suitcases, backpacks, and the odd golf bag or guitar case flowing by. He made his way back to her side and inquired about hers.

"Oh, there it is," she exclaimed excitedly, bouncing lightly on the balls of her feet. "The large brown one."

With a "pardon me" or two Marcus lowered a large shoulder and firmly muscled his way into the thick of the crowd, just managing to snag the old-fashioned, hard-shelled Samsonite before it got by him. He hefted it up and out of the crowd. He was no judge, but he calculated the old brute must weigh sixty or seventy pounds. How in the world had she managed it so far? he wondered. And what could she possibly have in it?

"Is your ride here?" Marcus asked, muffling a grunt as he lugged her bag through the crowd and into the open. The Amish girl smiled at his good deed from over the conveyor belt.

Mary Lou looked anxiously this way and that, peering down each end of the terminal and out the huge glass doors to the sunny parking lot. She was twisting a handkerchief nervously between her fingers. "No, I don't see them. Roger, my son, said he and the kids would be waiting. I wonder where they could be?"

"Well let's get our stuff out of the way while we wait," Marcus said as he hoisted their bags with another grunt and hauled them to a bench against the wall. "We'll just hang out till Roger shows."

As Mary Lou eased gently down and took a seat anxiety for her situation was quickly displaced by concern for his. "That's silly," she admonished. "I'll be fine. Besides, you have a brother waiting for you that you haven't seen in years."

He plopped down on the bench beside her. "Oh, there's no rush. I'd rather stick around 'til your ride shows up."

"Nonsense. I said I'll be fine. I'll just sit right here and wait for Roger. I'm sure he's just parking the car or got caught in traffic."

Marcus crossed his arms in mock severity. "I'm much bigger than you are, so unless you can move me from this bench it looks like we're waiting together."

He saw a brief wave of relief as it flitted over her features, and realized that despite her outward bravado she was nervous about being here by herself. She looked him over, sizing him up. "I certainly can't move you," she agreed, "so it looks like I'm stuck with you for now."

They both laughed and continued chatting off and on comfortably for the next fifteen minutes. Just down the way from the baggage area in the large foyer he saw a full scale replica of the Wright Brother's Wright B Flyer suspended from the ceiling. It looked impossibly frail and not at all air-worthy. He couldn't imagine anyone attempting a flight with it. How far had they gone that first time, 120 feet or so? Marcus wouldn't want to fly it twelve feet. Across from them there was a kiosk selling overpriced coffee and, against her protestations, he sprung for a cup for each of them. She liked hers straight black; Marcus took his with both cream and two sugars.

"If you're going to dress it up so much," she chided him playfully, "you may as well have hot chocolate."

He grinned and took a sip, jumping when it scorched his tongue. As he was leaning over and blowing to cool it off, Mary Lou said, "It's nice of you to wait with me." She took a drink of her coffee, oblivious to its searing heat. She smacked her lips in quiet approval. "As long as it's been, I'd just think you'd be in more of a hurry to see your brother." She took another drink, her attention still focused on her cup.

Yes, he was stalling and he knew it, he just hadn't wanted to admit it to himself. He was stalling because deep down he wasn't sure he was ready to see Rolland. Yes, he was his brother and he would do just about anything for him, but things had ended very badly on his last visit three years ago, and he just wasn't convinced either he or his brother were ready for any kind of reunion yet. He knew from experience that emotional wounds heal slowly, with scars that might never fade completely.

He considered explaining to Mary Lou that he had flown all the way across the country because Rolland's landlady in Wayne, Ohio, had called bitching about him being two months late with the rent. Marcus hadn't known (but wasn't the least bit surprised) that his little brother had put him down as a reference and emergency contact. The landlady hadn't heard from him or seen him in months, and the place outside of Wayne looked like shit, she complained: grass was overgrown, trash was everywhere, and strangers kept snooping around. She wanted her rent, dammit, and someone needed to clean that place up – it said so in the lease!

He also considered telling Mary Lou that he'd been hesitant at first to call Rolland's cell phone, but once he started dialing and it kept going immediately to voicemail he couldn't stop calling. He must have left Rolland a dozen messages, the first ones short and hesitant, "Rollie, this is Marcus – call me." Later ones were more urgent, more insistent, "Rolland, I mean it. Call me back right away!"

Nothing. No return calls, no contact.

Marcus had dithered around for nearly a week before he couldn't stand it any longer. No matter what had taken place in the past he knew he couldn't live in peace on the west coast without knowing what was going on with his brother. He had booked a flight that day and flew out the next, the red-eye connecting in Chicago, continuing on to Dayton.

But now that he was here, only twenty or thirty miles away, he was having a hell of a time completing the trip.

He pursed his lips pensively and turned to Mary Lou, but was saved from an all too personal confession by the sound of a young girl's voice yelling, "Gramma!" Through the glass sliding doors burst a cute ten year-old girl with blond pigtails, followed by an older, bored-looking teenage boy with bangs in his eyes, and a harried, irate, slightly pudgy man in his mid-40s. Roger and the kids had finally arrived.

Mary Lou gave Marcus' knee a quick pat and stood to greet her family warmly, hugging the young girl and kissing the reluctant teen. "Ahh, gramma," he mumbled, rubbing away the lipstick away with the back of his arm. Roger was cursing the airport traffic system, saying he'd been stuck on some godforsaken loop and kept missing the short term lot. And when he'd finally found it there were no spots and he'd been forced to exit, circle around again, and park in the damn long term section. Partway through his rant he glanced over and saw Marcus sitting there with Mary Lou's baggage, and he stumbled to a halt, his features wrinkled in obvious bewilderment. He looked back and forth between them.

Mary Lou quickly took note of his expression and explained genially about Marcus and how he had helped since their arrival. Roger looked dubious for a second, then shook Marcus' hand and grudgingly thanked him for assisting his mother. Still muttering curses about the traffic patterns and the morons who designed them, he snapped at his teenage boy to grab his mom's bag. "Come on, Jeff, let's go, let's go. Parking's expensive."

Marcus stood and gave Mary Lou a brief hug, the top of her head not even reaching his chin. She thanked him warmly for his help and wagged a finger at him. "Now you go see your brother. Remember," she said, casting Roger a rueful sideways glance, "family's important - no matter what they're like or what they've done."

With that she was out of the terminal, leaving Marcus with nothing but a fond memory and conflicting emotions. He watched as they went out the door and hustled across the street into the parking area, disappearing among the army of parked cars and SUVs. Marcus stood there, a solid, solitary figure, his arms crossed. Passengers flowed around him as if he were a rock in a stream. No discernible change came over his expression, but a minute later he strode purposefully to the rental car window, picked up the keys to a mid-sized Chevrolet, and walked out into the bright late morning sunshine.

Chapter 2

The thirty minute drive on the country roads from the airport to the Village of Wayne proved uneventful. He passed the time surfing radio stations and checking out the six inch tall, dew-spattered green shoots of corn that blanketed the surrounding fields. The green was so bright and vivid in the late morning sunshine that it almost hurt his eyes to look directly at it, like a sea of glistening jade. In about two or three months the corn would be so tall a driver would feel as if he were hurtling through a tunnel of eight foot tall rustling stalks, with nothing else visible but the road ahead and the sky above.

The geography in this part of Ohio was a complex terrain of valleys and hills, along with large expanses of fields and some clumps of woods, holdovers from an earlier time. He drove over several small tributaries with names like Raccoon Creek or Possum Falls. Twice he got stuck behind farmers pulling manure spreaders from one field to the next, with a stench so powerful that even with the car's vents shut and the windows cranked up tight his eyes still watered. When he finally managed to pass the tractors the farmers waved genially. Marcus guessed they were laughing inside, knowing full well that their cargos were spreading olfactory malaise in their wake.

He topped a final hill and saw Wayne spread out thinly below him, a forlorn gray and brown smudge that soon coalesced into a collection of low buildings. He had grown up about fifteen miles outside of Wayne, in a small frame house out in the country. As kids he and his brother would pile into the family sedan with their parents and head into town for shopping expeditions each Saturday, and back again for church on Sundays. At first the two boys had loved it, treating the short car ride and final destination as an adventure, enjoying all the relative hustle and excitement of downtown Wayne and seeing all the different people, poking their noses into different shops, playing tag with friends in the square, staring in mute fascination at all the fresh meat at the butcher shop. The IGA grocery store was one of their favorite stops as each brother was permitted to pick one treat, whatever they wanted. Marcus always went straight for the candy aisle and the Hershey chocolate bars, but for some reason Rolland had a terrible time making a decision. Several times he was simply unable to make a choice and had to leave empty-handed, upset and angry with himself. On those occasions Marcus would feel sorry for him and break off a few rectangles of his Hershey bar and share once they got back in the car. His father would shake his head and grumble at Rolland, but their mother would smile and gently touch his dimpled cheek.

But that fondness for Wayne quickly lost its sheen after the death of their mother. She had meant everything not only to the two boys, but to her husband as well. He had loved her immensely, desperately. When she died their father was so crushed by grief they quickly found that, among his other shortcomings, he was not a man geared to handle raising two young boys. More often than not Marcus had been in charge of the house and raising Rolland while his father drifted deeper into depression and alcohol, getting more abusive as the years dragged on. The drinking binges turned nastier and more violent, many times to the point where the Wayne police had to lock him in the drunk-tank for the night. That meant that Marcus would have to beg a ride into town and bail him out in the morning, a fact that quickly made for juicy gossip in the small village. The jeers and laughter were harsh, almost physical lashes that stung and burned. The boys suffered through them whenever they came into town, from their classmates at school, or even on those rare times that they attended church. It got to the point where they simply stayed away, a self-imposed exile. From that time on and forever after, Wayne signified humiliation and scorn to both of them, and Marcus vowed he would move away and never return.

He crossed an old bridge flaked with rust that spanned the slow-moving Stillwater River before continuing up into the village. Wayne was built in a ragged half-moon shape along the riverbank, with streets and residences sprouting from the center of town in a pattern similar to the layout of Washington D.C. Glimpsed from above it looked like half of a broken-down wheel, complete with irregular spokes radiating out from the oldest part of town, the courthouse and city park. Marcus drove slowly down the old-fashioned main street, with its two- and three-story red brick buildings that lined the sidewalk. Many of them, as much as a third, he guessed, were vacant, their windows dark or covered with yellowing, fly-specked paper, "For Lease" signs taped to the glass. There were several sad but hopeful-looking craft stores, an old Ace Hardware store, and a few bars with dusty neon bar signs flickering in dark windows. The only true sign of life was a restaurant called Foley's Diner on the main drag. Through the large plate glass window Marcus could see people sitting and eating, drinking coffee from plain white mugs. The remainder of downtown looked tired and grubby, forgotten, as if the rest of America had passed it by. He doubted if even a Wal-Mart could survive in this godforsaken place. It was a fading town already on life support, just one arthritic step away from admittance to hospice.

He quickly passed out of the business district into more residential neighborhoods, and after a few more blocks he was out of town completely. He hadn't realized it but his shoulders and arms had been hunched up and tense as he drove through Wayne. Now that the village was behind him he began to relax as he took deep, cleansing breaths. Marcus simply did not like the place and never could understand why Rolland lived here. If a place could project a colored aura then certainly Wayne's must be a smudged, dirty brown, perhaps tinted with ochre. He was relieved to see it fading in his rearview mirror.

Sighing, he turned left at the next intersection on Bradford - Wayne Road, not too far from Rolland's now. He thought back to what Mary Lou had said at the airport, that family was important no matter what they were like or what they had done. Try as he might he couldn't get her words out of his mind, even though in his case the concept of family was certainly overrated, especially when it came to his father.

Then there was that last time, the worst one ever, when his dad had him pinned against the wall by the neck, eyes bloodshot and unfocused, beer and cigar stench blowing in his face every time he exhaled, his nose a patchwork of blue veins, and his huge fist was pulled back, back, intent on inflicting as much damage on Marcus as he could, and then -

A sudden horn blast snapped Marcus from that horrific memory and back to the present. He viciously whipped the car back into his lane, narrowly avoiding an oncoming red pickup truck. The driver of the pickup mouthed something and flipped him off, speeding past, kicking up gravel from the berm. Marcus wiped a shaky hand over his forehead and it came away damp with cold sweat. The near hit should have been the cause of his sudden shakes, but he knew better.

Another mile passed. Marcus began to recognize a few landmarks and realized he was very close. Small two and three bedroom shacks were popping up in little clusters, like mini-neighborhoods huddled against the encroaching woods and fields. A select few had been cleaned and tidied up, with updated bushes and flowers, perhaps a fresh coat of paint, but they were the exception. Most were old and untended, houses but certainly not homes, places where people didn't live and love but merely existed. Their troubles weighed too heavily upon them to worry about siding and shingles, grass and gardens. Like his own home long after his mother had passed away, these houses suffered from sway-back roofs and peeling paint, littered with trash, peppered with old cars and trucks. Some were on blocks, thick weeds sprouting from broken windows and sprung trunk lids. At one shockingly pink shack two overweight, expressionless men sat on the porch, cans of cheap beer grasped tightly in hands. Their empty, fogged gaze followed Marcus like hunters tracking game. The bare ground around their feet was littered with empty cans, the red and white kills of their morning's efforts. Marcus made no eye contact and continued driving.

Immediately after a gentle bend in the road he saw Rolland's house. It sat by itself on the left side of Bradford - Wayne Road, with only one other house nearby, directly across the street. His brother's place was a small frame house, two bedrooms, one bathroom, a kitchen, and a living room. Some would have called it a cottage. The last time Marcus had been here it had looked pretty good, with the yard nicely tended and the white paint bright and clean. Now the grass was tall and overgrown, with Rolland's old Honda Civic off to one side, partly obscured by weeds. Marcus slowed, hit his signal, and turned in. Old newspapers littered the driveway, dozens of them in their yellow and white plastic wrappers. One of the bags popped like a gunshot as he drove over it. The mailbox, he noticed, was stuffed to capacity and then some.

He sat in the rental car, hands at ten and two. He contemplated the house, focusing on the front door. He kept expecting - almost willing - his brother to open the door and step out, long blond hair down to his shoulders, an easy smile on his tanned face, looking so very much like a younger, more carefree version of Marcus himself. He'd have a great explanation for the unkempt condition of the place, the reason he hadn't made rent for two months, for not answering his phone. He'd have all that. He'd have reasons for everything and they would make perfect sense, at least in his brother's own eyes. Marcus continued to stare at the door. Nothing happened. His heart was beating loudly, loud enough that he was sure anyone in the car with him would have been able to hear it, too.

Damn, he thought. An hour ago I couldn't bring myself to see him, and now I wish he'd just waltz out the door.

He slowly got out of the car, gravel crunching underfoot, and briefly surveyed his surroundings. Nothing moved around the small white house. It was so quiet and still that Marcus found it unnerving. He glanced back at the house across the street and saw a curtain in the picture window quickly, furtively, move shut. Someone over there was keeping an eye on him. He stared at the now curtained window but there was no further sign of life. Why so shy? he wondered.

He walked up to Rolland's house, took a deep breath, and then opened the wooden screen door. He knocked, the sound sharp and loud in the stillness. He waited as his ears strained for any noise from inside. There was nothing, no noise or hint of movement. He knocked again, louder this time. After a few seconds of no activity he cupped his hands and peered in the window but could only make out vague shadows and shapes in the darkness.

"Rolland!" he shouted through the glass. "Rolland! You here? Rolland? It's Marcus!"

There was still no sound or movement from inside. Mumbling an apology to the nasty landlady he put his hip to the door and gave it a shove. There was a slight cracking, some splintering of wood, and the door pushed open almost noiselessly.

As his eyes adjusted to the gloom he groped around on the wall and found the light switch. He fully expected it not to work but to his surprise it did: the local power company must be more forgiving than the landlady. The overhead light in the tiny living room came on, the naked bulb revealing devastation on a grand scale.

"Son of a bitch," Marcus whispered, his heart sinking.

The room had been completely demolished, as if a massive hand had picked up the small house and given it several hard shakes. Couches and chairs were flipped over, and a cheap bookcase was toppled onto its side. The old tube television was face down on the floor, destroyed, gray glass scattered under and around it. The stereo was smashed and lay in a heap, wires and other electronics sticking out like copper and plastic entrails. Ashtrays had been smashed against the walls, dried husks of cigarette butts littering the ground. Marcus took a step in and glass and debris crunched under his shoes. A thick layer of dust blanketed any solid surface. Nobody, he surmised, had been here for a long time. If possible, Marcus' heart sank even lower and a nauseous feeling settled in his gut as if he'd drank sour milk. What in the hell had happened here? he thought, followed up with the now familiar question: And where the hell was Rolland?

A quick check of the two small bedrooms and bathroom revealed the same level of destruction. As Marcus began to inspect the damage more thoroughly he found that not only was everything toppled and pushed over, but all the furniture had been sliced open methodically: each cushion, each chair, even the footstool had been eviscerated, the stuffing groped through and emptied, foam and wool ticking like dirty snow scattered on the floor. This was not a random act, not vandals, he thought. This was someone searching for something specific, bit by bit and piece by piece. What it might be he had no idea, but he had to assume they hadn't found what they were looking for since each room had suffered the same fate.

In the small hallway between the two bedrooms he noticed with some interest that the attic door in the ceiling was open. The searchers, whoever they were, had been very thorough. Looking down he saw some muddy footprints on the worn carpeting. No, make that two different sets of footprints. One was small, much smaller than anything Rolland could wear, and the other set was huge. Marcus put his own size twelves next to the dirty print and was shocked at how much smaller his shoe appeared. The other must be a size sixteen at least. *Wow.*

He spotted a corner of a picture frame sticking out from under the couch. Both the glass and the frame itself were broken. As he carefully picked out the shards he saw it was a picture of the two of them taken four years ago at Balboa

Park in San Diego. They were sitting on the ledge of a large fountain, the spraying water behind them a blurred silver and white against their clear images. In the photo they could almost be mistaken as twins, even with Rolland's longer hair and Marcus' more sober mien. There was no mistaking their Germanic heritage, with their bright blue eyes, blond hair, and strong shoulders. Marcus was a little huskier, slightly broader through the body mainly due to age and working out, but otherwise the similarities were remarkable. He smiled because he remembered that immediately after the picture was taken Rolland had good-naturedly tried to yank him back into the fountain and a splash war had erupted. Some of the children around them had joined in the fracas, and soon anyone within fifty feet was soaked and laughing. He grinned as he blew off the specks of glass and carefully put the picture in his shirt pocket.

Walking through the disaster in the kitchen was more problematic. *Dammit to hell,* he thought. Utensils, pots, pans, and broken dishes were tossed indiscriminately about. A large rectangular oak table was overturned. The fridge door was open, light still on. Fortunately it looked like his brother hadn't been much for stocking up on groceries since there wasn't anything too nasty left in there. He found a few cans of beer and some old rolls in a bag, now fuzzy and black with mold. Adding to the mess were the bags of flour and salt that had been broken open and spread across the counters, floor, and even the walls. Whoever had done this looked as if they had left the kitchen for last, and by this time had been pretty pissed off. This looked less like searching and more like destruction for destruction's sake. He felt as if he were walking on a gravel driveway as he crunched through the debris.

He finally made it to the back door and stepped out of the gloomy kitchen. The late afternoon sunshine was still so bright that for a moment he had to shield his eyes. The small backyard, only about thirty feet deep, terminated in woods that ran for a half mile or so down to the Stillwater River. The river meandered around through the woods and after heavy rains it could be heard even from here. The grass was easily a foot tall, with overgrown dandelions and goldenrod vigorously vying for the ministrations of bees and butterflies. He looked left and saw a doghouse, one large enough to house Sam, Rolland's German shepherd. It was relatively new and in good shape, made of wood siding and real shingles. He didn't recall it being there before.

A doghouse? he wondered. That was odd. Rolland treated Sam better than most parents treated their kids. Hell, Sam even slept in the same bed with him. What the hell was he doing with a doghouse?

Curious, he moved closer for a better look before stopping abruptly, stumbling back a step. The sun suddenly felt hot on his forehead and the sickening feeling of dread he'd been suffering intensified tenfold, pulsing through him in hot waves. His knees nearly buckled.

"Oh, shit," he mumbled his tongue thick and suddenly dry, like an old kitchen sponge left to bake in the sun.

Connected by a chain to the doghouse were the partially decomposed remains of a large animal, a filthy blue collar bright against the matted fur. Part of the grayish-white ribcage was exposed, and shiny green flies danced and hovered around, their buzzing easily audible in the still country air. The skull appeared to have been smashed in. There was enough rotting fur left on the skeletal shape to identify a black snout and brown body. Staring at it Marcus was certain the remains were Sam. His eyes welled up as he stood before the forlorn, sad shape. He knew that if his brother had allowed something to happen to his beloved pet, and that Sam was still out here like *this*, then he was in even more trouble than Marcus thought. In fact, if he'd left Sam out here then he was terrified that… No, he couldn't complete that thought, couldn't let himself go there, not now, not yet.

There he remained for some time, thinking, hugging himself tightly as if he were cold, while the bright afternoon sun beat down indifferently on the two of them.

Chapter 3

"I want to report a missing person."

Marcus sat in the basement of the courthouse in downtown Wayne. There were three small, dank rooms there dedicated to the W.P.D., the Wayne Police Department. The first was a small vestibule with a tiny bullet proof window, over which was hand-painted a gold banner proclaiming: "W.P.D. – to Serve and Protect". Down a short hallway was the single holding cell, and across from that was the actual office.

Marcus was there in the office seated in a gray metal chair with green vinyl upholstery. Some sort of heating pipes ran in crazy patterns around the ceiling, keeping the room unnaturally warm. Periodically they clanked or hissed loudly, loud enough to make Marcus jerk in surprise. A poster on the back wall warned of the Top Ten Most Wanted people in that part of Ohio, complete with black and white grainy photos. It seemed the majority were on the list for failure to pay child support. However two were wanted for armed robbery, and one for attempted murder. The attempted murderer peered back at Marcus with large glasses, a receding hairline, and a scrawny chicken neck, looking about as dangerous as an accountant ticked that the books wouldn't balance. Two desks and three other chairs were jammed in that small space, which left about five square feet for visitors. Marcus wasn't claustrophobic by nature, but all of the forces at play here – the heat and tiny space, the damn banging pipes, and his heightening concern for his brother – all combined to make him very uncomfortable, very edgy.

Then there was the Lieutenant.

Lieutenant Donald Doncaster was in his mid- to late-thirties. He was of medium height, sported a severe crew-cut, and had no doubt been stocky his whole life with a linebacker's sturdy build. However whatever athletics or activities had managed to keep his weight at bay were no longer sufficient. It was now to the point where the cop's muscle was quickly shifting to fat. It showed in his cheeks and forehead, but especially in his neck. As he leaned back in his chair, arms crossed, chin against his chest, his neck was puffed out wider than his ears, making his head appear too small for his body. His dark eyes were close together, like crocodile eyes. The way he squinted, unblinking, made Marcus feel as if he were guilty until proven otherwise. That, or he was just angry at something or someone. He had a cheap Bic pen in his hand and kept clicking it again and again. *Click-click, click-click.*

Angry, Marcus concluded. He just looks pissed.

Doncaster's steel desk was completely barren expect for one small picture frame and an empty In Box made of black steel. The frame was facing away from visitors. The Lieutenant stared at him, his thumb working the Bic pen vigorously. *Click-click, click-click.* He leaned forward slightly. He smoothly took a small black spiral bound notepad from his chest pocket and made some initial notes.

"Name, please," he said, his voice flat and without inflection.

"It's my brother, Rolland. Rolland Schmidt," Marcus replied.

Doncaster drew a quick line through what he had just written. "No. Your name, please."

"Oh. Marcus Schmidt."

"And the missing person?"

"My brother, Rolland Schmidt," he repeated.

Without lifting his eyes, Doncaster asked, "And why do you think he's missing?"

Marcus told him everything that had happened so far: the call from the landlady, not being able to contact Rolland's cell, the wrecked house, and especially Sam and how he had found him. The cop paused and looked up at that last point, his eyes a question mark.

"Rolland would never let anything happen to Sam," Marcus explained. "He loved that dog. And to just leave him out there like that...well, Rolland would never do that. He would've at least buried him." He took a breath, then repeated, "He loved that dog, probably more than anything."

Doncaster continued taking notes, his script very tiny and precise, almost childlike. After a few minutes he looked up again.

"When's the last time you saw or spoke to your brother?"

Marcus looked away. "Several years ago."

Doncaster's left eyebrow lifted fractionally. For him it was an extravagant expression. "Several years ago?"

"Yes, years. We had a...falling out." He didn't feel the need to go in to any details.

The Lieutenant looked coolly at Marcus for a moment. *Click-click, click-click.* "But you flew all the way from the west coast, just like that?"

"Well sure," Marcus stated, locking eyes with the policeman, "we're brothers. So yes, I did."

The two men continued staring at each other. Eventually Doncaster broke eye contact and directed his attention back to the notebook. He slowly and methodically made a few more entries. Marcus was quickly taking a dislike to the Lieutenant.

"Now, I need some contact information from you."

Marcus dutifully dictated his cell phone number and his home address in San Diego. He was starting to get antsy, feeling his temper beginning to rise and his grip on the arms of the chair tighten. The palms of his hands were sweating. Honestly, he never expected Doncaster to jump up and start barking orders into his radio, never thought this would be a high-powered police headquarters hopping with activity, phones ringing, people shouting, crooks being harshly interrogated and read their Miranda Rights. Not here, not in Wayne. He knew on all reasonable levels that these scenarios were the stuff of TV dramas and buddy cop movies. But at the very least he expected some sense of urgency or action from the man, some show of concern. The chair under him creaked as he shifted his weight forward. Control, he thought, jaw tight. Keep your cool.

Doncaster deliberately closed his black notebook and leaned back, his neck puffing out like some fleshy iguana.

"So what's next?" Marcus asked. He started to reach for his shirt pocket. "Do you need a picture? You didn't even get a physical description of him. How are you supposed to know who you're looking for?" Marcus noticed that his voice had crept up a notch in volume: his composure was slipping. He fought to keep himself steady. His anger was a nascent fire and Doncaster's indifference was a wind fanning the flames.

Click-click, click-click. The cop pursed his lips, thinking, then appeared to come to a conclusion and opened the side drawer of his desk. He flicked through some papers before finally bringing out a standard manila folder. He double-checked the name on the folder then slid it across the desk with one thick finger. Marcus didn't immediately take it but reached for it warily, like someone inspecting an exposed wire, unsure whether it would shock if touched.

"What's this?" he asked, although he was pretty sure he knew already.

"Open it."

Marcus concentrated on the folder for a full five seconds, and then slowly flipped back the cover. Stapled to the upper left hand corner were two unflattering color photos of Rolland, a side view and a front view. There were a series of numbers under each picture. It looked like his brother had been in some sort of brawl, which was not like him at all: both of the brothers were fairly large and imposing. While growing up that had usually been reason enough to make would-be attackers decide that a physical solution wasn't the best option after all. But there was no mistaking that Rolland's left eye was puffy and his lower lip was crusty with blood. There was a visible knot on his forehead as well. He looked older to Marcus. Older, and a little sad.

Marcus carefully scanned the attached paperwork and some earlier mug shots. He didn't understand all of the police and legal jargon reported there, but he didn't have to. He picked out enough – operating a vehicle while under the influence, public intoxication, some type of theft conviction, and of course drugs, in this case marijuana – to confirm that his brother was well known to local law enforcement. And by local law enforcement, that apparently was Lieutenant Doncaster. He thoughtfully closed the folder and slid it back across the desk.

"The last time I saw your brother," the cop said, finally deciding to impart some information, "he had just gotten beat up pretty bad. We found him a few blocks from here one night, unconscious behind some bushes near the courthouse. I think he crawled there trying to hide."

"Hide? From what? What happened?"

Click-click, click-click. Doncaster didn't look comfortable sharing. "I'm not sure. We think it was some drug deal gone bad but we never did find out for sure. A witness placed him with some Mexicans earlier in the evening. They'd been drinking at one of the downtown bars." He shrugged, a nominal lifting of his shoulders. "Your brother wouldn't tell us what happened. Says he didn't remember who beat him up."

Marcus pointed at the folder. "And you arrested him for what?"

"Public intoxication. It was as much for his protection as anything else. I slapped him in the holding cell overnight." He tilted his head across the hall. "If he'd gone home there'd be no telling what could've happened. You know where he lives. Outside of town, middle of nowhere. If someone wanted to continue where they'd left off…"

Marcus understood. "How long ago was this?"

Doncaster spun the folder around and glanced inside at a date. "About six months ago. I saw him two weeks later at the hearing. He looked better then. His eye was just a little swollen. Judge fined him a few hundred bucks and issued community service. Trash pickup, I think."

"What about the rest of the charges listed?" Marcus asked.

The Lieutenant pursed his lips. This was all public record so he wasn't divulging any secrets. "There were several times he was suspected in some house and garage thefts, but we couldn't place him at the scene for sure. There was one count of receiving stolen property, and a possession charge, a small amount of marijuana. There were a few times he was suspected in boosting cars as well. Two public intoxication busts.

"But I'll give you my two cents, too. Your brother was a trouble-maker, and was always into something. I had a lot of run-ins with him, and that's not a good thing. He was either in trouble, or was surrounded by it."

Marcus sighed, leaning back and rubbing his hand over his mouth. "Rolland had a…rough time as a kid. Our mom died when he was young, and our dad, well, wasn't much of a dad," he admitted. It was hard for him to share family history with anyone, especially an ass like Doncaster. "His ideas of right and wrong were always a bit fuzzy, and he didn't handle peer pressure well. But," he said, "that doesn't change the fact that he's still missing. I mean, come on – the trashed house, the late rent, his dog. I know something's happened to him."

Doncaster shook his head slowly. *Click-click, click-click.* "Listen – your brother is a legal adult. Okay, so he took off. People do that all the time, especially his type." Doncaster made the word "type" sound foul, like some puke he had to hose off the floor of a holding cell. "There's nothing I can do about that. Now, if we find for sure that something happened to him, or there are some outstanding warrants, then we can start looking. Right now there's nothing I can do." He stood up.

"Now wait a minute..." Marcus began, temper flaring higher. "You mean you're not going to do anything at all?"

"That's right, I'm not."

Marcus stood up fast and the metal chair screeched as it kicked back. The noise was doubly loud in the cramped room. Both men were standing now. He was much taller and found himself looking down on Doncaster, but the cop didn't budge an inch. "Listen, I know my brother, and -"

"And nothing!" Doncaster grabbed the folder and slammed it back in the drawer. "Your brother is an adult and can head off to Timbuktu if he wants to. And frankly," he added, his own voice rising in volume, "he's been a pain in my ass and if he's gone from my jurisdiction that's just fine with me. Look around you – I don't have a lot of help around here, and the fewer troublemakers I've got to watch out for the better."

Marcus stood there fuming. "Thanks for all your help and concern," he said in a tight voice. "I guess I'm on my own then."

"At this point, yes," he said. He sat back down and absentmindedly adjusted the picture frame on his desk. It had been nudged an inch or two out of place in all the commotion. He slid the Bic pen back in his top pocket. Marcus turned and walked stiffly out. He refrained from slamming the door, but just barely.

"You want to look for him?" the cop coolly recommended to Marcus' stiff back as he passed through the vestibule. "You might want to start with Foley's Diner."

Chapter 4

Seething, Marcus stormed up the steps and out of the courthouse, into the bright light of day. It was quite clear that he would receive no help from the fine Wayne Police force. Muttering curses under his breath he made his way back to the parked rental car, only to find a red envelope tucked neatly under the driver's windshield.

"A parking ticket?" he snapped. "No time to help, but one of his boys can issue me a damn parking ticket?" The red envelope in his hand matched the color of his burning anger. Slowly, leaning against the car, he worked to calm down. He stuffed the ticket in his pocket and took three deep breaths, then got behind the wheel, pulled out and drove off.

As he drove through town, still fuming about the circumstances surrounding Doncaster and the parking ticket, he noticed with surprise that it was almost four o'clock in the afternoon. He had been up nearly all night on the flight to Dayton and hadn't had a moment's rest since arriving. Fatigue was battering him like a strong headwind sapping a runner's strength, and he began to feel a little shaky and weak since he hadn't eaten anything since the two tiny bags of pretzels on the plane.

He passed Foley's Diner and looked in the window again. He could see waitresses in white uniforms standing around chatting casually, a few customers scattered about. He had no intention of stopping in now and following

Doncaster's final advice, if for no other reason than spite. Perhaps later, he told himself, but not now.

Instead he pulled up in front of the Ace Hardware store, parked, and went in. He made several purchases from the sullen, mumbling teenager behind the counter, including two candy bars from a rack by the cash register and a six pack of bottled water. He put the items in the trunk and made his way back out of town. Marcus could feel the tension drift from his muscles as Wayne faded to an indistinct brown smear in his rear view mirror. God he really did hate the memories associated with that place.

Arriving at Rolland's he got out of the car and pulled the bags from the trunk. He noticed that the curtain was pulled aside again on the house across the street, more brazenly this time since it never moved under his gaze. He dipped his head in a silent greeting and only then did the curtain slowly drift closed.

Back inside the house he surveyed the destruction anew. He had half hoped – irrationally, he knew – that it would look better upon his return. But of course that wasn't the case and if anything it seemed worse, though certainly that had to be his imagination. He was so exhausted, and the devastation was so complete that he could barely figure out where to begin. He felt overwhelmed, which was not like him. He also knew himself well enough that he couldn't rest, couldn't consider anything else, without making a reasonably orderly haven first.

"Gotta start somewhere," he finally mumbled, critically surveying the room. He settled on a plan of attack and methodically went about it.

He began by picking up all the easily identifiable trash as well as anything broken beyond use or repair, which encompassed a lot. The old tube style TV, now deceased, he hauled out back. One of his purchases at the hardware store had been a box of large heavy duty trash bags and he started by filling up one, then another. The remains of the radio and several lamps and some destroyed pillows took one entire bag. When he was done he had three bulging bags tied up securely in a neat and tidy line behind the house. As he considered his next move he ate one of the candy bars and downed a bottled water. The chocolate was soft from the warm air of the house but tasted exquisite. He seriously considered the second one before putting it in the fridge.

"Easy does it," he told himself. "Save it for later."

Next he scoured the wreckage for anything resembling a vacuum cleaner. Finding nothing but a cheap broom he worked to sweep up the living room, even though the worn carpet stubbornly resisted his most vigorous attempts at cleaning. He flipped all the furniture upright and managed to force enough of the stuffing back into some of the cushions so they were at least serviceable. After the rest of the furniture was in place, and only then, did he sit down on the couch and allow himself the other candy bar. It was cooled off and a little less soft but equally delicious. He made himself eat slowly, savoring each bite. He absently licked his fingers and wished he had bought a dozen instead of just two. The living room had all the class and feel of a college dorm now, he thought, but it was an improvement.

"Yeah, a pin-up for Better Homes and Gardens," he declared.

A glance at his watch proclaimed he had been at this for nearly three hours. It was now nearly eight o'clock Ohio time. Marcus sat on the couch and took another long drink from his water. He closed his eyes. He meant to take a few minutes and think through what little he had done so far and to plan his next steps, but instead he immediately and quite unintentionally fell asleep. The bottled water slipped from his lax hand and dribbled on to his lap, soaking his crotch. He didn't notice a thing.

Seven hours later Marcus jerked once and sat up. He looked around madly for a moment, confused and completely unsure where he was. His hair was sticking up on one side and he couldn't understand why his pants were damp. A few seconds passed before he recognized his location - then it all came flooding madly back. He sat back and exhaled noisily, his lips vibrating like a diesel engine. He rubbed his hands over his face. Reviewing his current predicament was depressing: it was the middle of the night, he was in Rolland's ratty house in a town he hated, he had no idea what had happened to his brother, and he was certain the local authorities were going to be less than helpful. Just perfect.

As he contemplated his situation depression began to settle over him. He peripherally understood that his mood was due in large part to exhaustion, travel, and uncertainty, not to mention frustration. Regardless, his heart was a heavy rock in his chest. He stared at the ceiling, his thoughts somber and black. A large white moth had somehow made its way inside and was beating itself relentlessly against the bare incandescent bulb, oblivious to anything but reaching its goal, unaware that to do so would likely mean its own demise. The shadows it cast against the walls were ragged and strobe-like, causing the entire room to twitch as if alive. The effect was both disturbing and eerie.

He sat that way for a while, time passing in its measured way. He absently watched the moth. Every time it hit the light bulb he could hear a tiny *ping* and it would lose altitude, tiny wings beating madly, before gathering itself back up and trying again. Finally, exhausted, it could take no more of the heat. It fluttered to the floor like a tiny scrap of Origami, too exhausted to follow its instincts any longer. It twitched weakly near his feet.

Marcus was impassive, staring vacantly at the moth. His face betrayed no emotion but his forehead was furrowed, the only outward sign of his emotional state. It was irrational, he knew, but the injured moth at his feet was suddenly the focus of his ire. Its nearly silent fluttering was like a cymbal crashing in his ears, like a thousand eagles screeching around his head. This insect, this non-sentient creature devoid of self-awareness, was suddenly the focus, the proxy, for Marcus' anger and frustration. It would be quick and easy, he knew, to do away with this thing. Just a little pressure with his heel, one push, and that would be it…

Instead he scooped up the moth and stalked stiff-legged to the front door. He flung open the screen and angrily tossed the insect out into the dark morning. The air was cool and populated with country noises: crickets, some spring-peepers, and a large truck downshifting several miles away on the state highway. Marcus let the night air blow gently across his face, a soothing balm that worked to gently loosen the knot of his foul mood. He leaned against the door jamb for several moments before he finally let the screen door gently shut, leaving the night to its own devices.

Back inside now and wide awake he wondered what he could do at three in the morning. He decided it would help his mental state to have more of the house in order, so with restrained enthusiasm he tackled the disaster that was the kitchen. Starting, he knew full well, was the hardest part, and it took him several minutes to know where to begin. He settled on the "nuclear option", which meant tossing out everything and beginning anew. With a heavy sigh he grabbed the trash bags and began chucking in anything that wasn't nailed or fastened down. A clean slate was the best solution here, and if he found later that he needed something that he had pitched, well so be it: he could buy a replacement.

Hours passed and finally the kitchen was vastly improved. A quick inventory found he had saved several glasses, a toaster, one pan, and two small pots. He had also salvaged several cheap utensils and a single bamboo mixing spoon that had "Pampered Chef" embossed on the handle. His only bowl looked like half a soccer ball with a goofy face on the side. Everything else – the old bags of salt and sugar, the moldy buns from the refrigerator, all the detritus left on the counters, walls, and the floor - had gone in to the bags that continued to line up out back like well-trained soldiers. Marcus was certain the trash collectors would forever curse his name come the next collection day. He had swept and mopped the kitchen floor several times trying to get rid of all the floor grit, and he was reasonably happy with the outcome as nothing crunched underfoot any longer. He crossed his arms and surveyed his handiwork, satisfied that he had done the best he could. The kitchen was at least serviceable now.

He snapped his fingers. "Oh, one last thing," he recalled.

He grabbed the remaining bottles of water and put them on the center shelf of the refrigerator. They were the only item in there and they looked damned lonely, but it was a start. Only a trip to the old IGA grocery store could help.

Sunlight was slanting in through the grimy windows, a muted yellow-orange that illuminated the kitchen and living room in a soft glow, washing out the hard edges and masking much of the damage. Dust motes drifted lazily in the air, their patterns random and uncharted. Marcus heard birds outside singing. He looked out the kitchen window into the backyard and saw the doghouse, half obscured by tall grass and weeds. He knew what was there and what had to be done - but he was having a tough time bringing himself to do it. He'd rather scrub the entire house from top to bottom with a toothbrush than face the task that lay ahead

He tentatively headed outside to the rental Chevy and popped the trunk. It opened with a muted *ka-chunk*. He pulled out his final purchases from the Ace Hardware store in town: a short handled shovel, a canvas tarp, and some thick plastic gloves. Head bowed low he began his gallows-walk to Sam's doghouse.

The dog's desiccated corpse was alone and unmolested since it was too early for the flies to be up and around. Marcus unfurled the heavy canvas tarp and gently covered up the body. In life Sam had been a big dog, fully ninety pounds. This husk that remained was nothing close to that but it still required a fairly large hole in order to be buried properly. Marcus dug through the dark, rich earth, one heavy shovel-full at a time, until he had a trench four feet long and three feet deep. The sun was higher in the sky now and getting hotter by the second. He flipped sweat from his forehead as he finished the grave and rested momentarily against the shovel. He looked at the forlorn ambiguous shape under the tarp and couldn't help thinking that he was not just burying Sam, but somehow laying a part of his brother to rest as well.

With the gloves on he pushed the tarp and body into the hole. They resisted at first before finally breaking free and sliding stiffly in. The sound the bundle made coming loose from the grass was like an old envelope being opened, the ancient glue on the flap finally tearing free. He caught a whiff of a hot, foul, musky smell, like the fleeting stench from some old road kill, but it was mercifully wafted away by the light breeze. Marcus bunched the excess tarp in too then unhooked the chain from the cleat on the doghouse and coiled it up. He placed it neatly on the canvas and proceeded to re-fill the grave with dirt. There was quite a bit left over, even mounded as it was. It was a sad end, he thought, to a wonderful companion. He wished again that he knew what had happened.

While Marcus wasn't particularly devout he did feel the need to say a quick, sketchy prayer of farewell. Afterwards he jammed the shovel in the ground and went back inside to get cleaned up. There was more work to be done.

He had nearly forgotten the sorry shape of the bathroom. So after another trash bag sat outside dedicated to cracked shampoo bottles, soaps, and ruined toilet paper, he finally managed to take a shower. Fortunately there were several towels that had somehow avoided the worst of it. After fifteen minutes in a hot shower he felt decidedly improved. He shaved and dressed, then hopped back into the rental car for a quick trip to town. When he returned – two hundred dollars lighter in the wallet, courtesy of the local IGA grocery store – he was able to stock the cupboards and refrigerator with enough food to keep him going for a week or two. Using his one remaining salvaged pan he whipped up some scrambled eggs and toast. The eggs were slightly over-cooked and the toaster only browned one side of the bread, but it qualified as one of the most satisfying meals he'd enjoyed in recent memory.

After cleaning up his dishes he went back outside to have a better look around. Since arriving he'd only been inside the house and near its perimeter, so he felt he should make a more thorough inspection of the immediate area. He also figured he'd pop on over across the street to meet whoever was living behind the curtained window. They weren't too social, that was clear, but if they were always this nosey they might have seen or heard something. Marcus didn't have much else to go on right now.

Stepping back out into the late morning sun it looked to be a wonderful day. The morning dew had already burned off and the nearly cloudless sky was a solid sheet of blue. Marcus meandered around outside the house looking for anything out of the ordinary, anything that might tell him more than what little he knew. He ambled through the back yard, swishing through the tall grass that grabbed at his ankles, and stopped at the ragged tree line. Walking to and fro he finally spotted a small, indistinct path into the thick woods where some ground cover had sprouted up. Unfortunately everything else was so overgrown that he couldn't force his way through. He'd need a machete to hack through that mess. He gave up on that for now, promising to try again later.

He went back to the front of the house to inspect Rolland's Civic. The little black four door sedan was splattered with bird droppings and both front tires were flat. The windshield was permanently fogged a nacreous white in the upper corner of the driver's side. On the front seat were several CDs with handwritten labels of bands that Marcus only vaguely knew. They were probably pirated over the Internet, he thought disapprovingly. To him pirated music was no better than outright theft. Far be it for Rolland to actually purchase a CD from a store. He shook his head. He hadn't seen any car keys in the house, and in the jumbled mess that remained they could be anywhere, or they could be with Rolland for that matter. He hoped he hadn't thrown them out by accident during one of his cleaning binges.

At the mailbox he pulled out twenty or more letters – mainly bills, from the look of things – and several catalogues. The envelopes were yellowed and crinkled from age and exposure to the elements. Most of the catalogues were from odd military surplus outlets selling all types of knives, guns, blankets, and tents. He'd never seen so much camouflage and military gear before. It was amazing what someone could buy through the mail or online these days.

Standing in disbelief he flipped through the stiff, crinkly pages and was shocked at what he saw. He spotted an evil-looking rifle called a Hungarian FEG AMD AK-47 Folding Stock that looked right out of a modern-day war movie or video game. And what the hell was this? A Vietnam era semi-automatic rifle called an AR10 308 Carbine with Collapsing Stock? Who in their right mind needed this type of arsenal, he wondered. Machine-gun pistols, sniper rifles, Rugers, Panthers, Sig Sauers? It was unbelievable! All this was available through a catalogue? There was also a flyer for a gun and knife show at a Dayton arena, but looking at the date Marcus noted that it had already come and gone. He was nonplussed and couldn't imagine what Rolland was doing with any of this. Had his brother undergone some serious personality changes since the last time they had been together? He checked out the address, hoping it read "Occupant," but it was indeed addressed to his brother. He felt a twinge of guilt, knowing that he had cut Rolland loose three years earlier and anything could have happened in that time. He resolved to throw everything but the bills in the trash once he got back inside.

As he returned to the house he glanced over his shoulder to see if the curtain was open across the street. It wasn't, but Marcus figured there was no time like the present and trotted over, arms still laden with Rolland's mail. This house was nearly as run-down as Rolland's, but it struck him that the neglect was somehow different. Here at least it appeared that a loving touch had been at work for many years, that possibly the maintenance load had slowly become too much for the homeowner: from the neat rows of bricks lining the weed-choked landscaping, to the heavy, intricate, eagle-shaped bronze door knocker, to the paint just now beginning to peel from the eaves, he could see that this home and property were sliding inexorably, sadly into disrepair. The yard had a threadbare, thinning appearance, like the arms of an old, decaying easy chair. Marcus felt something at his feet and looked down. Twining itself around his ankles was a black and gray striped cat. He reached down to pet it, afraid that it might spook and take off, but instead it purred loudly and pushed its head into his hand, as if saying, "Yeah, that's the stuff." Marcus set the mail down and gently scooped up the cat and scratched behind its ears. The purring became as loud as a low-flying airplane.

Still holding the cat, he rapped on the front door, waited an appropriate amount of time and knocked again. There was no answer and no sound from inside. He tried once more, this time with the eagle knocker. The sharp, metallic clang was loud, almost painfully so. If nobody answered that, he thought, they were either deaf or dead. He waited for several moments, straining to hear something, anything. He thought he heard a light footfall, the slightest rustle of fabric brushing fabric, then nothing. With a sigh he ruffled the cat's ears one last time, put it down, then gathered up the mail and headed back to Rolland's. He vowed to try again later.

Back at the house he pondered his next steps, but after some consideration came up empty. He knew in his heart he should take Doncaster's advice and head over to Foley's Diner, but he was still too pissed at the Lieutenant to just follow along like a leashed dog. Instead he decided to try and empty his mind for a while and go with something physical. In this case, since he had no equipment and there didn't seem to be an exercise facility within a four county area except the small Wayne YMCA, he opted to lace on his running shoes and head out.

Marcus hopped into the rental car and drove down his brother's road two miles, marking his running route. He spotted what had once been an old driveway now choked with weeds and grass. Whatever house had once stood there was long gone. He used the driveway to turn around.

Back at the house he changed into running shorts and a T-shirt, along with a newer pair of Adidas running shoes. He figured he could put the four miles under his belt in around 30 minutes or so. No need to overdo it, he thought, but he wanted to push himself enough to smooth out some of the physical and mental kinks. He pulled the damaged front door shut, hearing the broken jamb groan a bit with the effort.

The surrounding countryside was quiet with few sounds besides his steady, heavy breathing and the *slap, slap* of his rubber soles on the hot asphalt. He ran in the left lane, facing traffic, and kept to the faded white line next to the berm. This section of Bradford - Wayne Road was straight and flat, the corn and soybean fields on either side only occasionally marred by a lone house or barn. His body was operating as designed and he could feel a thin sheen of sweat begin to form all over him, the perspiration cooling him as he ran. The late morning was warm but not hot so he kicked it up a notch, his feet feeling light and fleet. Anyone listening to his shoes hitting the road might not have noticed the slightly increased tempo of his pace but Marcus could feel it in his thighs and lungs. He did a rough calculation in his head and figured he had just knocked off thirty seconds per mile, and was down to about a seven minute pace. Not too shabby, he thought, mildly pleased.

At the old driveway he turned around, crossed the road, and started back. He kicked his pace up one more level as he neared the end, reveling in the fluid dynamics of his body and how all the disparate components operated in conjunction. The wind in his face felt wonderful and the strong finish was the perfect end to a solid workout. He slowed to a jog, then to a walk. Rolland's house was a hundred yards or so away. He crossed back over to the right side of the road.

The run had accomplished what he had hoped it would. His head was clearer now so he was able to compartmentalize his anger, allowing him to think more logically about the situation. He knew now that it was time to put aside his extreme dislike for Doncaster and check out Foley's. He had no idea why the cop had recommended that course of action, but Marcus was out of ideas and had nowhere else to turn. Besides, his ability to prepare meals was quite limited at the house and he was looking forward to a good lunch. Overly done scrambled eggs and half-cooked toast could only go so far.

As he cooled off Marcus heard the sound of an engine steadily growing louder behind him. Looking over his shoulder he could see a red pickup truck – possibly the same one he had nearly hit yesterday – coming toward him. Normally Marcus wouldn't be too concerned, but a closer inspection through the windshield revealed that the driver was paying a lot more attention to his cell phone than what was on the road in front of him. He watched the driver, who was laughing into his phone, and realized with a start that the pickup was bearing down on him and wasn't going to swerve. Marcus was used to inattentive drivers and sometimes felt he had a target on his back while out on runs. The side of the road here plunged in to a deep culvert four or five feet wide and several feet deep, the bottom of which was muddy and weed-choked. Not an ideal destination. Marcus gave the pickup truck a last baleful look, knew the driver had no clue he was there, then swore loudly and jumped. The truck roared past.

He landed with a thud on the far side of the ditch, his teeth clacking together with the impact. Gravel peppered his legs as the truck raced by. A quick look at the receding tailgate revealed two things: the word FORD in dirty white letters, and an Ohio vanity plate that read, oddly, "Driver 8". Marcus brushed some dirt off his knees and watched the truck pass the house and disappear around the bend.

"Idiot," he muttered.

Brushing himself off he realized he was on the outskirts of the woods behind his brother's house. The trees were smaller and sparser here, which meant that for twenty or thirty yards the edge of the culvert was fairly free of vegetation. He considered jumping back to the road but wasn't sure he could make it without the panicked adrenaline burst. Besides, this area was more shaded and cooler than the road and he was still hot from the run. He began walking along the ditch toward the house, pushing aside a sapling or shrub to get through. A drop of sweat meandered into his eye and briefly stung. Dragonflies silently darted around the tall weeds at the bottom of the ditch, their purple and green gossamer wings nearly invisible in flight.

Twenty feet further on he saw a glimmer on the ground, a bright wink of light, like a glint of sun reflecting off a mirror or shard of glass. At first he dismissed it as a gum wrapper or broken bottle, but as he got closer he realized that wasn't it at all. He bent down to inspect the object. It was a Visa credit card stuck corner-down in the hard dry ground. The bright reflection had come from the sun bouncing off the holographic Visa logo on the front of the card. Brow furrowed, Marcus picked up the credit card and inspected it. The name on the front said Matthew M. Kazmierczak and was issued on a credit union out of Missouri. The expiration date was current but he noted with interest that there was no signature on the back. How in the world, Marcus wondered, had a credit card from Missouri ended up stuck in a forlorn patch of dirt in western Ohio? He inspected it in greater detail, then stuck it in his waistband and walked on.

Marcus found he still couldn't penetrate the woods to any degree so was forced to back off his initial plan to find a way around the thick woods. Farther down he located a narrower part of the culvert and jumped back across to the road, then walked to the house. Once inside he slipped the credit card into his wallet, unsure what to do with it. He knew he should probably just cut it up and trash it, but something, some voice in the back of his head, was telling him not to be so hasty.

Another shower made him suitable for a trip back to town for lunch. The day was turning even warmer and the sun was very bright. He slid on his sunglasses and went out. The Chevy's air conditioning was cool and welcoming on his face. He reluctantly pointed the car towards town.

It was just after noon and the lunch crowd at Foley's Diner was in full swing. When he opened the door and walked in the aroma of cooking wafted over him. He took a deep breath and smelled the standard Midwestern menu items – burgers, fries, the usual greasy suspects – but he also noted more southern smells, Mexican smells. Black beans, fresh tortillas, and salsa, for starters. His mouth watered and his stomach gave an immediate, audible rumble.

Foley's Diner had been an institution in Wayne for decades. It had originally been simply Foley's Tavern, where working-class men paraded in after work to drink, smoke, laugh, and occasionally fight with their friends. The bar had changed hands several times in the last decade, finally being purchased two years earlier by a Wayne native named Sal Black, a young serviceman freshly home from a stint overseas in Afghanistan. Sal and his wife, a pretty Mexican girl five years his junior, purchased Foley's for a song from the previous owners who had let it fall into disrepair. Having lived for years on sub-standard military rations and MREs, Sal's dream was to open a nice family restaurant in town. In his words, "everyone deserves a nice place to eat." He dumped his entire savings into refurbishing the tired bar, sat back, and waited for customers to flock in for his traditional menu of American classics. They never did. Not until his wife took over the kitchen and imbued it with her own touch, one full of Mexican and Spanish flair, did it gain in popularity. The new menu was a hit with both the locals and the growing Latino population, to the point where on nights and weekends the line to get in snaked out the door and down the sidewalk. Foley's Diner became a new Wayne institution.

Upon entering he found himself in a small vestibule where several padded benches were set up for customers to rest while waiting for a table. One of the benches was occupied by a young couple and their two children. There was also an antique podium to the left where he was expected to sign in and wait his turn. Marcus wrote his name in his precise script on the yellow pad and sat. A few minutes passed before a cute young blond waitress inspected the list, then called out, "Fox, party of four?" The couple gathered up their kids and followed the waitress in to the dining area, leaving Marcus alone.

As he waited for a table he wondered again why Doncaster had directed him here. There seemed to be nothing inherent in this place that would help him locate Rolland. Through the doorway into the dining area he could see waitresses hustling around waiting tables as waitresses everywhere did. There was a narrow window at the back where he caught glimpses of a Latino short order cook moving fast and efficiently, snatching written orders from a small counter and tossing plates of food up with amazing speed and dexterity. It was an impressive display of organized mayhem. Sal ran a tight operation.

The same blond waitress popped back into the vestibule several minutes later and consulted the ledger on the podium. She looked up at Marcus, did an obvious double take, her blue eyes growing wide, then quickly ducked her head and referred back to the list of names. Her voice cracked and she said in a shaky voice, "Schmidt? Party of one?"

Marcus looked around again, one eyebrow raised: he was still the only one there. He shrugged and followed her to his table.

There were booths along the left wall and tables scattered throughout. There was also a breakfast bar on the right. Three or four people, two of whom were Hispanic, stared at him openly as he slid in to a booth at the far end of the room. Marcus wasn't sure what they were staring at, but assumed it was because he was no longer a local and hadn't been around for years. A few conversations died, cut off sharply, guillotined in mid-word. He knew Wayne didn't enjoy much of a tourist trade and in a small town such as this just about everyone no doubt knew everyone else. A stranger, even a townie from way back, was probably big news. He gave a mental shrug and looked over the lunch menu. The chicken fajitas looked promising. He hoped they tasted as good as everything smelled. He was famished and ready for a real meal.

The blond waitress took his order, deposited a glass of water and some utensils, and quickly scooted off. The normal murmur and background chatter slowly resumed. Marcus watched several other waitresses moving about, taking orders, bussing tables, chatting up customers. One particular server with a dark complexion, long, raven-black hair, and almond eyes caught and riveted his attention. First and foremost Marcus was struck with how very pretty she was. Her dark skin, the color of *café con leche*, or coffee with milk, contrasted sharply with her white server outfit. She was quite obviously of Mexican descent with just a touch of some indigenous Mayan in her features. He could detect it mainly in her high cheekbones and the slight hook of her nose. He couldn't help himself; he was immediately smitten. He stared at her as she moved smoothly between several tables, smiling brightly and talking with her patrons. Her arms were laden with a pile of dirty dishes and she expertly plucked up several more from a table. She turned and walked toward Marcus.

Two steps later their eyes met and she stuttered to a stop, her shoe squeaking on the tile floor, face wide open with shock. Emotions flew across her features with tornado-like speed: surprise first, followed quickly by hope and a split second of joy, then something else. Fear? Marcus couldn't understand. Why would she be scared? Before he could devote any thought to it the plates in her arms suddenly became unbalanced and several from the top of the stack toppled. They hit the ground with a crash, white ceramic shrapnel and leftover food flying. Orange juice from a shattered glass splashed on the leg of a nearby patron and he yelped in surprise. She remained rooted there, her face a complex palette of emotions.

There was a collective groan from the rest of Foley's at her misfortune. She looked down at the mess, glanced back at Marcus, then down again. She seemed torn and unable to decide what to do next. Finally she turned and rushed back to the kitchen and disappeared inside. A minute later another waitress came and cleaned up her mishap.

Meanwhile Marcus' food had arrived. The cast iron fajita plate was sizzling, the onions, chicken, and green peppers still cooking in a thin dark sauce. The waitress needlessly warned him that the plate was hot. She also deposited a plate full of rice, frijoles, lettuce, sour cream, and bright green guacamole. A third plate held four hot tortillas wrapped in thin aluminum foil. Keeping an eye out for the pretty Latina waitress, Marcus layered in a generous helping of each ingredient and dug in. The chicken was tender and moist, browned just right. Okay, he admitted between bites, this meal beats the hell out of my scrambled eggs and toast hands down.

Ten minutes later nothing was left but the scoop of guacamole, which he had never much liked. For the first time in a long while Marcus felt truly satisfied by a meal. He patted his stomach, confessing that he had a soft spot for good Mexican food. This meal had certainly qualified as that and more. He had kept one eye open for the Latina waitress throughout lunch, but he hadn't caught so much as a glimpse of her since her dish mishap. His original blond waitress came back.

"Are we still working on that?" she asked, smiling nervously and pointing at the guacamole.

"No, I'm done. Thanks."

She laid the bill on the table. The amount was very reasonable. "I'll take that when you're ready."

Marcus dug out his wallet. He noticed her nametag said, "Hello! I'm ALICE." He was about to ask Alice who the waitress had been but just then he spotted her talking to the short order cook through the narrow window. They were having a heated discussion of some sort. He was distracted enough that he grabbed the first credit card he found and handed it to Alice.

"Thanks," she said. "I'll be right back," and she scooted off.

The cook and the waitress were no longer talking, and crane his neck as he might Marcus couldn't spot her anywhere. Damn! He hadn't even caught her name from her nametag. Alice quickly came back with a slightly embarrassed look on her face and handed him his credit card.

"Um, it was declined," she said softly.

Marcus was shocked. "Declined?" he asked, incredulous. "That can't be..." He took the card back from Alice and inspected it. Now it was his turn to look embarrassed, but also relieved. This wasn't his card, it was the one he had found near the culvert earlier that morning, the one issued to Matthew M. Kazmierczak. With an apologetic grin he handed her his own card.

"Sorry about that," he said, discomfited. "My mistake. Wrong card. Here – this one should work."

She accepted the new card and was only gone a minute. Upon her return she presented him with the bill to be signed. As Marcus quickly calculated an appropriate tip he looked up at Alice.

"That was a great lunch, thanks."

"Um, you're welcome," she replied nervously.

"This seems to be a popular place," he said, motioning to the crowd and smiling, hoping to make her more at ease with some small talk.

"Um, yes," she said, still seeming petrified.

So much for the small talk, he thought. He handed her the signed receipt. She took it, but Marcus held on to it as well. A brief mini tug-of-war ensued.

She looked at him questioningly, confused, the whites around her eyes showing.

"One last thing," he asked, still gripping the check. "That girl, the waitress who had the little accident with the dishes. She looks familiar for some reason. What's her name?"

Alice's eyes blinked very quickly, as if she were analyzing possible responses. Finally she said, "You mean Cassie? It's Cassie. Well, Cassandra."

Marcus wanted to ask her more – like why she was so obviously nervous, why was Cassandra stunned to the point of dropping dishes, why did some of the other customers seem shocked to see him - but she looked like a doe in the woods, ready to bolt at the slightest snap of a twig. He released the check and thanked her again. She quickly scurried off to the kitchen and he didn't see her again for several minutes. When she came back out to wait on other customers she wouldn't make eye contact with him. Cassandra never came out of the kitchen again.

Marcus spent another thirty minutes waiting and watching, then finished his water and left, still deep in thought. He knew how much he and Rolland resembled each other. The two of them had heard that their entire lives. Could that be the reason for all the bizarre, shocked reactions to him just now in Foley's? It just didn't make sense to him.

He was feeling slightly morose since he thought he had not accomplished anything, but in fact he had. Marcus had no idea, but he had shaken the nest, and the hornets were about to get angry.

Chapter 5

With no other leads to speak of and not much else to do besides cleaning Rolland's house, which served his need for organization but was nevertheless getting old fast, Marcus began taking many of his meals at Foley's Diner. He was hoping to catch another glimpse of this Cassandra person, to talk to her for just a minute so he could find out what she might know. He was certain there was something there, some reason for her distress. He had no idea what it might be, but he knew he had to talk to her about Rolland. He had a gut feeling she was a key player in all this. She had to be the reason Doncaster the cop had told Marcus about Foley's in the first place.

However, no matter how many times he stopped at the diner, no matter how often he hung around outside in his car or did a quick pop-in, she never was never there.

When he asked the rest of the waitresses at Foley's about her they were no help, and neither was Sal Black, the owner. They never allowed themselves to warm to him even after his many visits, and everyone there adhered to their strict policy of not sharing personal employee information. The only reply he ever got was that she was off for several days, out of town, visiting relatives. He didn't believe it. The entire staff kept him at arm's length, taking his food orders and serving his meals, but never moving emotionally much closer than what those perfunctory duties called for. He'd seen English butlers in movies that were friendlier.

"Good morning, Alice, how are you today?" he'd ask.

"Just fine, sir. What can I get you this morning?"

"Hmmm… I'll have the three egg breakfast, scrambled, with wheat toast."

"Anything to drink?"

"Yes, please. Orange juice, and a water. I'm going for a run later this morning."

"Anything else?" she would ask.

"Can you tell me when Cassandra will be back? I just want to talk to her."

"Sorry, you know we can't give out anything like that," she'd say with just a trace of an apology and a sad face. "I'll have your breakfast right out."

That was the best he could get. He hated being balked over and over, but it was tough to stay mad at her and the rest of them when he understood they were just doing their job. But he wanted something, a hint, some direction, anything! He even went so far as to ask several of the adjacent businesses downtown about her, including the indifferent teenager at the Ace Hardware store. While most knew who she was they either wouldn't or couldn't offer any additional information.

Out of desperation he even waited out back one evening behind Foley's. When the short Hispanic cook was done for the night and began walking down the alleyway, Marcus fell in to step beside him.

"Hi, good evening. Can I talk to you for a minute?"

The cook jumped when he saw Marcus, his heavy features screwed up in confusion, clearly not understanding the question. Sweat glistened on his forehead in the cool night air. "Lo siento, Señor, pero no entiendo."

"That's fine," Marcus replied in perfectly accented Mexican Spanish. "We can continue in Spanish, if you like."

The cook sucked in a breath like a hiccup, blanched and scurried away. Marcus was left in the dingy alley, calling vainly after him, watching the man's broad back as he practically ran away. His short legs moved fast as he kicked through some trash and litter on the ground. He turned left at the next street and was gone.

"Damn," Marcus exclaimed. Frustrated again by another failed attempt, he made his way back to the Chevy and reluctantly aimed it toward Rolland's.

Twenty minutes later he was in the house. He had little to do so he turned on the small radio he had purchased on the earlier trip to the hardware store. There were only a few interesting stations out of Dayton to listen to, so he tuned in to a classic rock station and set about tidying up what he referred to as the "guest" bedroom. *Rock You Like A Hurricane* by the *Scorpions* was just kicking in, the distinctive heavy opening guitar riff ringing out from the radio's small speaker. Marcus found himself singing along under his breath, "Here I am…rock you like a hurricane…" He refrained from performing an air guitar solo when the Scorpions really starting smoking. "The kitty's purring, it scratches my skin…so what is wrong with another sin… Here I am…rock you like a hurricane…"

He had only been working on the room for a few minutes when there was a heavy knocking on the door: three solid, authoritative booms. He nearly didn't hear it over the music, but the banging was so strong that it shook the walls of the little frame structure. More than just a little curious who would be at the door at this hour, and a little hopeful that it may have something positive to do with Rolland, he hurried over and threw open the door.

"Yes? May I help you?" Marcus asked.

There were several steps leading up to the front door outside, so squinting through the screen door into the dark he was prepared to look down on whoever was there. He was, however, stunned to find himself actually looking up into the face of a broad-shouldered man with long, jet black hair, hair that was parted in the middle and flowed down well over his collar. The man's face was partially obscured by shadow, but Marcus could tell even in the poor light leaking out from within the living room that his dark complexion was pock-marked and pitted, as if he had suffered through terrible acne or chicken pox as a teenager. His eyes were hooded by a heavy brow that gave him an almost Neanderthal-like appearance.

Wow - this guy is a damn Goliath, Marcus thought. He also noticed some furtive movement behind the big man. There was a smaller individual there, standing well back, his face and features concealed by the deepening gloom. Warning bells rang in his head and he suddenly had a bad feeling about this.

Then a fist the size of a cantaloupe smashed through the screen door and caught Marcus squarely in the chest, tossing him up in the air and throwing him backwards as if he had been yanked by a rope tied to a speeding car. The impact forced all the air out of his lungs with a tremendous "woof", and he felt as if his sternum had just been shattered. Windmilling his arms he stumbled, fighting to regain his balance, then tripped over the low coffee table and landed hard on his back. His head smashed into the wood floor with a loud *crack*! He saw a tremendous burst of white light and stars suddenly filled his vision. He dimly heard the final refrain belted out by the Scorpions *"...rock you like a hurricane...here I am!"* then mercifully everything went black.

Several years earlier Marcus had undergone a simple procedure at his doctor's office. While the procedure itself was relatively innocuous it had necessitated him being given a general anesthetic and being knocked completely out. He didn't remember a single aspect of the procedure itself. He did recall recovering from the general anesthetic. He hadn't woken up all at once, but had wavered in and out of consciousness for a while, with bits and pieces of events stuck in his mind, like flipping around and reading random pages of a book. He vaguely remembered the doctor peering in his eyes with a penlight, then later his nurse checking his blood pressure. Sometime after that he heard people talking in the next room. It was all quite fuzzy, as if he had witnessed it through a Vaseline smeared lens.

He was bleary now, not yet fully aware, still drifting, like he was coming around after general anesthetic again. Dimly he noticed that his head ached terribly. There was a tremendous pounding in his skull, like a sledgehammer striking the back of his head over and over. *Ba-bang! Ba-bang! Ba-bang!* It couldn't have been any worse if highway construction had been going on in there. He clutched and grasped at full awareness briefly, only to feel it slipping away again. He was fading quickly, he could tell, since the banging in his head was receding to a muted tapping. Then that too was gone and he was out cold once more.

Several more times he edged toward full consciousness only to slide away again. He felt like a drowning man clawing for the surface, managing a panicked gasp of air, only to be pulled back down as he witnessed the lighted surface above him grow small and dim.

He vaguely recalled answering the door, then... Did a huge fist really punch through the screen and knock him on his back? Really? Why the hell would anyone do that? He managed to lift his head an inch and a thick string of drool came away with it. He was still groggy, fuzzy, his brain feeling like it was stuffed with cotton. He opened his eyes a slit which served to kick-start the highway crew in his head – *Ba-bang! Ba-bang! Ba-bang!* – and he quickly forced them tightly closed. Despite his best efforts a moan oozed out between his lips. His chest ached too, especially when he tried to take a deep breath.

"He's starting to wake up," an impossibly deep and heavy voice said in Spanish. The voice spoke slowly, deliberately, the diction clear and precise.

"Good. It's about time," replied a second man, also in Spanish. His tone was higher pitched and laced with an edge of impatience. "You hit him too hard."

Still mentally operating well below par, Marcus tried to bring his hand to his mouth to wipe the drool away. To his surprise he found he couldn't complete this simple command. His hand wouldn't budge. Now that was damned peculiar, he thought. Why can't I move my hand? He willed his other arm to move with an equal lack of success. He was still too bleary to think straight, as if he were waking from a dream, but mounting anxiety was beginning to edge out his confused apprehension.

"Don't be absurd," said the deep voice. "Yes, I punched him, but he tripped."

"Yeah, right," replied the second voice sarcastically. "He tripped. You never know your own strength, do you?"

"Think whatever you like, you always do."

"Whatever."

Marcus tugged again at his arms, then at his legs. He jerked and pulled, but couldn't move or free himself. He yanked ferociously, struggling with all his might, teeth gritted.

"Oh, yes, certainly," said the deep voice right next to his ear. "He's awake now."

Headache or not he opened his eyes and immediately stifled a shocked yell. Not two feet away was the huge face he had seen through the screen door: long, lank hair, black and parted down the middle, framing a massive, square, cratered face with skin like partially melted wax. His brow was huge, shadowing narrow black eyes, eyes that stared at him like small black marbles. There was a mottled scar on his left cheek.

"You're awake," he rumbled, still in Spanish.

Marcus stared at the man, shocked, still speechless. He heard someone moving behind him, but couldn't turn his head far enough to see anyone else.

"We need to talk," the big man said simply, then stood, towering over Marcus. He brought a huge black cigar up to his mouth, lit a stick match on his thigh. He puffed slowly and patiently, in no apparent hurry. He drew deeply on the cigar. Blue smoke partially obscured his face, a ghostly haze that hung unnaturally still in the dead air of the house. He reached behind him and pulled a chair over. Sitting down he was still taller than a standing average person.

"I apologize for the forceful entrance," he continued, "but we needed to, shall we say, get your attention."

Marcus was lying face-down on the heavy rectangular kitchen table that must have been dragged into the living room. His wrists were tied with thin, sturdy nylon rope and secured underneath to the table legs. The cords looked like they had been cut from the blinds in the bedroom. He wasn't able to see his legs but guessed they were bound in the same fashion.

Keeping his voice as steady as he could, Marcus asked in Spanish, "Why am I tied up like this? What the hell do you think you're doing?" Unintentionally his voice increased in volume with the last few words.

The big man raised a finger the size of a bratwurst. He waggled it back and forth. "Now, now – we will ask the questions. You will simply supply the answers. First, some introductions." He placed his palm to his chest. "You may call me Señor Gonzalez, and you may refer to my associate as Señor Hernandez."

Hernandez, still standing out of sight somewhere behind him, snickered.

"Second, I feel I should give you some background information on myself," Señor Gonzalez said as Marcus continued to strain against his bindings. Peripherally Marcus noticed that his captor used formalized Spanish as opposed to the familiar mode. He also noted that the man spoke quite well, his speech smooth and almost eloquent. It certainly belied his exterior appearance. "As you may have already determined I am not originally from around here. Where I grew up I was a simple farmer, working the land and earning a meager living. However, I was always as you see me now," he continued, sitting up and showing his full size. Marcus guessed he nearly topped seven feet in height. He had never seen anyone so tall before. "But I have always been a gentle man, slow to anger. Peaceful." He sat back down and the chair groaned ominously.

"Until one day," he said, black eyes clouding at the memory. "I went in to town for some seed and supplies and while there decided to enjoy a drink. There was another man in the tavern. This man was drunk, even though it was the middle of the afternoon. He was a large man as well, although not as large as I, and I believe he felt he needed to prove something. Regardless, he tried to start a fight with me even though I had done nothing. I ignored his taunts and jeers, dismissed his attempts to become physical, and was about to leave. Then he did something truly foolish. He broke a bottle – much like you see in your American movies – and swung it at my face. That is how," he said, pointing one of those bratwurst fingers at his cheek, "that is how I got this scar."

He shifted in his chair, sitting back. He puffed on his cigar slowly, savoring it. Every so often he looked at it, rolling it between his fingers as if communing with the dark tobacco. Despite himself, despite his situation, Marcus was listening.

"And that is when I picked the man up over my head, and broke his back over my knee. I will never forget the sound it made, like walnuts being crushed under my heel." His black eyes grew distant and thoughtful, but there was no joy in them. "I knew from that point on that I was no longer a farmer, that I had a different calling. It was then that I was sought out by certain individuals, and from that time on I have been in their employ. I do not enjoy violence, no, no, and I've rarely had to resort to such behavior again, but I know that it is in me – " he thumped his chest once – "should I ever need it."

Marcus strained at his bonds again, feeling them cut into his wrists. The table legs creaked under the pressure. After five seconds of struggling he relaxed, breathing heavily. Beads of sweat had popped out on his forehead like fat drops of glycerin, dampening his blond hair and running into his eyes. Panic was setting into him in earnest and his heart hammered in his chest, his stomach clenching wildly.

"What do you want from me?" he panted, staring into Gonzalez's black marble eyes.

"Then we have Señor Hernandez," the big man continued, ignoring the question. "You do not need to know anything about him, except for one thing: unlike me, he enjoys violence and causing pain. That is why he is here."

Before Marcus could object or say anything the unseen Hernandez grabbed Marcus' collar from behind and yanked hard. The fabric of his shirt resisted for a split-second before tearing in half, completely exposing Marcus' back. Marcus yelled in surprise and anger.

"And now," Señor Gonzalez said flatly, almost apologetically, pointing with the lit end of the fat cigar, "we shall find out how much you do know."

Marcus heard a hissing, whistling sound behind him and pain exploded across his back. His entire body snapped taut, the muscles and tendons standing out like a weightlifter's when pushed to the limit. His eyes were clenched tight and all air seemed to have been expelled from his lungs.

There was a slight pause, just enough to allow Marcus to draw a deep, shuddering breath. Then the hissing, whistling sound shattered the silence again. The second time was in some ways worse than the first since he knew what was coming. Upon impact his entire body went rigid, as if he were strapped to an active electric chair. He numbly felt a slithering on his flayed back as something thin and rough was dragged across it.

"Yes," Gonzalez said softly. "That was a whip. I doubt you have ever been whipped before, have you? No? It is not something many people have experienced, I dare say. And you handle the pain very well, amigo. You did not scream or cry out. I have seen men stronger than you scream for mercy at the first taste of the lash. Well done."

Marcus' nerves were raw, waiting, waiting for the whip to fall again. His eyes were still screwed tightly shut. Sweat bathed his entire body as if he had been left too long in a sauna. His arms and legs twitched and jerked uncontrollably.

"Now that you have been suitably…primed, shall we say," he continued, his bass voice still soft, almost caring, "I think it is time that we talk."

"Talk?" Marcus muttered, still in Spanish. "Talk? What…what the hell do you want? Talk about what?"

"We'd like to know where your brother is," Gonzalez stated.

Marcus opened his eyes again. His back felt as if it had been slashed open by knives and doused in rubbing alcohol. "Rolland? This is all about Rolland?"

"Exactly," he replied, happy and grinning. "Rolland. We would like to know where Rolland is." He had trouble pronouncing the name, rolling the R in Rolland and giving the double "Ls" more of a "Y" sound. It was not a typical Spanish name.

Marcus' mind raced madly. They were all trying to find Rolland, but he didn't think these two would likely accept a simple "I don't know" as a suitable answer. Damn! Out of sight behind him he knew the whip was poised, ready to strike if they didn't hear what they wanted.

"Why are…you looking…for him?" he gasped in Spanish, stalling, the words coming out in bits and pieces.

The whip cracked across his back again. This time Marcus almost did scream out in agony. His eyes were shut so hard he was seeing red and blue spots. Nothing happened for twenty or thirty seconds before Señor Gonzalez spoke again.

"As I mentioned, we will ask the questions, and you will give us the answers. Or Señor Hernandez" – he nodded behind Marcus – "will be happy to use the whip again. Is that clear?"

After a few seconds to catch his breath, Marcus nodded his head. Sweat puddled on the table under his face and under his chest.

"Good," he said, clapping his huge hands together cheerfully. "What do you know, Señor Hernandez? He is learning already. Perhaps you will not have the pleasure of using your toy again, eh?" His cigar had gone out and he relit it with another stick match. The smell of sulfur mingled with the tobacco, a thick sinister odor.

"Hmpf," the second man grunted, disbelief and disappointment mixed together in that single syllable.

"So, back to our initial question. Where is Rolland? We know you are his brother, and we know you have had contact with him recently, or you would not have this."

Marcus cracked open an eye and saw that Gonzalez was holding up the credit card that Marcus had found stuck in the dirt, the one issued to Matthew M. Kazmierczak. Of course they would have rifled through his wallet and belongings while he was unconscious. The VISA card looked no larger than a matchbook in a hand the size of a catcher's mitt.

"What…? I don't understand," Marcus whispered.

Gonzalez quickly held up a hand, apparently to stay the whip. "It is quite simple. Rolland was taking care of some business for us involving cards such as this one. You could not have this in your possession without having contact with him recently. He has more cards such as this. Many more. They are ours, and we want them back. We will have them back." His low voice took on an edge. "So now you will tell us – where is Rolland?"

Marcus stared at the huge Mexican, and it dawned on him that no matter what he said, no matter what he did, this was not going to end well for him. He had looked into the eyes of Gonzalez and he knew – completely and with absolute certainty – that no matter what he told them there was zero chance of him making it out of this house alive. These men were brutal killers. At least one had killed before by his own admission, and he had little doubt the other had as well. This realization, this insight, made him decide on a course of action that he never thought would be possible in a situation such as this. He was done. He was done cooperating with these maniacs, no matter what they did. They were not going to get anything out of him – even though he had no useful information he could pass along. He closed his eyes and braced himself for the worst.

"Fuck off," he said in English, his teeth gritted.

Gonzalez stood quickly, the chair toppling behind him. It skidded across the floor and banged into the far wall. The huge man looked both chagrined and annoyed as he crossed arms larger than most men's legs. He worked the cigar around his mouth between huge, yellowed teeth.

"That's an unwise and unfortunate decision," he proclaimed. "I was hoping we could work this out quickly and amicably. Now I am afraid I shall have to let Señor Hernandez practice his skill a bit more. Then you will be happy to talk again."

Marcus heard the leather of the whip being drawn through the other man's hands. He mentally steeled himself for the impending lash, eyes clamped shut. But just then he heard a sound, far away but definitely coming closer by the second.

Gonzalez turned to the noise. "Police," he hissed. He looked down at Marcus, then back toward the sound of the siren getting louder. He chewed the cigar cruelly until the end was a pulpy black mess. He seemed to be weighing his options, as if considering how to perhaps take Marcus with them. His massive head swung back and forth between Marcus and the siren like a lion deciding between downed prey and an approaching hunter. Then he made up his mind and motioned to the unseen Hernandez with a quick, annoyed flick of his head, as if to say "time to go." He leaned down low to Marcus, his breath hot and redolent of cigars. The scar on his cheek pulsed an angry purple. Their eyes locked.

"We shall talk again, I think," he said ominously.

As he made his way toward the door, his footfalls heavy enough to shake the floor, Marcus managed to twist his head so he could see a portion of the room in the reflection of the dark window. He clearly saw the two men – one a giant, the other small and wiry and moving with a certain grace – preparing to leave. The small man looked toward him and for the first time Marcus was able to see his face, if only for a moment, in the reflection of the window. He sucked in a quick breath. That face! Son of a bitch, he recognized that face!

Then the door slammed shut, and they were gone.

The siren was close now, and he gratefully shut his eyes and waited.

No more than two minutes later Marcus could see the blue and red lights of a police car flashing through the window and splashing on the walls, illuminating the inside of the room like a dance hall. Moments later there was a knocking at the door, firm and authoritative. Marcus yelled out and assured whoever was out there that the coast was clear. Doncaster eased his bulk in the door and silently surveyed the scene before him. After a few seconds the Lieutenant made his way over and knelt down low so they were eye to eye. The cop's knees popped like bubble wrap as he squatted. His thick neck was bulging over his shirt collar.

"Damn." He stretched out the word, so it sounded like *day-am*. He brandished a small pocket-knife and began cutting Marcus loose. "What the hell is going on here? You pissed someone off pretty quick, considering you've been in town less than a week."

Marcus grunted as his bonds were cut and noted that they were indeed cords from the window blinds. That they had used something at hand led him to assume that his attackers had been working on the spur of the moment and with little advanced planning. Except the whip. He would never forget the whip and how it felt, like red hot razors across his back, and he shuddered before focusing once again on the present. Doncaster had to carefully slice the cords from around his wrists and ankles. His extremities were numb and wouldn't work well, the blood flow having been hampered by the tight bindings. His fingers tingled as he worked them, then began burning like frostbitten limbs regaining life. He sat up and massaged them gently, stiffly flexing them back and forth. His back burned even more now, and the shreds of his shirt were draped around his waist in a useless pile.

The two men stared at each other. "You going to tell me what happened?" the cop repeated. "Your back is a mess. If I didn't know better I'd say you'd been whipped."

Marcus started slowly. "Some maniacs broke in here looking for Rolland. They seemed to think I knew where he was." He didn't mention the credit card or what they had been searching for. "You're right. They knocked me out, tied me up, and one of them used a whip on me." He arched his back, moving it gingerly.

"A whip? You shittin' me?"

Marcus managed a small nod.

"Hmm. You need to go to the hospital?"

"No, I don't think so."

Doncaster stared at him, deciding whether or not to press the issue. He shrugged. "Whatever. Your choice, but it's probably just as well. I don't know how you'd explain any of this to them, or could even if you wanted to." The cop pulled out his black notebook and started taking notes with the Bic pen. *Click-click, click-click.* "Let's get some details while they're fresh in your mind." He proceeded to pepper questions at him for the next ten minutes. Marcus was truthful and forthright about the entire incident, only omitting details about the credit card and his last second glimpse and recognition of the second man. After Doncaster had filled several pages with notes he pocketed the notebook and the pen and looked piercingly at Marcus.

"That's it? Nothing else?" he asked. "You're not giving me too much to go on, you know. Two guys broke in here, one of them a giant, pock-faced Mexican. They tied you up and whipped you. You didn't see the other guy. Their names were Hernandez and Gonzalez." He paused then looked quizzically at Marcus. "Why would they do that? Why would they give you their names?"

Marcus gave a brief snort of laughter, not much more than a small lifting of his shoulders, then regretted the movement as pain flared across his back. "Saying their names were Hernandez and Gonzalez is like saying someone here in the States is named Smith and Jones. They're two of the most common Mexican surnames out there." Something hit him just then, something he hadn't noticed in all the commotion earlier: both of his attackers had spoken Spanish the entire time, not even worrying that he would or wouldn't be able to understand them. Somehow they had known he was fluent.

The stocky cop stared at him silently, noticing that Marcus had perhaps thought of something. The silence dragged on but Marcus held his tongue, for some reason not wanting to pass this latest information along. Marcus did finally oblige him, not with more information but with a question of his own.

"So, what brought you out here? How did you know there was any trouble?"

The cop grunted and looked perturbed that nothing more was forthcoming. He flicked his head toward the front of the house. "Your neighbor across the street called 911. Don't know how she knew there was a problem, but somehow she did. The 911 dispatcher told me the county boys were busy, so I went and took the call." He surveyed the table and the shredded bindings on the floor. "Good thing I did, eh?"

Marcus flexed his back. The pain was changing from a sensation of being cut by razors to a deep, lingering throbbing.

"Good thing. Thanks, and I mean it."

“It’s my job,” the stocky cop stated flatly. He unclipped his shoulder mounted radio and directed the dispatcher to disseminate a description of the giant Mexican to the various state and county police and sheriff departments. At the end of his verbal report he added that they were considered dangerous and to proceed with caution. Marcus couldn’t agree more.

“I’ll have the county boys keep an eye on you and the house for a while,” he said, wrapping up.

“Thanks, I appreciate it,” Marcus replied sincerely, still wincing as he explored his range of movement.

The cop shook his head as he walked to the door. “Only in town for a week and already a troublemaker. Unbelievable,” he mumbled. He glanced at the shredded screen door on his way out, still shaking his head. He sat out in the car for a few more minutes while he wrote additional notes, then flicked off his emergency lights and slowly pulled out, only to ease into the driveway across the street. Marcus watched as the cop went to the front door, which opened a crack. He couldn’t see much, but Doncaster did seem to write down some notes, nod politely, then stride back to the cruiser and depart. The yard was oddly silent and dark after he was gone.

Marcus walked around the house and made sure all the windows were shut fast. He also made sure the back door was locked, even going so far as to jam kitchen chairs under the doorknobs for extra security, especially the broken front door. Satisfied that he was secure as possible he found a length of two by four that would serve as a passable club, popped three aspirins, and lay down on the couch. He didn’t think he’d have any more trouble with his two intruders again tonight, but it never hurt to be prepared. If they wanted to have another go at him he would at least make them earn it this time.

Chapter 6

In spite of not being able to sleep well because of his aching back, the next morning dawned bright and clear, full of country noises: a tractor trundling by, birds singing happily, a distant lowing of cows. Awkwardly checking himself out in the bathroom mirror revealed three angry welts, each about ten inches long, crisscrossing his skin as if he'd been raked by the claws of some wild animal. There were several areas where the skin had been broken and crusted over with blood, and on top of that there was a splotchy blue-green cast all over that hinted at additional bruising to come. Three more aspirins took the edge off the throbbing enough that he could pull on a T-shirt. He purposefully chose a large, loose cotton one that wouldn't rub and irritate the wounds. He was absently muttering curses in both Spanish and English when there was a knock on the door. His makeshift club popped into his hand almost of its own accord, adrenaline pounding through his bloodstream. His stomach clenched.

"Who is it?" he asked, warily, making his way to the side of the door.

"Um, it's Otto," came a tentative male voice. "I'm a friend of Rolland."

Marcus was annoyed with himself: he wished again that he hadn't been absent from his brother's life for so long, otherwise he might have known if Otto was legit or not, friend or foe. He hefted the club.

"You'll have to excuse me if I'm a little leery of guests," Marcus replied. "I had a little trouble last night."

"Yeah, I know," Otto replied. "Don-Don told me. Something about a giant Mexican or something weird like that."

Don-Don? Marcus wondered.

"Anyway, I'm a friend and I know you're looking for him," Otto continued. "Can we talk? I'm…I'm really worried about him, you know?"

Marcus glanced out the window and could see a red Ford pickup in the driveway next to his Chevy rental. He paused, peering thoughtfully at the truck, knowing he'd seen it before. Then he eyed the license plate.

"'Driver 8'?" he asked. "You're 'Driver 8'? You almost hit me the other day when I was out running."

"That's me, Driver 8," Otto replied proudly. "And did I really almost hit you? Sorry about that. My bad, man. I don't always pay enough attention when I'm driving."

Marcus pulled the chair away from the door and opened it. Otto stood there, looking uncomfortable and nervous, his hands in his pockets. He was in his early twenties, sporting a bright yellow and black Columbus Crew soccer jersey. The young man did a little head flip to clear long bangs from his eyes. He looked a little like someone Marcus knew, but he couldn't place him.

"How do you know Rolland?" Marcus asked, leaning against the door frame, arms crossed, club just out of sight.

Otto was a little nervous. "We're friends, like I said. We've been friends for a couple years now. And, wow," he stated, staring at Marcus, "you *really* look like your brother. I mean you guys could be twins or something if your hair was longer."

"Yeah, we used to get that all the time."

"I mean, no wonder Cassie freaked out when she saw you. I'm freaking out right now."

Marcus started, suddenly very alert. He stood up straighter. "What did you say? Did you say 'Cassie'? Is this the Cassie that works at Foley's?"

"Sure, that's the one. She's his girlfriend. Or she was. I'm not sure now."

Shocked, Marcus further assessed the young man at his front door, and figuring himself a fairly good judge of character motioned him inside.

"Come on in," he said, not unkindly. "I think we need to talk. I could use some information, and some help."

Otto nodded and stepped over the threshold. He flipped his bangs out of his face again. Marcus motioned him to the couch and took a seat across from him, leaning the club against the chair. Otto stared wide-eyed at the two by four but didn't say anything. Marcus leaned forward eagerly, his elbows on his knees, purposefully keeping his tender back from making contact with the chair. Several questions fought for dominance in his mind as he looked into Otto's young, nervous face. He was dying to dive right into the heavy, meaty stuff, but intentionally backed off and started with a simple one, one he hoped would put Rolland's friend at ease.

"Otto, I'm glad you're here. You're right – I'm looking for Rolland, and I haven't had much luck so far," Marcus began. "But I have to ask you: I come from a family with rather unique names. Mine's Marcus, as you probably know, and of course Rolland. Our father's name is Egbert. But I've never heard of anyone here in the States named Otto before. Is that German?"

Some of the tension present in the young man seemed to loosen, like a tightly wound toy uncoiling several clicks. He looked relieved and eager to talk about this familiar ground. "Well, Otto is really just a nickname," he said. "And no, it's not German. My real name is Octavius, believe it or not." He watched Marcus' face carefully, waiting to see what he made of the name. Marcus looked interested so he forged on. "I'm the youngest of eight kids, and honestly I think my folks were running out of choices by then. Octavius means "eight" in Latin."

"Wow. Eight kids," Marcus said, shaking his head in mild disbelief.

"Yep. Eight kids, all boys."

"Your mom must have been a saint."

Otto laughed, an easy laugh of someone in their early twenties with limited responsibility, someone who had not yet had adulthood forced upon him. His thin face broke into a smile. "She is, really. But some of my older brothers helped a lot. Especially Don-Don. He was like a third parent, really."

"Don-Don?" Marcus asked. "You say that like I know him."

He looked slightly confused, his face scrunched up and head tilted to one side. "Well, yeah, sure you do. You've met him a couple of times, I think. Don-Don is Donald Doncaster, the cop. Don-Don was his nickname when we were all little."

Then it clicked, and now Marcus could see why he had looked vaguely familiar. There was definitely a family resemblance although Otto was much younger and leaner than the hefty Lieutenant. He was also much more personable.

"Yeah, your brother probably saved my life last night," Marcus admitted.

"Really?" Otto said, pride showing in his smile and eyes. "Cool. He's a good cop. I'm glad he helped you out."

Marcus nodded. "I'm glad, too. I don't think he likes me very much, though. At least that's the impression I got."

"Well, it's really not your fault," the young man admitted almost sheepishly, followed with a flip of his hair. The hair flip was so natural Marcus doubted he knew he did it. "It's Rolland's. You see, before Rolland came around Don-Don and Cassie were an item and had been dating for a couple of years. Then Rolland moved in and kind of stole her from him. Don-Don never really got over that."

Oh, ho, Marcus thought, mental light bulbs going off. That certainly explained some of the ice-cold reception he'd gotten from the cop.

"You've been in Don-Don's office, right? Did you see that picture his desk?" Otto asked, seemingly out of the blue.

Marcus thought for a second, back to his time in the basement office.

"Yeah, I did. I didn't really pay any attention to it, though."

"That's a picture of my brother and Cassie three or four years ago when they were hot and heavy. He can't seem to put it away. Just leaves it on his desk and stares at it." He shook his head. "It's not healthy, I don't think, but he can't get over her."

Marcus got up and headed to the kitchen. He grabbed two waters from the fridge and tossed one to Otto. The young man thanked him and took a long slug.

"Okay," Marcus said, changing gears, "let's talk about Rolland. What's he been up to? When's the last time you saw him?"

Otto took another pull from the water, gathering his thoughts. He stared at the water bottle, spinning it in his hands. Light from the window caught the water and shone dazzling, rainbow reflections on the floor at their feet, like a liquid prism. He sighed.

"Well, damn, I guess it's been months now," he began, almost apologetically. "We started hanging out about two, three years ago, and had a blast. You know how he is," Otto said. "Fun, funny, always ready for a good time. It was right after you and Rolland had that meltdown."

"Meltdown?"

Rolland's friend nodded, almost embarrassed to talk about it, as if he were revealing some dark family secret he wasn't supposed to know. He was having a hard time making eye contact. "Yeah, you know, when you were here and you caught him with all that pot and stuff? That meltdown. I came on the scene right after that, so soon afterwards that he was still really upset about the whole thing. He swore right then that he was going to clean up his act. And you know what? He pretty much did."

Marcus felt something twitch inside him. He was pretty sure it was pride, pride that Rolland had thought enough of their relationship to get clean. He also felt a strong pang of guilt for having stalked off and divesting himself of that relationship. He took a sip of water and clumsily motioned for Otto to continue.

"So what were you guys doing?" Marcus asked, clearing his throat.

"You know, parties, hanging out, stuff like that. We both did odd jobs here and there to make some bucks, but that was during the day. At night we had a lot of parties," he emphasized the word "lot". "We generally hung out here, and as long as we weren't too loud we didn't have any problems."

"And it doesn't hurt to have a brother who's a cop, either," Marcus observed.

Otto chuckled and flipped his bangs. His long brown hair was parted down the middle, almost an 80's style, and wavy. He wouldn't have looked out of place on a southern California beach. "You bet. Once in a while he'd have to come out and tell us to keep it down, but it was hard for Don-Don to do that because usually Cassie was here with Rolland. He didn't like that.

"But something changed a year or so ago," he continued. "Rolland and Cassie were together all the time, really doing the couple's thing. But they also started hanging out with a couple of Mexicans. I don't know if they were his friends or hers, but they were not the kind of people I was comfortable around."

"Why not?" Marcus asked, his interest piqued with Otto's talk of Mexicans.

"Well don't get me wrong," he insisted. "I like Mexicans as much as the next guy. I mean, heck, Cassie's a Mexican and she's great. But these guys," Otto said, his voice unintentionally getting quiet, "these guys were not nice Mexicans. I don't know who they were or what they were up to, but the more Rolland hung out with them the less I hung out with Rolland. Simple as that."

A sinking feeling in his gut made Marcus ask, "Was it drugs? Were they in to drugs and dealing?"

He screwed up his face in thought. "I don't know. Maybe. I don't know. Rolland swore he would never do that stuff again, not after you two had your…incident, but I was never comfortable around those guys, and after a while there were more of them. I felt, I don't know, out of place, especially when they were all talking in Spanish, Rolland included. It just wasn't that much fun anymore, so I stopped hanging around. I'd run in to Rolland at the store or Foley's, and we'd chat and catch up just like old times, but it never went any farther than that."

Marcus leaned forward. "So when's the last time you saw him?"

Otto was specific this time. "Just about two a half months ago, at Foley's. He and Cassie were fighting about something. She was crying, really upset. Rolland didn't look too good, either, and he didn't talk to me at all. Just stormed out of the restaurant, hopped into his Honda, and tore off down the road with Sam in the back seat. I never saw him again. Oh," he exclaimed, looking around excitedly, "what about Sam? I haven't seen Sam since then either."

Marcus wanted to dodge the question but felt Otto deserved the truth, as ugly as it was. He took a deep breath and explained how he had found Sam, dead, still attached to the doghouse. Otto sat back heavily in his chair, his thin face suddenly pale. He made some vague motions with his hands and almost dropped the bottle of water.

Marcus broke the silence. "And that's the last time you saw him?"

Eventually Otto said, "Uh, yes, that was it. I've talked to Cassie dozens of times, and she hasn't seen or heard from him either. That's what's really got me spooked."

Marcus had a sudden inspiration. "Do you by chance know where Cassie lives? I'd love to talk to her."

"Well sure," he admitted, perking up a bit. "I know exactly where she lives."

"Great. Let's take a drive, Driver 8."

Cassandra lived on the other side of town about fifteen minutes away. They chatted amiably on the way there, slowly getting to know each other better. The two of them clicked right off even though it was tough to carry on much of a conversation with the radio on and the windows down. At one point a song by the rock group R.E.M. came on and Marcus asked Otto if he knew the band or any of their music.

After pursing his lips and thinking about it, the younger man acknowledged that he did, a little bit.

"You know they have a song called *Driver 8*, don't you?" Marcus asked.

Otto's eyes opened wide. "No shit? Really? How cool is that?"

"Very cool. It's a good song, too."

"Wow. Man, I have got to download that when I get home."

The rest of the drive to Cassandra's was dominated by talk of music past and present, musical likes and dislikes and fads come and gone. Both laughed and said they despised Disco, although secretly Marcus thought Otto's hairstyle mimicked one of the band members of the Bee Gees, Andy Gibb's, very closely. Marcus enjoyed mostly alternative music new and old, and not surprisingly the young man was more into hip hop and heavier alternative, what he liked to call "angry white guy" music. From what Marcus could tell the old truck was only equipped with an AM / FM radio, so they listened to one the few Dayton stations they could lock in. Marcus thought Otto secretly didn't mind the classic rock or he would have retro-fitted a CD player or MP3 player, and more than once he noticed how the younger man would unconsciously bob his blond head to the music and tap out a steady drumbeat on the steering wheel. Marcus smiled and hummed along, a lover of music but a person who had been denied any real musical talent.

They turned on to Cassie's street, one of Wayne's many neighborhoods built in the 50s. The lots were small. Each of the one and two story frame houses was distinct in style and construction. Each was also quite distinct in its upkeep and maintenance: many were run-down and shabby-looking with peeling paint and overgrown lawns, while several others were meticulously kept. Otto pulled up to a white two story on the corner. It was nicely maintained with trim bushes and a split rail fence surrounding the small property. Otto turned and parked on the side street. Marcus saw a wooden deck on the back of the house, complete with lawn chairs and a grill. It looked like any of a million similar homes across the Midwest, fulfilling the American dream of homeownership.

"Well, here we are," he said.

Marcus nodded. "Nice place. Does she live here by herself?"

"No. She's got a few brothers here, too, I think. Sometimes they have some migrant workers spend a few weeks here. Her folks still live down in Mexico somewhere."

They parked and made their way to the side entrance. Otto assured Marcus that no one ever used the front door. Marcus discovered he was oddly nervous as they knocked. He could hear some muffled movement inside, people talking, and a loud TV commentator saying something incoherent through the walls. Then the door opened and Cassandra stood there in jean shorts and a red T-shirt. Her hair was pulled back in a ponytail which accentuated her high cheekbones and large, almond-shaped eyes. She had a small silver cross dangling from a fine chain around her neck, the silver a sharp contrast against the red of her shirt and her light chocolate complexion. Her eyes grew wide in shock as she looked from Otto to Marcus. He could see her knuckles grow white as her grip on the door increased.

"Hi, Cassie," he said brightly, smiling. "¿Qué pasa? What's up?"

She stood in the door, transfixed, her head swiveling from Otto to Marcus.

Otto forged on, his smile faltering just a fraction at the unexpected tension. "Long time no see. I've got someone here who wants to meet you." He indicated Marcus with a nod as he flipped his bangs out of his eyes. "Cassie, meet Marcus. Marcus, meet Cassie."

"Hi there," Marcus said softly, as if speaking too loudly would spook her.

At the sound of Marcus' voice her eyes grew even wider, although Marcus did not think that possible. He knew that not only did he look like Rolland but they shared similar vocal patterns as well. She looked over their shoulders at the street and houses beyond, seeming to scan the area for something or someone. Her cheeks were flushed a rosy red.

"Otto Doncaster," she said through gritted teeth. "What are you doing here? What have you done?"

He shrunk back half a step, confused and alarmed. "But Cassie, look who it is. It's Rolland's brother."

"I know who it is," she replied tightly, speaking as if Marcus weren't present. She had very little in the way of an accent. "He shouldn't be here."

A male voice from inside yelled, "*Oye. ¿Quien es?*" Marcus couldn't see the television, but he could hear a Spanish announcer describing the play of a soccer match. The commentator's voice rose in excitement as he relayed a player's shot bouncing off the goal post. Several groans and yells of dismay from inside quickly followed.

Cassie turned and replied simply, "*Está bien,*" then stepped outside and closed the door behind her.

Otto continued, befuddled but still intent on pursuing his good deed. "But Cassie, he's looking for Rolland, too. Maybe together you guys can find him. He's here to help."

This time she addressed Marcus directly. "You should not be here."

Marcus looked at her. "Why not? What's wrong?"

She reached up and fingered the silver cross. He could see her mind racing. She rubbed the cross between her thumb and forefinger.

"Why shouldn't I be here?" Marcus repeated.

"It's just that…" she started, then lowered her voice. "It's not safe, that's why."

Marcus took a shot in the dark. "Is it because of the big Mexican? Is that why?"

She stumbled back at this mention of his attacker. Her back hit the door with a thud. "You, you've seen him?" she stuttered.

"Yes, he and another man visited me."

"Yeah," interjected Otto. "They were at Rolland's last night. They busted in and were going to…"

He was stilled by Marcus' raised hand. "Let's just say we had a little discussion," he said, not wishing to go in to detail. Just thinking about it made his back burn even worse.

"Yeah, Don-Don got there in time to run them off," Otto said proudly, beaming. "No telling what would've happened if he hadn't shown up."

Marcus nodded. "Yes, it's a very good thing he showed up when he did."

Cassandra considered this for a moment, her lips tight, and then came to a decision. She glanced back inside the house then motioned for them to follow her. "Come this way, quickly," she ordered. She walked toward the back of the house and the two men followed her obediently. Marcus couldn't help but notice her trim figure as they headed through the backyard to a detached two-car garage. They entered a side door and stepped in to the gloomy interior. She flipped a switch and two bare bulbs feebly eroded some of the darkness. The smell of gasoline, oil, and old, cut grass permeated the space. An aging powder blue Pontiac station wagon was off to one side, the model with the raised roof over the back half with curved windows on the sides. He thought it was a '67 or '68. It said *Sportwagon* in chrome cursive letters and looked a lot like the one his dad had driven for years back and forth to work. The rest of the space inside the garage was taken up with bicycles and lawn equipment, including a beat up Toro lawn mower. She shut the door behind them and the light level in the windowless space retreated, giving mute permission for the gloom to return. She crossed her arms and stood before them, her feet spread shoulder wide. She faced Marcus, her eyes hooded and invisible in the darkness.

"Why are you here?" she asked, her voice flat.

"Well, Cassie, I -" he began.

"No. My name is Cassandra. Only my friends call me Cassie. I don't know you."

"Okay, fine. Cassandra," Marcus said, "it's pretty easy. I'm looking for Rolland and I hope you can help me find him."

"Hmph," she replied derisively, angrily. "So you're looking now? Where have you been the last three years, eh? Why weren't you interested in him all that time? He needed you then, too, but you were nowhere to be found."

Marcus didn't know what he had expected from her when they finally met, but it wasn't this. Her sudden verbal attack shocked him.

"Your brother looked up to you," she continued, her voice tight with emotion. "Idolized is too strong a word, but you were the successful one, the one that made all the right choices. You went to college, moved away, and got a job. He fought like hell to be more like you, and you just blew him off. And for what? For some stupid fight you had years ago? What the hell kind of brother are you anyway? What kind of man cuts off all ties with his brother for that long? Hell, you moved twenty five hundred miles away, so far that if you took another step you'd fall off a cliff into the Pacific Ocean." She was breathing heavily now, her emotions bursting to the surface.

Marcus felt his own emotions churning. She didn't know him, didn't know what he and Rolland had lived through with their alcoholic and abusive father. She didn't understand what substance abuse of any kind could do to a family. It was clear that these addictive tendencies ran in his family, and when they were together Marcus had done all he could to keep Rolland from falling prey to any of these vices. To discover that his younger brother not only used drugs, but *sold* them as well had been too much for him to handle. He had snapped. He had snapped and turned away from his own brother, because it was all he could do. He had been terrified what might happen, what he himself might do to Rolland, if he had stayed.

So he had left. He had left and never looked back.

Cassandra was staring at him, her expression furious and incriminating. Her cheeks were still flushed and her arms were crossed, her breathing loud in the dark, enclosed space. Outside a child rode by on a scooter, laughing at a friend. The temperature in the garage was pushing up the mercury. It would soon be stifling.

Marcus kept a tight rein on his temper, knowing that a shouting match would accomplish nothing.

"Listen," he said, his voice controlled and even. "I left because I had to. You're right – you don't know me and I don't know you. I'm not proud of what I did, and I'm reminded every day that I ran away and left him here to fend for himself. I feel like shit about it." He took a deep breath. "But I'm here now, and I'm hoping that together we can figure out what happened. Please – help me. I don't know where else to turn."

Her expression didn't change. She stood staring at him, a dusky statue with the red of her T-shirt and denim shorts muted in the dim light. Finally her arms relaxed a fraction of an inch.

"Fine. For Rolland," she said at last, grudgingly. "What do you want to know?"

Marcus held no illusion that her anger toward him had lessened in the least, but was grateful to be afforded this slight reprieve.

"Well," he started before realizing he truly didn't know where to begin. "Well, I guess, let's talk about the huge Mexican that visited me last night. What can you tell me about him? What does he have to do with my brother?"

At the mention of the intruder he noted that she shuffled nervously. Her arms shifted from being crossed in rage to almost seeming to hug herself, as if a sudden chill had stolen across her bare skin despite the thick, warm air of the garage. If she was thinking about Gonzales he well understood how she felt.

"I've only seen him twice," she said, her voice flat and distant. "It was about four months ago when Rolland and I were walking downtown on our way to Foley's. A car pulled up and your brother about jumped out of his skin when he saw who was in it."

"Gonzalez."

She shook her head. "Yes. Rolland made me stay back as he talked to this huge man with long black hair. He was so big he almost didn't fit in the car, and he had the seat reclined back so far it looked like he was in the back seat. They talked quietly for a minute, no more, and then the car pulled away. I remember that Rolland didn't move for what felt like forever but must have been only seconds. I called his name over and over and he didn't answer. I finally grabbed his shoulder and asked what that was all about, but he wouldn't say anything. I kept asking and he got so mad at me that I stopped."

"You said twice," Marcus said. "When was the second time?"

"Later, after Rolland came up missing. He came here, to the house, and demanded to know where he had gone. I didn't know. I mean, your brother and I hadn't seen each other much for a few weeks, we had pretty much called it quits by then. He – the big man – was very insistent, saying it was important that he find Rolland. He…he threatened me, told me that if he found out I was lying that he'd do…things…"

Marcus felt a jolt of pity for her. The giant would be terrifying to anyone.

"Things. What kind of things?"

Her hands fluttered in front of her vaguely and she looked up at him with haunted eyes. "Just…things, and not just to me," she replied, visibly shaken and upset. "I don't want to talk about it."

He waited for her to say more, but she didn't. "You said you and Rolland were fighting. What were you fighting about?"

She shook her head, as if coming suddenly back to the present. "Lots of things. Something had been going on with him, something that he wasn't telling me about. He had been on the phone a lot, and I think he was meeting with people I didn't know. He wouldn't tell me what was going on. That wasn't like him. He was usually open and honest with me."

"Was it the other Mexicans you guys were hanging around with?" Otto asked. Marcus had almost forgotten he was in the garage with them. The yellow of his Columbus Crew jersey was dimly visible in the faint light, like the last rays of the sun as it dipped below the horizon.

"Them? Oh, I don't know." She looked at Marcus. "Most of them were friends of you two when you lived in Mexico. Or friends of friends. They were here visiting and Rolland loved hanging out with them. Most of them have gone back now, or moved on, I think."

At the mention of Mexico and Rolland's friends, Marcus pursed his lips, reliving the final moments of his attack, the second he had glimpsed the smaller man's face. He purposefully hadn't told Doncaster about him, and he was afraid if he said anything now the information would make it directly from Otto to the Lieutenant. But it was potentially very important and critical to what was going on, and maybe it would make more sense to the others. He felt that the three of them were in this together now.

"Otto, I was not entirely…forthcoming about the attack on me," he admitted. "I didn't tell your brother everything. And I need you to promise not to tell him, okay?"

He was puzzled, the expression on his young, innocent face easy to read. "What do you mean? What else happened?"

"Well, while I was still, uh, tied down," he said, glancing sideways at Cassandra, "I told your brother I wasn't able to see the second man, the one who did the, uh, work."

"You saw him?" Otto exclaimed. "The guy who whipped you?"

"Yeah, just for a second. And I think I know who he is."

Otto looked from Marcus to Cassandra. "Okay, come on, man, you're killing me. Who the hell is it?"

Marcus took a deep breath.

"I think he used to work for my uncle in Mexico."

Marcus leaned against the Pontiac Sportwagon. "So how much do you guys know about the time Rolland and I lived south of the border? Do you know why we were there?"

Cassandra waggled her hand back and forth. "*Un poco*. A little. Rolland didn't like to talk about it much."

"Yeah," Otto agreed with a head bob toward her. "What she said. *Un poco*."

Marcus drew another deep breath in, held it, releasing it slowly from puffed out cheeks. He didn't even like to think about the past, and hadn't talked about this to anyone in years. He was very uncomfortable dredging it up even now, the memories still black in his mind.

"This will take a little bit, so you might as well get comfortable," he said. "We'll need to start several years before moving to Mexico. It'll make more sense then."

Marcus had been half-joking about getting comfortable, but Otto took him at his word and unfolded a battered old lawn chair he found hanging on the wall, one with green and white nylon banding. He sat and put his elbows on his knees, eager to listen. Marcus gave a fleeting grin.

“Okay, then. Mom died when I was fourteen,” he began. “It was a car wreck, ironically caused by a drunk driver with half a dozen prior convictions and no license. She was killed instantly. And the bastard who did it got off on a technicality.

“For the next six months or so everything ran pretty smoothly in the Schmidt household,” he explained. “Dad continued his job at the Honda plant fifteen miles away, but we began to notice how often he brought home a six pack, then later a twelve pack. He sat in the kitchen and drank one after another, getting plowed and smoking Swisher Sweet cigars, those cheap ones with the plastic tips. Then things began to deteriorate.”

“Our dad began to get belligerent, you know, turning into a mean, nasty drunk. After his evening twelve-pack was gone he’d stagger into our room. He was angry, not at us in particular, but just angry at the world and its injustices, I guess. He’d break things, throw things. He began pushing us around, mainly me since at fifteen I was about the same size as him. He hadn’t hit either of us, at least not yet.

“I was stuck being the ‘mom’ of the family,” Marcus continued wearily. “I was the only one who ever cooked a meal for us. I checked to make sure Rolland had his homework done and turned in. I was the one to show up for his track meets. I, uh, never got much of a chance to do anything for me, but that was okay, really. Rolland needed me, and dad was pretty worthless at that point. Then it got worse, mainly because he was so drunk he couldn’t even hold onto his job at the Honda plant any longer.

“That was bad on many, many levels. First,” he said, ticking points off on his fingers, “of course we had very little money because he wasn’t working anymore. Also, he was home all the damn time. The drinking started earlier in the day and lasted until he passed out. If he didn’t pass out and he ran out of beer, that was even worse. He’d take off and get into trouble at one of the bars here in town, or the cops would pick him up. I don’t know how many times I had to go bail him out of jail. Sometimes I'd leave him there overnight on purpose, just so Rolland and I could get some peace and quiet. God he hated it when I did that."

He sighed. "Rolland took to spending a lot of time at friends' houses, just so he wouldn't have to come home. I wish I could've done the same thing, but someone had to run the house, lie to creditors, and take care of dad. And he just kept getting more depressed and more violent. It was like watching him fall into a black pit.

"Until I turned sixteen. I don't think dad noticed that I was getting pretty big by then. In fact I was almost the same size I am now. He had to look up just to talk to me, but I think he was too drunk to notice.

"That's when my brother got brought home by the cops one night, and it all went to hell."

Both Cassandra and Otto were listening raptly, and both of them inhaled quickly then, their eyes wide. "Rolland had been caught stealing cigarettes with a friend. Turns out the two of them were working a tidy scam at the local Quick E Mart, where one would ask for help finding something, and while the clerk was looking away the other would stuff a few packs of smokes in their backpack. The surveillance camera eventually picked them up, and the next time they tried it they got busted. The owner wasn't going to press charges, but he called the cops anyway, mainly to scare the shit out of Rolland and his friend.

"But dad was hammered, drunk, and he just blew up," Marcus said. "As soon as the cops left he started pushing Rolland. Hard. Once he threw him up against the wall, and I thought Rolland was really hurt. And…and still he wouldn't stop. That's when I pushed back."

Marcus paused and his eyes unfocused, looking inward. "Neither one of us had ever dared to do anything to him before," he said, as if in explanation. "He always seemed so damn big and strong that we just didn't dare, no matter how bad we wanted to. But I had to do something. I pushed him and he tripped and fell down. He got up fast and pinned me against the wall by the neck. His eyes were bloodshot and unfocused, and beer and cigar stench blew into my face every time he exhaled. His huge fist was pulled back, and I swear I think he meant to kill me." Marcus involuntarily massaged his neck, his fingers digging into the flesh.

"And then Rolland grabbed dad from behind and tried to hold him back," Marcus whispered stonily. "He tried to hold him in a bear hug. You know, to stop him from hitting me. Damn, he was only thirteen years old and he was just a kid. Well dad blew up and went crazy. I'd never seen him so mad. He threw me away and spun around and hit Rolland in the face. Blood splattered everywhere, like a balloon full of red dye had smacked my brother in the nose. He fell backwards and our dad was on him, hitting him again and again. His fist was like this big, meaty piston, going up and down, up and down. We were both yelling for him to stop.

"I remember screaming at him but he wouldn't listen. I grabbed a table lamp from the nightstand and broke it over his head, and that got him up. He was like an animal and he came right at me. I punched him as hard as I could, right in the face. I really thought I broke my hand, but dad flew backwards, blood spewing from his nose and mouth. And I didn't stop. I grabbed him and punched again and again. I, uh, I don't even know how many times I hit him. Rolland was crying, yelling at me to stop now but he was still on the floor with blood gushing out of his nose. Finally I did stop. I was exhausted. Dad got up and staggered out." The vision of his battered father was crystal clear. He looked like a bull stabbed by the picadors, confused and bleeding, staggering. There was blood everywhere. "After that we didn't see him for three days."

"Holy shit," Otto stated. Cassandra stared at him mutely, brown eyes wide and round in the dark garage.

"Holy shit is right. Rolland saved my life, I really think he did. Dad was completely out of his mind and would have killed me, I'm sure of it," Marcus stated unequivocally. "When he came back three days later he was a mess. Two black eyes, his nose still all mangled up. He had a cut above his left eye and a few fingers were splinted. He wouldn't look at us, especially not my brother, who had his own black eye and broken nose. He didn't say anything but packed up some of our stuff and ordered us to get in the car. He drove us to the Dayton airport and put us on a plane. The tickets said *Merida, Mexico*. I didn't even know where the hell that was.

"That's when dad said he couldn't look after us anymore. We were going to go live with our mom's sister, our Aunt Mary in Mexico. We didn't have any other relatives, and Aunt Mary was going to take care of us."

Marcus noticed his eyes were welling up a little, and he fought the urge to wipe them with his sleeve.

"We begged him not to do it. He was the devil we knew and we had no idea what Mexico was all about. We pleaded with him but he gave our tickets to the lady at the gate and forced us into our seats. The plane took off, and *voilá* we were on our way to Mexico."

Now it was Cassandra's turn to break into his story. She was affronted and angry. While Marcus couldn't see her face well in the gloom he could read her obvious body language. "He just put his two sons on a plane for Mexico? What kind of a father was he?"

Marcus shrugged. "Not much of one, at least not anymore. He was mentally gone, checked out. Rolland and I just never realized how hard mom's death had hit him. They had been very, very much in love, and life without her just wasn't the same. He couldn't bear it. I've had years to think back on it. I can't forgive him for what he did, but I am beginning to understand what happened. I think."

The old Pontiac wagon creaked as he leaned against it. "So we flew to Mexico. My Aunt Mary met us there. She looked a lot like mom, only different. Like when you run into someone for the first time in years, at a high school reunion or something, and they've changed, but not to the point where you couldn't recognize them. And she acted different than mom, too. She laughed and talked a lot in a big, expansive way. Mom was a quieter person. More gentle and loving.

"Anyway, she took us back to her home then, and we started our new life in Mexico."

Thinking back, Marcus remembered the smells of Mexico more than anything. The smell of "hot", if heat could have a smell. Car exhaust. Lots and lots of people smoking. Cigars and cigarettes were ubiquitous, dangling from everyone's mouths and fingers like permanent appendages. But people seemed so happy. And everywhere was the aroma of food cooking, hot and spicy food. Fresh tortillas baking every morning in small *tortillarillas*, tiny shops where they made them every day, where wives and daughters and maids waited in long lines each morning to pick up the day's staple. There were small, out of the way, colorful red, blue, and yellow restaurants tucked between homes and businesses, run by families and serving delicious, simple fare that would eventually make his mouth water. Flowers were everywhere, beautiful flowers that he didn't recognize but which perfumed the air.

Their new home looked like nothing special from the outside. The houses were all built right up to and flush with the sidewalk, side by side, like brownstones but without the steps. Some homes had eight foot high walls out front, festooned with broken bottles and shards of glass across the top to serve as a deterrent to anyone rash enough to consider a climb. The front of the house was a pale, whitewashed sky blue, with a tremendous oak door bound with steel straps mounted in the middle. There were bars on the windows, thick steel bars mounted onto the house and looking as if they'd stop an army of conquistadors. But when they entered and stepped over the threshold their mouths dropped in shock.

Inside the house it was stunning. It was designed in a classic Spanish / Mexican fashion. Looking down from above it resembled a large open square, with the rooms surrounding a central courtyard on all four sides. It was two stories tall with a balcony that ran around the entire second floor. Vibrant flowers and shrubs in massive bright pots were everywhere. Most of the rooms were open to the bright courtyard. There was a blue and green ceramic tile fountain about ten feet in diameter situated in the middle of the courtyard. Water burbled up four feet before falling noisily back. After two days the sound of the splashing water receded into the background and they rarely noticed it again.

"We were shocked as hell," Marcus admitted. "We'd never seen anything like it before. It was gorgeous. And then we met our cousin, Santiago."

"Wait a minute," Otto interjected. "Rolland never mentioned that you had a cousin."

Marcus nodded. "Technically you're right. He wasn't our cousin by blood, but by marriage. Aunt Mary met our uncle, Javier, a few years earlier at some function here in the States. Uncle Javier – who Rolland and I always called El Señor - already had Santiago at that time. When they got married Aunt Mary moved down to Merida."

"Whoa," Otto said. "You call your Uncle 'El Señor'? Not very warm and fuzzy."

Cassandra nodded. "Yes, that's not that uncommon. It doesn't translate into English quite the same, but it's like calling him 'Sir'."

"Anyway," Marcus continued, "Santiago was a year or two younger than Rolland, but they hit it off pretty well. Santiago loved parading his American cousin around, and Rolland was just happy to have a safe and secure home to live in. We ended up staying there until Rolland was eighteen. That's, of course, where we learned to speak Spanish so well, too."

A car horn outside blared suddenly, causing all three to jump in surprise. After a second of intense listening where they stood as still as redwoods, they relaxed and Otto almost laughed in relief.

"It really was a nice place to grow up," Marcus continued. "Aunt Mary took very good care of us even though she hadn't seen either of us for years. She couldn't replace mom, but she knew that. And she liked having all of us around since El Señor wasn't there much and we kept her company. He had some job with the government or some other agency, we think, but we were never really sure what it was. He'd pop in every week or two for several days and he and Aunt Mary would spend a lot of time together. Then he'd be off again. We never could warm up to him like we did with her. He just wasn't that type."

Marcus paused. "But, that's where I swear I saw the second guy. I could swear he was a driver for El Señor."

Cassandra sucked in a quick breath. "Are you certain?"

Marcus nodded. "Yes, I think so. I only saw him a few times when El Señor was coming or going and I happened to be outside, but he had the same build and the same face. Thin, with a skinny nose and black eyes. If a rat had a human face, it would look like this. I could pick him out of a lineup today if I had to. He made me nervous even back then. And, I don't know, he moved very smoothly, like he was a fighter or an athlete."

"Like a cat?" Otto asked.

"Yes, gracefully, like a cat," Marcus agreed.

Cassandra then asked the obvious question: "So what is an employee of your Uncle's doing up here looking for Rolland? And why would he...treat you like that?"

"I don't know," Marcus said thoughtfully. "But I intend to find out."

"How are you going to do that?" Otto wondered.

"Simple," Marcus replied matter-of-factly. "I'm going to go to Mexico and ask him."

Chapter 7

In the truck heading back to the house Marcus asked him to stop at a little hole in the wall music shop downtown named TuneTime. He left them idling outside and was only gone for few minutes. When he came back he tossed a cellophane-wrapped CD onto Otto's lap. The young man held it up with a glow on his face.

"*Fables of the Reconstruction* by *R.E.M.*," he breathed, obviously pleased. "Is this the one with *Driver 8* on it? How cool is that?"

"You can play it when you get home," Marcus said, pleased at the young man's reaction. "Thought you might like to hear your song. I think it's track three."

"Play it at home, hell," Otto exclaimed. "Let's hear it now."

He reached across Marcus and popped open the glove box. Neatly mounted inside was a small CD player. He tore off the cellophane and popped in the disk, quickly cycling to the third track. Almost instantly the recognizable opening guitar riff surrounded them, followed by lead singer Michael Stipe's haunting voice belting out the first two lines:

Walls you build up, stone by stone,

Fields divided one by one...

As he looked over and saw Otto's head bob to the catchy tune he once again felt remorse settle over him at what had happened to his relationship with

Rolland. Yes, he understood that his brother had perpetrated the act that had divided them, but looking back Marcus could see how he had built the stone walls so thick it had seemed almost nothing could break them down. It frightened him at how easily a once unshakable sibling relationship like theirs had been frozen; where the absence of each other had so quickly and easily become the norm. It was much simpler to be on your own and not have to worry about someone else, he knew, so much easier to just take care of yourself. He feared that deep inside part of the estrangement had been some type of retribution on his part, a payback for everything he'd had to sacrifice while they were younger. This was a personal flaw he had never considered before, and, quite honestly, he didn't much care for this specific line of introspection.

"Wow – seriously great tune," Otto shouted over the music. "Is the rest of the CD this good?"

"Yeah, pretty much," Marcus assured him. "They've put out a lot of music over the years, but I like their older stuff better. It has a little more drive to it. Sadly they broke up not too long ago, calling it quits after being together for 30 years."

"Bummer on the breakup. But I got a feeling I'm going to be downloading new tunes tonight!"

Marcus smiled, not for the first time, at the young man's excitement and relative innocence. Although it seemed like several lifetimes ago, he recalled a similar sense of innocence that he and his brother had shared. He feared he would never feel that way again, and it saddened him.

Ten minutes later they were back at the house. Prior to leaving Cassandra's all three had shared cell phone numbers since Marcus had promised he would keep them up to date on his plans. Oddly, he was looking forward to talking to Cassandra again. He hopped out of the truck and came around to Otto's side.

"Thanks," he said. "I mean it. I couldn't have met Cassandra without you."

He smiled brightly. "No problem, man. Just let us know what's up and when you're leaving. I'll tell Don-Don to keep an eye on the place. And good luck. I really hope you find out what's going on."

Marcus waved and the red Ford drove off, the strains of *R.E.M.'s Can't Get There From Here* blasting out the window:

I've been there I know the way,
Can't get there from here,
I've been there I know the way,
Can't get there from here...

He chanced a quick glance across the street and noticed the curtain was pulled ever so slightly aside, just a crack. Casually so as not to alarm his persistent observer, Marcus walked across the street to the front door. He ignored the large eagle knocker and rapped gently with a single knuckle, waiting. Again he thought he heard some rustling from the hushed interior but no one came to the door, or at least nobody opened it. He leaned against the house and waited a minute.

"I just wanted to say thank you for calling the police last night," Marcus said, his head resting on the door jamb. "You probably don't know what a huge favor you did for me. If you ever need anything, anything at all, please just let me know." He remained leaning against the house, waiting. He noticed a slight movement in the bushes and the cat hopped up on the small front porch. It twined around his ankles, purring loudly. He picked it up and scratched behind its ears. The purring increased in intensity, loud enough to shame a cougar, and the black and gray tabby squirmed with pleasure. He strained again to hear anything from the interior, then, sighing, set the cat down. It looked at him with its accusing feline eyes, annoyed that the affection was already over.

Marcus trotted back to Rolland's. He was just about to head inside, his hand resting on the doorknob before he stopped, frozen. What if, he wondered, what if his attackers had snuck back into the house and were waiting for him? How stupid would he feel just waltzing right back in there for round two with those crazy bastards? It dawned on him then that he was going to have to start thinking this way, being more suspicious, looking around corners, watching his back, before making a move. This sudden need to be vigilant and hyper-aware of his surroundings was not only foreign but uncomfortable to him, however he knew his very survival might now depend on it.

He peered into the windows one at a time but didn't see anything so walked around the house. He grabbed another two by four from the trash and eased in through the front door. Carefully and quietly he walked around each room, makeshift weapon at the ready, his gut tight. His back throbbed anew, as if this return to the scene was enough to rekindle the fire in the raw nerve endings. After a thorough search he breathed a sigh, certain that he was alone. Home sweet home, he thought.

Marcus wandered back to the living room. He pulled out his cell phone and hit speed dial number four. After several clicks he heard three rings then a male voice answered.

"Hey, Dr. Schmidt, what's up?"

"Tony," Marcus said, "how's everything in southern California?"

Tony, or Dr. Anthony Barsalo, was arguably his best friend and co-worker in the Department of Latin American Studies at San Diego State University. He was about the same age as Marcus and had come on board at the same time. He was a short, swarthy young man of southern Italian descent, olive-skinned with dark black hair. His round, expressive face grew whiskers so quickly that by the time he finished shaving starting over again right away wasn't out of the question. They were frequent running partners and watched each other's backs in case of any university emergencies. Tony was as close as

Marcus got to a good friend. They were tight enough that some of the others in the department looked at the quite obvious German and Italian bloodlines and playfully dubbed them the Axis Powers. Since Marcus had a nameplate on his desk that simply said "Dr. Schmidt", Tony had started calling him by his title as a joke, and it had stuck between the two of them.

"It's fine," Tony replied. "You picked a good time to be gone. Summer school is a boring-ass piece of cake."

"You still okay covering my classes?" Marcus asked.

"Yeah, no problem, Doctor. But you owe me. Although there are a few fine looking co-eds in your morning 101 class."

"Hands off, you horny Italian. Can I ask you for another favor? This one's easy."

"Fine. I'll just add it to your tally."

Marcus smiled. "You've still got the key to my apartment, right? Can you head over there and get my passport out of the lap drawer on my desk and mail it to me?"

"Your passport? What the hell for? Hey, Ohio may seem like a different country, but it's not, you know."

Marcus didn't want to go in to details now. "I'll fill you in when I get back, okay? Can you just mail it to this address?"

"Hold on, hold on. Let me get a pencil. Okay, shoot."

Marcus rattled off Rolland's address. "Got it?"

"Yep. I'll get it in the mail tomorrow. Or do you want it overnighted?"

"Overnighted, please." Then another thought hit him. "Oh, and do you know anybody in the Business College? I've got a question that they may be able to help me with."

"Um," he thought a moment. "Yeah. Remember that inter-departmental shin-dig we went to last month?"

Marcus thought back. "Cheap booze, pretty good appetizers, and that one female prof from the College of Communications that passed out in the bathroom? Said her blood sugar crashed but the bartender counted eight dirty martinis?"

"Yeah, that's that one. I introduced you to Andy Lucas. He's a good guy. You two seemed to hit it off pretty well. Call him up."

Marcus thought back to the party and Andy Lucas...hmm, tall, thin guy, with glasses and blond wavy hair combed straight back. A sense of humor as dry as the Cabernet he'd been drinking. Marcus liked him. "Yes, sure, I remember him. What's his number?"

Tony passed along the phone number. They caught up for several more minutes in casual friendship, with Marcus reinforcing some instructions for class as well. As they disconnected Tony assured him he'd overnight Marcus' passport right away.

He dialed Andy Lucas' number but got his voicemail. He considered simply hanging up and calling later but decided otherwise. Marcus didn't generally like leaving messages, preferring instead to just call back, but with his pending trip to Mexico he was pressed for time. He wanted some answers sooner than later.

"Uh, hi, Andy, this is Marcus Schmidt. We met last month at that inter-departmental party. I was hoping you could call me back as soon as possible. I've got a question or two that maybe you can help me with." He left his number and hung up, feeling slightly foolish. It was quite possible that Andy wouldn't remember him at all.

Instead of waiting around and staring at his cell phone, willing it to ring, Marcus donned his running gear for another stint of asphalt pounding. He decided on a straightforward out-and-back route again since it was easiest for him and he already had the route marked. He had almost managed to forget about his wounded back until about five minutes into the run when sweat dripped into the cuts, causing them to burn anew. In total he was gone about an hour, and – after a quick inspection for any unwanted guests – he came back in and toweled off. He didn't notice at first but the message light on his cell phone was blinking red. He quickly called his voicemail and heard Andy's deep voice apologizing for missing him, and to call back at his convenience.

He hit redial and after a few clicks and a single ring was rewarded with Andy Lucas answering brightly. They quickly exchanged pleasantries. Marcus was honestly surprised that he was remembered.

"So what can I do you for?" Andy asked when they both tacitly agreed it was time to get down to business. "You're not calling from across the country just to hear my melodious voice, I'd wager."

Marcus chuckled. "True. I've got some questions about credit cards I'm hoping you can help me with. How much do you know about them?"

"I'm pretty sure my wife and the good folks at American Express are on a first name basis, but I doubt that's what you mean. What would you like to know?"

Marcus paused, thinking. How in the world could he explain what had happened so far without sharing way too much information? He didn't want to incriminate his brother in anything just yet. He mentally bantered around several options before settling on an abbreviated version of the truth.

"My brother is…not around right now, but I found a credit card at his house. I'm pretty sure it wasn't his, but belongs to someone in Missouri. At least, the card was issued by a credit union in Missouri. I used it once by accident and it was denied."

There was a pause on the other end while Andy thought, willing to play along. "Okay, first question that comes to mind is easy: does your brother know this person?"

Marcus pursed his lips and shook his head, thinking about the huge Mexican and what he had said. "I don't know. No, I don't think so. Like I said, he's not here and I can't talk to him about it."

"Oh. Okay, so why'd he have this person's card?"

"Good question. I don't have an answer to that."

There was another pause while Andy considered the limited information, and Marcus realized Andy Lucas was a man who thought long and hard before he spoke. He admired that.

"Okay," Andy continued, "let's move beyond that for a second. You said you tried to use the card and it was denied? You weren't trying to buy, say, a new car or something were you?"

"No, not quite. It was just for a meal here in town. I think the entire bill was less than fifteen dollars."

"Hmm. Look at the card, and tell me if it has the word "Debit" printed anywhere on it."

Marcus shook his head. "Sorry, I can't. I don't have the card any more. It was, ah, taken from me the other day. But I don't remember seeing "Debit" anywhere on it."

"Well this card has had quite the adventure of late, then, hasn't it?" Andy said. "I don't know what to tell you since you're not giving me much to work on. It could be a simple as a borrowed card, or as complicated as a stolen one. I'm afraid we may not have enough information at this point. I'm not sure exactly what you're looking for."

Marcus was getting frustrated at the lack of progress. "If I could talk to the owner of the card," he stated, "maybe he could tell me something. I just don't know how I can find him."

There was a three second pause before Andy said quietly, "You just want to talk to the cardholder? Well, there may be something I can do."

Several years earlier Andy Lucas had been tapped by his department head to teach a freshman course on Financial Responsibility at the university. It had been noted by many, including the mainstream media outlets and much of the university hierarchy, that tens of thousands of college graduates across the country were leaving school with crushing amounts of debt, not all of which was attributed to student loans. Credit card debt, once just a minor infection among a handful, had become a full-blown epidemic for students everywhere. Banks were well aware that if they issued a "starter" card with a low to moderate credit limit to current students there was a very good chance that the card would be used and the balance carried forward month after month, especially if the bank was savvy enough to periodically raise the available limit. If the graduate defaulted there was also a strong chance that mommy or daddy would make good on the debt, not wishing their offspring's credit rating to suffer. Many graduates were leaving the hallowed grounds of their colleges or universities, including San Diego State, with tremendous levels of revolving debt, debt that they couldn't hope to pay off for years or decades. Dr. Andy Lucas, recent addition to the College of Business, was directed to devise a curriculum on financial responsibility that every student interested in receiving a degree in business was required to attend. The problem was that Dr. Andy Lucas had very little idea how to do this.

In his methodical fashion and after much trial and error and dozens of phone calls, he managed to befriend an analyst at one of the big three national credit bureaus, Lee Abernathy. Lee, as it turns out, had a daughter who had recently graduated from a small private college, and unbeknownst to him had racked up some hefty revolving credit card debt of her own, mainly through pizza deliveries and runs to the carry out for booze and beer pong supplies. So he was more than a little sympathetic to Andy's plea for help. They had kept in contact ever since, even to the point of getting together once each year or so for long weekends. Their wives got along great, usually heading out on shopping sprees with, ironically, their credit cards armed and ready.

Marcus gave Andy the name on the mystery card – Matthew M. Kazmierczak – the credit union name in Missouri, and what he thought were the last four digits on the card itself, 6413. Marcus had recalled those four numbers because they were very close to an old street address from his youth.

"What are you going to do?" he asked Andy.

A slight pause, then, "Let's just say I have a connection, and leave it at that. Let me get to work, and I'll be back in touch soon, possibly today."

Intrigued, Marcus said, "Okay, deal. I'll be waiting. And I must say, you've got me curious."

Andy laughed lightly, more of a heavy breath out his nose than an actual laugh. He reiterated his promise to call back soon and hung up. Marcus wasn't sure why the business professor was so eager and willing to help, but he was certainly appreciative of the assistance. It could have been the general level of camaraderie many of the younger professors at the University shared, or it could have merely been a sense of adventure. Whatever it was he was thankful for the aid, vowing to himself that they'd get together for dinner or drinks when he got back to the coast.

Marcus was impatient for Andy to call, never letting the cell phone out of his sight for more than a second at a time. He managed to fix himself a light dinner while he listened to the radio, but ate it distractedly while he stared at his phone. What did we ever do before cell phones? he wondered between bites. He couldn't imagine being chained to a corded land line. In fact didn't even have a home phone back at his apartment in San Diego. That spiral cord could keep you shackled in place more effectively than steel chains.

Much to his dismay Andy didn't call back that night. With a deep sigh he resisted the urge to call him, then placed the phone next to the bed in the guest room and managed to finally fall into a fitful, restless sleep.

Weather-wise the next morning was a carbon copy of the prior day, but Marcus didn't take much notice. He managed breakfast and several chores, not tasting the first and moving mechanically through the second. At about 10:30 he was surprised when he heard a truck pull into the driveway, gravel popping under its heavy treads. A quick glance out the window revealed a brown UPS truck, complete with its shorts-wearing driver. The clean-cut man whistled tunelessly as he came up and knocked on the door, delivered a thick envelope with a smile and tip of his brown hat, and drove off.

Marcus pulled the tab to open the envelope and with a grin pulled out his passport.

"Nice job, Tony," he said to himself, smiling. "I can always count on you. Good man." He happily slapped his palm with the blue passport before slipping it in his back pocket. Properly armed he was now ready to make some travel plans. It was finally time to cross some boundaries, and hopefully get answers to some very pressing questions. He dialed his travel company and fifteen minutes later he had his flight to Merida all squared away for the next morning. He called Otto's cell phone to let him know his travel plans but was asked to leave a message. Grudgingly he did so, sharing his flight number and departure time, promising to keep in touch and to let him know if he if he found out anything of interest.

Five minutes after that Andy Lucas from the University called him back. Marcus pounced on the phone.

"Ah, we may have a problem," Andy said, his voice sounding unaccustomedly serious.

Marcus blinked, immediately concerned. "Problem? What's up?"

There was a two second pause while Andy marshalled his thoughts. "That credit card. Are you sure you don't know anything else about it?"

Marcus shook his head before he realized, of course, that Andy couldn't see the gesture. "No, nothing. I'm not even 100% sure Rolland had it. Someone else…told me he did. Sorry, but it's all really confusing. I wish I could tell you more."

There were another few seconds of dead air while Andy considered what Marcus had said. "Okay, hold on a minute while I conference in a friend of mine. His name is Lee, and he works for one of the big national credit bureaus. I'm not going to say which one since we'll probably discuss someone else's credit report and that's strictly *verboten,* not to mention contrary to the Fair Credit Reporting Act. But I talked to him yesterday and asked him for a favor. I shared the few facts we know, and he did some checking."

"Checking? What did he find?" Marcus asked, both wary and excited.

"I think I'll let him tell you that. He's the expert and I'd probably screw it up. Hold on a minute."

Marcus could hear a soft click as he was put on hold, then several more clicks as the three-way call was completed. Within seconds Andy's voice was back.

"Lee? You there?"

"Yes, I'm here," came a male voice speaking quickly.

"How about you, Marcus? You there?" Andy asked.

"You bet," he replied.

"Okay, great. Lee, why don't you start by telling Marcus what you told me. I think he'll find it very interesting."

"Yeah, sure," Lee said, talking fast, just a few notches below auctioneer level. "Just remember, you didn't hear any of this from me.

"I ran that name against our national database and came up with quite a few hits. Without a Social Security number it would normally be hard to pin down a specific person. However, with the addition of that rather unique last name, the credit union name and the last four digits on the account, I was able to pinpoint your Matthew M. Kazmierczak."

"Well that's great," Marcus exclaimed. He was trying to visualize what Lee looked like. He imagined a thin, prematurely-balding man with a bowtie and a large Adam's apple. He was sure that wasn't correct, but the image stuck in his mind. "So we know who he is?"

"Oh, yes, we know who he is and where he is. His credit report has warnings and consumer statements all over it. It seems your Mr. Kazmierczak was the victim of some pretty serious credit card fraud."

"What do you mean?" Marcus asked, his stomach clenching nervously.

"Well, first let me back up a bit. Have you ever heard of the term 'common compromise'? No? I'm not surprised. It's not a phrase the average consumer would be familiar with. A common compromise in the credit card world is a large database breach where thousands, even hundreds of thousands, perhaps millions, of credit card numbers and consumer identities are stolen by hackers. These database breaches are happening more and more all the time, even though the industry is getting more sophisticated in their defenses. The tougher we get, the craftier they get. They're damn smart, and damn persistent.

"The largest data breach came last year, when a payment systems company admitted that intruders hacked into the computers it used to process 100 million payment card transactions per month for over 250,000 merchants. In that hack the thieves had access to the databases for a month or more and included names, credit and debit card numbers, and expiration dates. Over nine million people had their personal information compromised on that one. A few years back another company, a retail operation, lost 94 million customer records to hackers. This sort of thing goes on all the time, and it's getting worse before it gets better."

Marcus was stunned and shocked. "Wait a minute. Isn't there supposed to be security to prevent this sort of thing?"

Lee snorted. "Security? Yeah, right. Next time you pull out your credit card check that black or brown magnetic stripe on the back. The technology associated with that dates back to the 1970s, and can be copied, duplicated, and stolen by any reasonably savvy teenager with Internet access and equipment from Radio Shack. Credit and debit card processors have come up with better and more secure methods to keep information safe, but the hackers keep coming up with ways around it."

"But if somebody gets my card and charges something, then who's responsible?" Marcus asked, still stunned. "I don't pay for that, do I?"

"Generally, no," Lee replied. "Banks and most financial institutions don't make you pay for that, they eat those themselves. They don't have insurance for those losses, they just come out of their budget each year. A small community bank probably suffers over $100,000 or more per year in fraud losses. You take one of the big boys, the huge national banks, and their annual losses are easily in the millions."

Marcus had a difficult time getting his arms around numbers of that size and scope. A professor's salary generally didn't include too many zeros and commas.

Lee went on to explain how a lot of this could be stopped if the big guns, VISA and MasterCard, would adopt the type of credit card with an embedded microchip, like the ones in Canada and the European Union. Those cards were virtually impossible to counterfeit, but the expense to them would be massive, he said. They would have to replace all the swipe readers in every business in the country, and make some tremendous infrastructure changes before they could do that. They'd rather go on with business as usual, since these losses didn't directly impact them anyway. They never paid for the losses, the issuing financial institution did.

There were a dozen questions rattling around Marcus' head, but first and foremost was how could such a business model continue? Something this prone to corruption and failure went against his organizational sensibilities. How much must a large bank make off credit and debit cards to be able to afford to pay for such gigantic losses? He was going to ask that very question when Andy Lucas chimed in.

"Tell him more about the credit card, Lee. Our Mr. Kazmierczak."

"Oh, right. Sorry, got a little off track there. From what I can tell from his credit report, Matthew M. Kazmierczak got hit with some credit card fraud four or five months ago. One of his cards – the one issued from that Missouri credit union – seems to have been involved in that big common compromise I told you about. Before anybody noticed he had about $10,000 or so in bogus charges against his VISA card. Mr. Kazmierczak demanded that we shut down all access to his credit report, and he put a consumer statement on there explaining what happened. We put some extra warnings on as well. He may have had a second card involved in it, too, from a local bank. Right now his credit's a mess while all parties involved get this figured out."

Marcus' head was spinning. Rolland, he thought morosely, if you were indeed involved, what have you done? Common compromises? Counterfeit credit cards? This was no penny-ante crime, not like shop-lifting or stealing beer from garage refrigerators. This was big time, full-fledged felony material. For crimes like this, Marcus knew, people got sent to federal penitentiaries and had their entire lives ruined.

"Consumer statements on credit reports as a general rule don't go in to too much detail," Lee continued. "They're not designed for that and you're limited to how many characters you can use. Mr. Kazmierczak's is no exception. But it does mention something about his credit card being used to buy gift cards at places like Wal-Mart. That's a pretty typical scenario for this type of scam: the fraudsters make the counterfeit card, go to a gas station or convenience store and buy something small to make sure the card works, then haul ass to Wal-Mart or one of the big box stores and max out the card on gift cards and other goodies. Those gift cards are as good as cash from that point on. They can be used to buy anything at all, whenever they want."

"This is crazy," Marcus said. "I had no idea this sort of thing went on, not like this. I've seen stories in the paper once in a while about counterfeiting, but I had no clue it was this bad."

"It's that bad and worse," Lee stated flatly. "I heard through the grapevine last week that a new scam was going on involving ATM cards, an area we had thought was pretty secure. The fraudsters attach a device to an ATM machine that skims the important data off that magnetic stripe I was telling you about. They also place a small web-cam nearby so they can read the customer's PIN number as they enter it. After that they dial in to the financial institution's voice response unit and change the PIN number. Then off they go to their nearest AMT and withdraw every last dollar of the card holder's money. Bingo. It's very, very slick."

Marcus thought he heard a note of admiration in Lee's voice for the criminal's ingenuity and creativity in these endeavors. He himself was simply feeling sick thinking that his little brother could be involved in anything this criminal.

That was when Andy Lucas stated the obvious, the one thing that doubtless all three had been thinking and that Marcus was afraid to verbalize, the big, massive, ugly elephant in the living room.

"So, Marcus," Andy said, "what in the world is your brother doing with a counterfeit credit card?"

Chapter 8

Marcus had enjoyed several days of excellent weather in Wayne, but the next morning the skies were heavy and thick, like masses of sodden cotton on the brink of exceeding the saturation point and ready to release their pent-up water in a massive deluge. The gloom matched his mood perfectly.

After hanging up from Lee Abernathy and Andy Lucas the day before, Marcus had made several phone calls in preparation for his trip. One was to the power company to pay the overdue electric bill. According to the mumbling, uninterested customer rep, the service was about two days away from being turned off. The second was to a locksmith in town. With some significant coaxing and the promise of a hefty tip, he convinced the man to come out that day and change all the locks. The locksmith, Al of Big Al's Locks and Bolts, not only changed the locks but also managed to repair the door jamb that Marcus had broken. He was wary of changing the locks once Marcus verbally slipped and admitted it was a rental property, but after several additional twenty dollar bills greased his palm Big Al's attitude did an abrupt about-face and he had all the work done in under an hour, humming very accurately rendered Rolling Stones songs the entire time.

Marcus tossed his suitcase in the rented Chevy then locked and dead-bolted the doors. He knew it wouldn't stop anyone from breaking in if they truly wanted to, but it should deter any casual attempts. He took one of Big Al's new keys and walked across the street. The key was as shiny as a freshly minted penny, its newly chiseled teeth sharp and clean as he rubbed it between his fingers. He rapped gently on the door.

"Hi. I'm leaving for a while, and I don't know how long I'll be gone. I had the locks changed, so if Rolland comes back while I'm gone would you please give him this?" He held up the key toward the window, not knowing if the reclusive soul inside could see or was even listening. He hung the bronze key on the eagle door knocker, where it winked brightly at him despite the overcast morning.

He waved as he walked back to his car. Just as he got in and shut the door the rain started, tiny drops at first, then rapidly increasing in intensity until it sounded like a dozen drummers pounding on his car. He switched the wipers on high and watched as they flew back and forth at breakneck speed, a pair of crazed metronomes keeping the beat. As he pulled out of the driveway he looked back across the street. He wasn't positive, but he didn't think the key was still hanging there. He smiled, his foul mood lifting a degree or two as he drove away.

Forty-five minutes later he arrived at the Dayton International Airport, turned the rental in, then made his way to the ticketing counter. As he walked up to check his bag he heard a voice calling to him from behind. He spun around and saw Otto and Cassandra there, waiting. There was a suitcase at Cassandra's feet.

"Hey, Marcus, glad you could make it," Otto called jovially, a huge smile on his narrow face. He shook some rain-dampened hair out of his eyes. "We've been waiting for you."

Marcus cocked a single eyebrow and gestured at the suitcase. "What's going on? Whose suitcase is this?"

Cassandra stood a little taller. Marcus noticed she had changed into a long tan and brown checkerboard skirt. Her white cotton blouse was adorned with mother-of-pearl buttons. Gone were the far more revealing shorts and T-shirt. The silver cross was still around her neck, glinting in the bright lights of the airport lobby.

"It's mine," she said firmly. "I'm going with you."

Marcus raised both hands up, palms out, as if to ward her off. "Oh, no. I'm going alone."

"No, you're not," she stated, taking half a step forward and staring up at him, her hands planted firmly on her hips. "I'm going too."

Otto laughed out loud. "Dude, you might as well give up. If Cassie says she's going, she's going. Simple as that."

Marcus frowned at the young man before turning back to Cassie. "Why are you so determined to go with me?"

"Listen. You may be able to speak the language, but you couldn't be any more conspicuous if you tried. A six foot two white guy with blond hair, in Mexico? You might as well hang a neon light around your neck. Please. I'm almost a native, and I can talk to people and go places you can't. I can help, and," she added, "I want to help. I want to find out what is going on and what's happened to Rolland."

Marcus looked at her resolute expression and knew this battle had been lost before it began. Plus, deep down he was rather pleased she'd be going with him, although if anyone had asked he would've had a hard time admitting it. He kept reminding himself that she was Rolland's girlfriend, or perhaps ex-girlfriend, and while the status of that relationship was apparently in a state of flux he had no intention of doing his brother further harm by attempting anything romantic with her. He vowed to himself right then and there that she was strictly hands-off until he heard from his brother that it was okay, that their relationship was over. But that didn't mean he couldn't look forward to her company.

He nodded yes and she smiled brightly then hugged Otto, followed by a quick peck on his cheek. Marcus shook the young man's hand and addressed him solemnly.

"Listen, I don't know how long I'll – we'll – be gone," he amended, glancing at Cassandra. "But be careful, okay? I don't know if those two maniacs are still around. Promise me you'll watch your back."

Otto laughed. "Nothing to worry about. I'll be careful, and besides Don-Don is still around to protect me from your Mexican Gigantor."

"Still, just practice a little common sense."

"Sure thing," Otto said, holding his three fingers up in a Boy Scout salute. "Scout's promise."

"Hmm. Were you ever really a Boy Scout?"

"Sure. For about a week, until they caught me and a few Girl Scouts in the basement of the church practicing CPR."

Cassandra gave him a light slap on the shoulder as a mock reprimand before hugging him again. They said their farewells. Otto sketched a salute and strolled out into the damp parking lot, whistling a tune that sounded remarkably like something from his new CD. Marcus grinned at his receding back, wishing that he and Rolland had parted company on such a high note.

With Otto gone Marcus turned to Cassandra. There was a moment of uncomfortable silence as the two of them realized that, while they were now travel partners, they were actually little more than strangers. As newly-formed as the relationship between the three of them had been, Otto had been the common denominator, the one constant. Now that he was gone that reference point was missing and there was a thick, clumsy awkwardness that both felt keenly.

Marcus coughed lightly. "Uh, well we should probably check in and get to our gate."

She nodded quickly, almost eagerly. "Yes, good idea. We should."

Both of them reached for her suitcase at the same time and bumped heads.

"Ouch," she said, rubbing her forehead.

Marcus was massaging his own. "Sorry, I was just going to get your bag for you."

"Thanks, but I'm perfectly capable of getting my own bag."

"Sure, okay, no problem," Marcus said, still rubbing his head. He thought back and recalled his last time at this airport with Mary Lou, the older passenger from Wisconsin he had befriended. She had been happy to let him carry her bag. He almost wished she were here now as it would serve to break up what could be a long, uncomfortable trip. He sighed and walked behind Cassandra as she headed to the ticket counter, her back straight and stiff.

Yes, this could be a very long trip indeed.

Their flight to Merida was not direct. There was no chance of that flying out of a mid-sized airport like Dayton. They first had to fly to Houston where they would change planes for the final leg of the journey. They found it was too late to move seats on this first flight so Cassandra was all the way up in row A5, while Marcus was near the back. He didn't know if he was happy or not at that arrangement, but was leaning toward happy. Or maybe not? Damn, he wasn't sure.

He was, however, quickly reminded why he didn't care for air travel. Due to his size he just didn't fit very well in the seats of coach class, or as he liked to call it, the "cattle pen". He was holding out hope that he didn't have anyone next to him so he could at least breathe a little easier and enjoy some elbow room. As the stewardess closed the door up front he surreptitiously pumped his fist in satisfaction that he had not one, but two empty seats surrounding him. He leaned out and looked ahead, up at Cassandra, and saw that she was sharing her row with two older businessmen in dark suits and ties. He thought about inviting her to join him, but before he could the plane was backing out and heading to the runway. Within minutes they were in the air, angling southwest.

Marcus noticed with pleasure that his back was feeling a little better and only hurt badly if he made a sudden movement or twisted it too far. However that did nothing to diminish the memory of the whip, nor the man who had wielded it. His eyes closed to slits at the thought. He began to consider what he might do if he managed to find the small Mexican, and it was not, he knew, going to be a conversation among gentlemen.

With all this free time and plenty of personal space on the flight, Marcus reclined his seatback and considered everything that had happened over the last few weeks. He began cataloguing what little he actually knew, ticking off the points as he went:

First and foremost, of course, Rolland was still missing. Not only did no one know where he was, but there were several groups looking for him, each with their own agendas. Marcus himself was searching, but now also involved were Rolland's friends, Otto and Cassandra, as well as the two attackers, Hernandez and Gonzalez. Lieutenant Doncaster was not, he mused darkly, but that was a different matter altogether.

Hernandez and Gonzalez had insisted that Rolland was somehow involved in a credit card counterfeiting scheme, and that he had more of the cards in his possession. These cards were either with him or possibly hidden somewhere. Either way his two attackers were eager – no, desperate might be a better word - to secure the rest of these cards, wherever they were. He didn't have a clue what they planned to do with them, and at this point he really didn't care.

The smaller of his attackers, the one known to him as Hernandez, had some past relationship with his Uncle in Merida. How was he involved in all this? He was a vicious little bastard, which was the one thing Marcus was certain of. He twisted in his seat, keenly feeling his aching back.

Lastly there was Cassandra. He straightened up and peered ahead over the tops of the seats so he could just see her jet-black hair a dozen or so rows in front of him. How did she fit into this complex arrangement? She was, as far as he knew, just the ex-girlfriend, but why had she insisted on coming along? Was that from some sense of guilt? Was she still emotionally attached to his brother? She kept insisting she wasn't, that the relationship had ended. He didn't have a good handle on her role in this, but knew he had little choice now but to watch it all play out. Besides, despite all this he found himself still very attracted to her, and not just on a superficial level.

He closed his eyes and tilted his head back, the deep thrumming of the jet engines delivering a constant stream of white noise that he could both hear and feel. The vibration served almost to numb his entire body, like a coin-operated massage bed at a cheap motel. Looking inward, into his past, he found himself considering his lack of a love life over the years. When, he wondered, had he last felt any kind of emotional attachment to a woman? Was it an inability to get close to someone, or was it just ambivalence to romance? He was surprised to find that he couldn't recall having any really deep feelings toward anyone in years, possibly longer. He sat up in his seat, not for the first time aware how emotionally bereft he'd been. He shook his head in silent, sad amazement. He was unable to recall a single meaningful, long-term relationship in college, as well as all through his time in San Diego. One night stands? Yes, quite a few. A handful of girls he had dated before drifting apart? Yes, one or two. Long-term, meaningful relationships? No, nothing to speak of.

Regretfully, almost wistfully now, he looked up at Cassandra, and rather wished he had invited her to sit with him after all.

When Marcus and Rolland were younger and their mother was still alive, it became a tradition of sorts at Christmas to give each boy, along with their other gifts, a small puzzle of some type. These were not flat, cardboard, two-dimensional cardboard puzzles with a bucolic or snow-capped mountain scene on the box, one that had to be painstakingly assembled piece by piece. No, these were generally small, intricately designed, three dimensional diabolical enigmas that both confounded and amazed the boys. Marcus easily remembered one about the size of a billiard ball, made of wood, built of twenty or more interlocking pieces of varying shapes and sizes. Completed, the ball was sturdy and tough, the slightly different colored wood pieces a tightly constructed mosaic. But once the keystone piece was removed the rest of the construct fell apart with no more adhesion than a box of toothpicks. It was up to the boys to reconstruct the ball, fitting a wooden shape here, sliding another there, twisting still another this way or that, until the keystone was reinserted, thereby locking the puzzle in place. Each year it had been a fun, anticipated challenge.

Some years it was a matter of hours, other times it could take days, before the final piece of the new puzzle could be pushed, clicked, or shoved in to its appropriate spot. Each time, whether it was a ball, a cube, or a clear Lucite pyramid, upon completion of a new and more complex puzzle the entire family would celebrate with cheers and laughter, usually with much hugging from their mother. The finished project would be proudly placed on the boys' bookshelf almost as a trophy to their ingenuity and diligence.

That was how Marcus was viewing his current situation. All the different players with all their various motives were the interlocking puzzle pieces. It was up to him to fit them into place so he could proudly display the finished product. But did he have all the pieces? Did he know what the final shape was meant to be? So far, he knew, he was nowhere close. He hoped this trip to Mexico would provide the answers.

Their flight to Houston landed without incident. The majority of the passengers had to disembark, including Marcus and Cassandra. Their next flight left in just under two hours so they wandered to their gate and found a pair of seats. The two passed the time in small-talk, both taking this opportunity to try and get to know each better. He could tell she was keeping her emotional and physical distance from him, although she did award him a thin family history, explaining that her parents were originally from a small town outside of Merida but had made the decision to cross illegally into the U.S. when her mom was pregnant with her. She was born in the States so was by law an American citizen, but when she was a teenager her parents had returned to their hometown. She had opted to remain behind and had been able to visit them just a few times since.

"They don't even know I'm on my way," she explained. "I'd love to go see them when this is all over. It's been a few years. I miss them so much."

"Sure, I understand. We can do that before we go back, certainly."

She suddenly became nervous and didn't want to talk about them anymore. Marcus tried to continue the casual chatting before giving up when she proved unwilling. He instead picked up the newspaper he had purchased at one of the ubiquitous newsstands at their gate. He scanned the paper and checked out the scores of some baseball games and looked over the business section. Then, mainly because of their upcoming destination, he settled on a story in the international section that described the increasing drug violence taking place in the eastern half of Mexico. He nodded to himself. Yes, he'd heard a lot about this over the last few years. It was an ongoing, nightmarish story that had been going on for decades. There was much discussion concerning two warring drug cartels. One, the predominant cartel known as Los Hermanos, based in the southern State of Michoacan, was making vicious and violent inroads into the Yucatan Peninsula. They were expanding their turf against the entrenched, old-money cartel based in and around Merida, El Grúpo. Thousands of drug traffickers had already been killed, he read, many decapitated and with their severed heads literally dropped in the other's territory. Almost that many federal agents, Federales, had been murdered too, along with hundreds and possibly thousands of innocent civilians. The governments of several states within

Mexico were calling on the U.S. and Mexican governments for assistance, citing the warring cartels' tremendous firepower and almost religious zeal. Typically they were much better armed than even the Federal Police. It seemed the viciousness of Los Hermanos was paying off as they were making deeper and deeper forays into the Yucatan. Every day there were reports of more violence, more shootings, more decapitations, people being burned alive, others being tortured to death. There were even reports of incidents in Merida itself. It was beyond ugly, and the author of the piece gave his own prediction that it would get worse before it got better, if it ever did. Marcus nudged Cassandra and pointed to the story.

"This El Grúpo, Los Hermanos drug war is pretty nasty," he commented, trying to break the chasm of silence between them with additional small talk.

She was busy filling in the boxes of a Sudoku puzzle from the paper. She put her pencil down and looked at the headline, *Fourteen Dead In Drug Cartel Shootout.* She shuddered as she read on.

"It's horrible," she stated. "Innocent people are being killed every day. Police are, too, unless they have been bought by the cartels. It's a terrible situation. Just awful."

"From this article it looks like the U.S. and Mexican governments are going to step up their efforts to stop it."

"Well, they say that," she replied. "But every time anyone in the cartel is caught or killed there are ten more waiting in line to take his place. There's so much money at stake that these people will stop at nothing to get what they want. They're butchers. Animals!"

Cassandra spat that last word with such vehemence that it caught Marcus by surprise. She sensed this and looked away, back to her Sudoku puzzle, her face flushed. For more than a minute her pencil hovered over the newsprint without moving. Marcus noticed a smudge on the page of her puzzle that wasn't there before, a single round splotch of water no bigger than the tip of his little finger. Was that a tear? he wondered. Was Cassandra crying?

Confused and unsure what to do, he started to reach out to her, to lay his hand on her shoulder and ask what was wrong, but she suddenly excused herself and hurried to the restroom. When she returned a few minutes later she had regained her composure. Her cheeks were tinged a blotchy pink. The Sudoku puzzle page was gone, nowhere to be seen.

Then the loudspeaker announced their flight was boarding. They silently gathered up their belongings and filed toward the maw of the plane, one by one and single file, herded by nylon turnstiles, thereby fulfilling Marcus' vision of cattle entering a pen. The newspaper article about Los Hermanos was left draped over the arm of his airport seat where it soon fluttered to the floor in a messy heap.

Their plane bumped to a rough landing at Merida International Airport ten minutes ahead of schedule. Marcus had dozed through the repeated announcements of their imminent arrival, and when they touched down hard it startled him so much he shot upright, eyes wide and confused. He took a deep breath after he had gotten his wits about him and looked toward Cassandra in the window seat to his right. Her lips were tight and she was pointedly gazing out the window. He was pretty sure she was trying hard not to laugh at him. He kept glancing sideways at her as they taxied to their gate, but gave up when their plane linked up to the airbridge and the door opened. En mass the passengers stood up in the cramped space and began gathering up their belongings. Marcus prudently waited in his seat until it was his turn since he had to uncomfortably hunch over in the narrow aisle. He motioned Cassandra to ease out and go ahead of him, and she did just that, her cotton skirt swishing back and forth as she walked.

Marcus noted right away that the airport was different than the last time he had been there. The terminal had been remodeled sometime in the recent past and looked quite up to date and modern. On his previous trip it really had resembled a dingy bus terminal more than a large, metropolitan airport. The newly updated pastel greens and blues were accented by swooping brushed aluminum highlights all along the walls. Skylights and huge windows let in the bright Mexican sun. It was a pleasant change.

The bored customs agent asked Marcus several perfunctory questions – how long did he plan to stay in the country? Was he here for business or pleasure? – then stamped his passport and motioned him to move along with a flip of his hand. The agent woke up when Cassandra approached, and to Marcus' slight annoyance he asked her many more questions and kept up a steady stream of conversation. Finally he smiled a big, toothy grin, stamped her passport, and waved her cordially through. Marcus had no intention of asking what that obvious flirting had been all about. They took the escalator down to the baggage claim area.

Fifteen minutes later they had their bags in hand, Marcus' black suitcase with the bright green ribbon rolling behind him. He had briefly considered offering to pull Cassandra's too, but thought better of it after her earlier rebuff in Dayton. They dodged masses of humanity heading in different directions and all seeming to be in a tremendous rush. Marcus heard several different languages besides English and Spanish, most notably German, which he could understand in a pinch, and French, which he could not. They finally pushed through a crowd gathered by the entrance and stepped through the automatic doors and onto the sidewalk, and only then did Marcus truly realize they were in Mexico.

The heat and humidity knocked into him, his shirt instantly sticking to his back. He took a deep breath through his nose and was amazed by how deeply he associated places with their mélange of scents and smells: car and bus exhaust, untreated by catalytic converters, was thick enough to see; tobacco smoke from a million inhabitants; fruits, mainly mangos and oranges, being cut up and sold by street vendors all up and down the sidewalks; deep fried foods; fresh tortillas; and a hundred other aromas that were too faint to be recognizable or simply unknown. The afternoon sun beat down on them mercilessly. He slid on his sunglasses.

"I wish I had remembered a hat," Marcus commented.

"Hmm?" Cassandra asked distractedly. She looked almost rapt as it had finally sunk in that she was back. Her dark eyes were alight with joy, an unabashed smile on her lips, almost as if she were a child in an amusement park. Her head was tilted slightly back so the sun warmed her face, her black hair glistened like a crow's feather in the bright sunshine. Marcus knew she'd been born in the States but he could tell that she felt Mexico was her home. He grinned at her serene expression before tapping her gently on the shoulder.

"Come on. Let's grab a taxi and head to my Aunt's house."

She blinked twice. "Oh, yes, of course. We should do that."

There were several dozen VW and Nissan taxis idling and waiting for a fare. Marcus motioned and the next one in line eased up. It was an old-fashioned VW Beetle, the type rarely seen in the States and not manufactured new since the mid-70s. There were tens of thousands of them chugging along here in Mexico, the distinct whir of their engines unmistakable, most on them painted white and sporting a green stripe around their midsection. None had air-conditioning and all were equipped with vinyl seats and no carpeting. It was bare-bones, cheap transportation in a nation where such a thing was sorely needed, Marcus knew, although the environmental cost of so much raw exhaust was tremendous. Smog was a perennial health issue, especially in the summer months.

"Ugh, I never cared for these cars," Cassandra said, beginning the multi-step process of folding herself into the back seat.

"I know what you mean. I fit better in the airplane than in these things. I'd forgotten how cramped these were."

"It doesn't help when I think how many sweaty butts have sat here before, either."

Marcus stared at her. "Well I never thought about it before now, but thanks."

The driver, a heavyset, very dark skinned man with a square face and sporting a traditional white cotton campesino shirt, popped open the front hatch of the VW and tossed in the majority of their luggage. The rest had to squeeze in with Marcus and Cassandra. Like many VW taxis the right front seat of the car had been removed to facilitate ingress and egress, which did help, and it also served as additional storage space once the travelers were in and seated. Marcus looked around but there were no seatbelts. With a practiced flip of his index finger the driver deftly reset his fare counter and the peso count began ticking upwards.

"*¿A donde van, señores?*" he asked, tapping a cigarette out of his case.

Marcus gave him his Aunt's street address. The man grunted and off they went, the noisy engine making casual conversation difficult. Their driver initially seemed saner than some Marcus had driven with in the past since he actually obeyed several of the traffic laws. He was fond of sudden, neck-snapping lane changes, however, and he treated his horn like a musical instrument, honking it artfully and flashing his headlights at other drivers in some sort of secret taxi brotherhood language. Marcus marveled at how all the taxicabs and busses seemed to drive like they each owned the road, yet there were very few accidents. He also knew to latch on to the vinyl handle and say a silent prayer each time they made a radical maneuver.

They continued on, and several times Marcus saw landmarks or streets that he recognized, especially when they crossed the Paseo de Mantejo, a beautiful parkway lined with shops, outdoor restaurants, and unique hotels. The colors of the buildings and awnings were striking in the bright sunshine: pastel blues and pinks, yellows, some ochres. But the predominant color, or lack of color, was white, and many of the buildings were almost blinding as they reflected the afternoon sun. He caught a fleeting glimpse of the twin steeples of the massive, ancient *Iglesia de Jesus* before it passed out of sight behind the Government Palace, a block long, two-story, open air structure. Then they were moving away from the city center, into more residential areas, and he knew they were getting close to his Aunt's home. Most of the streets were not named but numbered in a somewhat regular fashion so it was a relatively simple matter to know where they were.

"Why didn't you want to let your Aunt know we're coming?" Cassandra asked as she watched the houses rush by. "I mean, it's not like you live down the street and you just pop in all the time unannounced, you know."

Marcus nodded. "I know, I just don't want anyone knowing we're here. Not yet."

"Because of the short attacker, Mr. Gonzalez?"

"Mr. Hernandez, actually," Marcus said. "Gonzalez was the big guy."

"Whatever," she replied with a small grin and an eye-roll.

"I just think that the element of surprise is very important."

She nodded. "Okay, whatever you say. I hope she likes these types of surprises, that's all."

"Actually, she does."

Suddenly a pair of horns blasted and their driver made a spirited, high-speed swerve, jerking left then right to avoid an oncoming pickup truck. Marcus and Cassandra tumbled back and forth for a few seconds before the car stabilized, Cassandra with a squeal of shock. As the car leveled out they quickly and with muttered apologies untwined from each other and smoothed out their clothes. The driver screamed at the offender and shook a meaty fist his way as he mumbled curses under his breath.

Their driver lit his cigarette and blew out a plume of smoke. Most of it was sucked out the open window but a lungful or two drifted to the back seat. Marcus shifted nervously. Between the rough ride, the smoke, and Cassandra's proximity, he was getting more discomfited by the second.

Thankfully after just a few more minutes they turned onto his Aunt's street. The taxi slowed as they wound around the gently curving cobblestone road and the driver asked them to point out their destination. Marcus motioned when they arrived and they pulled to the curb. In no time their bags were on the sidewalk, the driver had been paid and tipped, and the old VW whirred away, a stream of grayish blue exhaust trailing in its wake.

Marcus stood rooted to that spot, watching the iconic white and green taxi diminish and then disappear around a distant corner. When he turned Cassandra was standing next to their luggage, her hands clasped in front of her, a question mark on her face. A few houses down a dog barked, and not too far away he could hear a woman's muffled voice singing an unfamiliar, rather melancholy tune. He nodded to Cassandra and looked at the massive wooden door. It was exactly as he recalled: solid oak stained dark, almost black, girded by steel straps across its face. The house itself was still a light pastel blue, as if it had been painstakingly colored with sky blue chalk. It was two stories tall and built right up to the edge of the sidewalk. He walked up to the door and rang the doorbell. Excitement and anxiety battled for dominance, and he was surprised to feel that his palms were damp. He heard a noise inside the entryway of the house, faint footfalls on terracotta tile, and then the doorknob turned and the door creaked open.

Chapter 9

Back in Ohio, Otto Doncaster was doing what he liked best – which was nothing at all, really, besides driving his Ford truck and listening to music as loud as the stereo would go. The radio volume went to ten, but he often joked that if he twisted the knob just a little harder he could force it to eleven. He had already listened to and memorized the music and lyrics to the R.E.M. CD; he didn't know why or how, but he'd always possessed an amazing and nearly useless ability to recall song lyrics verbatim after just a few plays. His mom was quick to point out that if he could do that he could certainly remember to empty the dishwasher or mow the yard, tasks that always slipped his mind. He was back to the classic rock radio station out of Dayton and right now it was playing *Rock the Cashbah,* by *The Clash*. He was dutifully drumming his hands on the steering wheel in time with the heavy beat. The window was down and the wind kept blowing his long brown hair into his eyes. He didn't care. He just kept driving and drumming, driving and drumming. Ah, life was good.

He thought briefly of Marcus and Cassie, and hoped that they were okay. He figured they were in Mexico by now, probably in Merida. He couldn't wait to hear what they found out. He made sure his cell was on and charged just in case they called. Damn, all of this was getting very exciting! He cranked up the volume another notch, and it actually did move slightly past the tenth notch.

Right at that moment he had no real destination in mind, nowhere he absolutely had to be. He had recently picked up some hours at the Riverside Beer and Wine Drive-Thru but he didn't go on duty for several hours yet, so the afternoon was his. *Rock the Cashbah* faded away and *The Who's* venerable *My Wife* came on next. Slightly off-key but not concerned in the least, he sang along.

Give me police protection, gonna buy a gun so I can look out for number one.

Give me a bodyguard, a black belt judo expert, with a machine gun...

A few blocks later he pulled into the town's one and only McDonald's and waited patiently in line at the drive through. When his turn came he eased up to the speaker and heard a muffled, static-filled voice asking for what he thought was his order. He marveled that in this day and age no one could design a system with better sound quality than this. He and Rolland had both thought of themselves as audiophiles, true lovers of music and sound reproduction, so this poor display of fidelity bothered his acoustic sensibilities. He leaned out the truck window to place his order.

"Hi, there. Yes, I'd like a Big Mac, a Quarter Pounder with cheese with no onion, a large fry, and a Coke. Oh, and an apple pie."

The buzzing voice repeated what he thought was the correct order, so he said thanks and pulled up. The girl at the window slid it open.

"Oh, hi, Otto," she said brightly. "How's it going?"

"It's going," Otto said, smiling. Her name was Jenna and she was a cute blond a few years his junior. He thought she was still in high school, a senior, and according to the rumor mill she had recently broken up with her long-time boyfriend. Hmm, he mused, they'd always been on good terms, although she was kind of a jock, and he most certainly was not. He had a fond memory of a lot of leg and a tall, athletic build. He might have to follow up on this later.

Jenna looked around the cab of the pickup truck.

"You the only one in there? This is a lot of food for one guy, especially a guy as skinny as you."

He laughed. "Just a little snack," he assured her, trying to sound both casual and manly at the same time. Damn. He didn't think he pulled that off very well. He vowed to practice later at home. He unconsciously flipped his bangs out of his eyes with a gentle shake of his head.

She leaned on the counter as they waited for his food – the no onions on the order took a few extra minutes. She had brown eyes, not blue, he noticed, which was a little quirky for a blond, and she had a nice smile. He asked her about the crappy intercom system. She laughed.

"When we talk into it we crinkle paper by the microphone at the same time," she said, looking mock-secretive. "We just like to screw with people. The intercom's really very good."

They both laughed and chatted easily for another minute. Much too suddenly for Otto's liking his order was bagged and ready to go. She turned away for a minute as she put some napkins in his bag and handed it to him. Otto paid, smiled a warm goodbye, and drove off. As he headed down the street he dug in the sack and pulled out his meal, the napkins, and his straw. He did a double-take and saw some writing on a napkin: it was a little smiley face next to a phone number. He felt a warm fuzziness in his gut and smiled wider yet. She wanted him to call her! Sweet! Driving with his knees he expertly entered her name and phone number in his cellphone, and hit SAVE. His grin was huge. Yep, life was good.

As he continued his aimless journey and munched on the first burger and some fries, he saw a black Cadillac SUV forty or fifty feet back in his rearview mirror. Come to think of it, he was pretty damn certain he'd seen that same SUV before he had stopped at Micky Ds, although he couldn't be one hundred percent sure. He sat up a little straighter, French fries held motionless in his hand. He purposefully turned left at the next street, a residential neighborhood of older homes. The Caddy slowed, but cruised on straight ahead. Otto exhaled nervously.

"Get a hold of yourself, son," he told himself. "You're wigging out here."

He stuck around the neighborhood and made a few more random turns but didn't see the Caddy again. He held a hand out in front of him, parallel to the ground, and watched it quiver and shake as if he suffered from Parkinson's.

"Rock solid, that's what you are, my boy," he mumbled sarcastically, pissed at himself for overreacting. Otto looked at the remainder of his food and decided his appetite had taken a hike. He carefully folded up and tucked the napkin with Jenna's number in his pocket, then stuffed everything else back into the McDonald's bag. He pointed the nose of the truck back toward the center of town, thinking maybe it wasn't a bad idea to drop in and see Don-Don for a few minutes. Yeah, a quick visit to see his big brother sounded like a super plan. He didn't want to admit how shaken he was by the false encounter with the SUV. Having a brother for a cop was sometimes a pain in the ass, but other times could be very handy.

Three blocks from the courthouse the low fuel light came on and he darted in to the first gas station he came to, Dan's Gas & Go, a combination gas station, convenience store, and car wash. Otto especially liked the car wash since it would accommodate his truck, and it did a pretty good job for only four bucks. He trotted in and tossed a crumpled twenty dollar bill on the counter.

"Sixteen bucks on number three, and a basic car wash."

The clerk barely looked away from a small television set long enough to take the cash and ring up the sale. Without so much as a mumbled thanks he handed Otto a receipt with a code on the bottom. Otto tipped a non-existent hat towards him before he went back outside and pumped his gas. When he was done he pulled around back to the entrance of the car wash.

Otto pulled up to the small kiosk outside the car wash. He entered the code from his gas receipt, rolled up the window, and shifted the truck into neutral. The conveyor belt bit and grabbed his tire with a soft bump, gently pulling him forward, all driving decisions now effectively out of his hands. It was almost eerie, he thought, looking at the steering wheel twitch back and forth as the truck moved ahead seemingly of its own volition. It was as if he had lost control of the thing he cherished the most.

The first of the clean water hoses soaked his truck, quickly followed by a foamy, multi-colored soap that looked a lot like pastel shaving cream but tickled his nose and smelled of citrus. Next came the traditional spinning cloth brushes that beat the top and the sides of truck and made the passenger compartment echo like the interior of a drum. There was one more foaming bath of some sort which completely covered his windows and dimmed the interior, and then came the final rinse.

As the truck continued its predestined journey and the jets blasted off the last of the soap from his windows, Otto thought he saw something. No, not something but rather someone. Whoever the person was remained motionless against the wall as the truck glided forward. As the last of the soap was powered away and the windows cleared completely, Otto's eyes widened in terror.

"Oh, fuck," he hissed under his breath. "It's the big Mexican."

The man standing with his arms crossed was enormous, looking as solid and imposing as a totem pole carved from an ancient Sequoia. Marcus' description of him was accurate but it just didn't do the guy justice - in person the man was freakin' gigantic! Otto ripped his eyes away for a split second, long enough to focus on the passenger door that was, unfortunately, not locked. Indecision or perhaps some ancient survival instinct froze him in place while his mind worked furiously to determine his next step. Meanwhile the truck still rolled mindlessly, mechanically ahead, until the passenger door and the enormous Mexican were lined up.

Their eyes met.

Reacting out of terror and self-preservation Otto lunged for the door lock. At that precise moment all sound seemed to cease and time stopped. No, it didn't exactly stop, but to Otto it began moving in super slow-motion, as smooth and clear as a high-definition football instant replay. Otto saw the rhythmic jets of water pulsing lazily back and forth across his windshield, the dripping water like transparent corn syrup on his windows. He could see the big brushes leisurely spinning near the rear of the truck, their dark cloth bristles stuck straight out from centrifugal force and rhythmically tossing water in exact crystalline spirals. The drops of water shimmered like liquid diamonds, each one dazzling and brilliant. It was quite beautiful. In that one instant, in that tiniest span of time no longer than it took a flashbulb to pop, he recalled Marcus' warning that he needed to watch his back. He saw his hand moving out and downward to slap the lock home. He was young, he was scared, and he was fast.

The Mexican was faster.

And just like that, time snapped back to normal and the roar of the carwash came flooding back. Like a serpent's strike the Mexican's hand shot out and ripped the door open in one smooth movement. Otto's hand struck nothing but empty air and hung out there, flailing, as if he were hailing a taxi. The giant Mexican casually opened the door wide and climbed into the cab, heedless of the water still spraying in the air. The truck groaned and tilted sideways under his massive bulk. He was so large he had to sit with his knees nearly parallel to the dashboard, his head hunched down low. Water dripped off the ragged ends of his long black hair. His hooded eyes were deep black pockets of coal, void of emotion or feeling. Otto mashed his back up against the driver's door, his legs working furiously to put nonexistent distance between the two of them. He madly scratched and groped with his left hand in a blind search for the door handle that seemed to have vanished. Like a man in the throes of a heart attack Otto's breathing was rasping and loud. Before he could find the handle the Mexican grabbed his shoulder, those monstrous bratwurst fingers digging in to

Otto's muscles, grasping down through flesh to the very bone. Escape at that point was impossible and Otto knew it; his body sagged in resigned defeat. The big Mexican leaned forward and Otto could see the pitted and pocked skin that Marcus had described, his complexion like melted wax. The ragged scar was almost black in the poor lighting. The smell of old cigars, wet clothing, and damp hair filled the truck's cab. The headliner was splotchy with water where the Mexican's head pressed against it.

Otto considered screaming, but just then the dryers kicked on and effectively drowned out any other sound short of a tornado siren. His captor somehow sensed his intention and squeezed harder, so hard that Otto was momentarily light-headed with pain and was certain his damn shoulder had been dislocated. He was so scared he nearly pissed his pants, and while he didn't he had a feeling there would be plenty of time for that later. His bangs fell in his eyes and simply hung there. The Mexican leaned closer yet. In heavily accented English, he uttered one brief sentence.

"We need to talk."

Chapter 10

The door opened and a diminutive older lady stood there, a thin cotton dress and apron over her blocky frame, a wispy halo of dark hair framing her round face. She appeared to be in her mid-fifties, but was probably closer to late forties. She was puzzled for a moment before recognition dawned and her dark eyes lit up with joy.

"Marcus!" she exclaimed.

They came together and hugged warmly. Marcus was so much larger than her that he could have been embracing a child. "Juanita," Marcus replied in Spanish, "I'd like you to meet a friend of mine, Cassandra."

Cassandra smiled at her. "Nice to meet you." She extended her hand, and Juanita quickly wiped her already clean hands on her white apron and shook hands awkwardly, holding Cassandra's with her own two hands.

"Nice to meet you as well," she said, using the formal mode of Spanish. "Come in, come in. The Señora didn't tell me you were coming."

"She didn't know," he explained, purposefully using the more familiar mode. "Our visit was spur of the moment."

"Well come in, come in," she chided. "Let's not stand here on the sidewalk all day. You must be hungry and tired. Would you like something to eat?"

They grabbed their suitcases and followed her inside. They were in a small foyer which led to a large living room. Marcus took it all in, happiness and joy suffusing him: this house was home to him, much more so than his old house in the States. He had spent many happy and safe years here with Rolland and those memories easily tumbled back upon him. He saw all the big, heavy, comfortable furniture, the artwork and tapestries on the walls, the colorful blue and terracotta tile. The only new item was a large LCD television that looked out of place, but it was situated off to the side and tucked out of the way. Looking around he never really noticed how well off his Mexican family was, much more so than most in town. Compared to an American household they would be considered upper middle-class, but here in Mexico they were doing well indeed. Perhaps because he'd been so much younger and less aware back then? Regardless, El Señor was wealthier than he thought.

Juanita continued into the living room and through a large archway into the dining area. She motioned for them to sit and disappeared into the small kitchen beyond. Marcus took his seat on one side, and Cassandra sat next to him.

"Juanita is the cook," Marcus explained. "She's been here, well, forever. I learned most of my Spanish from her, sitting on the counter while she prepared all the meals. She's very nice and helped me a lot, especially in the beginning. She was patient with me, talking slowly and simply, you know, like you'd talk to a child. She had no idea what a great teacher she was." He looked around curiously. "Naibi is the maid. I'm sure she's around her somewhere."

"She seems very sweet," Cassandra said.

"She is. Through and through."

Marcus didn't feel the need to explain this to Cassandra who no doubt knew it already, but much of Mexican culture was still based on an unwritten caste society. There were the educated and wealthy, and then there was, well, everyone else. A middle class as in the States and Europe nearly didn't exist here, although that was slowly changing. Juanita and Naibi were almost considered family members, but would never be part of the family. They worked long hours for little pay in lovely houses such as this, then in the evenings they went home to their own small, cramped homes. This was the norm and they would never dream of doing anything differently. It had bothered both Rolland and Marcus when they had first arrived as kids, but time and day-to-day living soon made it normal for them, too. After a while the guilt began to fade as well. After all, what teenage boys wouldn't love having all their meals cooked for them, their beds magically made daily, their laundry cleaned and pressed without ever asking?

This extended beyond the home, too. When he and his brother had taken bus trips to different parts of the country they had been amazed at the dichotomy between the classes. The bus lines always came to mind. Here were two major types of bus transportation available, the cramped, overcrowded and ancient school-type buses with no air conditioning and zero amenities on one hand, and comfortable, plush transportation that rivaled charter buses in the States on the other. The difference in ticket price between the two was not great, but those in the lower socio-economic class would never dream of riding in the nicer buses, no matter how small the difference in the fare was. Some things just weren't done.

Juanita quickly came back to the dining room and placed a steaming stack of fresh tortillas in front of them, then returned seconds later with some bowls of green salsa that she had undoubtedly made fresh that morning. Marcus thanked her heartedly and ladled some of the salsa onto a tortilla, rolled it up like a loose cigar, and quickly munched it down. The green salsa was spicy hot, *picante*, and would have cleared any sinus congestion he had. He watched as Cassandra did the same, her eyes alight with familiarity and joy. He grinned inwardly as she soon gasped and grabbed for a glass of water. Neither one of them were accustomed to the heat.

"So where's La Señora?" he asked between bites. Damn this was good! He had forgotten how wonderful fresh tortillas were, even though he didn't like to think that Juanita had probably stood in line this morning at 5:00 AM at the tortillaria down the street to get the day's supply. There had almost been food riots several years before when the government had threatened to cut off subsidies to the tortilla makers around the country. It would have nearly doubled the price of this staple, something the masses could not have afforded. The government had wisely relented at the last minute.

The little cook set down several bowls of fruit. Ripe yellow mangos, bananas, and plump oranges. Mangos had been Rolland's favorite, Marcus recalled. They were a pain to eat, but their taste was different and wonderful.

"Oh, she is out shopping, as usual," she replied. "I expect her back soon. El Señor is out of town on business, of course."

"What about Santiago?"

"Santiago is out and about," she said. "It's hard to keep track of him these days, you know."

"Is he still attending the university?"

She needlessly rearranged the flowers that adorned the table, fussing over them with fluttering hands. She stood back with her hands on her hips, glaring at the arrangement. Marcus could sense that she was nervous about something.

"Yes, I suppose. Now, what else would you like? Dinner is not for some time, but I'd be happy to fix you something now if you'd like."

Marcus rolled another tortilla and ate this one more slowly, savoring the texture and flavor. He eyed the oranges but decided against one since it was too messy for his liking.

"No, I'm fine. Cassandra?"

"No, thank you very much, Juanita."

She beamed, happy to move on to more familiar ground. She explained that Marcus was welcome to head upstairs to his old room and freshen up, while Cassandra could take the guest room down the hall from him.

"It's just the way you left it," she said. "There's so much room in this big old place, and we almost never have guests. Oh, I almost forgot to ask – where's Rolland? Will he be coming, too? I hope so." She had trouble pronouncing the name, as did most Spanish speakers. Soft R sounds were not in the Spanish language.

He hoped he didn't show any undue emotion, or give anything away in his expression, as he said, "No, he won't be coming. He's still up in the States."

She clasped her hands together and made a quick pout. "Oh, what a shame. I haven't seen him for so long, either. Well, please pass along my love and prayers to him the next time you see him."

"You bet."

She scurried off to other parts of the house and Marcus finished up. He and Cassandra gathered up their luggage and she followed him in to the courtyard, where they both marveled at the beautiful fountain surrounded by lush plants and flowers. Marcus would have been hard pressed to name any of the exotic flowers, but had always been enthralled by their brilliant colors. The water in the fountain splashed and burbled over the lip and down into the small pond below. They went up the outside staircase ("very inconvenient when it's raining," Marcus explained) and around an open walkway to the back portion of the house. The first door on the right was hers. His was next door.

"I know we've talked about this already, but you're sure they won't mind me staying here?" she asked in English, standing in the doorway.

"Of course not. My Aunt will love it. She doesn't have many visitors from the States, and she'll like having another woman around the house. Be prepared, however – she may insist on doing something horrible, like taking you shopping or something."

Cassandra smiled and laughed lightly, and Marcus found that he was really becoming quite fond of her laugh and her smile.

"Until then," he continued, "you might as well get some rest. It's been a long day, and dinner isn't likely to be until seven or eight o'clock."

"That's a good idea. A nap sounds rather nice. You'll wake me a little beforehand, so I can freshen up?"

Marcus nodded. "Sure. Whatever you like."

She smiled again and eased the door closed. Marcus stood there for a moment before making his way to his own room. Yes, he really did like her smile.

Marcus went back downstairs after dropping off his luggage. Juanita was right – his room looked just as he'd left it years before. He wanted to talk to the little cook some more, to pick her brain a bit, but she was nowhere to be seen. He walked around and called out her name several times, poked his head into several rooms, but to his chagrin was unable to find her. She had always had quite the knack for disappearing when she wanted to. He mollified himself by eating a few more rolled tortillas with salsa. The *picante* heat continued to pleasantly clear his sinuses.

Just then he heard the front door clunk open, and women's voices chatting amiably in Spanish.

"Aunt Mary?" he called out. The voices suddenly stilled, like a radio abruptly clicking off. He was sure he heard some whispers and then his Aunt strode in to the room, her arms laden with bags and packages.

She looked so much like his mother that his heart swelled. Back in the day anyone looking at them could have told the two were sisters, but where his mother had been a fairly simple and straightforward woman, never one to draw undue attention to herself, his Aunt Mary was much more cosmopolitan. In fact

Marcus' father had tagged her with a nickname or two: High Maintenance Mary, or Her Majesty Mary.

Her oval face was bronzed from years in the Central American sun, and her brown, wavy, shoulder length hair was artfully streaked with blond, the best salon hair that money could buy, she would quip. She was a little taller than his mother had been and her figure was still shapely due to trips to the gym several times a week, as well as never having had children. She loved silver and gold jewelry of any kind, and loved flaunting it, too: besides numerous bracelets and bangles she brandished rings on several fingers, both thumbs, and a few toes. There were times when she jangled as she walked, as if she had a pocket full of loose pesos.

When she saw her nephew she dropped her bags and threw her arms up in the air.

"Marcus, dear!" she yelled in delight.

She was also quite expansive, and Marcus loved her very much.

"Hi, Aunt Mary," he said warmly.

She ran to him, her red, high heel sandals *click-clicking* on the terracotta tile. She wore tight-fitting designer jeans, completely contrary to the cultural norm in Mexico for someone her age. Some things, she would proclaim resolutely, she would never change.

"Dear, what are you doing here?"

"Well to see you, of course."

She grinned and hugged him close. He could smell her perfume, and despite the personality differences between the two sisters he could have sworn it was the same brand his mother had worn.

"Dear, you never were a very good liar," she admonished, holding him at arm's length. "Are you here by yourself? Is Rollie here, too?"

That sobered him immediately. Before he could reply however Naibi entered the room, her arms laden with all the shopping bags, her high cheeks flushed pink with the strain. She flashed a brief smile when she saw Marcus. She was younger than Juanita, and thinner, her black hair pulled into a ponytail. She was quiet and very reserved. In fact Marcus couldn't recall her saying more than a few words at any one time. In her soft voice she welcomed Marcus back to the house. He thanked her politely before turning back to his Aunt.

"No, Aunt Mary, Rolland's not with me. In fact, that's why I'm here. Can we go sit somewhere and talk for a little while?"

Her smile flickered and an unwelcome look of concern clouded her joyful expression. Her brow knitted, showing wrinkles across her forehead that she would have preferred to keep hidden.

"Certainly, dear. Of course." She turned to Naibi and said in excellent Spanish, "Please make some fresh coffee for me and coffee with milk for Marcus. We'll take it in the courtyard."

"Yes, Señora, right away."

Naibi scurried off towards the kitchen while Marcus and his Aunt made their way out to the courtyard. They bypassed the fountain and threaded through a dozen large and colorful pots of flowers and trees. Nestled on the far side were a small table and two chairs, neatly shielded from view from all angles except the stairs and part of the balcony overhead. They sat opposite each other, the burbling and splashing noises of the fountain muted by the masses of foliage. She liked to sit here and relax, to read the paper, or just have a cup of coffee and enjoy the sunshine.

"So tell me, dear, what's going on? Where's Rollie?"

Marcus sighed, unsure how to get started. "He's missing. Gone."

"What do you mean, dear? Missing? I don't understand."

He began with the call from Rolland's landlady, his increasingly frantic calls to his brother's cell phone, and his arrival in Dayton. He then told her everything he could recall, and while he started off slowly and hesitantly he soon began talking in a torrent, as if his problems could be solved in the quick telling of the events. He described the condition of the house, his first encounter with Cassandra at Foley's Diner, and with some hesitation he replayed his meeting with Hernandez and Gonzalez. His Aunt gasped and her hand fluttered to her mouth. He moved quickly through his ordeal with the two attackers, providing more of a high level overview and avoiding too many details - until he got to the part about seeing Hernandez's face.

"I recognized him," he insisted. "I'm sure he used to work for El Señor years ago, as a driver."

"Javier? You mean he worked for my Javier?"

Marcus wasn't used to hearing his Uncle referred to as Javier. He nodded and said, "I'm sure it was him. I recognized his face, but also something else. His attitude, his cockiness. Something. I can't put my finger on it, but I'm damn sure it was him."

Aunt Mary was thoughtful. "What did he look like?"

Marcus described Hernandez. "Thin, with dark eyes and a slight build, plus a certain grace and athleticism. Like a dancer, or a gymnast. I would know him again immediately, I'm certain of it."

With a hushed sound of cloth brushing against the flowers, Naibi quietly sidled up with a tray laden with cups of coffee as well as cream and raw, light brown, heavily granulated cane sugar that had a natural, caramel flavor all its own. They paused in their conversation. His Aunt stirred in a teaspoon and added a dollop of cream. Marcus' coffee with milk, his *café con leche,* was fine as it stood. He took a sip and savored the familiar, traditional drink as it warmed him all the way down.

Searching her memory, his Aunt finally said, "I don't know, dear, he's had so many drivers and assistants throughout the years, this Hernandez fellow doesn't jump out at me. It could be any of a dozen men, and honestly I just never bothered to pay attention."

Marcus swore under his breath but really hadn't expected anything more.

"That's fine. I'd like to talk to El Señor about it as soon as possible. When is he due home?

"Oh, you know Javier," she replied with a little wave, half-jokingly. "He never tells me his schedule ahead of time. But he's been gone several days now, so I suspect he'll be back soon."

Marcus looked deeply in to the depths of his drink. The light brown liquid was murky, completely opaque. He set the cup down on the busy mosaic tabletop.

"Aunt Mary, I've never really known for sure, but what exactly does El Señor do for a living? Who does he work for?"

His Aunt laughed brightly and leaned back in her chair.

"Well, dear, if you must know, I've never been entirely certain myself. I know, I know, that sounds crazy and awfully naive, but when Javier and I first met I tried to find out. Even had to resort to using some of my more feminine wiles, if you catch my meaning." She winked playfully at him. "But Javier wouldn't crack, and it got to the point where I had to drop it or risk losing him. Besides, he's already tall, dark, and handsome, but now I get to throw *mysterious* in as well."

"So you don't have a clue?"

"Oh, no, dear, I have my suspicions. He's always so secretive about his work, so hush-hush. And then there's the big black SUVs with the drivers, as you know. And I can't say for sure, but I even think I've seen men in dark glasses in the house across the street, watching ours. My guess is that he's involved in government work of some kind, like the Mexican version of the Secret Service or the CIA."

Marcus gave that some consideration, and found it plausible but unlikely. After all, did Mexican government officials make the kind of money needed for a place such as this? He wasn't sure, but doubted it.

"Of course," she went on, "he could be working for some large multinational company and needs to keep a low profile for some reason." She shrugged her shoulders. "Hell, dear, he could be employed as a greeter at Wal-Mart for all I know, and honestly, the older I get the less concerned I am. All I know is that when he comes home we have a fabulous time and we pack in as much as we can since we both know he'll be gone in a few days. Why earlier this year we hopped a plane and flew to Miami for almost a week. He was out and about for two days, but I had the best time shopping and being back in the States." She leaned forward and crooked a finger at him, smiling conspiratorially. "You know what?"

"What?"

"I even had a Big Mac while I was there. Ah, Miami can be such fun. I hope we go back soon. Don't tell anyone about the Big Mac."

Marcus laughed. As much as he wanted to continue their discussion about El Señor and his employment status, he could see that she was tiring of the topic and wanted to move on. He would have time to circle back to that later. He took the opportunity to ask about his cousin, Santiago. She brightened, saying her step-son was attending university here in Merida and was in his last year of a business degree. He was as headstrong as ever, she assured him, and couldn't wait to get out in the "real" world.

"Since he's right here in Merida, does he come home often?"

"Oh, certainly, dear, usually once or twice a week. But he truly is his father's son – it's hard to keep track of him. Tall, dark, handsome, and mysterious, just like Javier." She smiled. "If I ever knew what they were really up to I'd probably die!"

A movement out of the corner of his eye showed Cassandra talking to Naibi on the outside staircase, back toward the front of the house. Damn – with all the talk about Rolland he had completely forgotten to mention Cassandra to his Aunt, though he was certain she wouldn't mind. He saw the maid pointing in their direction.

"By the way, Aunt Mary, I forgot to tell you. I brought a guest with me from Ohio. I hope you don't mind."

"Of course I don't mind, dear. Who is he?"

"She is – or was, I'm not sure – Rolland's girlfriend. Her name's Cassandra, and she came with me to help find out what's going on."

She placed a tender hand on his forearm. "Dear, you know I love house-guests." She turned to see Cassandra weaving her way through the flowers. "So I take it this is her coming this way? My, she's a beauty, isn't she?"

Marcus saw that she had changed outfits and now wore a floral print blouse with colors that rivaled the very blooms surrounding her. The skirt was a deep tan, the color of the beach just as the sun touches the horizon. She had changed shoes into red sandals with heels, the red matching several of the petals of her blouse. Besides the shoes it was a simple outfit, not showy or ostentatious, but on her it was a perfect combination of opposites. Her hair was loose over her shoulders, trailing down her back. The small silver cross was in sharp contrast to her skin. Her smile was warm but hesitant as she threaded through the flowers toward them. Yes, he had to admit to himself, she was a beauty. He was still unsure of her relationship with Rolland and whether there were still feelings there. Damn, he didn't know. He stood as she came closer.

"Aunt Mary, I'd like you to meet Cassandra. Cassandra, my Aunt Mary."

His Aunt stood and came around the wrought iron table, smiling, arms wide and welcoming. She embraced the younger woman warmly and with great bravado. After several seconds she broke the hug but held on to her hands.

"Cassandra, dear, welcome! I'm so glad you could come and help Marcus look for poor Rollie. I'm worried sick about him, and I'm sure you are too."

"Thank you for having me," she replied. "And please, call me Cassie. All my friends do."

Marcus shot her an accusing look which she returned with innocent eyes.

"Absolutely, dear – Cassie it is. So is there anyone else around looking for Rollie that I should know about?"

"Not around here," he said. "We've got another friend up in Ohio, but he should be laying low right now and staying out of trouble. His name's Otto."

Chapter 11

The barn was six miles outside of town, down a dusty side road and tucked against a band of trees at the end of a long, weedy lane. The trees were incongruous there all by themselves in a rather precise two acre rectangle while every other square foot of land for miles around was cultivated farmland, mainly soybeans, corn, and some hay. Its siding was splintered and gray, the color of road dirt, and it was quite evident that the barn itself hadn't seen a coat of paint in decades. The tin roof was bent and shredded on the ends from high winds that occasionally tore through that part of Ohio. What roof was left was also a dull gray marred with streaks of rusty brown, like coppery stains of blood leaking down its wounded flanks. The barn's attendant frame farmhouse had been demolished years earlier when an agricultural mega-cooperative out of Sweden had purchased the land but had had zero interest in maintaining the structures. The vestiges of its crumbled foundation could be seen nearby, dirty white slabs of concrete poking up through the weeds like neglected cemetery headstones. Through an uncharacteristic paperwork glitch the Swedes had never gotten around to tearing down the barn, tucked out of the way as it was, so Otto and his friends gladly claimed it for their own and subsequently named it the Party Barn.

In reality its existence as a party destination had been passed from one group of teenagers to another over the years like a treasured family heirloom.

When each older group headed off to college or left high school to join the workforce they would pass the secret of the Party Barn on to the next crop of younger teens, and then on to the next. It was the best kept non-secret in Wayne and the surrounding county.

On the whole the Party Barn was a great gathering spot. As remote as it was the sheriffs rarely made it out there, and with no other houses nearby and no one to complain it made the Party Barn a perfect place to hang out unnoticed. As an added bonus two or three cars could park behind it and be completely hidden from the road. Otto and his buddies had been there dozens of times, smoking, drinking, and generally carrying on. He had fond memories of the Party Barn, but that was likely to no longer be the case.

Inside the old structure it was very dusty and dim, with the late afternoon light from several broken windows failing to do much to push back the interior gloom. Thin threads of sunlight sluiced through gaps in the gray siding and illuminated jagged stripes on the floor, lending the interior the look of a massive jail cell. It smelled of tobacco smoke, stale beer, old vomit, and musty straw, much of the straw smell coming from a few dozen bales that were either stacked up against one wall or tossed indiscriminately about. There were huge sliding double doors which hadn't been opened in years and were in fact chained shut, as well as a regular door at the back. On the opposite wall there was an open doorway into a separate room, a separate structure actually, constructed of shiny ceramic bricks the size of cinder blocks and built on to the back of the barn. It had its own door out to the road. It had been a tack room decades ago, but the party-goers usually called it the tool room since they didn't know better. Back inside the main area three huge vertical timbers, each eight inches on a side, disappeared into the upper gloom and supported the heavy trusses and tin roof. The central of these three support timbers had an ancient, rusty ring affixed to it eight feet off the ground, and it was to this ring that Otto was tied by a thick white nylon rope.

Actually only his left hand was tied up high, his arm nearly straight up in the air due to the short length of rope. His shoulder throbbed in pain from being suspended so long. His right hand had been untied earlier and was now cradled up against his quivering chest, the last three fingers on that hand having been systematically broken one by one by a smiling Hernandez, the little man's dark eyes alive with pleasure as Otto's bones snapped with little cracking noises, like popsicle sticks breaking. Now his fingers were useless, puffy and swollen, angled in directions fingers were never designed to go. His left eye was crusted over with blood, swollen completely shut from where the small Mexican had punched him repeatedly. He looked like an inept fighter who couldn't remember to keep his guard up. His cheek felt altogether wrong, sunken in, and he had a really bad feeling his eye socket had been crushed. His sweat-sodden hair hung in strings down around his eyes.

Movement to his right made him swivel his head dumbly, his neck working in jerks and twitches. He coughed and saw red droplets splatter on the vertical support beam in front of his one good eye. Muddily, some vestige of his mind that was still processing on a normal level recognized that this could mean internal bleeding of some sort, but that trauma barely registered since so much of his body was in pain. He couldn't recall now how many times Hernandez had punched and kicked him in the face and gut. Ten? Fifteen? The coughing jarred something in his chest which caused a sharp pain to explode below his sternum. He started crying again, muffled sobs that shook his entire body. His tears seemed to burn as they touched his skin. So much blood was spattered on the central beam that it began to trickle down thinly, a gravity-warped Rorschach ink blot. Otto inspected the blot in a detached way and, oddly enough, thought it resembled a reclining naked lady, like the image he'd seen dozens of times on truckers' mud-flaps. He would have laughed but he was certain laughing would hurt as badly as coughing did.

Sitting on a bale of straw five or six feet away was Gonzalez, a large brown cigar clenched in his teeth, a box of stick matches near his hand on another bale. Otto's cell phone was next to the matches, tantalizingly close yet totally out of reach. Even sitting down the huge Mexican was almost eye level with the standing Otto. The scarring of his pocked skin was exacerbated by the streaky light within the barn. His long hair hung down on either side of his square face like open tent flaps framing empty darkness. Gonzalez stared at Otto dispassionately, saying nothing, moving only enough to take the cigar from his mouth. Smoke hung around him in the still air. He hadn't raised a hand against Otto, hadn't spoken a word since they'd arrived at the barn. That was Hernandez's job.

Otto heard movement behind him, the soft, careful padding of a predatory cat. He knew it was Hernandez and he tried to steel himself for whatever was to come. But all he could manage was to clench his eyes shut and try to hold back more tears. There was a sibilant, dragging sound, something being pulled through the loose straw that littered the barn floor. It was the whip. He knew it was the fucking whip.

Otto was pretty sure he was going to die, but strangely that wasn't the worst part of this ordeal. No, the worst part was that he had cracked so quickly and had told these two bastards everything he knew almost right away. He was ashamed that he had caved so fast, that he hadn't been stronger and at least made them earn what little he knew. His failure hung on his shoulders like a lead yoke that crushed his body and his spirit.

The hushed pacing behind him continued, back and forth, back and forth, like a lion determining the best angle of attack. Suddenly Hernandez's hot breath was on his left ear, not saying anything, just breathing slowly and evenly. He draped the whip over Otto's shoulder and pulled it gently back. With his one good eye Otto watched in mute fascination as the whip passed by his field of vision. It was made of tightly braided brown leather, he noted abstractedly, and as each inch slithered by its diameter decreased ever so slightly. The leather was worn in places, and even more telling were the darker smears which were certainly blood stains. Some of the blood had to be his.

When Hernandez had initially ripped Otto's shirt off, the young man remembered what Marcus had said and knew what was going to happen next. When the first lash finally came it was almost more than he could bear. He screamed out and his body went as rigid as one of the support beams. His eyes sprung open so wide showing so much white that his irises looked small and insignificant. Otto's thin body was locked in premature rigor mortis, his muscles straining, tendons and veins popping out so far they looked ready to pop. Then he sagged, a marionette with all its strings cut save two, the two that held his arms high above his head. He started talking then, fast and without hesitation, telling them about Marcus and Cassie and them heading to Mexico and anything else he could think of. But still the whip fell. And then the beatings began, with Hernandez asking again and again about things Otto knew nothing about: *Where were the credit cards? How did Marcus get the one card? Where was Rolland?*

Otto had no damn idea where Rolland was, didn't these people know that? He was looking for him, too! He didn't have a clue what credit cards he was talking about, either! He tried to explain that but Hernandez refused to accept this lack of new information and just kept going on about credit cards. Then the whip-wielding Mexican kicked a hay bale up and stood on it, untying Otto's right hand, and then pretty as you please he broke his pinky finger, *snap!* Otto was almost too shocked to react, his mouth hanging open stupidly. When Otto still couldn't produce answers he broke the next two fingers, *snap! snap!* The man was deaf to Otto's pleading and screams. Then the whippings began again, this time harder and with more ferocity. Then the hitting started. Hernandez just kept hitting him! Otto quickly lost track of the sequence of abuse, he just remembered talking louder and faster, shouting anything, trying to forestall more pain, trying to keep the goddam whip from his back.

Then Otto had blurted out between sobs that Marcus thought he recognized Hernandez, that he had seen his reflection in the window. Abruptly the whipping stopped. Otto couldn't see Hernandez but he noticed that Gonzalez sat up straighter on the bale of straw and he was pretty sure the two made meaningful eye contact with each other. Otto seized on the opportunity for any kind of respite and began babbling like an auctioneer, jabbering, pleading. He wasn't even sure he was making sense. He was both shamed and deliriously relieved that the assault on his broken body had ceased, and would have told them anything. Shit, he would have tried to convince them he was the damn Pope if that would've helped.

That was where they were now. The whip continued slithering over his shoulder until the end, with its three loose leather strands, slid up his bare chest and over his shoulder. The strands, quite ironically, tickled as they made their slow journey over his hyper-sensitive flesh.

Hernandez whispered in his ear, his English really quite good, "Marcus Schmidt is now in Mexico, yes?"

Otto nodded quickly, still ashamed but unable to help himself. "Y-yes, Mexico. Merida. Going to h-his Aunt's house."

"And the girl. She is with him." That last sentence was a statement, not a question.

"Cassie? Yes, she's there too."

He looped the whip around Otto's neck and began pulling slightly. The leather grabbed and snagged on his skin, not quite choking but heightening his already elevated sense of personal peril. He pulled the whip tighter around his neck as he stepped in front of Otto. Their faces were only inches apart. Through his one good eye Otto was staring at Hernandez. He could only focus on his eyes. They were cold and black, like the eyes of a fish found dead on the beach.

"And you say he recognized me? He knows me?"

Otto nodded vigorously, humiliated but unable to help himself.

"Yes," he gasped, his throat being slowly constricted by the whip. "He thinks you used to w-work for his Uncle. As a driver, or something like that. He went down there to find out who you are, to try and f-figure out what's going on."

Hernandez growled and flicked a glance at Gonzalez. The smaller man said something in rapid-fire Spanish, something that Otto had no chance to follow. The huge Mexican shook his head. *No.* Hernandez retorted with several quick words in anger. He turned back to Otto and grabbed both ends of the whip and began pulling. Otto's airflow was suddenly cut off as the leather dug in to his flesh. From the bale of straw nearby Gonzalez uttered one word, a command.

"*Basta.*"

Hernandez ignored the order and pulled harder. Otto's vision started to dim and he began feebly to strike his attacker with his mangled right hand. The pain in his hand was like it was being struck with a hammer over and over. The giant Mexican stood and towered over the two of them.

"*¡Basta!*"

Otto had been around Spanish speakers enough to dimly know that *basta* meant "enough". Hernandez growled again and released the whip. Otto's breath came rushing back in great gulps and he sagged against the support beam, smearing his own blood on his cheek. The small Mexican tore the whip away from his throat and both moved away, back toward the tack room. Otto heard the giant's heavy footfalls thumping on the barn's wooden floor. He stood there hugging the thick beam and cried silently. Each time he sobbed something in his chest grated badly and pain radiated outward, a red blossom of agony that flared before his face like a bright explosion.

A few minutes passed and he could hear an animated argument growing between his two attackers. He caught a word or two that he understood but no more. He thought he heard the word *muerto*, dead, but wasn't really sure. He didn't know if they were discussing what to do with him, or what they thought would happen to him. But he did know that he was in horrible shape and if he had any hope of surviving this he had to do something *now*.

Blearily he looked up at the rope securing him to the post. It was white nylon, not quite half an inch thick but strong enough to pull a car if it had to. There was no way of cutting or breaking that. There was nothing else in reach that could help him, nothing except…

The matches? Could he reach the matches?

Shit, there they were, an open box of blue tip wooden matches that Gonzalez favored to light his cigars. He turned slightly and looked back at the tack room. He could see Hernandez's back. He was talking animatedly to Gonzalez who was just out of Otto's sight behind the wall. The small Mexican kept gesturing back toward Otto, but his face was turned away.

Otto slowly reached out his right foot and tried to snag the bale. It was old and the bailing twine used to hold it together was loose. He stretched farther and felt his raised arm howling in pain. He was too damn far away! He felt as if reaching that bale were a metaphor for his life: he had never really been pushed, had in fact never pushed himself, always content to drift and get by. For the first time he knew with total clarity that he had to rise above the low bar he had always set for himself. If he didn't, if he couldn't, he would most likely die. Hell, he might die anyway, but he would at least give a shit for once.

He steeled himself and pulled against the nylon cord again, stretching, reaching. His shoulder and wrist thundered in pain, pushed beyond their natural design. His first three attempts to loop his shoe around the twine failed, but on the fourth he jerked hard and just managed to hook the toe of his sneaker around it. His body sagged in relief. Slowly, quietly, he pulled and the old bale inched toward him. Otto shot a glance back at his captors but they were still arguing heatedly.

When the bale was beside him Otto exhaled. Now what? He couldn't reach down far enough to get the matches. Chancing another quick look he nudged the box with his foot until it fell on the floor with a small clatter. He froze. To him the sound was louder than a dozen metal pipes falling from scaffolding on to concrete. Sweat dripped in his good eye and he impatiently brushed it away with his shoulder. The disagreement in the tack room continued unabated.

With his foot he slid the open box up against the beam and gingerly tried to slide it up to his ruined hand. He failed several times because the angle was bad and he was terrified that they would see his leg moving up the wooden beam. He worked at it slowly, his leg quivering with the effort. A dozen or so matches fell out of the open box and landed noiselessly on the wooden floor. Finally it was in reach and he stretched down and grabbed the box, quickly secreting it between his chest and the thick beam. He stopped and panted heavily, as out of breath as if he had just run around the block.

Hernandez started back in to the barn but Gonzalez grabbed his arm, his part of the conversation not yet finished. The smaller man tried to shake the hand off but was unable. Their voices were raised even higher as the argument over Otto's fate intensified.

"That's it, you big son of a bitch," Otto mumbled under his breath, his words slurred. "Keep that murderous little fuck busy…"

His long bangs partially obscured his vision as Otto looked down at the box pinned at his chest. So he had the matches, now what? Given time he could probably burn through the nylon rope and get free, but he didn't have that kind of time. Never mind that he could do little more than stumble ten feet right now. There was no way he could run from those two maniacs.

He looked around the barn at all the bales sitting here and there. He took note of the barn itself and what it was made of. He looked at the matches clutched against his chest, back to the straw, then back to the matches. Otto came to a decision.

Still moving slowly, he managed to pull a single match from the box with his thumb and one good finger. Any time he bumped a broken finger he grimaced in pain and had to hold back a yelp. Another look showed the two men still ignoring him. Hernandez seemed to be doing most of the talking, gesturing grandly with his hands and pointing this way and that. Otto gently ran the match up the side of the wooden support beam. With a sizzle and a smell of sulfur it hissed to life. He watched it for a split second before flicking it toward the bales of straw strewn about near the tack room. The match tumbled end over end but fell short of the mark, landing on the floor and quickly burning out. He cursed under his breath and tried again. This time he pressed too hard and the match simply broke in two. To calm himself he took a deep breath and quietly began singing one of the verses he had only that day learned from *Driver 8.*

"Way to shield the hated heat, way to put myself to sleep,

"Way to shield the hated heat, way to put myself, my children to sleep..."

The third match lit perfectly and Otto tossed it right away, while it was still flaring to life. It landed in the middle of several bales that were stacked up between him and the tack room. He was terrified that they would smell the sulfur, but the distinctive odor was trapped inside the barn itself.

Otto stared at the small wisp of smoke coming from the bales, wishing and praying, and then saw a tiny tongue of flame lick up. It caught on some loose straw and remained contained for several seconds. Suddenly he heard a muted *whoosh!* as if a gas grill had been lit, and the entire bale went up in flames. The suddenness of the fire shocked him, and he watched, transfixed, as the flames eagerly leapt from one bale to another, the dry straw better than any kindling. In seconds five or six bales were burning fiercely and smoke was filling up the ceiling far overhead. The flames snapped and popped madly.

The noise or the flames caught Hernandez's attention. He shot a glance back toward Otto and his eyes went wide with shock. He tried to rush back in to the barn but the conflagration was between Otto and the tack room, blocking his way. The small Mexican was desperate to find a way back in, sprinting back and forth like a trapped jungle cat that was unwilling to relinquish its prey. Otto would have gladly flipped him off if his fingers hadn't looked like mangled French fries that littered the floor of his truck. Gonzalez simply stood there with his arms crossed, his face cold and expressionless. Then the common wall between the tack room and the barn caught fire and the sudden heat pushed them back. He saw Gonzalez grab the smaller man's sleeve and pull him forcibly from the tack room door. Hernandez fought him the entire way but was no match for the huge man's raw strength.

The back third of the barn was fully engulfed with flames. There was a sudden rush of wind as the fire's voracious appetite sucked in air from outside, the noise like nothing Otto had ever experienced before, a primal, tyrannosaurus roar that gave him a more intense rush than any drug or alcohol ever had. For a moment he was transfixed in both shock and awe, stunned, before his situation hit home and he knew he only had minutes to get free. If he couldn't then all these efforts would have been wasted and Hernandez's wish would be fulfilled.

He tried to steady his quivering hand and grabbed another match. He struck it and held it up to the nylon rope. The angle was bad and he couldn't keep much of the flame to the white nylon. It singed slightly but little else. Smoke began filling up the barn and he started coughing. Each cough moved something broken or cracked in his chest and the pain made his hands shake even more.

"Shit! This isn't working," he mumbled angrily.

The temperature in the barn was up at least thirty degrees. Sudden inspiration hit and he clambered onto the bale Hernandez had stood on earlier. Now he could hold the nylon rope almost straight out, giving him a better angle to burn through it. He pulled out another match and struck it, again holding it up to the rope. He made more progress this time: the nylon sputtered and black, gooey tendrils dripped down, leaving angry red marks wherever they made contact with his flesh. Before he could burn through it the match went out. He quickly fumbled for another but the entire box fell to his feet, tumbling off the bale and on to the floor. He cried out and his head sagged, the very real possibility of defeat beating him down. He just didn't have the energy or the time to start over. The smoke was so thick he could barely see, and his wracking cough was a constant, steady drain on his remaining strength.

Then between blinks of his eye and the strands of his hair he saw one match had fallen out of the box and was perched on the waistband of his jeans. He carefully, slowly plucked it up between his good finger and thumb, like a mom using tweezers to ease a splinter from a child's finger. He lit it and held it up where he thought the rope was. The thick and acrid smoke was stinging his good eye so badly he couldn't focus. The match burned down to his fingers and he was afraid he had blown it, that he would soon die here, that they would find his charred corpse among the ashes of the Party Barn.

Suddenly there was a sensation of freedom, of falling, and Otto was on the floor, his face pressed into the ancient floorboards and bits of dirty straw and ash. The air was marginally better here, down low, so he took several deep, cleansing breaths and began army crawling to the bale of straw where Gonzalez had been sitting. He reached out blindly and grabbed his cell phone. He managed to flip it open but couldn't see any of the numbers or the display. He thought he remembered what he had been doing last on the phone. He said a silent prayer and hit what he hoped was the green SEND button. He kept crawling toward the door to the outside but still couldn't see anything. His sense of direction was shot. Was the damn door this way? Or was it over there? He heard a small voice from the phone.

"Hello? Hello?" came a girl's voice.

Coughs wracked his body again. Finally he managed, "Jenna? Jenna? It's Otto!"

"Otto? What's wrong? What's going on?"

"Fire! At the Party Barn," he coughed. "Help! Send help!"

"Otto? What are you talking about?" Jenna asked, her voice rising in panic.

"Fire at the Party Barn!" he repeated before he could talk no longer and his voice choked off completely. Wracking coughs consumed him as he inched toward the door he hoped was still there. He dropped the cell phone and continued crawling, oblivious to the debilitating pain in his chest, hand, and back. He may have passed out for a few seconds, he wasn't sure. Then fire roared behind him anew and the entire back wall collapsed on itself with a tremendous crash. Heat washed over him like a boiling ocean. In a flash the ends of his long blond hair singed, curling in small, black, crispy ringlets. New air rushed in and momentarily cleared out some of the smoke that had surrounded him like a clinging fog. Suddenly he saw it. There it was, the back door to the barn, not ten feet in front of him. It was open and beckoning him outside, a hazy rectangle of salvation. With a sense of renewed hope he dragged himself forward again, just inches at a time, his mind blank to everything but the nacreous doorway straight ahead. He was almost there when most of the roof gave way and slammed down in a mass of tin and flaming lumber behind him. Sparks and pieces of burning wood fell everywhere. He was no more than five feet from the doorway when something ungodly heavy fell and pinned his legs. His forward progress was over.

Well shit, he thought angrily. *That was damn close. I almost made it...*

And then, belatedly, *Wait a minute, how did those two whackos even know the Party Barn existed?*

Suddenly an old Ford Explorer tore up to the back door and a pretty blond girl leapt out. He could just make out Jenna's terrified expression as she ran toward the inferno. He saw her shielding her face from the heat, and then everything went black.

Chapter 12

Dinner at his Aunt's house was always a long drawn out affair, as it tended to be in many homes in Latin America. It began about seven o'clock with the three of them – Marcus, Cassandra, and his Aunt – seated around a tremendous rectangular dining room table while Juanita hustled about, scurrying in and out of the tiny kitchen, filling glasses, clearing plates, bringing in first trays of fruits and appetizers, as well as the ever-present tortillas. All this was followed by platters of hot, delicious, spicy food. Tonight the main course was tamales dripping in a deep red sauce. Marcus could tell that Cassandra was uncomfortable watching the diminutive cook handle all the food preparation and bussing. Several times she tried to lend a hand, but each time she was gently but forcefully rebuffed. Finally she had to admit defeat and sat down with a frown, her arms crossed. He was getting to know her better each day, and this was proof once more that Cassandra did not like to be stymied. He hid his grin as he watched her. Marcus understood how she felt about Juanita, however. He remembered his consternation at having the little cook wait on him hand and foot during his earlier time in Mexico. Sadly he also recalled how he began to secretly enjoy it, a guilty pleasure like shoplifting penny candy. Later he began treating her work as if it were completely normal and right - which it was, in this culture. Juanita efficiently topped off his iced tea and he gave her a small grin of thanks. She smiled back at him, her small white teeth bright against her dark complexion. She hustled back to the kitchen, constantly wiping her hands on her white apron.

Marcus and Mary kept up a steady stream of conversation, mainly revolving around his life in San Diego, work, and school. Twice she bluntly asked about girlfriends, and both times Marcus clearly told her there was no one right now, thank you, and he was doing just fine.

"A handsome young man like you, still single?"

"Yes, Mary, still single."

She looked at him appraisingly. "I don't understand. You're good looking, have a nice job, and live in San Diego, for heaven's sake. You're not gay, are you, dear? Not that there's anything wrong with that."

Cassandra snickered under her breath, hiding her face behind her drink.

"No, Mary, I'm not gay."

"Then what's the problem, dear?"

Marcus sighed in amused frustration with his aunt. Mary seemed to think his relationship status was a serious problem and was about to demand more detail when they heard the front door clunk open and closed. Santiago strode in.

He was almost exactly as Marcus remembered him, even though they hadn't seen each other for years. He was tall for a Mexican male, nearly six feet, and broad through the shoulders. His black hair was relatively short and a wavy on top. He would be considered good-looking to many, but much to his chagrin never handsome: his nose was a little too wide, and his cheeks sagged a bit too much. He would have jowls when he was older. But when he smiled he could light up a room, and with his boisterous and affable personality he was usually the center of attention - which was exactly where he wanted to be. He was mercurial, joyous and effervescent one moment, stormy and brooding the next. He was excellent at working a crowd. Santiago had forever made it known that his goal in life was to be a successful businessman just like his father. Marcus always believed he would make a great politician, or better yet a powerful Wall

Street broker. Yes, he had that desire, that burning *drive* to succeed. Marcus had always liked him but had never been great friends with him, not like Rolland. Santiago and Rolland had hit it off grandly from the beginning.

When his cousin saw Marcus his face quickly lit up with surprise and joy. He rounded the table and gave him a big, meaningful hug that lasted several seconds, much longer than a man to man hug would have lasted in the United States. When they pulled apart he held Marcus at arm's length, his face still alight.

"Cousin, it is so good to see you again," he said in English, his Spanish accent evident but not thick. Santiago enjoyed speaking English, and also enjoyed many things American: jeans, shoes, sports teams, and especially women. He could have had nearly any local girl he desired, but he was only interested in American girls. Blond American girls, if at all possible.

Marcus found his cousin's grin contagious and felt warmth spreading through him. This was his family, or as close as it came to a family for him. Some of the most enjoyable years of his life had been spent right here, in this room, in this house, with these people. Yes it was his Aunt who both was and wasn't like his mother, and his cousin, who was actually only a cousin by marriage. And then of course there were Naibi and Juanita who were family to him as well. None of them were his by blood, but what did that matter? His grin widened even further.

"It's great to see you, too, Santiago."

"I didn't know you were even coming," he said. "Mary, why didn't you tell me Marcus was coming?"

Aunt Mary set down the glass of wine she was drinking. "Why, I didn't know either, dear. I was just as surprised as you are."

Just then Santiago saw Cassandra for the first time.

"Well hello, my name is Santiago. You are a friend of Marcus'?"

Cassandra smiled. "Yes, my name is Cassandra. Nice to meet you."

"The pleasure is mine, I assure you." He bowed low with an elegant sweep of his arm. Marcus and his Aunt laughed at his over-the-top gesture. Santiago himself quickly joined in.

He took a seat next to Marcus and tapped his forefinger on the table. Juanita was there in a flash with an additional table setting which included a tall glass of ice and a bottle of Coke. Marcus was never one to drink much soda, especially here since Coke in Mexico had a different formula than its sibling in the States. Mexican Coke was thicker and sweeter, made from real sugar. He never cared for it but it was phenomenally popular here. Rolland used to joke that drinking a six pack of those babies would likely trigger Type II diabetes, and Marcus didn't think that was too far off.

As Juanita prepared his plate Santiago paid her no attention. He was focused on Marcus and Cassandra.

"So what brings you back?" he asked, taking his first bite of rice and refried beans. "It is always great to see you, do not get me wrong, but I'm rather taken aback that you showed up like this."

Marcus exhaled slowly. "It's about Rolland."

Santiago looked around, a quick smile on his lips, his eyes alight. "Yes, Rolland. Is he here? Did he come with you?"

He shook his head. "No, that's the problem. That's why we're here."

"What do you mean?"

"Rolland is missing." Again Marcus launched in to the story of how he came to be there. He was becoming quite proficient at it by now. He pulled no punches this time and for some reason shared details with Santiago that he hadn't even mentioned to his Aunt, such as more intense descriptions of the whipping. Santiago listened intently, eating methodically and tapping the table with his forefinger when he needed a plate filled or his Coke replenished.

When Marcus finished he drank some ice tea and took a breath. Santiago kept eating mechanically. Finally, "That is incredible. This man, this Hernandez, you believe he worked for my father?"

Marcus nodded. "I'm almost certain of it. I only caught a glimpse of him, but it was enough."

"Then we know what we must do, don't we? We will ask my father about this man, and find him. We will find him, and we will find out what he is doing and how he is involved in all this." He turned to his step-mother. "When is my father coming home?"

She shrugged dramatically, the wine in her glass sloshing around dangerously but somehow defying gravity. Not a drop was spilled.

"I haven't a clue, dear. Your father will be home when he's home, just like always."

Santiago accepted this with a grunt and turned back to Marcus. "We will have to wait. I doubt it will be much longer than two or three days."

Cassandra had been listening to this last exchange in disbelief. "We will have to wait two or three days?" she asked, incredulous. "There must be some way to get in touch with him before then? Certainly he has a cell phone?"

Santiago looked sideways at her, his eyes narrowed. "We do not disturb my father when he is away on business. That is the way it is. We will wait."

She looked from Santiago to Marcus. "Wait? That's crazy! This is really important! It's..."

Marcus' hand on her arm stopped her in mid-sentence.

"It's okay, really. I honestly didn't expect El Señor to be here. We'll wait."

Cassandra huffed once and shook her head. "I still say it's crazy. People are in danger here, especially you."

Santiago was beginning to get annoyed with her dogged persistence. "We will wait, and we will not discuss it any longer," he stated, cutting off any further debate. Then, softening, "Now, Marcus, fill me in on the rest of your life since we last spoke. And you can also tell me what is new in America these days."

The remainder of the meal was spent in easy conversation, family members catching up after several years of separation. Cassandra kept to herself, either content to let Marcus bond with his family or still angry at Santiago's summary decision concerning his father. Throughout dinner Juanita kept up the steady stream of delicious food, followed by *postré*, an ice cream dessert, topped off by several more platters of fruit before bringing out a tray filled with hot, dark coffee. When the coffee arrived Santiago pulled a pack of Marlboro cigarettes out and expertly lit one up. He blew the smoke up where the slow moving ceiling fan gently dispersed it. He offered one to both Marcus and Cassandra in an automatic gesture. They both declined.

Santiago laughed as he put the pack away. "Remember when Rolland I went out partying that one night? The night with the vodka?"

Marcus shook his head. "How could I forget it? You two idiots were drunk and walking down the street at two in the morning, singing *Gimme Three Steps* by *Lynyrd Skynyrd* at the top of your lungs."

"We were singing wonderfully," Santiago assured him with a wide smile. "Why the police didn't think so is beyond me."

"Then Marcus and I had to go bail you two Sinatras out," Mary said. "I told you the next time it happened you were going to spend the night there."

"That's right," Santiago said. "As I recall we made it a week before it happened again. The head jailer, Raul, I think his name was, and I were becoming friends by then."

They all laughed, even Cassandra. Their conversation continued, much of it revolving around good times Santiago and Rolland had had as kids. It was only about eight thirty but Marcus realized he was beginning to feel the effects of the day's travel, and two or three times he caught Cassandra artfully masking a yawn. He stood and announced he was calling it a night, thanking his Aunt and Juanita for the wonderful dinner. Cassandra stood as well.

"So what are your plans for tomorrow?" Santiago asked, staring at them.

Marcus shrugged. "Hadn't really thought about it," he admitted. "Our main goal was to get here and meet with your dad. With that on hold for now we're kind of open."

"Excellent. Here is an idea," he said, suddenly enthusiastic, his face lighting up. "Let us get up early, eat breakfast, and then go over to the market. I always enjoy that, and if I recall correctly you enjoy that as well."

"Sure, I guess. We can do that. Cassandra?"

"Why not?" she agreed. "Sounds fun."

They all agreed that a trip to the market sounded like a fine plan. With that both Marcus and Cassandra bade them farewell for the night and headed upstairs to their rooms. She smiled a fleeting, drowsy goodnight as her door shut. Marcus was certain he wouldn't be able to sleep after the several cups of coffee with dinner and the excitement of the day, but moments after he slid between the crisp white sheets he was asleep, his dreams punctuated by disturbing scenes of Rolland and Sam running from unseen antagonists, while gunshots rang out and a terrified Rolland was pleading over and over for help from his brother.

Chapter 13

Merida's main downtown market, or Mercado, was a tremendous, rambling, seemingly haphazard maze of vendors selling everything conceivable, from hammocks and blankets to live squid and hardware, from silver and turquoise to pirated DVDs. The Mercado was a huge building the size of a city block, bordered on each side by major streets. It consisted of several confusing floors of shops, stores, and stands, some having a feeling of permanence, whiles others looked like they could vanish like gypsies in the night. Restaurants and other food vendors were tossed randomly into the mix. There was a distinctly European flavor to certain areas, sometimes even bordering on Middle-Eastern. On a past visit he'd turned the corner from a high end jewelry shop and nearly collided with a jury-rigged butcher stand, huge hind-quarters of beef hanging from silver hooks, blood staining the counters and floor. The Mercado could be both bright and joyous or dark and eerie, all at the same time. The sounds of customers and purveyors of goods haggling over prices rang out, some appearing good-natured, others rising in volume as tempers flared when agreements couldn't be reached. Several areas around the outside rim were open to the elements with sunshine and warm breezes filling the air where people gathered at small tables smoking and drinking hot coffee, laughing, talking, holding hands, small children running and playing. When Marcus thought of the Mercado certain adjectives always came to mind: rambling, unsanitary, exciting, jumbled, and more than just a little crazy. It was old Mexico with no holds barred, not some sanitized version of a touristy Mexican market. Its mayhem and lack of organization should have rankled him to no end, but for some reason he couldn't fathom, it didn't. He had loved it then, and he loved it now.

It was not yet seven o'clock in the morning. Santiago had insisted on an early arrival before the heat of the day hit in earnest and the crowds made walking on the sidewalk or in the market a chore. Besides, he said, he wanted to peruse the seafood selection, and since the best of the morning's catch arrived very early it might be picked over if they waited until later. Santiago had a car but insisted they all take a taxi since parking was always a problem.

The green and white taxi, a Nissan this time, dropped them off on 56th street. Santiago paid him as they stretched after their time in the cramped car. With a chirp of tires on hot pavement the little four-door motored away, quickly blending in with the hundreds of other green and white vehicles tearing haphazardly up and down the street. Restaurants and cafés had tables right on the sidewalk, some within a foot or two of the curb. Every few seconds a car or bus rumbled by close enough for the diners to touch. No one seemed to care that a texting or otherwise distracted driver could take them all out in a split second. The smell of exhaust mingled with breakfast food and fresh tortillas. Marcus was always amazed at how the streets and sidewalks were so clear of trash and debris. They were as clean as in any prosperous town in the States.

The three of them stood on the curb across from the Mercado. Santiago glanced at his watch.

"We can head in or sit and enjoy a quick cup of coffee," he said.

Marcus didn't have anything specific in mind to buy and knew this day trip was mainly for fun and sightseeing. Because of that he didn't feel any need to rush in.

He shrugged. "I'm fine with some coffee."

"Me, too," Cassandra said, still looking a little bleary from the early start. Her white blouse was as bright as the white buildings surrounding them. She could have easily passed for a native.

They pulled up chairs at a small café and ordered from a clean-cut teenager with a white apron. He nodded repeatedly as he memorized their order, then scurried off and returned moments later with three large steaming cups and some cream. A bowl of the tan, thickly granulated raw sugar was there, too, and both Marcus and Cassandra spooned some in. The coffee lightly foamed as they added the natural sweetener. It was delicious.

"So, Santiago, how's life at the University? Almost done?" Marcus asked.

His cousin made a face. "At this point I think it is a waste of my time," he said. "I know all I need to, but my father insists I get that piece of paper. That, uh, how do you say?"

"Diploma?" Marcus offered.

He snapped his fingers. "Yes, diploma, that's it. He insists that I finish my degree and get a diploma. He says I will need it in the world of today."

"It's not a bad idea," Cassandra said. "I wish I had gotten one, but that wasn't possible."

"Why not?"

Cassandra explained her history, with her parents coming into the U.S. illegally, but how she was born there and grew up as a citizen. However, even though her parents held two, or even three jobs, there was never money for college.

"So I've been working since I was a freshman in high school, and then after school just kept working." She shrugged. "That's the way it was. College would have been a luxury."

Santiago nodded. "At least you are an American citizen. That will be very difficult for me to accomplish should I ever desire to attempt it. I'm afraid I will be stuck here in Mexico forever." He made a face.

Marcus said something about the grass always being greener on the other side of the fence, a common enough phrase in English. Santiago was unfamiliar with the idiomatic expression so he and Cassandra spent the next few minutes explaining what that meant while they drank their coffee. He nodded in understanding, although the entire concept of green grass, yards, white picket fences and such was foreign to him. Finally Santiago looked at his watch and announced it was time to go.

Even at this early hour the sidewalks were filling up with shoppers. In some places it was difficult to squeeze through at all, and the most common expression uttered here was "pardon me". Merida was a polyglot city filled with all types of people from around the world, mainly North America and Europe. Marcus heard English, French, German, some Slavic languages that he couldn't identify with any certainty, and Spanish from Spain, thick with its own specific accents and verb tense.

They made it to the corner and scurried across while dodging taxis and buses. All around them shops were beginning to open, their steel shutters being noisily rolled up, the sidewalks being swept or hosed down. The store owners chatted amiably with each other in their daily morning ritual. Once they made it to the other side of the street Santiago motioned them up a ramp to the second floor of the Mercado and in they plunged.

Inside it was much darker and cooler than on the sidewalk. The sound of buses and cars honking was suddenly muted, distant, as if a door had closed or a tremendous curtain had been pulled. The inside vendors were for the most part already set up and selling, and as the three walked past they were targets for each shopkeeper hawking their wares. Marcus was especially a target as it was obvious to all that he was a foreigner, perhaps a well-off one. Most vendors knew a smattering of English, and they had a few catch phrases they used repeatedly, such as "Almost free", or "Make you a good deal." Some would toss out the occasional remark in Spanish when the three of them didn't stop, not realizing that Marcus understood their language nearly as well as they did. Santiago was quite adept at ignoring them or sometimes shooting them a blistering look that effectively communicated his opinion of them. All the while Marcus and Santiago talked and laughed, sliding back into a comfortable state with each other even after so many years had passed. At one booth Santiago took a towel from a vendor's rack and quickly wrapped it around his head in a passable turban. The older man behind the counter stared at him in mild disbelief. Santiago bowed low to them, his palms pressed together.

"How may I serve you, master," he intoned, trying for an Indian accent.

Marcus laughed and quickly bought three apples from a fruit cart behind them. He tossed the apples to Santiago one at a time. He knew what was coming.

"You may juggle to amuse me and the queen," he said in mock seriousness, sweeping one hand towards Cassandra. "And do so very well or it will be your head."

Santiago grinned and began juggling the three apples, first in a standard shower pattern, then shifting gears and moving on to the more difficult cascade. Out of the corner of his eye Marcus watched Cassandra's expression as Santiago continued the cascade. She clapped her hands in amusement. Santiago ended his routine with a flourish, sending each apple high in the air, and then firing the first one around his back at Marcus, who was expecting it, and then another to Cassandra, who was not. A small crowd of people had gathered around and now applauded vigorously. Santiago took a deep, eloquent bow and tossed his apple to a little boy of about five who looked stunned and then overjoyed. The boy smiled and tore off through the stalls, his prize held high.

"Still haven't lost your touch," Marcus observed with a smile.

His cousin shrugged as he removed the towel. "Apples are easy. It's juggling everything else in life that I find difficult."

"You got that right," he admitted.

They kept walking around the upper level for a while longer, the two of them munching their apples. They passed by several hammock vendors and at least a dozen stores selling woven cotton blankets of all colors and styles. Two taco stand owners almost tripped them trying to persuade the three to stop and sample their fare. There were several higher-end shops displaying silver and turquoise jewelry that winked and glittered beautifully. Marcus thought Cassandra was going to get whiplash as she passed by the silver jewelry and he had to gently move her along with a hand on her elbow.

Several stalls down near one of the main exits was a butcher stand. Overhead rails ran around the large work area behind the counter, and there was an opening where the rail crossed above the pedestrian thoroughfare to an adjacent butcher shop. Hanging from ten inch long chrome hooks were beef or bull hindquarters and forequarters. Each quarter weighed well over one hundred and fifty pounds, others as much as two hundred. Some initial dressing was done in the one stand before each quarter was hooked and pushed to the other side when there was a break in the pedestrian traffic. There, with much grunting and cursing, it was manhandled off the hook and slapped down on large wooden tables. Next it was summarily cut up into steaks, roasts, or ground into hamburger. An interesting operation, he thought, wondering how many people had gotten clobbered by a hindquarter flying from one stall to the other. The three of them moved on toward the exit before Santiago stopped suddenly.

"I forgot," he said. "I wanted to get some fresh fish before it is all picked over."

"That's right, you did," Marcus agreed. "Let's go downstairs and we'll help you pick some up."

Santiago shook his head. "No, this will only take a minute. Besides, it smells very bad down there. Just wait right here and I'll be back."

Marcus and Cassandra nodded and he hurried off, back the way they had come. He turned a corner and was gone. There were interior steps back there that led to the lower level where there were all types of animals - chickens, pigs, goats, fish, birds – for sale, some alive, some not. And, he recalled, Santiago was right – it did smell very bad down there. He was content for both of them to wait right there. The butcher to his right swung a huge cleaver and sliced off what looked like a New York Strip from a larger piece of meat. When the cleaver hit the wooden table it made a solid "thunk" sound, almost like a lumberjack chopping wood. Marcus leaned against the counter.

"What do you think of the Mercado?"

"Well it's very interesting, that's for sure."

Marcus chuckled. "There are about a zillion US Federal food safety laws being broken here at any given time." He motioned toward the butchers with his head. "Seeing what's going on right here would send the FDA and the USDA into a righteous tizzy for sure. No refrigeration, no hairnets, flies everywhere."

"I know," she said, making a face. "We get so used to the way things are done in the States, we think it's the only way. But from what I know of you so far, I'd imagine that you would hate this type of place."

He was curious. "Why do you say that?"

She shrugged. "It's so disorganized, so chaotic. That just doesn't seem like you. But you like it here, don't you?"

Marcus shrugged. "You're right. I guess I do, and I've never known why. Maybe because it's so basic, so simple and straightforward."

She stood back and considered him. "Or maybe there is a bit of a wild streak hidden deep inside that organized exterior after all?"

He didn't know what to say to that. The Mercado was beginning to fill up with more people now, to the point that they were getting jostled by the crowd. The volume of noise from the vendors and customers alike was ratcheting up and the two of them had to talk very loudly just to be heard.

"So what do you say? Is there more to you than meets the eye, Dr. Marcus Schmidt," she said appraisingly.

“I doubt that. Pretty much what you see is what you get.”

She smiled lightly, then glanced in the direction Santiago had taken, through the throng of shoppers now filling the space. A look of concern crossed her face, shown in the tilt of her head and the pursing of her lips.

“What about him? Santiago?”

“What do you mean, what about him?” Marcus asked, not sure what she was getting at.

“I don’t know for sure. He’s got a nasty streak in him, I think. I just have a feeling about him. I’m afraid that back in Ohio he’d be the kid who got caught torturing squirrels in the woods or something.”

Now it was Marcus’ turn to grin. “Santiago? I don’t think he’d torture squirrels or anything else for that matter. But he is bound and determined to succeed in life, I’ve always known that and he’s never tried to hide it. I think he’s the kind of guy who knows what he wants, sure, and will go to great lengths to get it.”

She shook her head slightly, her hand straying to the silver cross around her neck. She rubbed it absently. An older couple brushed past and bumped in to her, mumbling an “excuse me” in Spanish as they moved on.

“I don’t know. There’s something there.”

“Keep in mind,” Marcus said, stepping back as three young children ran by laughing, “that he is a Mexican male. In this society, in this culture, that makes him king of the castle. Sisters, mothers, grandmothers, they all are culturally programmed to wait on the males hand and foot here, you know that. Plus his father has obviously been very successful, which I would think compounds his need to succeed.”

“Hmm. Very Freudian of you. I hope that’s it. He can certainly be fun and entertaining, but there’s something about him...”

“Okay, try this - next time dye your hair blond and it will be a different story.”

"Dye my hair blond? What for?"

Marcus smiled. "Santiago absolutely loves blond American girls."

He started to laugh as her mouth formed a perfect "O" and her arms crossed, mock-irritation suffusing her features. He thought she might decide to take a half-hearted swing at him. At that moment he heard several distinctive popping noises from outside, as if a car had repeatedly backfired. That was followed immediately by a sustained rattling, like a string of firecrackers going off.

"What the hell?" Marcus asked, looking around. Most of the crowd was oblivious to the sounds, busy laughing, talking, and haggling with vendors. But he saw a few inquisitive people glancing around in concern. Cassandra noticed the look in his eyes and tried with limited success to see over the heads of the people around her.

"Something's going on," he said, suddenly very uneasy. Those popping noises sounded very ominous. "I think it's time to go. Now."

"What about Santiago?"

"Damn. That's right. Why isn't he back yet?"

"What's going on?" she asked, her voice rising in pitch and the whites of her eyes beginning to show. She sensed that something was wrong, too. She gripped his shirtsleeve tightly.

Just then three deafening gunshots rang out, deafening because it sounded like they were right on top of them, there inside the market. The shots boomed and echoed throughout the large structure, making it impossible to pinpoint their origin. People screamed and began to scatter but were confused about what direction led to safety or perhaps into disaster. Dozens simply dove to the ground or ducked behind stalls. Mothers grabbed children and hugged them tightly, muttering prayers under their breath, shielding their children with their own bodies. Marcus tried to hold on to Cassandra's arm but a sudden panicked crush of terrified shoppers forced the two of them apart. She was pushed and twirled away like a scrap of paper in a tornado.

"Cassandra!" he screamed, but his voice was overwhelmed by the terrified yells of the hundreds of people scrambling madly around him. A small stand selling colored beads and cheap necklaces toppled over as someone collided with it, sending thousands of tiny glass and plastic beads everywhere. There was a crash as someone or something smashed into a glass display case in the next aisle.

Then Marcus saw two men moving fast and coming in his direction, their eyes twitching back and forth. They each held what looked like a black machine pistol of some sort, and were both dressed like anyone else in the market: one wearing jeans and a white *campesino* shirt, the other with a tan shirt and a black vest. Both appeared to be native Mexicans, their hair black and short, their skin the color of dark leather from years in the sun. They spoke quickly to each other, eyes still roving. White Shirt let off a loud blast with his gun into the ceiling of the Mercado and quickly scurried off to the left and out of sight. Screams of fear trailed after him like a roller coaster full of frightened riders.

Meanwhile Black Vest began walking forward quickly and deliberately, his gaze shifting this way and that, machine pistol held high. He fired off a short burst and fire spit from the barrel. A dozen copper, spent casings spun and hit the floor with eerily musical pinging sounds. Smoke wisps drifted in ghostly tatters from the end of the menacing black barrel. He strode forward another two paces then spotted Marcus, the American's six foot two frame and blond hair standing out as visibly as a roadside flare. The gunman cocked his head and stopped about fifteen feet away. He lowered his gun and leveled it at Marcus.

"Oye, gringo," he said, loudly enough to be heard above the din.

Marcus shot a quick look to his left and right. His back was up against the meat counter. He had nowhere to go. The hole in the end of the barrel was a stygian abyss no larger in diameter than a pencil, but looked as deep and bottomless as an abandoned mineshaft. A mother on the floor next to him cried out as her young son sobbed in her arms. Black Vest took another step toward Marcus. Sirens wailed in the distance, slowly coming closer.

They're not going to get here in time, Marcus thought, oddly emotionless.

Black Vest took one final step toward him and sighted down the barrel. He smiled, showing yellowed teeth. The tangy, sharp smell of cordite filled the area.

"Adiós, gringo," Black Vest said smugly.

A motion to the right caught Marcus' eye. Black Vest saw his eyes flick and he quickly shifted his gaze toward the movement. The Mexican's face erupted in shock and he spun the gun around instinctively, finger yanking back the trigger a split second before a one hundred and fifty pound side of beef on a stainless steel hook crashed into him with the force of a linebacker. A score of bullets slapped harmlessly into the hindquarter as it threw Black Vest into the butcher counter, flipping him head over heels, the machine pistol flying from his grip. Marcus heard a loud *crack* and some muted cursing as the attacker's head hit the concrete floor. The weapon crashed to the aisle and spun silently, its barrel still smoking, looking like the conclusion of a perverse, deadly game of spin the bottle.

Marcus leapt on the gun and tossed it harmlessly into a cart of meat scraps and waste where it landed with a wet smack. Then he turned and hurdled the butcher counter toward the Mexican, hoping and praying belatedly that the man didn't have a backup weapon. He needn't have worried as the stunned attacker was just picking himself up, groggy and wobbling, blood oozing from a gash on his temple. Marcus grabbed two handfuls of the vest and picked the man up and off the ground until they were eye to eye. The toes of the attacker's shoes dangled off the floor several inches and twitched, looking every bit like a man who had just been hanged. The Mexican's pupils were unfocused as he fought to regain his senses.

"Who are you?" Marcus barked in Spanish, anger pushing his composure to the limit. "What the hell are you doing?" He shook him violently.

Black Vest's head lolled for a moment until it dawned on him what was happening. He struggled in Marcus' unyielding grasp then started swinging his fists and kicking out with heavy shoes. Marcus took several glancing shots to his unprotected face before realizing this was not a very safe and sound arrangement. With a tremendous heave fueled by adrenaline he tossed the Mexican backwards into the next stand, almost clearing the low wall between the two. Black Vest flipped backwards as his heels clipped the wall. He fell in a crashing and untidy heap among some trinkets and magnets, most depicting the pyramid and other Mayan ruins at Chichén Itzá.

More sirens screamed outside and several others could be heard arriving from the rear of the market. People were up and running again, dragging children, their gifts and purchases left scattered and littered about on the floor. Marcus started toward Black Vest but stopped when White Shirt suddenly came charging back, gun still raised high. He fired a short volley into the ceiling while searching for his companion. Spent shells pinged to the floor, their bright copper sheen mixing with the colorful glass beads. Marcus quickly ducked low behind the butcher table.

"Carlos!" White Shirt yelled.

Oh, so Black Vest has a name, Marcus thought.

Carlos groaned and pulled himself to his feet, Mayan replica trinkets falling around him. Several of the ceramic ones smashed as he stumbled upright.

"*¡Vayamos!*" White Shirt screamed, rushing over and pulling his companion from the debris. "*¡Policía!*"

The blood on Carlos' temple was running freely down the side of his face. White Shirt grabbed his sleeve and pulled. Together they ran around the corner and out the nearest exit, Carlos doing so unsteadily.

Cautiously Marcus stood up and looked around. Other people were standing now, too, looking around warily, like wild animals at a water hole, ready to sprint to safety should danger reappear. A few children were crying, but for the most part everyone was quiet, still in shock, unable to believe what had just happened and how close to injury or death they had come. Suddenly Marcus remembered Cassandra. Where was she?

"Cassandra!" he shouted, his loud voice startling many of those around him. "Cassandra!"

"Here I am," she said, walking shakily from the other side of the aisle where the beef hindquarters were hanging. Her face was pale and she appeared to be in shock as well, but determined not to show it.

Marcus ran to her. He saw some smears of blood on her hands and white shirt, and for a split second feared she had somehow been hurt in the melee. His heart sank until he saw the hanging beef and put two and two together. He grabbed her wrists in his big hands.

"You did that. You pushed that meat into the gunman."

She nodded almost absently, as if she were not one hundred percent sure that she really had done it. Her eyes were slightly glazed.

"You saved my life," he stated, then unselfconsciously wrapped his arms around her and hugged. He was large enough that she almost seemed to vanish within his embrace. For a second she didn't react, then slowly her arms encircled his waist and she squeezed tightly. Her body quivered once, a single sob, the only one she would allow. They remained that way while everyone around them gathered their belongings, found relatives, retrieved their purchases, and began to exit. More sirens arrived outside and after another minute well-armed policeman in heavy black gear, helmets, and masks began storming the inside of the market. Their guns were drawn and they barked orders, taking no chances that other gunman might be inside. A dozen or so regular uniformed cops began rounding up witnesses and directing them outside.

A young, terrified Merida policeman with a black peach fuzz mustache, his voice and gun hand shaking badly, escorted both Marcus and Cassandra out to waiting vans. When the two of them were hustled from the Mercado Marcus realized his fondness for the market had been brutally torn from him forever, and he felt a stab of emptiness as he passed from its cool shadows into the harsh light of mid-morning.

Chapter 14

They were transported in an unmarked white police truck to a unpainted cinderblock building a few miles away. The heavy-duty vehicle rumbled over the old, pitted roads like a lightweight tank. The rear passenger section was windowless with a row of bench seats along either side. He and Cassandra and three other people from the market sat on one side, while heavily armed and armored police sat opposite them. They said little or nothing during the short trip, and kept their eyes locked dead ahead and their backs ramrod straight, weapons at the ready. The hot, cramped van ride would have been simply uncomfortable without them: with them it was nerve-wracking. Cassandra sat next to him in silence, one hand in her lap and the other rubbing her silver cross. Her eyes were nearly closed and her head bobbed back and forth with the motion of the van, as if she were on a small boat in choppy seas.

When they arrived at the cinderblock building the back doors of the van were flung open and they were motioned outside. With quiet efficiency the group was herded into the cool dim interior, which was not much more than a square, windowless room with red and blue plastic chairs, a dirty beige linoleum floor, and a ceiling fan that wobbled as it spun. Every time the blades made a revolution there was a tapping sound. *Tap-tap-tap*. To Marcus this place closely resembled most Drivers License Bureaus from any county in Ohio. The clicking of the fan, he knew, was going to get on his already-frayed nerves in a hurry.

As he looked around the plain, windowless room a door opened at the other end and a man walked out. He was tall and rather gangly, with a build much like a sixteen year old boy during his awkward growth stage, all arms and legs. He was dressed in dark blue and black fatigues that hung loosely on his frame, and wore a black policeman's hat atop his large round head. His hands were hidden by thin black leather gloves. Adorning each shoulder were muted blue and white patches that read *Policía Federal Ministerial* in small print, with larger letters below that spelling out "PFM". His hair was as black as an oil slick, but the rest of his features except his eyes were hidden behind a black plastic mask that obscured everything from his chin to just below his eyes. There were horizontal breathing slits across the front. It reminded Marcus of a paintball mask. It was impossible to determine his age, although from his bearing and voice Marcus guessed thirty or thirty-five.

While he stood there more people from the market were ushered in from other vans. Everyone looked both concerned and confused, and several appeared outright terrified. Seeing the man in the dark fatigues at the front of the room did nothing to calm their nerves. An older lady in very traditional garb had to be helped to her seat. She used a light shawl she wore to dab perspiration from her forehead while she rocked gently back and forth, muttering prayers under her breath.

When everyone was in and seated the man from the PFM took a few steps forward and cleared his throat. All eyes swung to meet his.

"Good morning," he said in Spanish, his muffled voice oddly deep considering his build. "My name is Special Agent Roberto Cruzado. I am with the *Policía Federal Ministerial*." He glanced over and saw Marcus. "You, sir. Do you speak Spanish? Can you understand me?"

Marcus nodded. "Yes." He was amazed at how quickly they had organized this round up.

"Good. I am with the PFM and we are investigating the incident at the market today. From a legal standpoint none of you should be concerned. It appears you were simply in the wrong place at the wrong time. One at a time we will escort each of you to the back room for some questions. Please refrain from discussing anything you saw or heard this morning with anyone else in the room: we would like to know what you saw in your own words, not what someone else thinks they saw or heard. Does everyone understand?" Heads around the room nodded slowly. "Good. Again, we will bring you back one at a time for your statement and to ask you some questions. This should not take long, then you will be free to go."

There were about fifteen witnesses seated in the red and blue chairs. Cruzado pointed to the end of the row of chairs at a bent, elderly man sitting there.

"You, sir, please come with me."

The old man appeared less concerned than just about anyone in the room. He grunted and heaved himself laboriously out of the red chair and shuffled through the door with no more trepidation than if he were heading out for tacos and beer. He was gone about fifteen or twenty minutes before he came back looking none the worse for wear. He was about to sit down again but paused and glared at Cruzado.

"Hey! How am I supposed to get back to the market?" he asked with a strong voice. "You brought me here. You going to take me back?"

Even with the mask obscuring most of this features everyone in the room could tell the PFM agent was slightly annoyed. "Fine. When enough of you have been questioned and can fill a van, we'll take you back." He pointed to the next person and motioned them to follow him. The old man nodded and sat down in his original chair, content to wait. He folded his hands in his lap and his eyes drifted shut. Remarkably, he appeared to doze.

Marcus counted heads and calculated that he had over an hour until it was his turn. Cassandra would follow him assuming they stuck to the order. He desperately wanted to talk to her, but the armed Federales around the room would have none of it. He was worried that something was wrong with her. She just sat there rubbing her little silver cross and staring at the floor. She wouldn't make eye contact with anyone, and never even glanced at Marcus. He almost put his arm around her, but just wasn't sure that was an appropriate gesture. Physically she was right there next to him, but he could tell that her mind was miles away.

Finally it was his turn. Marcus was happy to leave the bland confines of the room and the annoying ceiling fan behind. The PFM agent motioned to him with a curt nod and Marcus followed him to a small room that contained a gray metal desk and several more of the red plastic chairs. He was invited to sit and he did so. The room smelled musty, like a damp church basement he had frequented in his youth. The white walls were streaked with brown stains from dirty water that had repeatedly leaked from the ceiling. Special Agent Cruzado sat behind the desk and shuffled through some random papers. Head down while he worked, he held his hand out.

"Identification, please."

Marcus never went anywhere without his passport, and he passed it over warily, uncomfortable letting his it out of his possession even for a moment. The agent made notes for several seconds then began asking Marcus questions in Spanish, basic ones first such as name, address, and the like. It took him a moment but he finally noticed the dark blue color of the passport. The PFM agent raised his eyebrows.

"I expected a maroon passport. You're not German?"

Marcus shook his head. "No I'm not, but that's a common mistake."

"Your Spanish is excellent. I can barely detect an accent."

"Thank you."

The agent stared at him and waited for Marcus to elaborate, which didn't happen. The silence began to grow heavy and fat with expectations until Cruzado understood that there was no more information readily forthcoming.

"Do you know what the *Policía Federal Ministerial* is?" he asked Marcus.

"Not really, no."

"Think of us as something like your SWAT teams, or perhaps a civilian version of your Special Forces. While we officially report to the Federales we operate independently of them and focus one hundred percent of our efforts on fighting the drug trade. That is our one and only job."

Marcus nodded. "Not an enviable one, I'd say."

"Sadly, most times it's not." He glanced down at some hand-written notes he had taken. "From what I've heard from the other witnesses it seems you had a direct confrontation with one of the attackers. Please tell me about that."

Marcus shrugged. He told him how the events had unfolded, from the time they entered the market until after the gunman had run off, including Santiago's trip to the lower level of the Mercado. He didn't embellish his actions or what had happened, and in fact kept his narrative quite sparse and to the point. He did ask a question about the one shooter, Black Vest.

"The machine pistol he had. It looked a lot like the ones your men out there are carrying."

The PFM agent then surprised Marcus by reaching back and unhooking the clasp holding his mask on. He pulled the plastic off, then rubbed his cheeks and chin. He had a young face, unlined and clean shaven. Marcus corrected his first estimation of the man's age. He was at the most thirty. The agent continued scratching his boyish face.

"These masks. I hate them," he said emphatically, not answering Marcus. "The drug cartels are so strong and well-connected that even the men and families of the *Policía Federal Ministerial* are not safe. If they find out who I am or where I live my family's lives are in danger. We have to wear masks just to hide our features so we can't be identified."

He suddenly flung the mask across the room in anger. Marcus involuntarily jerked backwards in his seat. Cruzado didn't seem to notice.

"What has my country come to when even the police and their families are no longer safe? These drug lords kill, they decapitate, they kidnap, they 'disappear' their enemies and rivals! And why? Eh? Why do they do that?"

Marcus stared back at him. Cruzado's eyes were fiery with passion and hate. He rubbed his gloved thumb and forefinger together.

"Money. Always for the money. Because of the insatiable demand for drugs in your country, because of that demand, my friends, my fellow policeman, my countrymen, innocent people, thousands and thousands of people are killed each year. Mexican border towns are no longer safe for anyone, not even your own consulate workers. And these criminals are getting bolder each and every day." He pounded his fist on the table, then took a deep breath and steadied himself. "My apologies. This is not your fault, but the consequences of the cartels fighting each other, of fighting for land and access to the coastline north of us. It is tearing my country and city apart. Since your USA has been stepping up border inspections and controls, the drug smugglers have taken to the water. For that they need access to ports where they can work undetected, and the coast north of Merida has just that, right on the Gulf of Mexico and not too far from your states of Florida, Texas, and Mississippi." He shook his head again, sadly this time. "I fear that unless we are able to find a weakness, some way to break them up, then the country of my parents and grandparents will be no more. I have no illusions that I alone can stop them, but I need to find a way to slow their progress, to make them pay a heavy price for bringing their war to my city. I need to find a way. I must."

Marcus sat silent, knowing there was nothing to say.

"To answer your question," Cruzado continued finally, once more gaining his composure. "The gun you saw was likely a Heckler and Koch MP5, or an MP5K. It's a nine millimeter submachine gun. I imagine the one in the market either had the stock removed for easier concealment, or was an MP5K that comes without the stock from the factory. Ironically it is the same gun my men carry, and it's very popular with special forces groups like your Navy SEALs. It's German made. It's a very effective and efficient weapon, but then I would expect nothing less from the Germans."

Cruzado walked over and picked up the mask from the floor. The black plastic was undamaged. He held it at arm's length, absently, as if he had no clue what it was.

"You know what is even more ironic about the guns? With all the work your government does to prevent the cartels from bringing drugs into your country, they do almost nothing to make sure contraband is not smuggled out of your country and into mine. Do you know what your country's biggest export to Mexico is? Yes, guns! Guns of all types are painfully simple to transport across the border and into Mexico. Once they cross the border it is just a day or two until they are in the hands of the cartels."

He hooked the facemask back on, wiggling it from side to side until he was satisfied with the fit.

"What else can you tell me about the incident?" he asked, voice once again muffled. "Anything at all might be helpful."

"The guy in the black vest, the one that confronted me. His name was Carlos. That's what the one in the white shirt called him."

Cruzado raised an eyebrow, the only expression that could be seen on his covered face. "That narrows it down to about fifty million Mexicans, but it is something." He made a note on a piece of paper. "Why do you think he targeted you over anyone else?"

"I suppose because I'm a foreigner. A very easily identifiable foreigner. Blond hair, pale skin. Big target. Or maybe he just doesn't like gringos."

The agent almost chuckled as he took some more notes. His breathing was noisy and raspy through the mask. They talked for several more minutes while Cruzado scribbled down additional information, although there wasn't much else that piqued his interest. He asked for Marcus' temporary address and his cell phone, verifying that it would accept international calls, which it would. As he wrote it down next to the names and address of the other witnesses he paused in thought for a moment before moving on, his eyes focused on the address.

"Where are you staying while in Mexico? A hotel?"

"No, with my Aunt and her family."

"Your aunt lives here, in Merida? Is this where your cousin, this Santiago, lives as well?"

"Yes, she's my mother's sister. Santiago lives there when he's not at school."

Cruzado noted that on his paper, writing his cousin's name with a question mark after it, then he handed Marcus a business card emblazoned with the blue and white logo of the *Policía Federal Ministerial,* a phone number, and nothing else.

"If you think of anything, please call this number."

"Of course," Marcus assured him.

"I need something to help me stop these cartels. They are destroying my city. They are killing my people."

Marcus studied the card. "These cartels. Which ones are they?"

The agent leaned back in his chair. "There are two. El Grúpo we've had in Merida for many years, and we had something of an unwritten agreement with them, similar to what you and the Russians had during the cold war. Détente? Is that how you pronounce that? They were almost reasonable: we left them alone, and they left us alone. In its own way it worked. El Grúpo has been around for decades, and we had an understanding. There were no killings, except among themselves. There was peace, such as it was."

"Then what happened?"

"Los Hermanos, that's what happened," he answered. "They are a newer, vicious cartel based out of the southern state of Michoacan. They operated down there and never bothered anyone outside of the state, until they decided they needed access to the northern coast, just like El Grúpo. It is like putting two alpha dogs in the same room and tossing in a single piece of meat – they cannot abide by each other. They will fight and kill innocents and each other until only one survives. From what we can tell, for some reason El Grúpo has been slow to respond and now it looks like Los Hermanos may be getting the upper hand. And if not the upper hand, then they are without a doubt becoming bolder and more ferocious."

"Really? Why do you say that?"

"Because," he sighed, "it seems that the incident at the market today was just a diversion. While we were all there tending to that emergency a different squad of armed men attacked a main office of the Banamex Bank on the other side of town. They killed four guards and stole a huge sum of money. That is not El Grúpo's style. That has all the signs of Los Hermanos and a quick way to finance more terror."

Marcus remembered reading while at the airport with Cassandra about the killings and the mayhem the two cartels were causing. This incident fit perfectly with what he had read. Cruzado stood, signaling that the interview was over. Both men moved to the door. Marcus held out the business card.

"No name on the card," he stated.

"No, no name."

"And I bet your real name is not Roberto Cruzado, either. Is it?"

"Of course not," the agent admonished. "Why would I give my real name? That would be foolish."

Cassandra walked mutely passed him and Cruzado shut the door behind her. While she was away Marcus muttered "What the hell..." and pushed a plastic chair under the fan. Under the curious and watchful eyes of the Federales he twisted the entire fan assembly a quarter of a turn and gently released his hands. The obnoxious tapping noise stopped. Satisfied he jumped off the chair and sat back down. All the occupants of the room were looking at him with a mixture of bewilderment and curiosity except the old man who had gone first. He smiled a toothy grin and gave him a "thumbs up" with a bent and arthritic thumb. Marcus grinned thinly back at him.

Ten minutes ticked by and Cassandra walked back out, looking just as she had earlier, except perhaps slightly paler. He wasn't sure if she was still upset about what had taken place at the market, or if something else he wasn't aware of was at the root of it. Whatever the cause, she was withdrawn and quiet and still not making eye contact. She shuffled to her seat and sat back down. The metal chair leg shifted on the concrete floor and squeaked loudly, almost as if someone had stepped on a cat's tail. Several people jumped and the old lady with the shawl grabbed her chest with a gasp, crossing herself and mumbling.

One of the guards at the door took a quick head count and determined there were enough people to fill a van. He efficiently ordered Marcus, Cassandra, and several others out the door where they filed outside and into the waiting vehicle. The sun was bright after their time in the dim, musty room. Traffic, mainly white and green taxies, small pickup trucks, and buses hauling hordes of people, flew past in both directions. Exhaust was thick in the heavy air. Marcus helped Cassandra up and in, and the fact that she permitted his assistance served to increase his anxiety about her. Something was wrong, but what was it? For some time now there had been a niggling at the back of his mind that he had been considering, but had also not wanted to think about. Something unpleasant, a part of the puzzle that he hoped wouldn't fit but was afraid would. He would have to wait until they were out and somewhere they could talk.

They jostled and bumped their way back to the market and in no time the van pulled over and they disembarked. Everyone quickly scattered and lost themselves in the crowds that were still hanging around. Looking at the mass of people shopping, eating, and milling around Marcus inwardly marveled: they either didn't know about the shooting, he thought, or they just didn't care. It struck him as surreal that so much had happened to him, Cassandra, and the others, and this mass of humanity was oblivious to the mayhem that had taken place right here. Either way, he was eager to locate Santiago and get back to the house, if for no other reason than to give Cassandra a chance to rest and them an opportunity to talk.

"Come on," he urged her. "We need find Santiago and get you home."

He stood straight and looked over the heads of the throng that clogged the sidewalks and spilled in to the street, once again thankful that he was tall enough to easily do so. Several small, dark skinned Mexican children standing nearby stared at him, unused to seeing such a tall, blond man up close and personal. Their eyes and mouths were wide in amazement, as if they were in the presence of some Norse god. They shied away when Marcus looked at them, clinging tightly to the legs of their mother.

"I don't see him anywhere," Marcus told her. "I think our best bet is to get a taxi and head home."

Cassandra nodded. "That's fine," she said softly.

He nodded at her, happy that she was at least talking. He moved to the curb to flag down a taxi when he heard a muffled ringing noise and looked around. Cassandra perked up and tilted her head, listening, until she realized that it was her cell phone. She groped for it in her small purse and squinted at the incoming phone number, scrunching up her face, puzzled. Finally, at the fourth ring, she hesitantly flipped it open.

"Hello?" she asked, her tone thick with uncertainty.

Marcus couldn't hear the other side of the conversation over the traffic noise and the passing throng of people, but he saw her eyes pop open and her hand flutter to her mouth. The skin on his forearms tingled in sudden apprehension. She listened for several minutes before staggering backwards a step, bumping in to an old man carrying a sack of potatoes on his shoulder. He muttered something foul that Marcus didn't completely catch.

"Are you sure?" she continued. "Oh, my God. Okay, okay, I'll tell him. Please call back when you know more."

She slowly closed her phone and turned to face Marcus. There were tears in her eyes and her lip quivered. She tried to speak but her voice caught. Marcus' anxiety level jumped tenfold. He placed his hands on her shoulders.

"What is it? What happened?"

She took a deep breath. "That was Donald, back in Wayne. He..."

"He what? What is it?"

"It's Otto. He's been hurt. It's bad. Donald thinks your big Mexican got him." She told him about the fire at the Party Barn and what little she knew, that Otto was in Intensive Care.

Despair crashed through Marcus, a tidal wave of guilt and remorse. Otto wouldn't be in this mess if he hadn't convinced him to help. Damn it! He should never have left him back in Ohio unguarded and alone. He'd figured he'd be okay with his brother the cop around.

"Oh my God. What's the prognosis? Is he going to be okay?"

She shook her head.

"Cassandra! How bad is he?"

She sniffed. "They're not sure if he'll make it. They think he's dying."

Chapter 15

The taxi drive back to his Aunt's house was as nerve-wracking as always, that being the standard in Merida. Thankfully it only lasted fifteen minutes - but to Marcus it seemed like several lifetimes. He held on to the grab handle of the taxi with a sweaty grip, his other hand nervously fidgeting about, drumming on the seat or tapping out a staccato beat on his thigh. The thought of Otto in critical condition back in Ohio was tearing him up, his guts twisting and cramping as if he had eaten something that had gone bad. He had been mentally inching toward the very real possibility that something terrible had happened to his brother, but the thought of losing Otto as well was unthinkable. Cassandra had her head up against the filmy window of the taxi, oblivious as it bumped and thumped against the glass each time they hit a pothole in the road or swerved to avoid an unwary pedestrian. She gazed out at the passing cityscape blankly, her eyes unseeing and empty with scarcely more life than two polished marbles.

They arrived at Mary's house and Marcus paid and tipped the driver. No sooner had the taxi pulled away in a puff of blue exhaust than the big oak door burst open and his Aunt, Santiago, and Juanita charged out on to the sidewalk. Santiago hugged Marcus so hard it took his breath away and Mary rushed to Cassandra, throwing her arms around her like a mother to a lost child. Almost immediately both women started crying. Poor Juanita just stood there holding back tears and twisting her small hands in her cotton apron.

"Oh thank heavens you're safe," Mary said between sobs. "We were so worried about you. We couldn't find you, and the police were no help at all."

"Yes," Santiago said, so excited he had slipped back to speaking Spanish. "We had no idea what happened! One minute I'm down in the fish market and I hear screaming and gunfire! I tried to get upstairs to find you, to maybe help, but nobody could get upstairs. People, regular people, shoppers, wouldn't let anyone pass, saying it was too dangerous and that I'd be killed."

Marcus nodded. "Good thing you didn't. It, uh, almost got ugly up there."

He proceeded to give all three of them a brief overview of what had happened, from the moment Santiago left until the Federales and the PFM agent were done with them. Again, he skipped over details of his confrontation with the gunman, but felt no need to hold back Cassandra's part in saving his life. Aunt Mary's face lit up with astonishment and surprise. She dabbed tears from her face and looked Cassandra up and down, appraising her in an entirely new light.

"Nice job, dear. Well done."

Cassandra peeled herself off Mary and held out her hands as if to ward them off.

"No, really, it was nothing."

"Nothing?" Santiago chimed in, astonished. "You saved my cousin's life. You are a hero!"

"No! I'm no hero!" She turned and ran in to the house, disappearing inside, her footfalls loud on the tile floor. A few seconds later they heard a door slam shut. They looked around in confusion, searching for answers in each other's faces but finding none.

"What's wrong with her?" Santiago wondered aloud.

Marcus stood there, staring into the house. To himself he said, "I think I have a pretty good idea."

"What did you say?" his Aunt asked. "Perhaps I should go talk to her. She looks very upset. A nice glass of wine would probably help."

"No, I'll go," Marcus stated firmly, so firmly that it stopped Mary and Santiago in their tracks. "I think she and I need to talk."

The three of them remained there in silence as Marcus strode purposefully in to the house. After a few seconds they followed, but trailed behind as he walked up the steps to the closed bedroom door. He stood outside and rapped solidly four times.

"Cassandra? I need to come in."

"No, go away," came a muffled reply.

Marcus ignored her request and opened the door. She was lying on the bed with her face buried in the pillows. The bed was huge and she looked small and vulnerable, like a scared and tired little girl, her legs drawn up and facing away from him toward the open window. Marcus stared at her, feeling a sense of pity at what was to come. The door shut behind him with a clunk. She spun around on the bed, her tear-stained hair damp and hanging across her eyes.

"What are you doing in here?" she snapped, her face puffy and red. "I just want to be left alone."

He ignored her pleas and remained by the side of the bed, towering over her supine form. She sniffed and stared up at him, seeing resolve written in his expression as if it had been laser-etched in stone.

"We need to talk," he said, realizing as the sentence left his mouth that those had been Gonzalez's exact words to him.

She wiped her trembling hand across her face to clear the hair away. Mascara smudged and ran from her tears. Her eyes shifted left to right quickly, and she still couldn't meet his resolute gaze. She didn't answer him.

"We need to talk," he repeated.

She finally met his stare and their eyes locked. Something seemed to pass between them, some sort of tacit agreement. Slowly she nodded and moved to the side of the bed. She swung her feet down and sat on the edge, elbows on knees and her face cradled in her hands. Her black hair hung down and partially hid her face. He sat on the bed next to her. The mattress groaned under his weight and he sunk so low that Cassandra listed toward him. Their thighs ended up touching but neither made an effort to move away.

"You going to tell me what's going on? Why you're so upset?"

She sniffed again and didn't move. Marcus could hear her breathing. More than a minute passed before she said anything at all. When she did it was just a whisper, spoken so low he had to strain to hear her.

"My fault..." she said, her voice no louder than the breeze through the window. "It's my fault. Those bastards that attacked you, and now poor Otto...and then today. You were almost killed today."

Marcus kept his voice quiet. "Why do you say all that was your fault?"

"Because," she said softly, reaching in to her purse and pulling out her cell phone. She held it out in front of her, pinched between her thumb and forefinger as if it were infected with a malicious disease. "I've been talking to them the whole time."

As it turns out, "talking" was not entirely correct. She was reluctant to discuss it at first, but slowly it began to flow from her like a tap being opened, until finally the words were pouring out in a torrent.

"Since Rolland disappeared I've been receiving voicemails and text messages from someone. I don't know who it was. It was just a husky, low voice, but it spoke Spanish with a Mexican accent and he was very, very insistent that I follow his orders. I have no idea who it was or what he wanted, but I got the impression that he's used to having his orders obeyed."

"Why is that?" he asked.

"Besides his arrogance and the easy way he demanded and expected things, you mean? I don't know, it was just the way he spoke, I guess. It was as if he never even considered that his orders wouldn't be followed, couldn't imagine it." She paused and thought, and he could tell she was wracking her memory for specifics. "Except for one time in the beginning when he said he needed to find Rolland immediately, because things were heating up. Something like that."

"Things were heating up? What did he mean?"

"I never found out. And from that point on the messages never gave any extra details and rarely asked me to do anything at all. He was more interested in finding your brother and would check to see if I had any news. It was almost never anything else, until you came along..."

"Okay, what did he say in the beginning, to get you to follow his orders?"

She continued to stare at the floor. "That I was to do everything possible to help find Rolland, and if I didn't, then…"

"Then what?"

"Whoever it is knows exactly where my parents live here in Mexico," she finally blurted out. "They said if I didn't help find Rolland they would…hurt them. Maybe kill them. They described their house and town exactly. They know who they are and where they live!"

Damn. "So what did you do?"

"Well there wasn't much I could do to help them in the beginning. I mean, I had no idea where Rolland was or what had happened to him. Months had passed and I hadn't seen him, so I couldn't tell them much. I would get a voicemail or a text once in a while from him, asking a question, but that was it. I just texted back to the same number."

"And then?"

She looked directly at him. "Then you showed up, you showed up and I had to tell them you were here. I had to! I couldn't take the chance that they might find out you were in town and at Foley's and asking about Rolland and I didn't let them know. I just couldn't take that chance. I didn't know they were going to go to your brother's house and… and do things to you." She buried her face back in her hands, her shoulders shaking weakly.

Marcus kept his voice even and soft. "Don't worry about that now. What were you supposed to do with me? Anything specific?"

She shook her head. "No, I was just supposed to stay close to you in case anything happened, in case you found Rolland. Then I was supposed to report back."

"And did you tell them anything?"

"No. Well, yes – that you were headed to Mexico. I didn't say why, just that you were still looking for him. Whoever it is told me to go with you, to keep an eye on you. He said he'd be in touch."

Marcus kept her going and asked next about Otto, and why she felt that was her fault. Cassandra looked down, then up at the ceiling, as if asking for forgiveness. She explained that several days ago, right before they left, she had gotten another text, this time asking for a place outside of Wayne, somewhere in the country where someone could lay low and hide. She innocently gave them directions to the Party Barn, didn't think anything of it.

"I had no idea that they were going to do there!" she wailed, obviously distraught as guilt over her complicity in Otto's fate hammered at her. Tears flowed freely down her face, further smearing her mascara and lending her eyes a nasty bruised look. "And today in the market," she continued, "you were almost killed. You wouldn't even be here now if I hadn't told them about you in the first place."

Marcus gently reached around and put his arm around her shoulder. She stiffened at his touch, then bit by bit she relaxed, until eventually her head drifted to his shoulder, settling there. To Marcus it felt oddly natural. He took a deep breath, dreading what he had to say next.

Voice calm and soothing, he said, "Well, I had an idea that you were talking to them, whoever they are."

Her head popped up and she stared at him in alarm, the expression on her face changing from shock to shame then to something like aggrieved disbelief.

"*What?* What do you mean? I mean, how could you have known?"

He sighed. "The timing, mainly," he said delicately, his arm still on her shoulder even though she had pulled away. "The timing was just too neat and tidy to be a coincidence. I mean, a few days after I saw you in Foley's for the first time Gonzalez and Hernandez just showed up? Someone had to let them know I was there at the house. I thought maybe it was whoever lives across the street, but they seemed way too timid for that sort of thing."

"Across the street? You mean Mrs. Kerr? Oh, she would never do anything like that," she said dismissively. "She loves Rolland. He used to help her out all the time after her husband died a few years ago."

"Is that her name? Mrs. Kerr? I just didn't think she could do it, especially since she called the police when she thought I was in trouble. That wouldn't make any sense. And when you told me what happened to Otto, that was the second piece of the puzzle. He's been living there in Wayne the whole time, and they could've grabbed him any time during the last three months, but nothing happened until we got together."

"I never wanted anyone to get hurt."

"I know. And also," he said, moving on, "you were so insistent on coming along with me down here. Again, you hadn't even been actively looking for Rolland, and suddenly you were all hot and bothered to go with me. It just didn't add up. I figured they had something on you and were forcing you do this, but I had no idea what it was."

Her face twisted in confusion. "But if you knew all along…"

"I didn't know for sure, but it seemed likely, and I wanted you here by me anyway. Whatever lever they were using on you had to be a strong one, and I didn't want anything to happen to you because of me. Plus," he added, "I think it's better that you're with me than not. I think we can use this to our advantage."

She stared at him, fear for her family clear in her expression and the flinty look in her eyes. Her skin was pale and drawn, like ink-stained parchment stretched over bone. She pulled away and his arm fell to the bed.

"I won't do anything to jeopardize my parents' safety."

"I wouldn't ask you to. But I still think we can use this. I'm just not sure how yet, that's all."

"Just promise me you won't let them hurt my family."

"I promise, Cassandra. I also promise that I'll bring an end to this. Somehow."

She thought on that for nearly a minute before finally nodding in agreement. She rubbed her silver cross absently, gaining comfort and solace at its cool touch.

"Okay, and please - call me Cassie."

Marcus left her to get cleaned up, but before doing so he made her vow to keep the issue of the cell phone and her clandestine communications completely secret.

"But why?" she asked. "Don't you trust your family?"

"It's not that I do or don't trust anyone," he replied, shaking his head. "But this is something we need to keep to ourselves for now and we just don't know what's going on. Please promise me that you won't say anything, not to my Aunt, to Santiago, not to Juanita. And not to Donald back in Ohio, either, for that matter."

She looked at him sideways for a moment, then nodded hesitantly, agreeing, but still skeptical.

"Good. And one last thing – let's not discuss Otto and what happened to him, either. We need to keep that to ourselves for now, too."

"Why not? I don't understand."

He placed his hand back on her shoulder. "Do you trust me?" he asked simply.

She pursed her lips in thought. "Yes, I suppose I have to. Fine, I'll keep it to ourselves."

"Good," he smiled, relieved. "I'm going to head back downstairs and explain that you're just upset after what happened today and that you'll be down in a while. Please try to contact Donald and find out what you can on Otto's condition. We can discuss that later if you get through."

Cassie soberly agreed. With a final look at her smudged and splotchy face he headed downstairs. He noticed with satisfaction that her color did seem to be returning, That was a good sign.

Waiting for him were his Aunt and Santiago. Mary was drinking something tall and fruity that Marcus suspected contained a healthy dollop of rum, and Santiago was gripping a brown bottle of Pacifico beer in one hand, a cigarette in the other. They were both seated at the large dining room table. Juanita was nowhere to be seen. Concern showed on Mary's face in the creases across her forehead, like faint lines drawn with a fine pen. Santiago almost seemed carved from stone, so still he didn't even appear to be breathing. Both pairs of eyes swiveled up to greet him as he walked in. His Aunt heaved a heavy sigh when he told them that Cassie was fine, just tired and distraught over their ordeal.

"Well that's a relief, dear," Aunt Mary said. "She seemed so upset."

Marcus gave a slight shrug. "I don't blame her. It's not every day you're involved in a shootout and get hauled off by the Federales. That's enough to unnerve anyone."

"Except you, apparently," she pointed out.

Marcus didn't reply but pulled out a chair and sat down. He picked up an orange from the bowl and began idly spinning it on the table. Juanita magically appeared and asked if he'd like something to drink. He nodded, and seconds later she set down a tall glass of iced tea on a small cork coaster. He took a drink and lined the square coaster up with the edge of the table. They shared stories about the day and their experiences, although Marcus didn't go in to much more detail than he already had. The day's events were already beginning to fade from his memory, and he realized that elements of the experience that were clear just hours ago were becoming fuzzy, like old photos that dim and wash out over time. Later, much later, this too might become something they could joke and kid about, but certainly not yet.

Santiago still looked angry that he had not been able to get back up to their floor on the market to help out. It seemed to Marcus that his cousin was somehow personally offended that he had been unable to do something. Perhaps some sort of "macho" thing, he wondered?

"I should have been there with you," he said flatly.

"Why, so the shooters had more targets? I don't think so."

Santiago grumbled something under his breath and took a long pull from his beer. He vigorously crushed out his cigarette then lit another right away. Gray smoke engulfed his face before slowly drifting up and away.

"Those things will kill you, you know," Marcus told him.

Santiago waved him away. "You Americans, so safety conscious all the time: don't drink, don't smoke, don't eat red meat. Wine is bad for you, wine is good for you. Bah! Sometimes you have to grab the bull by the balls and live a little, you know. You can't be safe and sound all the time. Throw caution to the wind. Live and enjoy, that's what I say!" He took a long drag and blew the smoke across the table toward Marcus.

"Maybe so, but I prefer caution over excitement right now, thank you very much." Marcus waved the smoke away playfully and they both grinned at each other. "My life has been pretty damn thrilling lately anyway. Hell, I don't think I can handle much more excitement."

Santiago continued grinning and loosened up a little. His hunched shoulders relaxed and he sat back in his chair, still eying Marcus. He seemed to finally accept, grudgingly, what had transpired and his lack of a role in it.

"Santiago, dear," Mary said, "don't you have to get back to the University? You have class tomorrow, don't you?"

He made a face. "Yes, I should, but there's no rush. I'd rather sit and enjoy our limited time together. How often do we get to do this?"

"Not often enough, that's for sure, not with Marcus at least. If only we had Rolland here too, then it would feel complete." Mary lifted her drink as if in a toast.

"And father, too," Santiago reminded her.

"Oh, I forgot to tell you both," she said, her face suddenly lighting up with the news. "Your dad called this morning while you were gone and told me he'll be home tomorrow. Isn't that wonderful?"

Marcus sat up straight – the orange slowly stopped spinning and gently rolled to the center of the table where it came to a stop. He noted from the corner of his eye that Santiago sat up straighter in his chair as well.

"He's coming home tomorrow? That's fantastic news! Maybe I'll finally get some answers to what's going on after all."

"Yes, dear," Aunt Mary continued, "he called this morning while all those dreadful things were happening to you two. He said he'll be home by dinner tomorrow at the latest, but will only be able to spend the night before he goes back out." She made a small pout. "I do wish he could stay longer. I miss him terribly when he's gone."

"Excellent. With everything that's happened I don't think Cassie and I should stay down here much longer - we should get back to Ohio as soon as possible. We'll just relax around the house tomorrow and wait for him."

"Perfect, dear," she said brightly, looking forward to the continued company. "That sounds wonderful." Not for the first time Marcus wondered if he should be happy or concerned at his Aunt's situation here, by herself most of the time in a foreign country. He remembered an old adage he had once read: *Don't confuse wealth with happiness*. He wished his Aunt would take that to heart.

Juanita entered the room again and announced that dinner would begin in about an hour. Marcus' mood had improved and he realized he was ravenous, having not eaten anything since breakfast and missing lunch altogether. He was sure Cassie would be hungry by then, too, and wondered how she was doing up in the room. He hoped she had an update on Otto. While he was worried sick about him he worked to keep anything from showing in his demeanor.

Mary perfunctorily thanked the diminutive cook and was about to ask Santiago to fix her another drink to tide her over when he stood and announced he had changed his mind. He needed to get back to school after all.

"I just remembered that I have a quiz in Economics tomorrow," he apologized. "I will try to be here for dinner tomorrow night, however. It will be good to see my father again." He came around the table and kissed Mary on the cheek, then went and hugged Marcus warmly. Marcus caught a whiff of some sort of hair product that mingled with the cigarettes and beer. That double hit of vice smells gave him a nasty flashback of his father, although Santiago and his dad had nothing in common.

"Sorry to see you go," he said, still locked in the embrace.

"Please give my best to Cassandra, but I'd best be going. I have quite a bit to do."

A thin cloud of cigarette smoke trailed behind him as he exited the room, like a wispy contrail behind a passing jet. They heard the heavy clunk of the front door as it closed. Mary looked at the doorway where he had gone.

"Such a nice boy," she said, mainly to herself. "But just like his father – tall, dark, and mysterious."

Marcus couldn't agree more.

Dinner that evening was low-key. Cassie came down shortly beforehand and smiled shyly, apologizing for her earlier outburst. Mary was on her feet in an instant, arm around Cassie's shoulder, steering her toward the table in a very motherly fashion. Marcus had rarely seen his Aunt act that way before and guessed she didn't often have a daughter-figure to pamper and care for. He again felt a fondness for her that transcended so much else.

Marcus looked at Cassie and raised his eyebrows, silently asking if she had an update on Otto. She compressed her lips and shook her head negatively, a tiny movement that went unnoticed by the others. Marcus cursed under his breath.

Juanita served dinner quietly and efficiently as always, and they moved through their several courses in easy companionship. To Marcus it seemed as if they had been together for months instead of days, and he marveled at how easily this situation seemed to be the new normal. He began to wonder what it would be like when they got back to the States. Would being back there feel odd and uncomfortable after this?

With dinner finished they moved to the living room and casually watched some television, mainly to try and relax and take their minds off of recent events. Both Marcus and Cassandra laughed when they watched American shows dubbed into Spanish. Familiar actors' and actresses' voices were different, and were sometimes so far from what they were accustomed to it was difficult to watch.

"Wow. I have never heard Homer Simpson sound like that before," she remarked with a laugh.

Then a Mexican show came on, a long-running evening soap opera-drama. The women were all sexy and busty with lots of cleavage while the men were dark and brooding. It was like an American soap opera on steroids. There was quite a bit of thinly veiled intrigue and romantic skullduggery, but not much seemed to actually happen. The acting was for the most part over the top and not very good, at least to Marcus' tastes.

They flipped around a few channels and stumbled upon an American action movie from the 90s. Marcus smiled ruefully at the painful memory this film evoked. The movie was not dubbed over but ran Spanish subtitles across the bottom of the screen. He pointed to the television as the hero attempted to leap away from a runaway, derailed train.

"So, who here knows how Rolland came up with the name 'Sam' for his dog?" He was met with two blank looks as he expected, so he continued on. "Well, Rolland had just gotten Sam, and hadn't even figured out a name for him yet. He was trying out several but nothing seemed to be just right for the puppy. Then that very night this movie came on and something clicked. This movie, *The Fugitive*, was about a doctor who was accused of killing his wife. The doctor insisted a one-armed man had done it, but no one believed him. What not many people know is that this movie is loosely based on real events that happened in the mid-50s in a suburb of Cleveland called Bay Village. The real-life doctor in that murder was named Sam Sheppard, and he was accused of murdering his wife, Marilyn. One of Rolland's teachers in high school had been obsessed about that case, and talked about it all the time." He waited for any light bulbs to blink on with either his Aunt or Cassie, but none did.

"Don't you get it? His puppy was a German Shepherd, and here's this movie on television based on a guy named Sam Sheppard. It just clicked right then, and the name Sam seemed to be a perfect fit. So Sam it was."

Both Mary and Cassie smiled and laughed, although with the knowledge of Sam's ultimate fate Cassie was more subdued. Her smile was touched with sadness. He saw a bit of melancholy washing across her face, just a ripple, like a faint breeze agitating the surface of a pond.

"Oh, Rollie," Aunt Mary said, "that sounds so much like you. Just your type of humor. I wish he were here right now with us. That would be so nice."

Around ten o'clock they all decided to call it a night and both of them lightly kissed Aunt Mary on the cheek, which she loved, and went upstairs to their respective rooms.

"Any news about Otto?" Marcus whispered.

"No, dammit. I tried over and over to get in touch with Donald but I couldn't get him. Either the circuits were busy or he wasn't answering. I'll keep trying tonight and tomorrow morning."

"Speaking of morning," Marcus said as they stood outside her door. "I'm looking forward to a mellow day here around the house, just waiting for El Señor. Boring and easygoing would be quite welcome after what we've all been through."

Cassie readily agreed. "I plan on sleeping in until Naibi bangs on my door to make the bed. Then I'm not doing a thing. I'd like to help out around the house but I know Mary and Juanita won't let me. I'll guess I'll end up lounging around the courtyard."

They said goodnight and Marcus headed to his room, dozens of thoughts battling for dominance in his head. They dealt with secret communications, injured friends, and random shootings – but most of them revolved around the girl in the room next door.

The next morning Marcus really was awakened by a gentle knocking on his bedroom door. A check of the clock revealed it was still early, only a little after seven o'clock. He quickly rolled out of bed, tossed on a T-shirt to go with his boxers, and opened the door. He was surprised to see Naibi standing there, and he nearly laughed out loud as he recalled his last conversation with Cassie before bed. He restrained from asking if she were there to make the bed already.

"Yes, Naibi, good morning."

The maid smiled nervously and handed him an envelope. On the front were two simple block letters that looked as if they had been computer printed: M.S.

"What's this? Where did this come from?" he asked, looking it over. His heart skipped a beat. He could feel his respiration increase as if the air in the room were suddenly thinner.

"The doorbell rang a little bit ago, and this was waiting on the mat," the diminutive maid said quietly. "M.S., that must be you, yes?"

"Yes, it must be me. Did you see anyone outside? Could you tell who delivered it?"

"No, I couldn't tell. There were some of the neighborhood children playing in the street, but I couldn't see who did it. I didn't ask, though."

Marcus looked the envelope over again. "Thanks, Naibi." The young maid smiled timidly, shut the door and went on about her business.

He walked back to the bed and sat on the edge, holding the envelope with both hands as if it were some ancient artifact, both invaluable and terrifically fragile. The large M.S. was in simple Times New Roman font and unremarkable, and the envelope itself was one available at any discount or office supply store, even here in Mexico. With trepidation that he couldn't explain Marcus precisely tore off the end and pulled out a white piece of paper. There was a single printed paragraph:

> *I have information concerning your brother. Meet me at the Sagrado Cenote at Chichén Itzá today at 5:00. Careful – others are watching and following.*

He examined both sides of the note, but could find nothing else, no markings of any kind. He stared at it for several minutes while options ran through his head. Then he stood and began getting dressed, putting on shorts and tough shoes. He grabbed his wallet and passport and pocketed his phone.

"Looks like I'm going to see Mayan ruins today," he murmured, lacing his shoes tight and grabbing a ball cap to shield him from the hot sun.

"You're going where?" Mary asked incredulously.

Marcus had headed downstairs several minutes earlier to grab some coffee and a bite to eat before taking off. He had hoped to get out of the house without waking anyone, especially Cassie. The note didn't say so but he figured this trip was one he needed to take alone. He couldn't stand the thought of placing her in the crosshairs of any crazies again. But after half a cup of coffee and a few tortillas his Aunt had shuffled into the kitchen, her robe cinched tightly around her waist and her face sans makeup. This was not something she did lightly. He couldn't even recall ever seeing her "unprepped" before. It was a little shocking, like seeing a movie star up close and in person for the first time in unflattering light.

"Naibi told me you got some mysterious envelope. What was in it?"

Marcus paused before handing her the note. She read it twice then gave it back, her hand trembling slightly.

"So now you're heading off to some Mayan ruins in the middle of the Yucatan? Because this note says they know something about Rolland?"

"Yes, that's right."

"You know Javier is going to be here today, don't you? If you go to the ruins you might miss him. Chances are he'll be here and gone before you know it. Isn't this the whole reason you came to Mexico in the first place? To see Javier?"

"I know, believe me, I know. But this may be the most definitive lead I've had so far. I mean, it seems everyone including me is looking for him, and whoever this is –" he held up the note "- says they have information about him. I don't have any choice. I have to follow up on it." He rolled another tortilla filled with salsa and in three bites it was gone. A few more and he'd be on his way. He knew from past experience that it was about a two and half hour bus ride from Merida to Chichén Itzá, assuming he could get a first class direct bus. If not he'd have to settle for second class one, one that was bound to make dozens of stops along the way.

His Aunt poured herself a cup of coffee and stood there, leaning against the counter, her arms crossed tightly around herself. She looked older, frailer, and he realized how lonely she must feel sometimes. Marcus wasn't the only one with limited family, he knew. It dawned on him then that she could be terrified that something might happen to him. As infrequently as they saw each other that would still be one more degree toward near-complete isolation for her.

"You've considered, of course, that this might be a trap of some sort, right?"

"I know."

"And you're still going? And why all the way there? Why can't whoever it is just talk to you here?"

"I don't know. But I've been to Chichén Itzá several times before. The place is always packed with people and vendors. And there's a huge gift shop not two hundred feet from the Sagrado Cenote. I can't see anyone getting me all the way there just to do something to me. It doesn't make sense." If his Aunt were aware of what had happened to Otto, the issue of Cassie's secret phone calls and text messages, as well as the threats to her family, she would probably lock him down for good. He wisely continued to keep those facts held close to his chest.

"What am I supposed to tell Cassie when she wakes up? She's not going to be very happy with you."

"Just tell her the truth. I won't ask you to lie for me. If everything goes well I'll be home tonight before dinner is over."

"And Javier? What should I tell him?"

He washed down the last of his tortilla with coffee. "Hopefully I'll be back in time to talk to him, but if he has to leave just ask him about the man who attacked me. Describe him, tell him he was a driver of his for some time back when we lived here, and see what he remembers. Anything will help. I hope to be here to talk to him myself, but if for some reason I'm not just find out what you can."

His Aunt absently took a sip of her coffee and made a face. She spooned in a healthy quantity of sugar and then tried it again.

"Promise me you'll be careful. You and Rollie are like my own sons, and having one missing is killing me already. I don't want anything to happen to you. I just couldn't bear it."

Marcus finished his coffee and went to her side. He kissed her on the forehead. The faint trace of her perfume that was so much like his mother's tugged at his heart. Maybe it wasn't even perfume at all. Perhaps it was some inherent scent the two siblings shared? He checked his pockets one last time to make sure he had his wallet, cash, and identification. He carefully folded the note up and put it in his back pocket. The paper was so thin and insubstantial he couldn't even feel it.

"Of course I'll be careful. And anyway it's a public place. I'm sure nothing will happen."

Chapter 16

Dr. Marcus Schmidt knew all about the Yucatan Peninsula. After all, on top of living there for years he had lectured on the subject dozens of semesters in front of hundreds of undergrads at a time. The place was so unique and foreign to a kid raised in the Midwest that it had latched on to his psyche on his first visit, and from that point on had refused to relinquish its grip.

"The Yucatan Peninsula was born of a violent act nearly 65 million years ago," his lecture would typically begin. "It is widely believed that a massive comet strike, most likely the very strike that helped cause the extinction of the dinosaurs also caused the cataclysmic birth of the peninsula. The strike hit with the force of 10,000 nuclear bombs and was so violent and powerful that it forced that huge rocky landmass, roughly the size of Florida, to be explosively expelled from the boiling, tumultuous sea, as if Neptune himself had heaved it from the watery depths."

Also, he tended to get just a little over the top when he talked about it.

"The Yucatan is formed almost exclusively of limestone, and is cursed with only a thin three or four inch layer of rocky topsoil. Trees do not grow tall there, and most plants are stunted and short. Limestone itself is porous, meaning that water will not sit on the surface, but will soak into the ground. Because of that there are no true lakes, rivers, or streams in the Yucatan. The only continuous and reliable sources of potable water for thousands of years have been the occasional sinkholes, called *cenotes*." He pronounced it "sa-NO-tays". He would always pause here and write the word on the board. If he didn't most of the students would misspell it, putting an S in place of the C. "The Maya were no dummies, and nearly all Mayan cities were built around these cenotes. They ruled that part of the world for thousands of years and they, like anyone searching for an ideal building site, prized a steady and reliable source of clean water.

"Cenotes vary in depth and width, but most are roughly circular with sheer walls of exposed rock," he would continue, sketching a cenote on the blackboard. It looked like a bucket filled about a third of the way with water. "The larger ones are hundreds of feet in diameter and up, sometimes as wide as a football field. The surface of the water in a cenote is at or near sea level, so it's roughly 60 or 70 feet below the level of the land. In most the water is 40 to 50 feet deep, with a muddy bottom of silt and other debris." He would pause here to make a point. "If you were to fall in and survive the seventy foot drop, you would not be able to get out on your own. The sides are too sheer."

Usually here he would move to a large map of the Yucatan and point out highlights of these unusual geological formations, such as the Ring of Cenotes, the demarcation line of the original comet strike's crater, and he might even talk about how subsidence of the limestone actually forms cenotes, as well as caves and complex underground passages. Most of the time, however, he would notice a few students playing with their phones or nodding off, perhaps one or two actually sleeping, and he would sigh and move on, muttering, "Undergrads…"

"That brings us to one of the most famous cenotes in the world," he would say, raising his voice, trying to refocus their wandering attention. "The Sagrado Cenote, or Sacrificial Sinkhole, in Chichén Itzá." He would quickly dim the lights and project a huge picture of it on the screen at the front of the auditorium. From the expressions of those faces that he could see in the front few rows, he could always tell what they were thinking. It was the same thing he thought when he had first laid eyes on it years earlier, and it was the same thought that everyone had upon viewing it for the first time: *the Mayans actually drank from that?*

His trip to Chichén Itzá had been uneventful and actually rather peaceful. Fortunately he had managed to secure passage on one of the nicer bus lines, A.D.O, or Autobuses Del Oriente. It was air conditioned with comfortable seats and not very crowded, so he had an adjoining seat all to himself and could stretch out. The two and half hour ride took him out of Merida and on to the highway, a newer one which was nearly as smooth as a freshly poured driveway, a nice change from the Midwest and its annual spring pothole season. They stopped at a few pueblos, or villages, along the way to pick up and drop off travelers, but between those stops there was little to see except miles of stunted trees and the occasional abandoned hemp plantation. The advent of synthetic twine and rope in the 1970s had destroyed much of the natural hemp industry, and the plantations that dotted the flat landscape were for the most part derelict and vacant. Even so it was still possible to pick out the ordered rows of *agave* plants, the stiff leaves of which were used to make the fibers which in turn were made into all types of rope products. The plants were also used by the locals to make the popular alcoholic drink *pulque*. They marched off across the flat plain like squat, ordered soldiers, their pale green narrow leaves stuck in the air, forever fully at attention. It was a desolate, quiet landscape, but still beautiful in a lonely sort of way. For the most part only the highway and the electrical towers with their never-ending power lines showed that man had made any impression there at all.

When they arrived at Chichén Itzá that all changed.

The bus pulled up to the Welcome Center just before noon. It was about the twentieth in line and the parking lot was already humming with cars and tourist vans. Marcus had never seen so many cameras in one place before. Hundreds upon hundreds of people were milling about and heading in to the Welcome Center, and without any effort he heard a myriad of languages including English, German, French, and several mysterious Asian tongues. The Welcome Center itself was constructed of colored concrete, about three stories tall, and the twenty foot tall doorway leading in was shaped like a pyramid and painted a terra cotta orange. Once inside he quickly navigated through the throng, deftly dodging adults, kids, and quite a few strollers as well. He finally made his way to the admission window and paid the nominal entrance fee. The overwhelmed girl at the window handed him a green wristband and he headed through the turnstiles.

The first thing Marcus noticed were the vendors, scores, hundreds of them everywhere, their tables overflowing with homemade wooden masks, jewelry, T-shirts, blankets, and countless trinkets depicting all aspects of this archaeological wonder. On his previous visits they had not been permitted inside the grounds. Now they lined the gravel paths like groupies at a rock concert, vying for the attention and wallet of each passerby. At times it was difficult to walk through them they were so prevalent and tenacious. It was a change Marcus did not much care for: besides being terribly annoying, their presence seemed to defile the place in some way. He shook his head sadly and continued to push through. He walked on down the gravel path, trees arching overhead, their leaves casting flickering shadows that bathed the walkway in dancing, shifting chiaroscuro patterns.

About a quarter mile later he cleared the trees and there before him was one of the most recognizable structures in Mayan history. It was huge, rising almost eight stories above the flat, grassy area surrounding it. The conquering Spanish had named it El Castillo, The Castle, because they lacked a reference point for what it truly was. To the Maya it was called the Temple of Kukulkan, or Temple of the Feathered Serpent. Most everyone considered it a wonderfully preserved pyramid, but not with a pointed triangle like the iconic and massive Giza pyramids that rose majestically from the desert sands of Egypt. No, this pyramid seemed to have had its top amputated about three fourths of the way up and a square structure, a large room with a door on each side, placed there in its stead. A set of steps graced each side of the Temple, steps wide enough for a dozen men to stand shoulder to shoulder and ascend at one time. It was made of limestone, as were all the artifacts at Chichén Itzá, and its weathered sides were mottled with varying shades of light and dark gray. Hundreds of tourists milled around him, talking, laughing, staring in mutual awe, taking pictures – but he was unaware of their presence as he stared in wonder at the Temple. With the cerulean blue sky as its canvas it was magnificent, a testament to the skill, craftsmanship, and religious fervor of the ancient Maya.

A group of a dozen tourists led by a short, very dark-skinned Mexican guide with a wide-brimmed straw hat passed behind him and he sidled up closer to eavesdrop on their conversation. The guide spoke English and had a very thick Spanish accent, but his deep voice powered right through that impediment so that understanding him was actually quite easy.

"In 2007," Marcus heard him say, "Chichén Itzá was named one of the seven modern Wonders of the World. Chichén Itzá is Mayan for 'at the mouth of the well of the Itza', and was one of the most important Mayan political, commercial, and religious centers of its time. This city is home to several buildings, such as the one before you, that are remarkable for both their architectural design and religious and scientific significance. Besides this one, the Temple of Kukulkan, there are also the Observatory, the Temple of Warriors, and the Ball Court."

He turned and gestured grandly at the Temple of Kukulkan, almost as if he himself had had a hand in its construction. Peering more closely at the man's features Marcus could certainly make out distinct Mayan facial characteristics.

Hmm, he considered, perhaps his ancestors had indeed been a part of its creation after all.

"The Temple is one of the tallest and most notable structures in Mayan architecture. Many still call it a pyramid, but it was actually a temple where only the highest and most reverent priests were permitted to ascend to the top. It sits on a 182 foot wide rectangular platform and rises to a height of nearly 80 feet. Each side has 91 steps and the platform that crowns the pyramid is considered the 365th step, meaning there is one for each day of the solar calendar."

He stopped so a few of his charges could snap some pictures. He smiled at their oohs and ahhs. He then continued discussing how the Mayans had been masters of the heavens, possessing an incredible and uncanny knowledge of the movement of the stars, moon, and sun, and how the interplay between them all depicted the seasons, as well as the month and day of each year. They knew exactly when the equinoxes fell, so were prepared for either harvesting or planting. They could tell also tell when the next lunar or solar eclipse was set to take place. Marcus had always been very impressed with their vast level of knowledge. The guide and his charges moved off, the man sticking with his patter all the while. Marcus walked on.

To his left was another huge structure, one constructed of two towering walls over thirty feet tall and more than a hundred yards long, also of limestone, with a vertical stone hoop placed twenty feet high at midcourt on each wall. It was the Ball Court, topped by the Temple of the Jaguars, and was the largest of the many Ball Courts found in the Mayan empire. Accounts were unclear, but it was widely believed that some type of contest took place there over the course of one or more days, and that the winner was beheaded as a sacrifice to the gods. Marcus and Rolland had always joked that had they been playing they would have been the most inept contestants the game had ever seen.

Several hundred yards to his right was the Temple of the Warriors, a monstrous, squat, three-tiered structure surrounded by hundreds of stone columns and topped by what appeared to be a life-sized Mayan warrior reclining on something that looked amazingly like a chaise lounge, his head turned to survey the whole of Chichén Itzá.

Marcus would have loved nothing more than to poke around these and the rest of the smaller temples dotting the site, but he didn't think he could waste any more time. His only goal now was to meet up with the writer of the note, and to do that he had to head to the Sagrado Cenote. He kept walking, passing by several walls carved with scores of death-heads, their empty eye sockets staring blankly at him as he strode by. Shortly after that he entered a heavily wooded path leading to his destination. The path was about a quarter mile long and once again lined with vendors and their stands, each one trying his hardest to part Marcus from his money. He studiously ignored them, intent on being just one more tourist among the thousands passing by every hour.

However, against his better judgment he slowed as he neared a stall resplendent with silver jewelry. Hanging from a peg he saw a glittering silver cross on a fine chain. The cross was no more than in inch tall and was delicately inlaid with turquoise and onyx. Involuntarily he thought of Cassandra.

"You like the cross? It is silver," the vendor said in English with a thick accent. She was an older Mexican lady wearing a shapeless cotton dress and a shawl, the dark, wrinkled skin on her face looking like an apple left in the sun too long. Three small, dirty children twined around her feet and legs and ignored him, involved in some game of their own making. He approached and carefully cradled the cross in his hand. It was handmade and beautifully done. It flashed like a strobe light in the sunshine.

"*Sí, me gusta mucho*. It's very pretty," he replied in Spanish.

The old lady didn't miss a beat, switching languages on the fly. "Yes, it is very beautiful, and made just down the road in the village of Piste by local artists," she said in a throaty voice. "It is the only one that I have like that, very rare. Perhaps a gift for someone special?"

Marcus didn't answer but continued to examine it. The turquoise was pale blue with dark flecks in it, and the obsidian seemed to almost absorb light. He gently lifted it off the peg and held it out.

"How much?"

She named a price that was obviously too high, knowing full well that it was time for verbal fencing as they both jockeyed for the best deal. He countered with a slightly lower price, a token gesture, really, and she hastily agreed. He knew this might be the only sale she would make all day and he didn't have the heart to beat her down further. The cost to him was minimal but she had three additional mouths to feed. He paid her in American dollars, which she deftly disappeared in a pocket, then plucked the cross from his hand and slid it into a small wax paper bag. There was no receipt. She smiled and thanked Marcus, then promptly forgot about him and moved on to an Asian couple who were ogling a silver paperweight shaped like a jaguar. As he left they were both trying to converse in broken English, their only shared language.

He slid the small bag in his shirt pocket and wondered if he could actually give it to Cassandra. His feelings for her were growing stronger and more confused with each passing day, but those feelings were still overshadowed by the guilt that weighed upon him. She had been Rolland's girlfriend, dammit, and he couldn't do anything else until he got his brother's blessing. That was not up for debate. He had done too much to Rolland already, he knew, and just couldn't bring himself to hurt him again. Even so, he only had to close his eyes and involuntarily he would see her face, her smile, feel her head on his shoulder and smell her scent, the touch of their legs as they sat on her bed. He smiled inwardly, wondering what she had done when she discovered he had left her behind this morning. She would not be happy with him when he got back to the house later, he knew, and would certainly let him know how she felt about it. He moved on then. The weight of the cross against his chest, just below his heart, was profound. He almost considered canceling the sale, but looked again at the small children and kept walking instead.

He continued down the path and a little farther on it opened up and he was there, and it was just as amazing and bizarre as he had remembered it.

The Sagrado Cenote was over a hundred yards in diameter, roughly circular, its sheer sides of stratified limestone looking like a huge, vertical paper tube whose sides had been crushed and buckled by a tremendous force. Vines and roots festooned its sides and dangled down, some all the way the sixty or seventy feet into the water. An ancient Mayan platform of some sort was perched near the closest edge, and the remains of a small, twenty by twenty foot temple stood to the left of that, only two of its walls still standing. But what always caught his eye, and the eye of anyone seeing it for the first time, was the water itself: it was a bright, pea-soup green, an unhealthy color caused by thousands of years of plant material being washed into and decomposing in the warm water. This was what caused the universal reaction among his students and anyone else seeing it for the first time: *the Mayans actually drank from that?* Not only would no one want to consume that, few in their right mind would want to touch it at all. It looked foul and putrid and its perfectly still surface showed no signs of life. Not a ripple disturbed the placid, smooth waters, and it seemed almost as if it were solid, like the bright green felt on a pool table. It was as alien to most people as the surface of the moon, and despite that – or because of it – it always enthralled Marcus.

There was a permanent gift shop to the left and he bought a bottled water which he sipped as he walked around. He found a spot in the shade where he had a good view of the path and anyone coming or going. He sat down on a rock outcropping and pulled out the note. He read it again:

I have information concerning your brother. Meet me at the Sagrado Cenote at Chichén Itzá today at 5:00. Careful – others are watching and following.

He checked his watch and saw that it was only a little after one o'clock, so he sat back and prepared himself for a long wait. More groups of tourists and their attendant guides wandered by, all of them snapping pictures of the Cenote and its still green waters. He heard their murmurs of delight and disgust at its appearance, and he had to smile. Despite his run-ins with Hernandez and Gonzalez and the incident at the Market, he wondered specifically what the author of the note meant, that others were watching and following. He certainly hadn't seen anything or anyone suspicious so far, and the throngs of people wandering around paid him no more attention than to any other of the obvious tourists. This train of thought also led him to wonder again about his brother, and not only what had happened to him, but what he had been up to. Whatever he had been involved in it must have been hugely important to someone since they were willing to go to all this trouble. It was important enough to kidnap, torture, and kill for, and it obviously had something to do with stolen credit cards. During the bus drive over he finally had some time to think, to consider everything that had been happening since his arrival in Wayne. With the limited facts at his disposal he was just beginning to piece together some of what was going on, or so he thought. He still needed more, and he was hoping against hope that whoever was set to meet him here today could fill in some of those blanks. If all went well this could be a major turning point for him.

A different guided tour moved his way, this time made up entirely of Mexicans visiting a proud national treasure. The guide was a younger man in a white shirt open at the chest and wearing a New York Yankees ball cap. He was directing his charges into the shade by Marcus and wiping sweat from his face with a red bandana.

"The Sagrado Cenote is the reason Chichén Itzá is here in the first place," he said. "The Mayans needed the water to survive. Back then it was not green like this, but clear and clean. It only changed after Chichén Itzá was abandoned and the jungle reclaimed it."

An older man in the group spoke up. "I thought it looked like this because of all the human and animal sacrifices that took place here."

The guide waved both hands in front of him at chest level. "No, no, that is a common misconception. The Mayan people were extremely intelligent and they knew that such sacrifices on a regular basis would foul one of their only sources of drinking water. There have been about eighty remains of children and men and women found in the mud at the bottom of the Cenote, but this city was inhabited for nearly 600 years, so human sacrifices did not happen on a regular basis at all. Perhaps only in the most dire of circumstances, such as during a drought when they might make a sacrifice to *Chaac*, the rain god.

"Recently archaeologists discovered a series of underground caves, some of which terminate right here at the Sagrado Cenote, which can be accessed just under the surface of the water. The finds are so new very little has been done with them yet. The ancient Mayans believed that the caves were *Xibalba*, or Realm of the Dead. The rain god Chaac lived there, as did *Ixchel*, the goddess of fertility. Xibalba was a stinking, fearsome place, where the recently deceased had to pass trials to move on to their final afterlife."

The young guide moved closer to the edge of the Cenote. He mopped his face again with the bandana and lit a cigarette.

"The Mayan priests started exploring these caves nearly a thousand years ago," he said, punctuating his talk with his cigarette and using it like a pointer, gesturing downwards. "Some of the caves are filled with drawings and paintings, and some contain alters and entire rooms made of stone blocks carried from the surface. Many of the caves are filled with water, but some are dry.

Others can only be accessed with great difficulty through small openings, some from right here at the Cenote."

A young Mexican girl in the group gave an involuntary shiver. The guide and several others laughed at her.

"Archeologists are not certain what the caves were used for, but they have found human skeletons, pottery, some tools, and sculpture. Most of what they have found has been left exactly as it was, in situ, so to speak, so scientists can continue to study them exactly as they were so many years ago. Research is moving slowly."

The young girl shuddered again at the thought of the caves directly beneath her feet and what horrors may or may not have been perpetrated below her in the distant past. During his studies Marcus had seen pictures of those underground labyrinths and the bizarre underground land the Mayans called Xibalba. It was a dark and dismal place where sacrifices and strange rituals had occurred, spurred on by zealous priests and superstitious leaders. Some of the rooms were completely submerged while others were high enough above the water table that they were forever dry. There were sudden drop offs and dead ends that made the caverns potentially lethal to the unwary. While some of the caves had ceilings vaulted so high they seemed to soar upwards like those in a European cathedral, other passageways were so snug and tight that it was necessary to crawl on hands and knees in order to pass through. Marcus didn't consider himself claustrophobic but the thought of spelunking around those black chambers held no allure for him. He much preferred the above-ground mysteries of the Maya.

Finished for now, the young guide and his group moved away toward the air conditioned gift shop, no doubt intent on checking out the souvenirs and taking a break from the heat. A small Mexican boy of no more than five or six years old hung back and stared at Marcus, obviously intrigued by his pale skin and white-blond hair. His brown eyes were huge as he looked at Marcus sitting on the rock. He took a hesitant step forward and Marcus couldn't help but smile at him. He held up a hand. The little boy paused then slapped his own hand against Marcus' in a high-five, then laughed and scampered off after the rest of the group, pointing back and calling after his mother.

A half hour passed and there was a lull in the activity around the Cenote. Evidently people were eating lunch or just wandering around elsewhere, but for whatever reason suddenly Marcus was the only one there. He could hear some muted chatting by the customers and the employees of the gift shop down the way, but for the moment there was no one else in sight. With only a little effort he was able to imagine that he was suddenly transported back in time, to the height of the Mayan empire with Chichén Itzá as its hub. The bright green water appeared to magically clear, becoming as blue as the Caribbean waters a hundred miles to the east, and the jungle surrounding him faded away, replaced by even rows of cultivated corn, beans, squash, and chili peppers. The small, deteriorating temple at the edge of the Cenote was suddenly whole, its gray limestone bricks sharp-edged and true, its roof sound. He could hear distant chanting coming from the Temple, a low murmur as the citizens prayed to their gods, among them Chaac and Ixchel, and the occasional cheer as crowds witnessed a life and death contest on the distant Ball Court.

He was so engrossed in his reverie that he didn't notice when a small figure detached itself from a gnarled tree by the gift shop and gracefully moved towards him, making no more noise than a cat carefully stalking prey through tall grass.

The era of the Maya had been violent and superstitious, filled with mystery, rampant religion, brutal wars, and a reverence for death. Marcus did not wish to live in that time, but to be able to view it as it was, to peer in to the lives of the Mayan people and their long-dead culture, called to him in its own peculiar siren song.

He sat there on the lip of the ancient Sagrado Cenote, eyes half-lidded, his mind elsewhere, when behind him he heard a bit of gravel shift, just a soft crunching sound as of a careful footfall. He sensed a presence behind him. Marcus began to jerk upright, but at that exact moment felt something sharp and cold against the side of his neck. He froze, cursing liberally under his breath. Keeping pressure on his neck the figure slowly glided around until they faced each other. Marcus gazed into the cold dead fish eyes for the first time.

"I thought we would meet again," Mr. Hernandez remarked casually. "How's your back feel?"

Marcus said nothing but inside he was raging at himself. How could he fall for this simple ruse? His Aunt had even warned him that the note might be a trap. Damn!

Hernandez took a graceful step back and motioned for Marcus to stand. At full height he towered over him but the shorter Mexican was undaunted. He either didn't notice or care about the height disparity. In his hand was a long thin knife with a six inch black blade. The dappled sunlight seemed to be absorbed by that evil-looking steel, like a black hole that sucked in any light that strayed too close. He held it loosely in his right hand. With his left he opened up the light jacket he was wearing, which revealed several holstered pistols as well as the handles of at least three more blades. Marcus understood: even if he tried to flee, Hernandez had enough firepower to cut him down, along with other innocents as well. He nodded once at the smaller man to show his understanding of the situation. The two of them stared at each other for several moments, and if Hernandez was waiting for a sign of fear it was not forthcoming.

Finally Marcus broke the tense silence. "What do you want?"

Hernandez didn't immediately answer. He flipped the blade in the air several times, never taking his eyes from Marcus, but deftly catching the handle of the knife each time. He cocked his head at Marcus like a curious dog, perhaps confused at the lack of a response. The dark skin of his face was unnaturally smooth save for some tiny wrinkles around his eyes, but no laugh or smile lines marred his complexion. His skin reminded Marcus of the fake, perfect complexion of a mannequin. His black hair shone like a crow's feather in the sun. It shimmered purple where the light struck it directly.

"We have unfinished business, you and I," he said.

Marcus refused to show a reaction but he knew well what the man meant. He was still internally cursing his stupidity, running it over and over in his head like a mantra.

"We are going to leave this place. You will walk in front of me and we will move slowly to the exit. I will be behind you. If you attempt anything foolish I will shoot you."

"You won't find out what you want if you kill me."

The corners of Hernandez's mouth flicked upwards once, a twitch, really. The movement was faster than a snake strike. So he could smile, in a manner of speaking, Marcus realized.

"So be it," he said, his voice oily.

Marcus nodded once and his shoulders slumped and his chin dropped, resignation clear in his body language. Hernandez's black eyes shone in triumph and he tilted his head to the side, motioning Marcus to move on. Marcus took one step then stopped, holding up a finger.

"I've got one question."

"No questions," Hernandez stated flatly, astonished that Marcus had the gall to even speak. "Start walking."

Marcus ignored him. "Why did you have me come all the way here? You could've saved us both a lot of trouble and told me to go somewhere a lot less public and closer to Merida. I would've done it."

Hernandez was becoming annoyed. "What are you talking about?"

Marcus slowly pulled the note from his pocket and held it out. "This. The note. Why did you tell me to come all the way here?"

"What are you talking about?" Hernandez repeated, looking quizzically at the piece of paper. "I wrote no note. I've been following you for the last two days, waiting to get you alone."

Marcus continued to hold the paper out. It flapped gently in the small breeze. "You didn't write this, telling me to come here?"

"No. Enough of this. Walk."

But Marcus didn't budge. "If you didn't write it, then who did?"

"I don't know and don't care. Now *move*!"

Marcus thought for a second, and then nodded to himself. He crumpled up the note into a tight ball and before Hernandez could say or do anything he threw it at the little man's face. It hit him on the cheek, just below his left eye. As his attacker flinched backwards in shock and his eyes involuntarily tracked the paper projectile, Marcus' other hand whipped out and grabbed the knife hand at the wrist. Hernandez growled in disbelief and anger and jerked twice trying to get free, but Marcus' grip was fierce and unyielding. A brief and silent power struggle took place, the two of them locked in place, immobile, as rigid as any of the ancient statues of Chichén Itzá. Marcus squeezed so hard his arm shook with the strain. He was gratified when he suddenly felt something pop in Hernandez's wrist. The knife fell from the now limp hand and clattered on the uneven rock, bouncing a few feet away. Grimacing in silence through the pain, Hernandez quickly understood that he would not win this particular battle. His free hand shot underneath his jacket for one of his many backup weapons – but Marcus was prepared for that. He grabbed a fistful of his attacker's jacket and spun like a discus thrower, putting his legs and back into it, yanking Hernandez off his feet. The smaller man was tossed up and out, into the open air, toward the edge of the Cenote.

But as he was being spun Hernandez managed to latch on to Marcus' arm with his good hand. The force of the throw was too strong and the smaller man couldn't maintain his grip, but it was enough to overbalance Marcus. He found himself suddenly peering wide-eyed at the rocky outcroppings and serene water below, water that looked like a tremendous putting green. Hernandez sailed up and over the side and then quickly dropped from view without a sound. Marcus arched his back and pin-wheeled his arms madly, almost comically, trying to regain his equilibrium. But gravity prevailed and he toppled over the edge like a giant tree being felled. He peripherally witnessed the still-spinning Hernandez smack awkwardly into the soupy green water seventy feet below with a tremendous splash, and less than three seconds later Marcus himself hit the now troubled water feet first and sunk deep, deep underwater. Cold darkness closed over him like a verdure shroud.

Chapter 17

Cassandra was supremely pissed.

The morning had started off so well. She had woken up gently about thirty minutes earlier, slowly, luxuriating in bed, feeling the soft cotton sheets against her warm skin. She was in no rush and was content to lie there peacefully, stretching her arms, legs, and back a little bit at a time, relishing this time alone with no real agenda and no place to be. She arched her back like a cat, her arms extended and her hands balled into fists, then relaxed her muscles and settled back in the bed with a satisfied sigh. She and Marcus had no plans for the day, she knew, save waiting around for his Uncle to arrive. That thought disturbed her, because it brought back memories of her past deceit, the months-long communications she had been having with the mystery man concerning Rolland and, later, Marcus. She screwed her eyes up tight at that, hoping to squeeze away both the memory and guilt at what she had done. It didn't work. The deceit gnawed at her.

That train of thought also led to her feelings about Rolland and Marcus. She *had* been in love with Rolland at one time, of that she was sure: he was fun, affectionate, without pretense, and a wonderful lover, too. But people and relationships change over time, and she and Rolland had drifted apart there in the end, weeks before he vanished. Looking back she realized she had been more in love with him than he had been with her, although this lopsided aspect of their relationship hadn't dawned on her until recently. She probably still loved him in some way, but it was distant now, detached, like a long-ago high school crush. She knew they would never be able to go back to what they had. That saddened her, the knowledge that that chapter in her life was over.

Which brought her to Marcus.

So much like his brother, and yet he was so completely different. He was complex where Rolland was more transparent, determined where Rolland was carefree. Physically they were almost twins, eerily alike, but there was much more to Marcus deep inside. For some reason he refused to open up to her and she sensed he was holding himself back emotionally. She could tell that he found her attractive and had feelings for her, that much was evident, but he wouldn't let himself act on those feelings. She had never met anyone like him, and she was acutely aware that she was falling for him a little more each day – would probably have fallen more deeply already if only he would let her.

She rolled over and buried her face in the pillow. Karma be damned. Why did life have to be so complicated?

Sounds of the morning penetrated the thick door of her bedroom: Juanita moving around the kitchen and clanking pots as she prepared the morning's breakfast, Naibi humming over the gurgle of running water as she freshened up the plants lining the second floor walkway, Aunt Mary's muffled voice, her words vague and indistinct. Outside she could hear cars and trucks rumbling down the road. The yeasty smell of fresh tortillas from the tortillaría up the street wafted gently through her window and made her stomach rumble ever so slightly. This was what finally stirred her enough to begin her day.

She changed into her jeans and a plain cream-colored crew neck T-shirt. She realized that if they stayed any longer she was going to need to do laundry or go shopping for more clothes. She made her way to the bathroom and brushed her hair and teeth, then applied a little makeup: nothing too extravagant, just some base and a little highlighting here and there. She knew she'd be seeing

Marcus in a few minutes so she wanted to look nice, but not too over the top: many Latina girls painted it on to the point where they looked like hookers, and that was just not her style. She was more conservative than that. She pulled her black hair into a neat ponytail.

Satisfied, she trotted lightly downstairs and found Aunt Mary sitting quietly at the big dining room table, a cup of coffee in her hands and an odd, concerned expression on her face. Despite this Cassandra gave her a warm greeting, inquiring about her night.

"Oh, it was fine, dear. And yours?"

They chatted amiably for a few minutes, passing the time comfortably like two people who had known each much longer than just a few days. Meanwhile Juanita hustled out with a cup of coffee and some rolls, *bolillos*, which were fresh and hot from the bakery a few blocks away. Juanita would have picked them up on her way to the house earlier this morning, prior to her arrival. Cassandra spread some jam on one and ate it with her coffee, a strong brew that was much better than anything she could find back home in Wayne. The cup was warm between her hands.

"So, where's Marcus?" she asked. "I thought he'd be down here by now."

Mary sighed. "Now don't get too upset, dear," she warned after a pregnant pause.

Cassandra was instantly alert, the back of her neck suddenly tingling. "Upset? Why would I get upset?"

"Because Marcus left this morning, several hours ago."

So now of course she was beginning to get upset, and worried as well. "What? Left? Where did he go?" She swiveled her head this way and that, as if he were hiding somewhere in the room and she could spot him if she looked hard enough.

Mary proceeded to tell her about the note and where Marcus had gone, and more importantly why he was determined to go alone. Cassandra stared at her with wide, unbelieving eyes, her hand straying to the cross around her neck.

"No! I can't believe it. He wouldn't go without me!" she said, her voice loud. She didn't add "We're in this together," although she certainly felt that way. She had already lost Rolland. She couldn't stand the thought of something happening to Marcus as well. Not now, not again! She tried to tell herself that it was irrational and the circumstances were completely different: Rolland had vanished as if someone had plucked him off the face of the Earth, whereas Marcus had only taken an ordinary bus to a busy tourist attraction a few hours distant. She tried to convince herself that the two incidents weren't in the least bit related, but she couldn't separate them. Anything out of the ordinary was suspect now. She stood and began pacing the room, Mary watching her stalk back and forth, full of sympathy but for the moment devoid of answers.

"Sorry, dear," Mary said. "I told him you'd be angry, but he insisted that he go alone."

"You bet I am," she said, her voice two octaves higher than normal. She heard it but couldn't stop it. She was pissed. "How could he do this to me? Leaving without me! That note could be from anyone! It could even be from one of *them.*" She didn't have to elaborate on who she meant – they both knew.

Mary made sympathetic noises, her coffee cup held in front of her like a shield. Her eyes looked haunted and she suddenly appeared older, tired. Her lust for life seemed somehow diminished.

"Hasn't he figured out by now that whatever is going on here is serious? Whoever is behind all this is not playing around. Two people together have a much better chance if something goes wrong. Ooh, that pig-headed, selfish…"

Cassandra continued to stomp around the dining room, alternately cursing Marcus for leaving solo and berating herself for sleeping in and missing him. Juanita stole a glance into the room and quickly backtracked, wisely staying clear. Cassie stomped and ranted for five minutes before finally beginning to wind down, her temper subsiding to a low simmer, a pot of boiling water turned down to "warm" - still hot and potentially dangerous, but no longer scalding. Eventually she slumped into a chair, for the moment drained. Mary reached across and patted her arm.

"Why would he do this? It's crazy," Cassie said. "He should know better by now."

"Dear, saying I know how you feel sounds hollow and corny, but I do."

Concern and fear were clearly written in the lines creasing Cassandra's forehead, in the turn of her mouth, the pallor of her skin. She continued to rub the silver cross at her chest.

The older woman took a deep breath and held her gaze, then looked away, over Cassie's shoulder at the lush garden behind her. She could have been gazing a million miles distant, into another world. "Dear, let me tell you something I don't talk about to anyone. I know I come across like a ditzy blond when I'm talking about Javier and his life outside this house. I know that. But the truth is I'm terrified every single time he leaves, and I hold my breath each and every minute he's gone. I pout and worry and feel sick to my stomach and can't sleep. That's why I tend to, shall we say, tip a few too many. I'm a wreck." She sighed, forcing a tight smile. "But when he finally walks through that door," she said, motioning toward the front of the house, "my heart leaps and I curse myself for being a fool, and I run in to his arms and all is right with the world again."

Cassandra sat up a little straighter, interested. "Then?"

She clasped the younger woman's hands tightly. "And then he leaves and I do it all over again."

"How? How can you do that over and over? Emotionally, I mean."

Mary pulled away and grasped her coffee cup again, her shield once more firmly in place. "Different people show their concern in different ways, I guess," she said. "I fret and worry, you get angry. It's what we do when we care for someone."

Cassandra began to protest, ready to distance herself emotionally from Marcus in a knee-jerk reaction, but then she paused: peering inward she knew for certain that she *did* care, maybe more than she knew, and it was high time she began to press the issue. She had already drifted apart from one person she loved. She couldn't let someone else she cared about slip through her fingers. Did she love him? No, not yet. At least she didn't think so. Even though Marcus was reluctant and couldn't take their relationship to the next level, it was time for her to take the initiative and move them forward - even if she had to drag him kicking and screaming. Yes, she would do it!

"Thanks, Mary."

She smiled broadly and leaned back in her chair, her effervescent nature quickly returning. "You're quite welcome, dear. Now I know it's still early morning, but I can whip up a batch of mimosas if you like. I've tried to teach Juanita how to make them but she just can't get the hang of it. Anyway, it's almost like drinking juice, and makes mornings like this so much easier to bear."

Cassandra grinned despite herself, her anger sloughing away like an unwanted skin. Her color had returned and most of the worry lines melted away from her forehead, banished for some later time. She realized she was still fingering the cross around her neck so she forced her hand down to her side. Hanging on the opposite wall, she saw, was an antique mirror filled with spidery black veins, one corner fogged a silvery gray. Her reflection in the hazy glass was indistinct with blurred edges, like an old photograph slightly out of focus. She smoothed her hair while touching up her ponytail and considered the plain T-shirt and jeans she was wearing. Hmm. Perhaps a bit more make-up wouldn't hurt, she considered. Just a smidge, and maybe some lipstick, too. It was time to primp. She turned to Mary.

“Do you have a blouse I could borrow? Something…nicer than this?” She plucked at her beige shirt with a sour expression.

“Well of course, dear. Come with me and let’s see what I have. You’re a little bustier than I am, but I’m sure I can find something.” She perked up. “Ooh, this could be fun. We may have to go shopping.”

They laughed conspiratorially, like two recently matured schoolgirls prepping for their first prom. Any remaining tension in the room quickly drained away. They stood and were heading towards Mary’s room when they heard the front door clunk open then decisively close with a bang. A deep voice, not speaking loudly at all but quite easily heard, said, “Mary, *donde estás?*”

Cassandra saw Mary’s face light up. “It’s Javier! He’s home!”

She ran towards the front of the house, Cassie all but forgotten.

Chapter 18

The air in Marcus' lungs exploded outward in green-tinged bubbles when he struck the water, which from that height felt like slamming into thick, drying concrete. Stunned and battered, it took a few seconds before he could gather his wits about him enough to look up. There he saw the bubbles dancing toward the murky surface so very far above his head, seemingly miles away. The impact from falling seventy feet had nearly knocked him out. While he didn't have time to take inventory for serious injuries he felt shooting pain lance into his right shoulder and neck. An old phrase leapt into his mind: it's not the fall that hurts, it's when you hit the ground. Or water, in this case.

Basic survival instincts took over and he feebly kicked for the surface, still dazed. The dappled, hazy green light up above grew slowly brighter, but not nearly fast enough: his air was essentially gone already. The water temperature, very cool down below, increased dramatically as he ascended until it was nearly bathtub temperature. His chest was on fire, burning as if he'd inhaled flames, while he simultaneously fought the primal urge to suck in something, anything, even water. The edges of his vision began to darken in a pulsing rhythm, keeping in time with his thundering heartbeat. He gritted his teeth to hold back the frantic desire to breathe.

I'm not going to make it, he thought darkly.

Then his head burst through the soupy green water and into the humid air. He sucked in huge, gulping mouthfuls of the blessed stuff. His burning lungs recovered almost instantly, even the hot air feeling cool and glorious. Marcus felt relief course through his body as his hands and feet tingled with the influx of fresh oxygen. He remained where he was for a few moments, content to simply breathe and weakly tread water, his right arm stiff and sore. He had never been so conscious of the act of breathing before, ever. He weakly swam to the side so he could grab on to the limestone wall, its ridges and striated layers providing ample and easy handholds.

About ten feet away he spied Hernandez flailing weakly, his face bobbing up and down and sinking more often than not, water spraying from his mouth as he gagged and choked. The airborne mist from each cough spawned ephemeral rainbows in the sunlight that quickly dissolved away as if they had never been. It was quite obvious the man couldn't swim. He coughed softly and seemed to weaken suddenly, his head silently sinking beneath the surface while his hands splashed ineffectively. Marcus stared at the spot where Hernandez had been, watching impassively as the man's arms and then his hands slid under water, with only a rippled disturbance on the surface marking the spot. He swore under his breath. He knew in his gut that he needed the man alive so he could garner some useful information from him, find out what this was about and who was behind the whole mess. But he was torn between pulling him up from the depths or just letting him drown and being done with him forever. Pragmatism battled against the sheer satisfaction of knowing the little lunatic was gone and out of his life. Satisfaction lost out.

Cursing, he pushed off and dove down where he thought Hernandez should be. He forced his eyes open in the thick greenish water and caught a shadowy glimpse of him about ten feet down and to the left. The man was still kicking feebly but making no progress, his eyes closed, face tilted down. His black hair waved around his head, dancing slowly like dark seaweed in a gentle current. A fine trickle of bubbles escaped his flaccid lips and nose.

Marcus quickly swam around and grabbed his collar from behind with his bad arm, saving his good one for swimming. His shoulder throbbed but two strong kicks found him breaking through to the surface with Hernandez limply in tow behind him. God the man was heavy! It must be all that extra firepower he was carrying. Marcus hauled him to the side and latched on. Was Hernandez even breathing? He certainly hoped so – he knew how to administer mouth to mouth, but he was in no position to do that while clinging to the wall. Not to mention the abhorrent thought of placing his mouth on the maniac's lips.

Thankfully the little man coughed, water spewing from his mouth and nose. He retched a little more and started splashing and panicking, his eyes huge and round, an unaccustomed look of terror on his normally emotionless face.

"Settle down, settle down!" Marcus commanded loudly.

Hernandez was still terrified and not listening, madly grabbing on to Marcus with both hands. With frenzied strength born of panic he tried to climb on top of him, pushing the bigger man down under. Marcus gasped and fought back, his own strength just barely equal to the smaller man's manic struggles. He managed to claw his way back to the surface and with one quick motion slapped Hernandez across the face with a stinging blow.

"Get a grip! You're going to kill us both!"

Hernandez froze and his face went cold, his eyes narrowing to the merest slits, like cracks in a sidewalk. From his reaction Marcus figured that he wasn't used to being treated like that but he couldn't care less. He needed him to be composed and in control or there was a good chance both of them might die right there in the Cenote.

"You're back now?"

Hernandez tilted his head back and forth a fraction of an inch, a barely perceptible nod. His hair was matted down, smooth and slick, like an otter's fur. His breathing had calmed. The one cheek was bright red from the slap.

Marcus nodded. "Good. I'm going to try and get someone's attention. I don't think anyone saw us fall."

The little man cocked his head sideways and looked at him again in that cold, calculated manner he had. Water dripped down his face. "Why did you save me?"

Marcus ignored him and looked upwards. The rocky sides of the Cenote were not perfectly sheer after all, but angled up and out slightly near the top, like a huge funnel. Anyone up on the ledge would still have to look out quite a ways to spot them down here, flush against the wall as they were. He needed to swim out toward the middle before he could be seen. Anyway, he wasn't as concerned about their survival now since the air was warm and the water was even warmer, plus he had always been a fairly strong swimmer. If they had to they could cling to the wall for some time until they were noticed and rescued.

"You have not answered my question," Hernandez said flatly.

"Believe me, not saving you was my first choice, but I need you alive so you can tell me what's going on here. Who's behind this whole thing."

"I will not tell you anything."

Marcus met his gaze evenly. He knew Hernandez was baiting him but didn't care. "I think you will, when this is all done. Or maybe I'll just turn you over to the Federales and let you explain everything to them."

"I will not go with the Federales."

He knew he should just ignore him and concentrate his efforts on getting out, but the little man was too damn smug and infuriating. "Why are you so interested in my brother? What credit cards do you guys keep talking about? What was he doing for you?"

"Your brother was nothing more than a tool. An errand boy."

"What do you mean? What was he doing?"

"He was an errand boy who stole from us, and then lost his nerve."

"Lost his nerve doing what?"

But Hernandez was done talking and would say no more. With his left arm he held on to the wall, while his right was concealed underwater. Marcus resisted the urge to grab the man and shake him, demanding more information. Fine – if he couldn't coerce any more from him now he would just do it when they reached the top. He made himself turn away and prepared to push off and swim out to where he could be seen from above, hopefully catching someone's attention. A quick movement and a sudden splash of water from Hernandez caught his eye. Marcus instinctively twisted sideways and backwards, away from him. As fast as he was the stubby silver blade in Hernandez's hand whipped out and still sliced his cheek, just below his left ear, not cutting deep but leaving a three inch gash that began to bleed freely. Marcus cursed and slapped a hand to his face. When he pulled it away it was covered in blood. Damn, he had forgotten to disarm that little maniac! If he hadn't moved when he did the blade would likely have slashed through his carotid artery, probably severing his windpipe as well. He would have died in moments with his blood mingling with the ancient green water.

"You crazy little bastard!" Marcus yelled, pushing back and out of range from the knife, his free hand still to his cheek. The water around him felt the same temperature as his oozing blood. "I'm trying to get us out of here!"

Hernandez grinned lightly, showing his small teeth, white and even. It was the most expressive he had seen the Mexican's face. His eyes were alight, dancing black motes. "I will not go with the Federales, and neither will you."

He lunged again but the element of surprise was long gone. His natural speed and grace were blunted by the water so the thrust came up short by several inches. Marcus seized the opportunity. He could have played it safe and simply headed out into the Cenote to stay clear of Hernandez, but he was sick and tired of dealing with the little lunatic. He enjoyed a much longer reach and was more at home in the water. That gave him the upper hand. When Hernandez pulled the knife back to try again Marcus surged forward, pulling himself with his right hand, the hand holding tightly onto the rocky side. He swung his left fist as hard as he could. He put not only his shoulder and back into the punch, but all his anger and frustrations as well. As he swung it dawned on him that if he missed he would be leaving himself wide open for an easy knife thrust. It didn't slow him at all.

He didn't miss. He caught the smaller man squarely on the jaw, just below his ear. The impact jolted up his arm and across his back, causing another shot of pain to flare across his right shoulder. It felt as if he'd just broken his hand but he didn't care. It had been worth it. Hernandez's head snapped sideways, the knife tumbling from his limp fingers. Marcus saw it glitter and flash like a darting minnow as it sank into the gloom. The little man's eyes unfocused and his grip on the side slipped limply away. He fell backwards with a small splash. Before Marcus could react he dropped beneath the surface and was gone, swallowed up by the silent green waters of the Cenote.

A short time later a forty-seven year old American tourist from Corydon, Indiana, noticed a figure treading water and yelling something from down in the Cenote. Intrigued, he ambled back to the gift shop where he casually asked the young salesgirl behind the counter how to get down there so he could swim, too, as it was dang hot out there. With his thick country accent the clerk thought she had misunderstood him.

"I'm sorry, Señor, there is no swimming permitted in the Sacred Cenote."

"Ya'all better tell that to the fella' splashing around down there."

It took her a second to register what he had said, but when it finally clicked she sprinted from behind the counter to verify his story. It only took her another second to spot Marcus waving his arms and yelling for help before she was back in the gift shop frantically dialing the Welcome Center. Ten minutes later a uniformed rescue crew arrived, expecting the worst. They were visibly disappointed to find the lone victim alive and swimming peacefully. They had a rope ladder dropped down and a minute later Marcus climbed up, wet, tired, and very much by himself. No one in the gathered crowd noticed when he quietly moved away and picked up a crumpled piece of paper, then surreptitiously kicked a wicked-looking black knife over the edge. It hit the water without a splash and sank to the muddy bottom, gone forever.

When Hernandez finally regained consciousness he felt a rush of panic. It was so dark he could see nothing, no movement of his own hand before his face, no variations of the absolute blackness, nothing. He feared he had somehow gone blind. When he closed his eyes and squeezed tightly he saw deep purple smudges and other imaginary dark shapes and whorls, all conjured up by his mind. But when he opened them again they all vanished into the Stygian darkness. It was dark, death-dark, as dark as a sealed coffin buried six feet underground.

He was lying on his stomach on what felt like a rocky incline. Most of his body was still in the water, but his head and shoulders were out in very damp, humid air. When he moved little splashing noises bounced and echoed around him, seeming to come at him from all sides. Hernandez – whose real name was actually Ramón Calderon – had no idea where he was or how he had come to be there. His last cogent thought was of fighting with that *cabrón* Marcus Schmidt in that disgusting fucking sewage water in the pit. Calderon had tried to slice him and…

…and Schmidt had connected with that huge left hook. He had actually touched him! Twice! No one touched Ramón Calderon! He took a moment to massage his jaw and felt several teeth move and a shooting pain lance up the side of his face to his ear. That big Yankee bastard had probably broken his jaw, too! Dammit! He wasn't clear what had happened next, but Calderon knew he must have somehow tried to swim or crawl to the surface. Instead he had ended up here, wherever here was. He had no knowledge of the extensive network of caves and tunnels running throughout that part of the Yucatan, or that several terminated right there under the waterline at the Cenote. His inability to swim had made him try to climb the limestone wall back to the surface, but in his semi-conscious, nearly drowned state he had clambered into the mouth of this cave instead.

He stood, but it took much more effort than he thought. Soaking wet his clothes were weighing him down, not to mention the extra twenty or thirty pounds of armament he was carrying. His legs were unsteady as he trudged in the direction he considered "forward", out of the water. He shrugged out of his heavy jacket and dropped several pistols and two more knives at his feet where they clunked solidly on the rock. He took another step and smacked his forehead on something hard. He barked out a yell and saw stars swimming in his vision, but they did nothing to alleviate the absolute darkness.

A sudden inspiration struck and he pulled out his cell phone. He flipped the device open and the little screen's blue glow illuminated an area four or five feet in front of him. Calderon felt a rush of euphoria when the hardy phone still worked at all after the dunking, proving that he wasn't blind at least. But any additional hopes of an easy rescue were quickly quashed when he saw the *No Service* indicator. He heard his breathing coming hard and fast and felt his heart hammering in his chest. He forced himself to remain calm, but several deep cleansing breaths didn't do much to help. To regain his self-control he began planning what he would do to that bastard Schmidt once he got out of this place. His revenge was involved, gruesome, and quite entertaining. It included pliers, bolt-cutters and much, much screaming. He would paint himself with Marcus Schmidt's blood. Ah, he could already feel his heart slowing as calm spread throughout him, and that was good – but first he had to find a way out. Survival, then revenge, in that order.

Using the cell phone as a flashlight he looked around. He had whacked his head on a low outcropping of rock. As he surveyed his surroundings he discovered that he was in a low cave of some sort. Behind him was nothing but water and total darkness, the roof of the cave sloping down and meeting the black water somewhere beyond the meager range of his light. He nervously shied away from that direction, refusing to retrace his steps that way. Much to his chagrin, Calderon had never learned to swim. He couldn't imagine going back there into that horrible, wet darkness.

He ducked low and stepped into an open space. The roof above was too distant for his weak light to touch, but he found the gritty floor ahead was relatively level. He moved forward in a shuffling step, carefully placing one foot in front of the other. He looked to the wall at his right and nearly jumped backwards in shock. What the hell? Bright, vivid paintings of gruesome ancient ceremonies were rendered there, horrific depictions of mutilations and beheadings, where genuflecting mortals were pleading for their lives before huge and terrible Mayan deities. The gods were garbed in heavy blue and purple robes and were displayed with multiple piercings of their noses, ears, and tongues. Gold jewelry adorned their bodies, garments, and headdresses. They wielded massive blades. Several humans at their feet had already been decapitated, snakes sprouting from their severed necks like flowering trees. These paintings had never seen the light of day so were as vivid and bright as the moment they had been completed, hundreds or thousands of years earlier. Despite his outward calm Calderon was shaken. Under other circumstances he would have enjoyed the horrid depictions, but not now. What kind of hellish place was this? he thought to himself.

He walked on slowly, his planned revenge on Marcus beginning to dissipate ever so slightly as the enormity of his circumstances began to weigh on him. For perhaps the first time in his life he was beginning to feel the nascent twinges of something, some emotion he hadn't experience before. He recognized it as true, absolute fear, and he did not like it.

He came to the end of the large cavern and found a small, obviously man-made doorway carved from the rock. He had to crawl to enter it. He did so, scraping skin from his knees and hands on the rough surface. Any sound he made echoed back to him a dozen times. In the dim blue light of the cell phone he spied what appeared to be a rectangular altar made of fashioned, carved stones, while scattered around it were large piles of sticks. As he shuffled toward it he pulled up short. They were not sticks, but bones, human bones, tangled up with molding scraps of clothing and hair. Two skulls were set atop the altar, their black eye sockets staring back at him dispassionately. He was not easily spooked but nevertheless quickly skirted the altar and hustled forward, through a wide doorway that opened into an even larger cavern, a cavern so big that his blue light couldn't touch any of the walls or the far side. Ahead was such a deep black that it could have been nothing or it could have been a tremendous chasm leading to the deepest bowels of the Earth itself. He nervously moved forward, shuffling quicker now, fear gnawing at him and displacing some of his earlier caution. Suddenly his cell phone screen flickered. He tried but couldn't stifle a high-pitched yelp as he held the display to his shivering face. Water from his hair dripped a single drop on the screen where it ran down like a solitary tear. The little battery gauge in the corner was gone, replaced by a tiny blinking red warning light. The screen flickered, grew dim, and then died completely. He was left in total darkness.

Terror shredded his self-control. He spun around then sprinted, panic-stricken, his hands outstretched. He bounced off a wall. He ran again before he careened off the doorway and back into the altar room. His breathing was ragged and punctuated by wet sobs that caught in his throat. He smashed face-first into the altar, tripping over the littered bones which sent him sprawling, tearing flesh from his hands and knees. Blood spewed from his nose and mouth but he didn't notice as he jumped up and ran wildly again. He stumbled to his knees on the coarse rock, almost as if he were praying. At that moment he looked hauntingly like a figure from the paintings in the other room, like a mortal about to be sacrificed to a hideous Mayan god. He shakily regained his feet a final time and ran blindly, banging into the altar and bruising his hip before careening wildly into the large room beyond. He suddenly found himself tumbling over the edge of a sheer twenty foot drop. With a horrified scream he twirled and crashed down and felt something snap on impact. His left leg was broken, shattered and useless. He whimpered and cried, writhing around and clutching his wasted leg. Calderon heard hollow, empty clattering noises surrounding him, a haunting sound like a thousand deathly wind-chimes. Tentatively, terrified, he reached out a shaking hand and discovered he had landed in a huge natural pit filled with what felt like more sticks, some as large around as his wrist. He knew they were bones. Hundreds, perhaps thousands of bones. He would never know but he had fallen into a ceremonial dumping ground where those sacrificed to the rain god Chaac had been tossed hundreds of years ago. He tried to stand but his leg was ruined and he fell back down, bones clattering dryly all around him, their jagged ends piercing his flesh. Blood spurted from a dozen wounds, made all the worse by his panicked thrashing.

Calderon screamed, and then screamed again, his tortured and terrified voice lost forever among the ancient dead of Xibalda.

Chapter 19

Marcus hung around the Cenote until nearly seven o'clock before finally calling it quits and trudging dejectedly back to the Welcome Center where he caught a bus back to Merida. His clothes had dried a few hours earlier but they were crusty and smelled foul, a combination of swamp water mixed with sweat. Even worse, his pants and underwear chafed. The cut on his jaw ached, and even with the butterfly bandages holding it together it still oozed if he moved it too much. He was feeling dejected and miserable. He pulled the crumpled note from his pocket and smoothed it flat, rereading it yet again.

Why had someone sent him this note and then not shown up? he wondered yet again. Hernandez hadn't been involved, that much was obvious. The crazy little bastard clearly had no clue what Marcus was talking about. Not a single soul had approached him the rest of the time at the Cenote, except for the tourist from Indiana who laughed hysterically when he found out Marcus had simply "fallen in".

"Shee-it, son," he had remarked, looking at his cheek where the rescuers from the Welcome Center had bandaged him up. "You're lucky to be alive. That coulda' killed ya'. You need to be more careful."

Marcus had agreed, promising to watch his step in the future. The tourist slapped him jovially on the back and walked away, still chuckling.

He gently folded up the note and pocketed it again. He felt he was right back where he had started that morning, except for the very real possibility that he would never have to worry about Hernandez again. That fact almost made his day. Almost.

The bus had been underway for over an hour and a half with Marcus alone in a seat near the front. He did little more than think as he gazed absently out the window at the terrain. Just outside the Merida city limits the bus driver began downshifting, slowing down. Curious, his fellow passengers started murmuring amongst themselves and a few craned their necks to look ahead for the problem.

"Oh, damn," Marcus muttered.

Parked across the two lane highway ahead were three cars in a blockade, all branded with the blue and white logo of the *Policía Federal Ministerial*. Five well-armed men stood facing the bus, motioning it to a halt. They were wearing the black body armor and masks of the PFM. The bus slowed further and pulled to the side of the road with its emergency flashers clicking in a steady rhythm. There were no other cars in sight.

One of the PFM agents walked up to the bus driver's window where they spoke in muted tones for a minute. The driver nodded nervously a few times. Marcus could see a line of sweat running down his neck and into his shirt. The driver looked over his shoulder directly at Marcus and motioned him to come closer. With a sigh he complied.

"You speak Spanish? Very good. These men outside want to talk to you," he said in a whisper so shaky he could barely talk.

Marcus simply nodded. "You're sure it's me?"

"They described a huge blond Gringo and were going to search the bus for him. I didn't want to upset the rest of the passengers. It is you, yes?"

Marcus nodded. "I'll go talk to them."

"Good. I will wait, unless they tell me otherwise. Not that I can move," he added, pointing to the cars blocking the road.

He patted the driver's shoulder and stepped out as the door hissed open. The outside air was beastly hot after the air-conditioned bus, causing his Cenote-fouled shirt to reek again almost immediately. There was no breeze to stir the stiff leaves of the agave plants as they dutifully stood at attention along the road and diesel exhaust from the bus hung like fog in the still evening air. The humidity was so thick he could have been walking through hot water. The PFM agent motioned him to the center car and opened the back door for him. Marcus slipped inside. The car door clunked shut as solidly as a cell door.

In the back seat with him was Cruzado, the agent he had spoken with after the incident at the market just the day before. His mask was off inside the vehicle, his identity secure behind the deeply tinted windows.

Without preamble he said, "So I'm in my office and I hear a report about a big blond Gringo having to be pulled from the Sacred Cenote at the ruins. Curious, because that is my nature, I do a little more checking and find that it was you. The reports don't mention much of interest besides that, except for one eye-witness who apparently no one believed, a little boy from the gift shop who said he saw this Gringo and someone else fighting, and that you both went over the edge."

Marcus didn't say anything. He stared at the young agent's round face. His eyes were in shadow and impossible to read, like windows in a darkened house.

"Oddly, there is no reference to anyone else being rescued, and you were the only person brought back up out of the water. The report makes no mention of anything else, besides the obvious fact that you suffered no injuries except a gash to your face." He peered sideways at the cut along Marcus' chin. "Strange that you could suffer such a wound from a fall into water, from whatever height. To me that would appear to be a knife wound of some sort, and I have seen my fair share of knife wounds." He paused and waited for a reply. Marcus just shrugged.

"Now I would not normally concern myself with clumsy tourists, as I have bigger problems, but when the same person is involved in two odd incidents in two days then I begin to wonder. An investigative policeman many times has to rely on his intuition and mine tells me something larger than these two seemingly unrelated occurrences is going on here." He leaned forward and his brown eyes burned into Marcus, trying to see inside his very soul. "So tell me, Marcus Schmidt, exactly who are you and what are you doing in Mexico?"

Marcus paused. Even before he had been rescued from the Cenote he had been rehearsing what he might say should something like this happen, although he certainly hadn't expected it so soon. He had never considered himself an accomplished liar but he had to make Cruzado believe that he was nothing more than a bumbling tourist with very bad luck. How convincing could he be? If the agent suspected anything and pushed, did more digging, Marcus was afraid the lives of Cassie's parents could be in jeopardy and his search for Rolland could be sidetracked or stopped. He couldn't let that happen.

Just then a sudden terrifying thought struck him. He still had the note in his pocket. That would be, at the very least, challenging to explain if he were searched. So he kept to the facts – just not all the facts.

"Listen, agent Cruzado," he began earnestly, always keeping eye contact. He placed his right hand on his chest in a gesture of sincerity. "I'm just a tourist here visiting my Aunt and cousin. The girl with me had no desire to visit the ruins – she's pretty shaken up from yesterday, as you can understand – and since we're leaving in the next day or two I went ahead and visited them myself."

He went on, not elaborating overly much, and sticking to the truth about ninety percent of the time. He kept making eye contact with the agent, and actually managed some self-deprecating jokes about tripping over his own feet. Cruzado sat and listened intently, but Marcus couldn't tell if he believed him or not. He described in detail his fall and barely making it to the water's surface, and how he had to yell and shout until he was noticed. He claimed to have no idea how in the world he had cut his face. A rock on the wall of the Cenote perhaps?

"And that's it, unless of course that guy from Indiana spreads my name around and someone in California finds out about it. My friends at the University would never let me live it down! Otherwise I'm not telling anyone and I just want to get out of these smelly clothes."

Cruzado continued staring at him in complete silence, the only sounds in the car the drone of the engine and hum of the air conditioning. Marcus knew better than to keep talking now that he had said his piece, so the silence dragged on and quickly became uncomfortable. His natural instinct was to hold his tongue, but he didn't want to raise any additional suspicions in the agent's mind. He decided to break the deadlock.

"So, can I go now? I'm probably stinking up your car, and I really don't want to stain your upholstery. It may never come off."

Cruzado ignored his attempt at humor. "You realize of course that here in Mexico I can take you in to custody and hold you indefinitely? We have no Miranda Rights here. I'm sure it would be several days at least until your consulate was notified and took any action."

Marcus forced himself to look shocked. "What? Why?"

"And I am tempted to do just that. There is something about you, Marcus Schmidt, something that does not make sense. As cavalier as your story is, something is not adding up and I'm giving serious consideration to keeping you in my hands for at least several days while we figure this out."

Marcus began to protest again, but Cruzado continued.

"But I'm not going to. The drug war between El Grúpo and Los Hermanos is getting worse. There was more fighting on the outskirts of Merida today, north of town. Several of my agents were killed as well as some cartel members and a dozen civilians. Two other PFM agents were found decapitated near the coast. Several groups threw Molotov cocktails in bars frequented by cartel members. The total projected dead this year because of these cartels is expected to be more than 7,000. Yes, 7,000!

"So the war continues to heat up, and from what we can tell El Grúpo can't seem to figure out what to do or how to react. They may be too bureaucratic and unable to move, I don't know. They may simply be too frightened. What I do know is that I don't have the time or resources to concern myself with you now. However," he emphasized, "I think it would be very wise if you made plans to leave Mexico right away. Tomorrow would not be too soon. Do we have an understanding?"

He considered another protest, then stopped himself and nodded. "I don't see what the problem is, but we were planning to go home tomorrow anyway."

"Good. So unless you have any information for me, or can help me put an end to these killings, I do not want to hear your name or see you again. Is that understood?"

Marcus nodded. The agent knocked on the glass and the door was opened. Hot air billowed inside, air so hot it felt as if a kiln had cracked open.

"If we cross paths again it will not go well for you, Marcus Schmidt. Say adios to Mexico. Oh, and get some topical antibiotics for that cut before it gets infected. Any pharmacy will do."

The remaining agents slid into the waiting cars then pulled away, their tires murmuring on the hot tarmac. Marcus was left standing there in the scorching evening sun, watching as the vehicles were slowly swallowed up by heat mirages shimmering off the blistering blacktop. In less than thirty seconds they were gone. As he boarded the bus the driver looked at him with wide eyes while the passengers resolutely looked away, as if they were scared of him. The clicking emergency flashers were silenced and the big diesel engine pulled the bus back down the road, the agave plants still standing in silent, eternal attention.

Chapter 20

Otto Doncaster felt like Grade A crap.

He was only dimly aware of his surroundings but knew he had to be in the hospital. He ached all over. No, he didn't just ache. He hurt like hell through and through, from his hair down to his feet. Each pain point was specific and individual, like some sadistic witch doctor was practicing new and interesting acupuncture techniques with an Otto voodoo doll. His head and jaw were banging, his throat felt as if someone had taken a power sander to it, his eye and cheek just ached, his chest was killing him anytime he moved at all, and his legs alternated between screaming agony and itching like mad. Grade A crap, yeah that pretty much described it.

As if through cotton he could hear the steady beeping of several machines. He imagined they were somehow all connected to him and keeping track of his vital signs. He didn't know what all the vital signs were, but he had watched enough medical dramas to know that was what they did in hospitals – they measured vital signs. As long as no one was screaming "stat!" or "he's crashing!" he figured he was having an okay day.

His mind was rather fuzzy as well, and he found he kept napping and sliding in and out of consciousness on a pretty regular basis. He had no clue what day it was and in fact had just recently begun even noticing the difference between waking and sleeping. The only way he marked the passing of time was when a nurse popped in to check out more of his vital signs. Sometimes they talked to him in reassuring tones, which was nice, other times they simply puttered around and tapped one of the lines attached to his arm or fiddled with one of the machines that was outside his very limited scope of vision.

That morning he had discovered something wonderful. One of the nurses had placed a small device in his good hand and told him something. He hadn't caught much besides the few words "push the button". He figured it was a button to call her back, but when he tested it a wave of sheer and utter wonderfulness flooded through his body, as if someone had dipped his insides in warm, glowing honey. He pushed the button a few times before he realized it was not the call button at all, but a morphine pump set up so he could have some control over his own pain relief.

Wow, he thought drowsily. I need the home version of this thing.

In between his fuzzy times he was aware that he had visitors. Jenna, dear Jenna, was there a lot. He had no idea what had happened after blacking out at the Party Barn – and wasn't too clear on what had happened before, truth be told – or what she had done to save him. But she seemed to have adopted him in some way. She was at the hospital way more than anyone, usually sitting and talking to him, watching TV, or just reading. She had been there earlier that morning, stationed at the foot of his bed, leafing through some textbooks before going to school, and if tradition held she'd be there after school, too. She visited a ton and he loved her for it. Whenever she leaned over him her long blond hair fell across his chest and sometimes she put her hand on his forehead. When she did that he was afraid one of his vitals would spike and a nurse would rush in with a crash cart or something. It hadn't happened yet, but that didn't mean it wouldn't.

Of course his folks and his brothers had been there a bunch, too, especially Don-Don. His brother always looked so solemn and grumpy, which, Otto had to admit, was basically what he looked like ninety percent of the time.

He kept asking Otto questions about what had happened and who had done it, but Otto's throat wasn't quite ready to cooperate yet. Add on top of that all the drugs in his system and he wasn't really sharp enough to answer with more than a grunt or a raspy moan. That seemed to upset Don-Don more than anything and he would sit there and *click-click* his pen waiting for Otto to get with it. Eventually he would jam the little notebook into his pocket and hustle out the door with his belt equipment jangling and his neck all red and puffy. Otto wished he could help out, he really did, but his mind and the rest of him didn't want to connect just yet. It was as if his body was a big organic circuit box and several of the breakers between his head and throat were still tripped. Much as he tried to talk he just couldn't generate the correct current to overcome the shorted out parts. He really hoped that would improve in time: how could he sing along with his tunes in this shape?

And speaking of music, that was cheesing him off more than anything right now. He could hear something "music-ish" from what he guessed was the nurses' station down the hall. They had it tuned to some god-awful Muzak station that played nothing but rehashed versions of classic rock and Top 40 songs, only they screwed them up and made them all frou-frou and laced with corn syrup-drenched cotton candy. It made him want to gag. Right now he could hear Van Halen but it was set to harps and cellos. Really? Were they freaking serious?

The Van Halen song mercifully ended with a whimper and another one began. He tried to concentrate on the sappy beginning and shift it to his own reference point, but it sounded so beyond the original he couldn't make the puzzle pieces fit. Perhaps what he needed was another little shot of morphine. Hell that might not help matters a whole bunch, but it certainly wouldn't hurt! He pushed the button and a flood of delicious warmth spread from his arm out through the rest of his body in pulsing waves. His mind seemed to grow fuzzy. No, not fuzzy exactly – but if his thought processes were normally clear cut and sharp, the drug rounded down all the corners and edges, as if a mental router had buzzed them off. He lay back in his bed and dozed again, all anxiety medicinally vanquished.

Some time later he awoke and found a doctor at the foot of his bed reading his chart with a practiced eye. The doctor was a young man not all that much older than Otto, with straight blond hair parted at the side and combed over. It was longer than most doctors his age would have kept it, but on him it looked good and probably helped Otto relate to him. Otto would have laughed if could have managed it: the guy looked like some soap opera doc after a rough night, what with the blond two day growth he sported on his chin and cheeks and the compassionate albeit red and puffy eyes. He was short and stocky and his face was tired, but he had a pleasant, weary smile, the kind that doctors have when they were on their third shift in a row and were a little punchy. He came over to the side of the bed and sat there. It sagged with his weight.

"Hi, Otto, I'm Dr. Wilson. Feeling better today?"

Otto managed a slight nod. He tried to talk but nothing came out.

"We recently moved you out of the ICU and into the critical care area since you seem to be over the worst of it. How do you feel?"

Otto managed another slight nod. His communication options were limited.

Dr. Wilson smiled warmly. "That's great. You gave us quite a scare, you know. I'm not sure if you know what happened, but it was touch and go there for a while."

Otto stared at him, trying to form his eyes into question marks, as if to ask, "Please, tell me more. You have my undivided attention." Somehow the young doctor got the message. Perhaps he had taken mind-reading as an elective in medical school.

"You were in pretty bad shape. Crushed orbital eye socket, five broken ribs, a cracked jaw, broken fingers. Not to mention the contusions and second degree burns to your legs, along with the smoke inhalation. Your throat was burned by the extremely hot air, which is one of the reasons you can't talk right now. We also had to intubate you and place you on a ventilator for a while due to smoke inhalation. Your voice should come back in few days, a little bit at a time.

"What gave us the biggest scare was the internal injuries and bleeding caused by your broken ribs. One of the jagged ends did some real damage in there, including nicking a lung. You're really very lucky to be alive, and I think your friend Jenna should be given a lot of the credit. From what I've pieced together it sounds like you owe her quite a debt."

Otto knew that he did. He knew it very, very well, and would like to thank her somehow. Different, numerous, pleasant ways came to mind.

"Since you're out of ICU I went ahead and authorized the use of the morphine pump, which should help mitigate your pain. We'll start cutting back the available dosage in a few days, but for now go ahead and use it as you see fit. You can't get too much and overdose, and it'll certainly help out."

Yeah, baby, Otto thought. You bet your ass. Keep on pumping.

"I'll be back to check on you later, and the nurses will keep tabs on you as well. If you need them just go ahead and push the button on the side of the bed – " he pointed to a red button built in to the handrail on the side, near his good hand " – and they'll be right in. Okay?"

Otto nodded weakly again, wishing he could say something.

"Great. I'll be back later."

After he was gone Otto decided another nap was in order, although it just sort of happened on its own. When he awoke the first thing he noticed was the daylight outside his first floor room was long gone and the streetlights were on. There wasn't anything for him to do so he concentrated on trying to recall the events of the last few days. He managed to piece most of it together, from when he first met Marcus at Rolland's house, to the horrible time – he shuddered, his stomach cramping – in the Party Barn. He felt a terrible pang of regret at the loss of the Party Barn and was afraid he'd forever be known as the shithead who'd ruined the fun for everyone. Damn.

Most of all he kept thinking about Rolland. He missed him. The guy was arguably his best friend for years, and he wished he were here right now. He missed his sense of humor and his eagerness to party with no strings attached. He missed how he made talking to girls so easy, his talent as an awesome wing-man, and the musical camaraderie they shared. Rolland was a guy who laughed easy and fast and was a blast to be around. Had it really been more than three months since he'd seen him?

Then there was Marcus. It was freaky how much Marcus looked just like his brother, almost to a T. Personality-wise they were nine thousand percent different, that was for sure. Regardless, he really liked the guy and knew if he could help out then perhaps Marcus could find Rolland. There had to be something, some little clue or nugget that he could think of to help, something he hadn't thought of already. Hooking him up with Cassie had been a great start, but he wanted to do more. There had to be something! Come on, Otto, knock the fuzz off your melon, he chided himself. Think!

As he wracked his brain for some way to help his eyes drifted over to the darkened window. There were some bushes and a few small trees out there that were blowing slightly in the wind. The branches danced in the dark, their twisting leaves catching the light from his room like water shimmering over a silent waterfall. It was a soothing visual and he stared at it hypnotically. The drugs in his system prohibited any long bouts of true concentration so he found he had to work to stay focused. His legs itched like mad and the side of his face ached desperately, driving him to distraction.

Outside at the nurses' station another sappy version of some classic rock song came on. He knew the tune, even as marshmallow-cream as it was, but just couldn't put his finger on it. He was pretty damn sure it was a Led Zeppelin hit from the 70s, but the guitar riff had been replaced by freaking violins, he thought darkly, so it was hard to place it for sure.

He screwed his one good eye up in deep thought but the name wouldn't come to him. Angry with himself he exhaled deeply and relaxed, looking back out the window. The leaves continued their convoluted dance and he imagined he could see shapes and images in their movement. In fact, if he tried hard enough he thought he could even see a face peering back at him, a large brown mottled face framed by long black hair, maybe even with an angry purple scar on one cheek.

His heart rate shot from a steady eighty five up to one fifty in the span of two seconds. The even *beep beep* of the heart monitor suddenly spiraled into a crescendo like a pinball game gone berserk. Warning chimes clanged loudly by his head and at the nurses' station.

Shit! Was that the big Mexican? Not again!

Then the face was gone, replaced once again by the gently blowing leaves. He fumbled for the call button but accidentally pushed the morphine pump instead. No, no! Damn, he had meant to call the nurse, not hit the joy juice. But ten seconds later, just as the pain drug suffused his system and started to knock him out, a pretty Asian nurse with the name "Susan" on her badge hustled in to check him over. As she quickly took stock of his condition and vital signs he remembered the name of the sappy Muzak rock song. It was *Black Dog* by *Led Zeppelin*. That was when it finally came to him, the clue he had been searching for: Why was there a doghouse at Rolland's? Rolland would never let Sam sleep in a smelly old doghouse. Marcus had told him the poor guy was still chained to it when he'd found him. There had to be some other reason for it, although for the life of him he couldn't understand why. He had to let Marcus know about this bit of weirdness so he could check it out when he got back from Mexico. Maybe there was something there… The doghouse…

The morphine's warm honey washed over and through him and he drifted away. Susan was still checking him over with a worried look, unable to determine what could have caused such a spike in her young patient's vitals.

Chapter 21

Marcus had envisioned many different scenarios upon his arrival at his Aunt's, but he certainly hadn't foreseen this one.

He let himself in the large front door and made his way back toward the kitchen, calling out for Juanita and his Aunt without any luck, forgetting for the moment how late it was and that Juanita had most likely already gone home for the day. First thing on his mind was to get out of these smelly clothes and into a hot shower, then raid the kitchen and get a bite to eat. It was nearly ten o'clock and it had been a very long day. He felt drained, both mentally and physically. He moved into the dining room. At that moment Cassandra rounded the corner and they stopped and stared at each other.

Oh, boy, here it comes, he thought, bracing for her certain wrath.

Instead she strode purposefully toward him and enveloped him in an emotional embrace, her body pressed tightly to his, her head against his chest. He could feel her breasts pushing into him and his heart skipped a beat. After only a second or two he returned the embrace, and there they stood for nearly a minute, no verbal communication taking place but an encyclopedia's worth of information being exchanged. His head was turned toward the antique mirror on the wall and he found they were perfectly framed in its hazy glass, like a sepia-tinged portrait. Finally she pulled back and looked at him.

"Your cheek. Oh my God, what happened to your cheek?"

He stared at her. It struck him anew how very pretty, how beautiful, she was. Tonight there was something about her, something different. It wasn't necessarily physical. She was absolutely radiant, her immediate concern for him not marring her inherent beauty but actually enhancing it. Her dark hair, usually pulled back into a ponytail, was fanned out over her shoulders and fairly glowed. He gently brushed a stray lock over her shoulder and it dropped back into place like fine silk.

"You know about the note?" he asked softly, reluctant to disrupt the moment.

She nodded. "Your Aunt told me about it."

"Well, there was no one there. It was a wild goose chase. I stayed put until after seven o'clock and nothing."

She was visibly crestfallen. Together they shared a moment of silent frustration. "But wait," she said, her mouth pursed in confusion, her forehead wrinkled. "If there was no one there, then what happened to you? And –" she added, taking a step back " – why do you smell so bad?"

So much for the moment, he thought with a laugh. He smiled at her and plucked at his shirt. "This is the smell of the Sagrado Cenote, I'll have you know. You should be more reverent."

Now her eyes widened and her hand fluttered to her mouth. "You fell in? And how did you cut your cheek?"

Marcus gently took her elbow and guided her upstairs. "Come on. I'll explain as we go but I have to get out of these clothes and into the shower. I had to tip the cab driver extra or he wouldn't even let me in his car, much less take me home."

Together they walked upstairs and Marcus began the story of his long day, beginning with Naibi bringing him the note first thing that morning. He showed her the crumpled paper which she read and reread several times before giving it back to him. As he tossed it on the bed and began undressing Cassie looked away, out the single window at the darkened roofs of the houses down the street. He wrapped himself in a towel and by tacit agreement she joined him in the bathroom, averting her eyes as he climbed into the shower. The moment the water hit him the stench grew stronger, as if it were determined not to succumb without a fight. He scrubbed vigorously at all the nooks and crannies of his body, painfully aware that he was naked and Cassie was just a few feet away, separated only by a thin sheet of colored vinyl. He gave serious consideration to cranking the hot water over to cold just to help keep certain physical changes in check but kept up a constant stream of chatter instead. Steam hung thick in the air, warping all sounds in the small bathroom in odd, cavern-like ways. The water burned when it made contact with his cheek and his right shoulder was still mildly aching from the fall. There didn't seem to be any permanent damage there, thankfully.

"So what do you think Hernandez meant, that Rolland was an errand boy who stole from them?"

Hot water pelted his face and he spoke a little louder to be sure he was heard. "I don't know, but it confirms that he was involved with them. I'm sure it has to do with the credit cards the other one, the big guy, Gonzalez, mentioned before."

"I wish he would have told you more," she said, her voice tight in exasperation.

"Me, too, but I was lucky he gave me as much as he did."

She paused then, as if gathering her thoughts. "And you said that after you hit him, he just, um, sank?" Her voice cracked as she said it. She couldn't help herself – she was uncomfortable talking about the man's apparent demise, no matter what he had been like in life. Of course she had never had the pleasure of his ministrations, like Marcus had.

He had no such compunction, especially considering the several interactions the two of them had shared. "Yep. It was the oddest thing. He sank like a stone, didn't float at all and he never resurfaced. Personally I don't think we'll be seeing him again, and I'm fine with that." He turned off the water and reached out for his towel. She handed it to him from the other side of the curtain, and in that instant their hands touched. That moment, with his flesh scrubbed clean and hyper-sensitive, with his imagination already in overdrive, it was as if an actual electric shock had passed between them. It was both delicious and sensual. Marcus was stunned: he was certainly no teenager longing for a haphazard touch of feminine flesh, no virgin terrified of his first sexual encounter – he had been with plenty of women in his time, but he had *never* felt that before! He almost jerked his hand back and as it was he fumbled and nearly dropped the towel.

"Uh, sorry," he mumbled.

"Sure, no problem," she said quietly in return, as if she too had felt it.

He began to towel himself off. "Um, so, where's Aunt Mary now?"

Cassie laughed nervously and said, perhaps a little quickly, "Ever since Javier got here they've been in the bedroom. You should have seen them. They were like horny high school kids with no parents at home. He barely gave me a glance before they took off and I haven't seen them since. That was hours ago."

Marcus wrapped the thick white towel around him and stepped out of the shower. Cassie was standing there, and she briefly looked him up and down before she caught herself and concentrated on his face. He noticed she was wearing a rose colored blouse with Mother of Pearl buttons that revealed much more of her cleavage than normal, and in fact he just realized how much cleavage she had. The silver cross around her neck glistened with condensation from the steam and was almost white against the darker skin of her chest. There were faint beads of moisture caught in the fine hairs on her arms. Her dark eyes were wide.

They crossed the hall into his bedroom and he gathered up some clean clothes. The room was dark, lit only by the light from a bedside table that left the corners in shadow. The single window was now dark as well. He heard an odd sound behind him that he couldn't identify and when he turned around Cassie was standing there, her face flushed and her breathing heavy. He shot a quick glance at the dresser against the wall and saw her silver cross laying there, the fine chain hanging off the side and swinging slowly. He had never seen her without it before.

"Cassie, I..."

She stepped forward and pressed a finger to his lips. It was warm against his skin, almost hot. With her other hand she tilted his face down towards her and they kissed. Again Marcus felt that electric tingle, although it was much stronger and pervasive this time, as if an actual current was grounding through him wherever their skin touched. Their tongues probed, tentatively at first and then with greater urgency. Marcus suddenly found his arms wrapped around her as of their own volition and he nearly picked her up off the ground. His breathing came fast and hard and he felt a tremendous wave of passion and desire for her smash in to him, a tsunami-like sensation he had never felt with any woman before. His mind ceased to function in its regular measured and rational way. All its energies were focused on Cassie, the dance of their tongues, the crush of her breasts against his chest and the way their hips moved together in a singular rhythm.

Then they were apart, but only long enough for both of them to attack the buttons on her shirt. They were panting, almost frantic, and several of the white buttons that proved too stubborn were ripped off, flying across the room and clattering noisily on the terra cotta floor. On some level he expected her bra to come next, but she wasn't wearing one. His hands each cupped a firm, heavy breast and she hissed in a deep breath, leaned her head back, exposing her throat in a gesture of both submission and arousal. Her jet black hair was shining like moonlight on still dark water.

He quickly moved to the bed and with one swipe of his arm tossed all his smelly and soiled clothes onto the floor. He put one hand in the small of her back and the other behind her neck, and lowered her to the bed. He quickly settled next to her. They kissed and explored each other more intimately, not as frantic now, but with greater passion and intensity. He marveled at how smooth her skin was and how she reacted to a touch here, another one there. She rolled on top of him and shed her blouse completely, revealing herself to him. She leaned forward and shook her hair down so that it partially hid her face. Only her eyes, bright white, could be seen. Her breath came hot and fast.

Marcus reached up and touched her cheek, then ran his finger down her neck and between her breasts. He meant to push himself up with his free hand, but as he put his hand down his ears and mind registered a noise, a tiny crinkling sound, as of paper rustling. He stopped and looked and saw it was the note from the morning, the note directing him to the ruins, the note talking about seeing Rolland again. Suddenly his ardor melted away, his desire for her still strong but once again locked up as tightly as valuables in a vault.

She noticed the change instantly. "What's wrong?"

"Cassie, I can't do this. Not now…not with Rolland still missing."

"I don't understand. Why not?"

He exhaled loudly and looked at the ceiling. "It's hard to explain."

She crossed her arms over her breasts, hiding them. "Try me."

"Really? Now?"

"Yes, right now."

His head thumped back against the bed and he stared upwards blankly, a sudden look of sadness crossing his face. He sighed. "Okay. When I left Rolland three years ago, I had just had it with him, and I didn't care if I ever saw him again. I was done with him. I'd put up with his bullshit for years, and I was just done with him. I went back out to California and didn't care if I ever saw him again.

"Looking back now I know how stupid that was. Those were three years that he and I will never get back, and that's a lot of his life that I missed out on. Part of that life was you and him. You two were…together, almost right up to the time he disappeared."

Cassie leaned over and put her blouse back on. She began buttoning it back up and looked momentarily bemused when she noticed two of the buttons were missing.

Her voice was tight and controlled, but barely. "I told you already that we had pretty much broken up already. I hadn't even seen him for weeks or more by then."

Marcus nodded. "I know, I remember. But while you may think it was over between you two, I can't be sure Rolland thought that."

"So? What do you mean?"

"I mean, that until I hear from my brother that you two were over and done, I just can't be with you. I just can't. I've messed up too much with Rolland already – I can't screw him over again. I won't."

Cassandra stared at him for several moments, then huffed and rolled off the bed. She angrily snatched the silver cross from the dresser and fastened it back around her neck. She stomped to the door then turned and leveled a finger at him.

"I told you your brother and I were done, Marcus Schmidt. Don't make me say the same thing about you and me. Don't be stupid and ruin what could be."

With that she spun and stormed out of the room, slamming the door with such force that the crash reverberated through even the solid old walls. Marcus slowly stood and gathered up his old clothes, and as he did so he felt something in his shirt pocket: it was the silver cross he had purchased from the old lady at Chichén Itzá, the one with the inlaid obsidian and turquoise. He gingerly slid it from the wax paper bag and stared at it, noticing that it seemed to have lost much of its brilliance and was just dull and lead-colored. He sighed and put it back in the bag, then absently tossed it on the dresser. He lay back on the bed and stared sightlessly upward, as if there were no ceiling and he could read the answers he was looking for written in the cold stars overhead.

Marcus woke the next morning around nine o'clock, still on his back and with the towel wrapped – albeit loosely – around his waist. A quick look in the mirror above the dresser showed his short blond hair sticking out at truly amazing angles, an effect a punk rocker from the 80s would have to work hard to achieve. He frowned and tried smoothing it with his hands but it stubbornly refused all his efforts. He glumly surrendered and walked to the bathroom where hot water and a brush put it back in line. He also brushed his teeth and shaved, the morning routine welcome.

Back in the bedroom he noticed that his foul clothes had been spirited away while he had been in the other room and anything in the pockets had been neatly laid on the dresser next to the wax paper bag containing the cross. The bed was tidily and expertly made as well, the bedspread perfectly aligned and parallel with the floor. He silently thanked Naibi and guiltily knew he would sorely miss her behind-the-scenes work when he got back to his apartment in the States. He dressed and walked downstairs for some breakfast, acutely aware how hungry he was since he had never managed to grab anything the night before. And that of course reminded him of Cassie and how badly he had handled *that* whole episode. He didn't blame her for being pissed at him, and he wished belatedly that he had thought enough ahead to have a heart to heart with her and explain everything before they began ripping her clothes off. He had no idea what kind of reception he would get from her this time. His timing, or lack of it, sucked.

No matter what he had told her last night about Rolland, he realized this morning that he couldn't get that electric tingle and the amazing look and feel of her body out of his mind. Marcus felt a twitch in his groin. He resolutely vowed to pack those images and sensations away in a sterile and barren part of his consciousness, the same place he kept uncared for and unwanted information like IRS tax returns and car insurance policies. He had very limited success.

When he got to the dining room his Aunt was already there and seated in what he had come to know as "her seat". She was drinking a cup of coffee, a small Danish of some kind next to the daily paper she was reading. Juanita was humming and clanking dishes and such around in the kitchen. His Aunt looked up when he walked in to the room. She appeared tired but very relaxed and happy. A stray wisp of hair dangled down in front of her forehead.

"Well good morning, dear, how are you?"

He kissed her offered cheek and sat down. Juanita magically appeared at his side with café con leche, a Danish, and some sliced bananas and strawberries in a bowl. She smiled at him and whisked herself back to the kitchen before he could say anything but a fleeting "thank you". Yes, he would miss her and this, too, he thought with a pang.

"Good morning, Aunt Mary. I'm fine, thanks."

She peered sideways at his cheek, which was still being held together by the same butterfly closures. She motioned at his face with her coffee cup and an artful lifting of one eyebrow.

"You want to tell me about that, dear?"

He sighed, not terribly in the mood to recount the previous day's events, but he owed her that much. He gave her the Crib Notes version, omitting his and Cassie's aborted and disastrous late night encounter. While she listened she slowly folded up the newspaper bit by bit and neatly laid it on the table, then sat there and gripped her coffee cup in both hands. Her knuckles were white against the blue ceramic of the cup when he got to the part with Cruzado stopping the van on the highway and his strong "advice" to leave the country as soon as possible.

When he had finished he drank some coffee and they were both silent. Juanita's humming drifted into the dining room. Upstairs he could hear Naibi vacuuming one of the rooms, probably his.

"So then you're leaving today?" she asked, referring to Agent Cruzado's firm recommendation. He could tell she wanted to talk more about yesterday but was holding herself in check. "You haven't found out very much about Rollie yet though, have you?"

"I've got about all I can, I think. I need to talk to El Señor before we go, if that's okay. That's what I came for in the first place, really. After that I think we should leave. That was made pretty clear to me yesterday."

"Of course, dear, by all means I think you should listen to what he said, although I'll miss you terribly." She sighed and took a slow sip of her coffee. "Javier should be down soon. He's just finishing up in the shower and getting some things together before he leaves. Again."

Marcus nodded. Inventorying his findings he knew that he had uncovered some scattered information about Rolland and this entire mess, but all it really did was serve to highlight how little he actually knew. He had to fight back his disappointment at this lack of material success since he had first shown up in Wayne. How long ago had that been? It felt like years, but had really only been a matter of, what, weeks? So much had happened to him in that short span of time.

The two of them were quiet then, a little melancholy that he would soon be leaving and aware how long it might be before they would see each other again. For the moment they were content to eat breakfast in each other's silent company. If he caught sight of his Aunt out of the corner of his eye he was still shocked at how much she physically resembled his mother. At times her mannerisms were also amazingly similar, too, such as the way she held her head when she read the paper, or the graceful and languid way she would rise from the table. He once again marveled at how much this place, and these people, felt like home to him. He would do everything he could to not wreck that. These relationships were too important to him, his only anchor to what most people considered a normal family life.

Marcus devoured his initial breakfast offering and Juanita brought out several more plates of food. She patted his shoulder as he thanked her again around a mouthful of fresh tortillas, scrambled eggs, and additional servings of fruit. The diminutive cook had never quite gotten the hang of scrambled eggs, but they still weren't too bad.

"So, dear," his Aunt asked at one point. "I notice Cassie's still upstairs. Is she coming down for breakfast soon?"

He muttered something around a mouthful of food and downcast eyes. She peered at him with a quirky, questioning expression, but he didn't elaborate and she thankfully dropped it.

A few minutes later he heard dress shoes clacking on the floor tiles and he looked up from his plates, the fork filled with scrambled eggs held halfway to his mouth. El Señor strode in to the room.

He was a handsome man; there was simply no arguing that point. Like Santiago he was tall for a Mexican, right at six feet, and kept himself in surprisingly good physical condition. His black suit was impeccable, tucked in just right at the waist then flaring out to accentuate his shoulders the way only an expensive, tailored suit can. His hands were huge, the only aspect of him that seemed out of proportion at all. On his right hand was a brilliant diamond ring; on his left was his wedding band that seemed dull and tired by comparison. On someone else a diamond ring that size would have looked gaudy, but on him it just seemed to fit.

He was blessed with the looks of a network anchorman, his facial features even and symmetrical. His thick black hair was combed straight back so that his prominent widow's peak seemed to point straight down at his nose, directing attention to the center of his face and to his eyes, which sparkled over high cheekbones. His chin was square and solid, and he bucked Mexican convention by sporting no facial hair. He was a man who filled a room with his presence, a man that most people liked to be around. Marcus had never been able to warm to him, but he, like nearly all others, was nevertheless drawn to his strong personality. His Aunt's face brightened when he swept in, like a flower opening to the morning sun.

"Javier, dear, good morning," she said in her very fluent Spanish.

He smiled and went to her side, kissing her warmly. He placed his hand on her cheek as he kissed her, the diamond ring winking. Her shoulders slumped gently in pleasure in a voiceless sigh.

"Good morning, my love," he replied, also in Spanish. He spoke and understood English quite well, but never deigned to speak it in his own home, his castle. He walked back around the table and extended a hand. Marcus stood and grasped it firmly. His palm was dry and his grip was very strong.

"Good morning, Señor, it's good to see you," he said.

"And you, too, Marcus." He moved to the head of the table and sat down, and in an instant Juanita was at his side with black coffee and toast. He paid her no attention as he took his first sip and the little cook silently vanished back in to the kitchen. The two men exchanged pleasantries for a few minutes and then El Señor came to the point. With him it was nearly always business first.

"So, Mary tells me your brother has gone missing, and that you have suffered through several rather bizarre incidents both here and in the States. Is that true?"

"Yes, sir, it is."

"And that you think one of my old drivers is somehow involved? Tell me - why do you think that is so?"

Marcus shifted in his seat, suddenly nervous under Javier's steady gaze, as if he were a teenager again. There was nothing threatening or in any way menacing in his Uncle's words, actions, or demeanor, but Marcus felt a tickle of anxiety nonetheless.

His Aunt had already apparently briefed her husband, but Marcus went ahead and explained in more detail what had taken place at Rolland's house and then at the Sagrado Cenote. He described Hernandez very thoroughly, from his outward appearance to the fluid and athletic way he moved. When he dove into greater detail about the small attacker – his almost unnaturally smooth skin, his hard, pitiless eyes, his violent nature – Javier's eyebrows raised and his eyes unfocused, his thoughts momentarily elsewhere. He tapped his large forefinger on the table, much as Santiago had the day before.

"This man was proficient with a whip, you say?" he asked.

"Yes. Very. And he was fond of using it, too."

The front door clunked open just then and the two men paused to see who it was. Santiago walked in, almost tentatively, his smile nervous and a little twitchy. He looked quickly from Marcus to his father, his gaze swinging back and forth like a man at a tennis match. He relaxed a notch or two when he determined they were simply talking and at ease. Javier didn't appear to take note of his son's behavior.

"Hello, father," he said.

"Santiago, what a nice surprise." He stood and gave his son a perfunctory hug, a gesture with little sincere warmth, one given out of habit as much as anything else. The younger man gave his step-mother a peck on the cheek.

"So this man, Hernandez, he was short, very ruthless, and he moved like an athlete? You think he was a driver for me a number of years ago, correct?"

"Yes, that's correct."

Juanita served Santiago some coffee and a plate of the pastries. He ignored both her and the food and watched the other two men with wary interest, and stared frankly at Marcus' wounded cheek. He had an antsy, edgy look about him, as if he were dying to ask what had happened but didn't dare interrupt the conversation. Mary was also listening intently but had a more benign expression on her face. She nibbled at a pastry.

"Well, if my guess is right, then your attacker was Ramón Calderon, and he was indeed a driver for me a number of years ago."

Marcus' heart leapt. Perhaps he could finally find out what was going on here, what the connection to Rolland and these crazy people was.

"But I'm sorry to say he was only in my employ for a short time. He was too, shall we say, unstable and prone to violence to be effective at his job. I had to let him go almost immediately."

Marcus tried to hide his disappointment. "Damn. That sounds like our man. Why did you let him go? I mean, what else can you tell me about him? Who was he?"

"Oh, that's easy," Javier said with a casual flip of his hand. "I know all about him. He was very famous in this part of Mexico. He was a killer."

Marcus sat back in his chair in shock until he realized what El Señor really meant. In Spanish he had used the word "matador", which translated literally into "killer" in English. But as in all languages a single word could have two or more meanings, and in this case Marcus realized he intended it to signify a bullfighter, the man who wore the brilliant suit of lights and *bicome* hat, who several hundred years earlier would have been considered a courageous, valiant warrior. While modern day matadors were not held in as high esteem as in the past they were still gifted athletes who had to be quick, graceful, and very talented to survive the "corrida". A slow or clumsy matador did not enjoy a long life.

"That would explain a lot," Marcus mused out loud. "His expertise with the whip and the fluid, athletic way he moved. His violent personality."

El Señor nodded and took a sip of his coffee. "He was only with me for a few months, as I recall, and there were several incidents where he was too aggressive while in my employ. He was quick to anger when a more diplomatic approach would have served us better. I recall an incident where a passerby simply tapped my parked vehicle with his hand, innocently, and Calderon attacked the man. We had to pull many strings and call in some favors simply to keep him out of jail and us out of the news. He had a temper and was trouble, and we were happy to be free of him." He tapped the table again and looked at Marcus. "Many years ago I learned – if someone is not working out it is best to cut them loose sooner than later. Always remember that." He shook his head at the memory. Then, changing gears, he asked, "And you said he never surfaced again in the Cenote after he attacked you with the knife?"

Marcus pointed at his wounded cheek. "After he gave me this and I hit him, no he didn't. He sank like a stone and he never came back up. If I had to guess I'd say he was dead." It felt odd to speak like that, to refer to someone's demise as easily as he might talk about the weather or a sports score, especially a death that he himself had likely caused. He involuntarily traced his sliced jaw with a finger, but still couldn't bring himself to feel any remorse at the man's presumed death.

Javier nodded sagely, but not very sadly, and his voice didn't reflect any distress. He pursed his lips. "What a shame. He was quite famous in Mexico for his skills in the ring. A pity he was somehow involved in all this and came to such an end."

Marcus didn't think it was such a pity, but he kept that opinion to himself.

"Honestly, I had no contact with him after that," Javier continued, "and I don't recall seeing his name again in the papers or elsewhere. You didn't talk to that agent, this Cruzado, about him then?"

"No, I thought that might cause more, ah, trouble than I could handle," Marcus admitted.

Javier nodded again, and Marcus thought both father and son seemed to relax a fraction, as if they had been silently holding their breath. Santiago was staring at his father with a deliberate, steady gaze, his coffee and pastries still untouched before him. He lit a cigarette and took a deep draw, holding it in his lungs for several seconds before blowing it steadily out. The glowing red end of the cigarette twitched ever so slightly in his grip and the smoke twisted and writhed in front of him like an ephemeral, coiling snake.

Javier said, "Well done and I agree. The law in Mexico is not as, shall we say, *defined* as it is in the States, and you could have found yourself in some significant legal trouble. As it was," he remarked, pointing at Marcus' cheek, "I think you should consider yourself extremely lucky to have survived your encounters with this Ramón Calderon. It sounds like he was quite experienced in all this, and perhaps more vicious than even I knew."

Marcus nodded and gingerly touched his wounded face. "I agree. I'm hoping you can tell me something else, anything, really, about him. Rolland was somehow involved with this Hernandez, this Calderon, as well as the huge guy, Gonzalez. Hernandez told me my brother was no more than a tool, an errand boy, someone who stole from them. I'm assuming it has to do with the credit cards they've mentioned, but I don't know for certain."

Javier sipped his coffee and thought briefly. "No, nothing else, I'm afraid. It was years ago and I had no reason to keep track of him. I'm sorry I can't be of more help to you. And I certainly don't know anything about any credit cards. Again, I'm sorry."

Marcus slumped slightly in his seat. "Yeah, me, too."

"But I wish you the very best luck with finding your brother. That is very distressing, and if there is anything I can do please tell me."

There was a heavy silence then while they all digested the fact that Marcus and Cassandra's trip to Mexico had likely been a bust, that little or no additional information had been uncovered. The only positive that Marcus could see was the possibility that Hernandez was dead and would not return to threaten them again - although the other one, Gonzalez, was still lurking out there somewhere. As liberating as the man's death was, Marcus was no closer to the truth than before. Depression settled upon him again as he realized how little progress they had made.

Javier broke the silence. "Let us not dwell on this anymore. You are here, safe and sound, and we should rejoice in that much at least."

Much as Marcus didn't feel like rejoicing he managed a thin smile. Mary chimed in and spoke of Cassandra and what an adorable couple they would make, which caused Marcus to quickly change the subject to general happenings in the States and, more specifically, his life at the university. Soon they were all talking and laughing more easily, even Santiago, and they kept Juanita bustling in and out of the kitchen with more food and drink. The mood in the dining room lightened appreciably.

"So tell me more about this girl, Cassandra," Javier said. "Where did you meet her?"

"In Wayne at a place called Foley's Diner. She's a waitress there, but her parents actually live not too far away from here, outside of Merida."

"Really?"

"Yes, and as much as she'd like to see them while we're here, I'm afraid we've worn out our welcome and need to go back. Hopefully when all this is over I can make it up to her."

As the chatting continued and they fell in to their familiar routine of years past, Marcus suddenly had a very strong, almost fervent desire to ask El Señor about his work and what he actually did for a living. For some reason he couldn't fathom he felt he needed to know this now more than ever. He waited for a pause in the conversation, prepared to simply go for broke and ask flat out, but at that precise instant he made eye contact with Santiago. His cousin stared back at him, wide-eyed and tight-lipped, and very subtly and firmly shook his head side to side little more than an inch, with a firm, non-verbal "no". Marcus raised an eyebrow in a silent response, but Santiago looked away and jumped into Mary's chit-chat about some shopping expedition she was planning. Then the moment passed and Javier stood up.

"I will be leaving in a few minutes, and will be gone for a week or more," he said. "As you said, you will be going back to Ohio sometime today?"

"Yes," Marcus confirmed, "that's the plan. Our flight is at two o'clock this afternoon."

There was a heavy knock on the front door and Javier checked his watch. "Ah, yes, there is my driver now. Naibi!"

The shy maid silently slid into the open doorway adjoining the courtyard, her hands clasped nervously in front of her and her eyes partially downcast.

"My bags are packed and at the front door?"

She nodded wordlessly.

"Excellent." He touched the corners of his mouth with his napkin and tossed it on the table. He shot the cuffs of his jacket with a practiced motion. "Mary, my love, please see me to the door."

Mary sighed deeply and slowly stood, her palms against the table, pushing herself up as if she were pushing away a tremendous weight. She moved deliberately around and took his outstretched hand. He extended his other hand to Marcus, who stood and grasped it firmly in his own. As before his Uncle's grip was strong and dry, almost too strong. Had Marcus been a smaller man, or unprepared, that handshake would have been uncomfortable. The two men locked eyes.

"Good luck finding your brother. I hope for the best, but sadly I fear the worst."

Marcus didn't quite know how to respond to that, so he said nothing.

Javier released his grasp and moved toward the front door, Mary a step behind and clearly in tow. He patted Santiago's shoulder as he passed, then was gone, his absence making the room somehow seem smaller. Marcus could see the huge front door open, and caught a glimpse of a large black SUV waiting outside. He couldn't see the driver through the blackened glass, but if history was any indicator then there were several more people inside. For a moment he saw Javier and his Aunt framed in the bright doorway, their black silhouettes coming together as one irregular shape as they held each other in a long embrace. Then he was gone and the door was shut with a resounding boom, almost like a mausoleum door closing. His Aunt walked quickly up to her room without a word, her eyes and face red, a hand shielding her face.

Marcus watched her go but didn't fully comprehend her emotional reaction, having not been privy to the talk she'd had with Cassandra the day before. But as he thought back over the conversation he had just completed with his Uncle, he found it a little odd that El Señor had never once uttered Rolland's name.

Chapter 22

The rest of the morning was a blur of activity. Santiago wished him the best of luck and gave him an unabashed hug before he readied himself to go, saying he had to get to class. About the same time Cassie came downstairs and he embraced her as well. She hugged him back, albeit with less enthusiasm. He was out the door in a swirl of cigarette smoke and a traditional colloquial farewell, *qué le vaya bién*. After he was gone and they had a moment to catch their breath, Cassie sat and Juanita brought her some breakfast. The diminutive cook hustled back to the kitchen where they could hear her humming an old Mexican folk song. Marcus suddenly realized they were alone. He almost wished someone else would join them in the room, but of course no one did. He sighed and cleared his throat.

"Cassie, about last night…" he began hesitantly.

She stopped him with a raised hand and he stumbled to a halt.

"It's obvious you have some…issues to work out," she said evenly, no anger evident in her voice or manner although there was no overt warmth to speak of either. "Until then I think we should take a step back and wait and not push anything."

Marcus sighed heavily. "Thanks. I was afraid…"

"I'm not done yet," she said, more firmly this time, taking control of the conversation. "You're not off the hook, mister. I think we could have something very special together, you and I. I like you, Marcus Schmidt, I like you a lot. But," and she raised a finger and pointed it directly at him, centered on his chest, "like I said last night, your brother and I were finished before he disappeared. If discovering what happened to him will settle this once and for all then we've got even more reasons than ever for finding him." She softened slightly. "But I'm not going to wait forever. This is not open-ended and can't go on indefinitely. I can't do that. Do you understand?"

It took him a second, but he nodded in both comprehension and admiration. She continued to surprise him. He found himself more attracted to her all the time, which made last night even more confusing and uncomfortable. She was fiery, emotional, and unpredictable, and at that moment it was all he could do to resist the urge to walk over and kiss her.

"Is that a deal?" she asked finally.

"Yes, sure, it's a deal. I can't ask for anything better than that."

"You're right. You can't." She exhaled and smoothed the silver cross at her chest. "Now let's get to work." She pulled out her cell phone and gestured to it. "I got a call from Donald this morning – that's why I was late coming down for breakfast – and he filled me in on Otto."

Marcus pulled up a chair beside her. His voice was eager and anxious.

"And? How is he? Is he better?"

She patted his hand, her demeanor softening further.

"Yes, he's doing better and the doctors have their fingers crossed that he'll be okay. He is still in Recovery and will be there for several weeks yet, they think. But he is getting better. However, for some reason last night he got very agitated at something, but he's been unable to talk because of damage to his throat and vocal cords."

Marcus twitched as if jabbed with a needle when she described their young friend's condition. She noticed but pushed on.

"He finally got some girl named Jenna, whoever that is, to get him some paper and a pencil, and he wrote one word with his good hand. Doghouse."

He sat back, confused. "Doghouse? What the hell does that mean?"

She shook her head. "I don't know, but he wrote it twice and this Jenna told Donald that she finally figured out that he insisted we know about it. He thought it was important for some reason."

Marcus wracked his memory for a moment and his thoughts circled back to his brother's house in Wayne. "Well there's a doghouse in the backyard at Rolland's, right where I found Sam's body. In fact Sam's remains were still chained to it. I remember thinking it was odd that he owned a doghouse for Sam at all. I mean, hell, he treated that dog better than some people treat their own kids. But honestly I haven't really given it a second thought as busy as we've been with everything else. What in the world would a doghouse have to do with anything?"

"Beats me. That's all I know, that he thought it was important for some reason."

"Come on," he said, standing abruptly, "We need to get ready to go. I want to get home and look at that doghouse."

She took a hurried sip of her coffee. "I wonder what's so important about this doghouse? I don't understand."

"I don't either, at least not yet. But if Otto thinks it's so important that he went through all that to tell us, then it's something we need to check out."

Now that they were preparing to leave a sudden thought came to him from something he and El Señor had discussed. "Wait a minute – I promised you that we'd visit your parents while we were here. We need to do that."

Cassie shook her head. "No, not now. Cruzado told you to leave, and besides I don't want to draw any more attention to them than we have to. I'm already worried sick about them, but I'd rather get this mess cleaned up first. There will be time for visits in the future."

He knew how hard it must be for her not to see them, especially as geographically close as they were. Again he was tempted to kiss her right then and there, which would certainly violate the deal they had just made. He settled for gently placing his hand on hers: the electric tingle was still there, but it was softer, mellower, less urgent.

"Thanks. When this is over I promise you we will come back. That's my deal to you, okay?"

She nodded mutely and together they went upstairs to gather their things. They had a long trip ahead of them but finally had some direction. As Marcus methodically checked his room to make sure he hadn't forgotten anything one thought kept impinging on his mind and bouncing to the foreground: Doghouse? Why would Otto be so insistent that they check out the doghouse?

Aunt Mary came downstairs to see them off. She was the picture of perfection once again and showed no outward signs of her previous emotional outburst. Her oval-shaped face was artfully done up, the highlights in her brown hair shimmered. Marcus thought she could have graced the cover of any glamour magazine, and he again felt the emotional tug as he witnessed the ghost of his mother in her features and movements.

"Dear, it's been wonderful having you and Cassie here, and you know you are welcome back anytime."

Marcus gave her a long hug. In the middle of the embrace he thought for a second that he felt her breath hitch once, but when they pulled apart her countenance was steady and composed. He had never been able to figure out if she felt emotional displays were weak, or if she was simply afraid that if she started crying she might not be able to stop. Regardless, as she looked up at him her eyes were clear. She patted his chest with an open palm.

"Be sure to take care of Cassie, dear," she said. "She's a dear, and you two would make a wonderful couple."

"Mary!" Cassie admonished, but her tone was light and playful.

"What? Well, you would," she insisted with a smile. The two women hugged as well, and while out of Marcus' earshot they whispered a few sentences to each other. Mary tenderly touched the younger woman's cheek and then called for Naibi and Juanita to say their own goodbyes. The small cook came out of the kitchen wiping her hands on her cotton apron. Naibi quietly entered the room with her head down. Both wished the travelers well, and Marcus had to insist that Naibi not carry their bags to the curb.

As they stood on the sidewalk waiting for a passing cab, he looked around. He saw the house with its monstrous, steel-banded door, wrought ironwork protecting the windows, and the solid blue walls. For some people a structure like that could be seen as a prison, but for him it had always been a sanctuary, a safe refuge against life's cruelties. It had been a home to him and Rolland when they had nothing else and nowhere to go. For some children having to move there would have been a traumatic event beyond their comprehension – losing not only their home, friends, and family, but their country and language as well. But to Marcus it had been a revelation, an epiphany. It had not only released him from the burden of caring for a drunken, violent father, but had permitted him to be an actual teenager for once, responsible for no one but himself. He had embraced the culture and people to the point where it had become not just his passion, but his vocation.

These people were his family, not only Mary and Santiago, but Naibi and Juanita, too. They had shown him and his brother unconditional love and affection from the onset, taking them in and caring for them as if they were their own. He would never forget them and what they had done.

A green and white Nissan cab approached them and he broke from his introspection long enough to flag it down. It whipped over to the curb and screeched to a stop, its engine chugging and misfiring, purple smoke burping erratically from the tailpipe. The burly cabby roughly tossed their luggage into the trunk. Initially he looked to Cassie for instructions, bypassing the obvious gringo, and was visibly shocked when Marcus spoke to him in perfect Spanish, telling him their destination was the airport. He smiled: so many times people jumped to conclusions based on stereotypes and insufficient information, and so many times they were wrong. The group said their heartfelt goodbyes again, promising to keep in contact. After the two of them had clambered inside, the taxi pulled away and roared off like a robber from a bank heist. Marcus twisted in his seat and looked back, watching the blue house fade from sight and feeling a bit emptier than before.

The trip to the airport was uneventful besides a few of the standard gut-wrenching moments in traffic. The decibel level in the cab was high enough to cover their conversation, but not so loud they couldn't talk. Even so they spoke in English, their agreed upon common language.

"You have a wonderful family there," Cassie commented.

He nodded. "Yes, I do. My brother and I were very lucky to have them."

They traveled several more minutes in silence, both content to dwell within their own thoughts and not minding the occasional lulls in conversation. Marcus was trying without much success not to think of her next to him, especially when a swerve or bump in the road caused their legs or shoulders to touch. His mind was telling him one thing – *no, no, off limits!* - but his heart was telling him something quite different.

"Did Donald say anything else about Otto?" he finally asked.

She blinked twice, as if coming out of a dream. "Ah, no, that was it. I didn't have a very good connection, and I really don't like talking to him more than I have to."

He considered leaving that live wire alone, but figured talking was probably better than the train of thought he had been trying to avoid. "Why? Didn't you two used to date, back before Rolland?"

She swiveled her head to look directly at him, her ponytail whipping over her shoulder. Surprise was clearly written on her face.

Marcus smiled. "Otto told me you two used to be an item, some time ago."

She trained her eyes forward again, her mouth tight. "Otto talks too much."

He laughed. "Probably, but it did clear up some questions I'd had earlier, like why he was always pissed at me, even though he didn't even know me."

She gave a derisive sniff, not quite a laugh. "That's one of the reasons we broke up. I couldn't even smile at anyone in Foley's or anywhere else without him getting all bent out of shape. It was ridiculous."

He nearly said, "I don't blame him", but the judicious side of his nature won out and he held his tongue, merely nodding sagely. He'd never considered himself the jealous type before, but perhaps that was simply because he had never found the right woman. Would he be jealous of her now? He glanced back at Cassie, thinking. He wasn't so sure, but he had a nagging feeling his reaction wouldn't be any different from Doncaster's.

Cassie pursed her lips and stared evenly at him, as if she were trying to divine his thoughts. He met her gaze with innocent eyes, as bland as if they were watching a boring documentary. Finally she broke eye contact when he raised his eyebrows at her questioningly and he breathed a sigh of relief.

They traveled in silence for a few minutes while the taxi driver weaved in and out of traffic with practiced ease. The inside of the cab smelled faintly of fried food. A cheap blue and white plastic Madonna was glued to the dashboard and looked at them with an empty, lopsided gaze, as if she were eternally confused and slightly befuddled. The burly driver had the radio tuned to a sports channel where multiple voices heatedly talked over each other about a Mexican National soccer game from the night before.

Marcus turned to Cassie again. "Have you had any more contact with…whoever it was that was texting and calling you?"

Cassie looked at him once before returning her focus on the road ahead. They passed dozens of tiny shops, *tiendas*, with kids playing outside on the sidewalks. People were standing around talking and laughing. A small market on the left was fronted by several vendors cooking local dishes, and the smell of tortillas and salsa drifted into the car's open windows. She finally shook her head.

"No, nothing since my text to him about the Party Barn."

"But you've still got the number, right?"

"Of course. It's still in my phone."

He nodded. He was starting to formulate next steps, some way of bringing this to a close once and for all. The plan was in an early embryonic state, little more than vague shapes seen moving through a fog bank, but he finally had some idea what he wanted and what he needed to do. It was one of the family's Christmas puzzles all over again, however this time he was the person in charge of the design, he was the puzzle master. Whatever he did, however he managed to bring this to a conclusion, he needed to keep everyone safe and out of harm's way while still concentrating on finding Rolland. The shapes in the fog were ephemeral but the more he methodically thought about what to do the more defined and distinct they became.

Minutes passed and he saw Cassie staring at him out of the corner of his eye. The skin of her face was tight with concern, her mouth a compressed line.

"What?" he asked.

"You. You're planning something, aren't you? I can tell."

No sense avoiding it, he thought. "Yes, I am."

She leveled a finger at his chest. "Don't forget your promise. Whatever you do, whatever you're planning, you won't let my parents come to any harm. You promised."

"Believe me, I remember. If it looks like anything could happen to them I'll back off. I don't want anyone hurt, but we have to figure out a way to end this thing."

The look on her face still held traces of doubt, but he could tell that deep down she knew he was right.

"As it stands now none of us are safe," he continued. "Gonzalez is still out there, as well as God knows how many other people, including the man behind the texts, the guy in charge. None of us, including your parents, are safe until we shut this down and stop them. It's time we end it, and hopefully," he said with a sigh, "hopefully along the way we'll find Rolland, too."

Her hand drifted to the silver cross at her chest and she rubbed it while she digested what he had said. The silver winked sunlight at him and he intensely recalled her taking it off the night before and what that had meant. So absorbed was he by the sight of her that the taxi and the outside world retreated from view, moving far away. For a short time it was only the two of them there, momentarily insulated from the horrors and troubles of the outside world. Finally she nodded, a tiny, almost imperceptible movement of her head, and he knew she was on board.

"Yes, I agree," she said.

"You trust me?"

"Yes, I trust you. We have to stop this once and for all. We have to."

As he reached out and took her hand, lowering it from the cross, she raised an eyebrow in surprise. He held both her hands in his: they were trembling ever so slightly, quivering like an injured bird. He held them, his strength combining with hers. There wasn't anything romantic in this gesture; rather this was a show of solidarity and mutual strength. They remained that way until they arrived at the airport. He didn't let go until the taxi driver opened the back door and gruffly demanded his fare.

They passed the time at the Merida Airport watching the scattered televisions that were hanging from the walls and ceilings. The top story was of a firebombing at a local warehouse that was suspected of belonging to El Grúpo. More than a dozen workers had been killed along with a score of attackers and several policemen. On the other side of town six men were found, their hands bound, efficiently and cleanly killed with one shot to the back of the head. Marcus remembered Cruzado's heartfelt assertion that his city was being torn apart, destroyed by the cartels and their violent ambitions. He couldn't imagine being charged with putting an end to this horrific bloodshed and what he would be going through day after day, worrying not only for himself, but for his men and family, too. Cassie sat there as if carved from ice, stunned and silent, thinking about her parents and the danger they were in as well.

"We'll figure something out, I promise you," he whispered to her reassuringly, like a doctor consoling an ill patient. She didn't answer but leaned against his shoulder as if to gain fortitude from him. She pulled her haunted gaze away from the news reports and stared out over the busy tarmac where baggage handlers were busy loading suitcases of all sizes into the belly of the plane. He felt the tension in her body slowly lessen.

Soon afterwards the flight attendant began the boarding call. They gathered up their carry-on items and got in line. Forty minutes later they were in the air and headed northwest toward Houston. Five hours after that they landed at the now-familiar Dayton International Airport. Their traumatic experiences were behind them and already beginning to fade, as if they belonged to someone else.

But as withdrawn as Cassie had become, Marcus was even more so. Several events from their trip south of the border were bothering him, and the more he thought about their time in Merida the more worried he became. He stroked the wound on his cheek: it itched now, forever to leave a visible scar. He was afraid that the puzzle pieces he was working into place involved people he loved. That potential scarring was worse than any physical wound he could possibly suffer.

It was dinner time when he finally dropped Cassie off at her house. They walked to the door together, Marcus having graduated to carrying her bags. He waited until she checked inside that all was well before he would leave. Her brothers were in watching television and they greeted her distractedly but warmly, almost as if they weren't aware she had been gone. He set her bags on the threshold.

"I'm going to the hospital to check on Otto," he told her.

She nodded in mute agreement, expecting it, and told him to call her afterwards. He hesitated, unsure what to do next, before finally giving her a quick peck on the cheek. It brought a fleeting smile to her face. He again marveled at how much he loved to see her smile, and how wonderful it would be to see that on a regular basis…somehow.

Back in the rental he drove the several miles to the small county hospital, but was balked from seeing Otto by a large nurse named Millie blocking his way as effectively as a left guard protecting a quarterback. Visiting hours were over and no amount of cajoling could convince her to let him pass. In an angry funk he stalked off to the rental car. He steamed in silence as he drove back to Rolland's quiet house in the country, his thoughts focused squarely on Otto but involuntarily drifting over to Cassie whenever his concentration lapsed.

He didn't know what he expected to see as he pulled up to the house – Rolland standing there smiling, the yard trimmed and neat, the Honda Civic cleaned up and ready to roll – but nothing had changed. It was still the same sad house, the only difference that he could see were the addition of several more bagged newspapers scattered about the driveway. The mailbox was stuffed with more envelopes and magazines. He sighed and eased the car in and slowly got out. The sun was low in the western sky and it threw odd shadows from the trees onto the dirty white siding of the house, making the dingy structure look like a fledgling artist's charcoal sketch, all blacks and whites with no shades of gray. The leaves on the trees surrounding the property were motionless in the still evening air with the only sound the ticking of the car's cooling engine. When Marcus shut the door several birds squawked and jumped out of the bushes nearby. They circled once and were gone, faint motes in the sky.

Marcus dug the house key out of his pocket. It was still as shiny and bright as a penny soaked in ketchup, the edges sharp and unforgiving. Instead of going straight in he methodically checked around the house, looking for signs of forced entry or anything else that might be amiss. In the backyard the grass was even taller but Sam's mounded grave seemed a little flatter, as if the dirt had settled or rain had washed some of it away. Perhaps the earth was already claiming his remains and before long the mound would be gone altogether. He looked long and hard at the doghouse but resisted the urge to inspect it just yet. He needed to be satisfied that he was alone and no one was watching before he made any moves towards that. Content that the place was secure he circled back to the front and unlocked the door. He glanced at the screen door and noticed the hole where Gonzalez had punched him a week or so ago. His sternum no longer hurt, and remarkably neither did his back: not only was Hernandez gone, but the remnants of his ministrations had nearly faded as well. Good riddance, he thought, walking in and flipping the light switch.

Inside nothing had changed. The place still looked like a college kid's rental house, what with the mismatched furniture, lack of wall hangings, and a general air of shabbiness. Sure, it had never been much to look at even before those two maniacs had trashed it, but right now it was home and he was determined to make the most of it – starting with something to eat. How long had it been since he'd eaten? He couldn't recall.

The IGA milk had expired yesterday so he poured that out – no sense taking chances. The eggs had another week on them so he scrambled four and made toast, flipping the bread in the malfunctioning toaster so both sides would brown. He had added a little cheese to the eggs so they had some extra body and flavor, and he had to admit to himself that he was getting better at this each time. Belatedly he wished he hadn't poured out the milk.

Full, he unpacked and made sure the house was bolted up tight. It wasn't very late but he didn't have anything to read and the television was just a random heap of electronic flotsam in the trash bag out back. He turned the small radio on and tried to find something decent, but with all his diligent channel surfing he only found commercials or talk radio. Disgruntled as well as tired from the long day of travel he decided to call it a night. He planned on checking out the doghouse first thing in the morning. Maybe, just maybe, he could finally get a clue as to what was going on. And Mrs. Kerr across the street, he really needed to talk to her. That was tops on his agenda as well. He at least had the next day roughly mapped out.

As much as he thought sleep would elude him, he was wrong. He was out in less than a minute.

Marcus was up and around first thing, anxiety and excitement pushing him along better than a stiff tailwind. After a quick shower and a bite to eat he was dressed and ready.

He stepped out the back door. It was early-morning quiet, the type of quiet that was nearly unrecognizable to someone used to the city and its inherent, underlying hum and buzz. Dew collected on the toes of his shoes and quickly soaked through to his socks as he made his way around the yard. The long, thick grass made a swishing noise against his jeans and tugged at his ankles as he walked. He went and stood before the doghouse.

It was large, as it would have to be for Sam. It was constructed of tan painted wood with real shingles for a roof. All in all it was in better shape than the house, he mused grimly, surveying it with his hands on hips. This didn't surprise Marcus in the least, seeing how his brother had doted on his dog. He took a last look around and saw no one so he began his inspection. He walked around the perimeter and looked up under the eaves, running his hand into out of the way places. He completed his circuit without success. Back at the front he stared at the dark opening, hesitant for some reason to proceed. Finally he got on his hands and knees and stuck his head in the door.

It took several seconds for his eyes to adjust to the gloom, and when they did he sighed deeply, touched. Up against the back wall was a ragged piece of blanket and two chew toys, one a yellowed plastic pretzel and the other a fake rolled up newspaper that said "The Daily Growl" in chipped black letters. He remembered those from his last trip here. Marcus took a deep breath and tried to look around, but he was limited by the tight doorway and his broad shoulders. He flicked on a flashlight he had brought with him and shined its harsh, objective light inside. He saw nothing else but some dirt and tumbleweeds of Sam's hair in the corners, not to mention plenty of spider webs up high. With a grunt he withdrew and brushed wet grass and dirt from his knees. He scowled in concentration. Otto had insisted that something was peculiar about the doghouse being here, and when he thought back to his arrival a few weeks ago he remembered he had felt the same way. Rolland was not a guy to keep his dog outside without a reason. So what was it doing here?

Marcus circled it again, doing a more thorough job of peering in all the cracks and dark places. He found nothing more exciting than an abandoned mud-dauber wasp nest under one of the eaves and several more spider webs. Frustrated, he went back to the front and stared at it. Well, if there was nothing visible outside, and nothing to be seen by looking in the doorway, then perhaps…

He got back down on his hands and knees and stuck his arm in the door and up toward the apex of the ceiling. Due to the awkward angle and his size he couldn't easily reach up very high. He couldn't see a thing, either. As he continued to grope around his hand brushed something hard and cold. He stretched farther, the edge of the door cutting into his shoulder, until he hit it again. With two fingers he managed to grab hold of whatever it was. He palmed his find and brought it into the light, staring at it.

It was a key, but looked nothing like a standard house or car key. The flat part, the blade, was short and stubby, not more than half an inch long. The body of the key was round and made of orange plastic and had the number 45 embossed in it. He held it up and looked more closely but could see no more distinguishing markings. He decided it must be a locker key from a bus terminal or airport. It was obviously of critical importance to his brother, but how in the world was he supposed to figure out where it went? Even more important, what was locked in it? As he stood there in Rolland's backyard with his feet wet and his knees dirty, he felt his heart beating faster in his chest and a tingle ran down his spine, as if a feather had been drawn down his back. He didn't know exactly what he had found or what it signified, but it was something, and something was better than nothing. He closed his fist on the newfound treasure and felt its sharp edge against his skin. Yes, he thought, elated, this was something!

He pocketed the key and went back inside, a visible bounce in his step. His knees and hands were filthy, and he needed to get cleaned up for his visit across the street. The reclusive Mrs. Kerr was next.

Chapter 23

Her house and property were unchanged from the last time he'd been there, the air of continued entropy clearly evident. The grass was overgrown and weeds were jubilantly winning their relentless war against a lawn that had been well-maintained for years, possibly decades. The paint on the eaves was peeling in big, curled pieces that could easily pass for dirty white taco chips. Some large branches from a nearby tree littered the yard. It was a senior-citizen's home that was simply too much to keep up. Like an Alzheimer's sufferer who had only recently been hale and virile, the deterioration was both inexorable and heart wrenching.

As he approached the front door some overgrown yews by the porch rustled and the black and gray tiger cat poked out its head, its eyes blinking and sleepy. Marcus knelt down and extended a hand, making soft noises. The cat slowly stretched and padded to him. He picked it up, scratching expertly behind its ears, much to its pleasure. He stepped up to the door and knocked gently.

"Mrs. Kerr?" he said. "Are you home? I'd like to talk a few minutes, if I could."

As on his previous attempts he thought he heard the slightest rustling inside, as of fabric brushing against fabric. He waited a few moments and tried again.

"Mrs. Kerr? I'd just like to talk, that's all. Please."

There was no answer. He felt frustration building inside him and forced it back down, taking a few deep breaths to help. He knew he needed to be calm and in control if he had any hope of talking to her. He turned and leaned against the doorjamb, the cat still purring loudly in his arms. His eyes were unfocused on the middle distance as he spoke again.

"I'm just trying to find out what happened to my brother, Mrs. Kerr. I don't know where he is or even what he's been up to for few years. I've been searching everywhere and doing everything I can, but I can't find him. I'm hoping you can help me, somehow."

He waited for nearly a minute, then sighed and gently put the cat down. It rubbed once against his leg and slowly sauntered back into the bushes in a very leisurely, unhurried, completely cat-like fashion. Marcus shoved his frustrations down even deeper and sat down on the step with a huff, determined not to leave until she agreed to see him, however long it took.

Then he heard a faint *click* and he turned around. The front door creaked open three inches and a face, or small section of one, was peering at him through the narrow opening. Several tiny, wrinkled fingers were on the door, holding it open, and a single bright blue eye, its corners wrinkled like a dried out apple, was peering out from only four and a half feet up from the floor. He stood up slowly, afraid she might spook and vanish back into her home like a skittish mouse at the threshold of its hole.

"Mrs. Kerr?" he said softly.

The blue eye bobbed up and down in the tiny slit of the open door. When she finally spoke her voice was oddly firm and strong, not what he'd expected at all.

"Yes, young man, I'm Mrs. Kerr."

He stayed rooted to his spot. "Hi. I'm Rolland's brother, Marcus."

"I know. I've been watching. And listening."

He nodded and smiled, relieved that they had at least progressed this far. "Can we talk a little bit?"

She didn't immediately answer, but the bright blue eye slowly blinked once, twice. Seconds passed while she thoughtfully considered his request. Meanwhile the cat emerged from the bushes and nudged its way through the narrow opening and into the house. She may have taken that as a sign because she opened the door wider, standing behind it all the while as if it were a shield.

"I suppose so, young man. Mr. Whiskers likes you, and that says a lot. Come on inside and let's talk."

He smiled and walked to the door.

"Oh, and would you like a Twinkie?" she asked.

"Um, sure," he replied as he stepped inside.

"Good. I'll brew us up a cup of coffee to go with it. I do love a good Twinkie with my coffee."

Inside the small one-story house he felt as if he had time-warped back thirty years. There was a big console television in the corner that certainly only got VHF channels. The walls were covered in yellowed wallpaper, a complex and busy pattern of blue Greek urns and statues that was peeling back in more than a dozen spots. Several huge recliners and a couch were positioned in a symmetrical pattern and aimed generally at the television, their dark velour fabric worn thin on the arms and stained darker where heads had rested a myriad of times. A scratched coffee table and matching end tables were of ornate dark wood, probably cherry, but now the finish was nearly black with age. An old-fashioned touch-tone telephone was perched on the far end table. The tan carpeting was dingy and matted down where a million steps had trod again and again, on a Sisyphus-like trail from the living room to the kitchen. Dust covered much of the flat surfaces and cobwebs clustered boldly in the corners, no longer concerned about remaining out of sight. There was a kitchen chair with chrome legs and a yellow seat and back cushions, oddly incongruous, positioned by the curtained picture window: that was her spot to watch life, what little there was, as it passed by outside her home. He also detected a medicinal, musty smell that reminded him of hospitals or nursing homes, a combination of cleaning fluids and mold. The general sense of decay outdoors had oozed inside and was in the process of relentlessly taking over, like fall releasing its grasp to winter.

Mrs. Kerr herself seemed to be falling into disrepair along with her property. She was tiny, certainly less than five feet tall, and so frail a sudden breeze might have toppled her. Her shoulders were stooped and her back was bent, as if carrying even her own diminutive mass was too much for her old bones to bear. She shuffled slowly toward a door at the back of the living room, along the matted path in the carpet, to what Marcus correctly assumed was the kitchen. She wore a thick brown bathrobe that buttoned up to her neck with white plastic buttons. It touched the floor and swished softly as she walked, which was certainly the sound be had heard several times from the other side of the door.

"I'll brew us some coffee. Please make yourself at home."

He nodded and watched her go. Her white hair was thick and perfectly coifed, so perfect it had to be a wig. She wore makeup in an attempt to hide age spots and her lipstick was unevenly applied with a shaky hand. But he looked at her bright blue eyes and saw clarity and intelligence, and an analogy came to mind: just because an old car's body was rusty and dented with washed out paint, he shouldn't assume the engine wasn't smooth and strong. It was too early to judge Mrs. Kerr.

He looked around at pictures hanging on the walls and sitting on end tables. Most were faded and dim, grainy with age, but in many he could see a smiling young woman, very pretty and petite, with her arm around a thickset, smiling man sporting great teeth and jet-black hair combed straight back. He knew it was Mrs. Kerr and her husband. The photos progressed in time, sometimes jumping years or even a decade, but in each one the couple was happy and smiling. Even the later ones where he could look through the photographic shell to see the current Mrs. Kerr, they still looked serene together.

"These pictures. Is this Mr. Kerr?" he asked loudly, making sure his voice carried to the other room.

Water ran and there were some clanking sounds before she answered. "Yes, that was Mr. Kerr and me. We would have been married sixty five years next month."

That helped him place her age, which he guessed was early eighties. This photo looked like the two of them in front of the Grand Canyon, and another was of her husband grilling in the driveway of this very house. Other people were around him, smiling and drinking from cans of beer that were opened with pull tabs, not flip tops. They were sitting in aluminum folding lawn chairs made of green and white webbing. The photographer had caught him flipping a blurred hamburger in mid-air. He was concentrating on the burger patty, not looking at the camera. He had on a white T-shirt, and his arms looked large and muscled. Even in the later pictures when his hair was thinning and losing its color, he was still a big, imposing figure.

A few minutes later she came out carrying a brown tray. On it were two cups of coffee, some milk in a tiny, chipped container, and a sugar bowl. Stacked to the side were four Twinkies, still snug in their clear cellophane wrappers. The bright yellow snack cakes were unnaturally bright in the dark room. The tray shook in her hands as she slowly moved forward so he quickly stepped up and gently offered to take it from her. He set it down where she indicated, on the coffee table. She motioned to the couch.

"Let's both sit here, on the davenport." Its springs creaking ominously as his weight settled. She eased down gently into her spot, facing the television, as if moving too quickly were contrary to her nature or simply beyond her ability. The cushions didn't compress under her slight weight.

She looked directly at him, stoic and secure in herself, her initial timidity gone. He had to remind himself again that just because she was old that didn't necessarily have any bearing on her mental acuity. Those bright blue eyes were piercing and true. While there was no malice or artifice in her gaze, it was nevertheless a little unsettling and he resisted shifting nervously on the couch. Then her eyes softened and she smiled, as if she had somehow scored a point in a game he had not intended to play. She sat back on the couch with her coffee cup and saucer in her hands. The cup trembled ever so slightly and the black liquid danced, concentric rings moving across the surface. There was more to Mrs. Kerr than he had initially thought, he realized.

"Have a Twinkie?" she said, motioning to the tray.

Now that they were actually in front of him he couldn't imagine eating one of the cloying snack cakes. He instead reached for the coffee and loaded it up with cream and several spoonfuls of sugar. She looked at him sadly, disapprovingly. He remembered Mary Lou back in the Dayton Airport and her reaction to his coffee preparation back then, and wondered if it might be time to work on taking his coffee straight black.

"No, thank you." He motioned to his cup. "This is just fine."

She expertly peeled back the wrapper from a Twinkie and bit in to it, washing it down with her black coffee. She took her time eating it, like a special treat.

"Fine, but they're better than coffee cake, and they never go bad. That's why I buy so many of them at a time. I can't remember ever having a stale Twinkie."

He let her chew in silence for a minute while he drank his own. It was very strong, even with the milk and sugar. He considered adding more of both to cut it down in strength but he couldn't bring himself to do it under her steady gaze. She finally swallowed and set her cup and saucer down. She placed her hands in her lap.

"So, how can I help you?" she asked. She looked him up and down, as if she were appraising him. "Rolland told me quite a bit about you over the years. In fact I almost feel I know you."

Marcus raised an eyebrow. "Really? What did he say?"

She leaned back against the arm of the couch. "Oh, he was very proud of you, you know. You were the successful one, even if you were a bit of a stick in the mud. Graduated top of your class in high school and college, then on to graduate school and then off to get your doctorate. You were always the driven one between the two of you, of course, and he loved to talk you up to whoever would listen. He was so happy when you got that job in San Diego, he couldn't stop talking about it. So proud. I had to finally tell him to stop. I was tired of hearing about it."

Marcus' throat threatened to clench. He took another drink of the coffee.

"He was quite a nice young man, you know," she continued, very sure of herself and her opinion. "Mr. Kerr died just two years ago, and after that Rolland would come over and help me out whenever I needed anything. I remember," she said, softening and smiling at the memory, "when I got a VCR for Christmas from a friend, and had no idea how to work the damn-fool thing, Rolland came over and helped me record all my stories when I had bridge club. That way I could watch them when I got home. That was so wonderful – I could watch them and skip through all those pesky commercials. It was quite a treat." Her face sagged a little at the thought of her dead husband, and she tamped her eyes gently with a crumpled tissue from her bathrobe pocket.

"Stories?"

"Well, yes, my stories. You know, the soap operas. I hated missing a single day, and I didn't have to after he showed me how to record them. And when the yard got too much to handle he would come over and mow it for me. And he'd trim hedges, pull weeds, whatever I needed. I tried to pay him for his work, but he only wanted me to make him dinner once in a while." She leaned forward and patted his knee. "He was especially fond of my Salisbury steak and potatoes. That was his favorite. Such a nice young man. A bit of a wild streak in him, I have to admit that, but a nice young man anyways."

This was a side of Rolland that Marcus never knew. His memories were parked in a time when his brother was in his early teens, during those black days with his father. More than anything he recalled Rolland doing his best to stay away from home with all its conflicts and fights, and for the most part succeeding very well. It was refreshing to hear he'd been positively impacting someone's life.

"Sometimes he would just come over and we'd sit on the front porch and have coffee and he'd smoke. Mr. Kerr was gone, and most of my friends had passed on, too, and it was hard for me to get out and do anything." She sighed. "That's the worst part of getting old, you know - when everyone else is gone and you have no one to talk to. I look at the obituaries in the paper every day, almost like a challenge, to see who else has passed away before me." She stared at her coffee cup and sighed again.

"Anyway, he'd come over and we would just socialize, like in the old days before Mr. Kerr passed on. He couldn't bring Sam over, of course, since he and Mr. Whiskers didn't get along very well. But even with his help the house and grounds became too much to take care of. And since he hasn't been around I'm afraid nothing much has been done." She gazed around the room sadly, as if truly aware for the first time how the house was slowly falling apart. Her full age showed then, and he saw again just how tiny and waif-like she was. Wedged into the corner of the couch she looked to him like a little girl of no more than ten or eleven, a little girl who was lost and alone.

Marcus set his own cup down. "Mrs. Kerr, how long has it been since you've seen Rolland?"

"Oh, heavens," she said, snapping back from her reverie. She thought and ticked off time in her head. "I'd say at least three months, maybe a little more.

Since before that really bad thunderstorm we had. I hadn't seen much of him before that even, but it certainly has been since then, I'm sure."

"Thunderstorm?" Marcus asked.

"Oh yes, it was a doozy. There was so much crashing and banging I thought the house would cave in. Lots of thunderclaps right in a row, boom, boom, boom. I was sure we'd lose power that day, but we didn't."

A nasty notion struck Marcus. "Are you sure it was thunder? Could it have been something else? Like gunshots maybe?"

Mrs. Kerr's crystal blue eyes locked on him. "Gunshots? Well, I suppose. It was hard to tell what with the rain and all, but now that you mention it I guess it could have been gunshots. I do know what those sound like."

Something in Marcus' expression triggered a reaction in his hostess, because she paused before sticking her hand down in between the couch cushions. She withdrew a small, nickel-plated Derringer. Marcus drew back in surprise. The pistol gleamed in the palm of her hand. The tiny wooden handle was finely burled walnut. She handled it with familiarity, always aiming the two tiny barrels away from them both, her finger never straying toward the trigger.

"Young man, don't look so shocked. Mr. Kerr was in sales and was gone for days and sometimes weeks at a time," she chided. "He made sure I would be safe here in the country and he taught me to shoot. There's also a shotgun behind the front door and .223 gauge varmint rifle in the kitchen. I'm no Annie Oakley, but I'm not bad either. If anyone is going to pester me they will most certainly regret it. I may sometimes act overly cautious, but I'm not afraid to protect myself or my property if I have to, trust me."

He nodded slowly, impressed. "Okay, then. So they could have been gunshots?"

She mirrored his nod. "Yes, I suppose they could have been, but I wasn't thinking along those lines at the time."

"What else can you tell me about that night? The night of the storm."

She considered his question before answering as she neatly tucked the small pistol back between the cushions. His eyes kept straying to the slight bulge there and whenever they did she would smile, her done up lips looking distorted.

"Nothing else, really. Your brother had changed somehow before that. He didn't come over much, and there were a lot of cars and people coming and going from the house. Not the regular people, either. I didn't see his friend's red truck any more, and most of his visitors were foreigners, Mexicans, I guess. They came and went all the time, sometimes at all times of the day and night. I don't know what they were up to, but to me it seemed to be they were up to no good."

"Why do you say that?"

"I don't know, really. But why would they sneak around like that at all hours? They just seemed to be up to no good."

Interesting. "Perhaps you can tell me about the doghouse. Do you know when and why he got the doghouse?"

When she shook her head her hair never moved, staying stiff and close to her scalp like a helmet. "That was the oddest thing," she admitted. "It just showed up one day some time ago, and I asked him about it. He didn't really answer. He said it was for Sam, but that didn't make any sense. He almost never chained him up there since Sam always lived with him in the house. Said he picked it up at some garage sale, but I could never figure out why he had it, honestly. Rather a silly purchase, I'd say."

They sat in silence for a few moments with her opinion hanging in the air. Marcus of course now knew why: it was a rather clumsy attempt to hide the key outside of the house and to use poor Sam as a guard against anyone getting too close. That ploy had essentially worked but at the cost of Sam's life. He felt the key's irregular shape in his pocket as it pressed against his leg, its presence irritating him like a splinter in a finger. He dug in his pocket and pulled out the key. He held it up.

"Mrs. Kerr, have you ever seen a key like this before?"

She pursed her lips and cocked her head sideways. Her bright blue eyes trained on the small key with its orange trim. She squinted at it.

"No, I'm sorry to say I haven't. Is it important?"

Disappointed but not surprised, Marcus sighed. "I'm not certain, but I sure think so. Rolland had it hidden in the doghouse."

"Well then, sounds like you have your next step, doesn't it? Find out where the key goes, and perhaps you can find out about your brother. Seems pretty obvious to me." She reached for the tray and held it up toward him.

"Are you sure you won't have a Twinkie?"

As anxious as he was to head back to the hospital to see Otto, not to mention finding time to be with Cassie, Marcus felt obliged to stay and keep Mrs. Kerr company a while longer. They sat and talked for nearly an hour, covering topics ranging from current events, where she was very well versed, to sporting events. She was especially keen on college football and was a die-hard Ohio State Buckeye fan since that had been Mr. Kerr's alma mater. At one point she motioned to the picture of her husband grilling hamburgers. She always referred to her late husband as Mr. Kerr.

"That was a tailgate party before the OSU – Michigan game. That was always the highlight of the fall, you know, and if the Buckeyes lost he'd be in a terrible mood for days. We've had a wonderful run of late, running over Michigan pretty handily, which would have made him so happy."

They talked idly for a few minutes more before Marcus finally told her it was time to go, but he promised he would come over in the next few days and help out around the place, much as his brother had done. That seemed to perk her up significantly. Her eyes twinkled and she told him she would start a "honey-do" list. He belatedly wondered what he had gotten himself into.

She walked him to the door and squeezed his arm, thanking him for coming over and apologizing for not letting him in earlier.

"There are a lot of bad people out there, and prepared or not I just need to be careful," she said, looking back toward the couch where the Derringer was hidden. He glanced behind the front door and saw the shotgun, a smaller .20 gauge pump action Ithaca, its long blue barrel covered with a thin patina of dust. He had no doubt that the varmint rifle was in the kitchen as she had said, and wondered what other surprises she had in store. Tiny though she was, he had a feeling she was not a lady to be trifled with.

As he walked out the door and said his goodbyes Mr. Whiskers pushed out between his feet and trotted into the overgrown yard, intent on terrorizing any small rodents or birds he could find. Marcus felt a momentary kinship with the cat: they were both on the hunt; only unlike the cat's relatively harmless quarry Marcus' prey had already proven to have deadly claws. The door clunked shut behind him and as he walked away he looked over his shoulder to see the curtain flick open. Mrs. Kerr was again rooted in her spot in the yellow chair, watching the world drift by, taking it all in. He waved and trotted back across the street.

A quick and uneventful drive to the hospital landed him at the front desk of Recovery. Millie the large nurse glared at him from behind her counter as he walked past, and he smiled endearingly at her as he headed to Otto's room. It was lunchtime so orderlies and candy-stripers were pushing carts of food covered in metal lids and cellophane wrap down the halls and into rooms in an odd sort of haphazard precision. He entered room 120, pushing the heavy wooden door open quietly. There was Otto, asleep in bed.

His young friend was still hooked up to several blinking, beeping monitoring devices. Marcus was no doctor so much of what he saw was incomprehensible to him. Some bagged, liquid medicines and saline solution mixtures hanging from poles were systematically being administered through a drip chamber. His face was still heavily bandaged, his casted arm kept elevated by a set of pulleys. The steady beeping from the machines was slow and measured, even soothing. His bruised face had largely cleared up, although much of it was still concealed by the thick layers of gauze, and his long hair stuck out at wild angles from under the wrappings. He looked more peaceful than Marcus thought he would, although his face was pale from so much recent time indoors.

No one else was in the room so Marcus sat in one of the two heavy chairs along the wall and was prepared to wait until he woke up. Twenty minutes ticked by before a nurse, an Asian girl named Susan, came in and looked him over. She jumped, startled, when she saw Marcus, and then smiled at him as he grinned back at her in apology.

"Sorry," he said, "didn't mean to scare you."

"Oh, that's okay. I just didn't see you there. Are you family or friend?"

"Friend. How's he doing?"

She checked a few vitals, looking over the bags of fluids as she referred to his chart. She tapped the drip chamber and consulted her watch before making a few notes.

"He's doing much better, really. I think the worst of it is over, although you'd have to ask the doctor for any details. His doctor is," she glanced at the chart, "Dr. Wilson, but he already made his rounds for the morning. He won't be back until later this afternoon."

Marcus nodded thanks as she smiled and hustled out, on her way to her next charge. The door closed with a silent thump, cutting off some sappy Muzak from just down the hall. He thought it sounded like an Aerosmith hit from the

80s. He sat back down to stare out the window at the tall shrubs just outside. The day was bright and clear but the room inside was dim and in shadows, on par with his mood as he stared at his stricken friend on the bed.

Another hour or so crept by in peace and he took advantage of the down-time by resting in the chair. He really hadn't had much spare time to just sit and think, and he needed this break to look back over recent events. He had conflicting feelings about his brother: he knew that he had been involved with something way over his head, something involving counterfeit credit cards, Mexicans, and most likely guns. But he also knew that the Rolland he had known before, the caring, light-hearted Rolland, was still there. Mrs. Kerr had confirmed that. He shook his head. Really, when it came right down to it, he didn't know what to think anymore.

The door eased open and a tall, cute blond in her late teens or early twenties came in. She wore a baggy T-shirt and what appeared to be flannel pajama bottoms and boots. Her blond hair was pulled back in a ponytail. She was lugging a heavy green backpack over a shoulder, and he noticed with interest some gauze wrappings around her wrists and hands. She saw Marcus sitting there and her brown eyes narrowed in concern.

"Who are you?" she demanded, moving protectively to Otto's side.

Marcus hid his amusement and remained seated, not wanting to startle her by standing and showing his six foot two inch frame.

"I'm a friend of Otto's. Marcus Schmidt. Rolland's brother."

She squinted at him and he could see the wheels of suspicion turning inside her head. She frowned and edged even closer to Otto's bed.

"I don't know you and I don't know this Rolland person. I think you'd better leave."

He held up his hands as if in surrender. "Are you Jenna? Are you the girl who saved Otto from the fire?"

She tilted her head to one side. "Yes. Why?"

"I want to thank you for that and tell you how much I appreciate it. Otto's a great guy and he was helping me out and he got caught up in all this. I never would have forgiven myself if anything…permanent had happened to him. This," he said, motioning toward the machines and bags of medicine, "is bad enough. I hate seeing him like this."

Jenna relaxed, the tension slowly lifting from her shoulders. Her hand drifted to the assist bar on the bed, closer to Otto, and her face softened. Marcus could see how pretty she really was then, and how much she cared for his young friend. He didn't know if they had any history together, romantic or otherwise, but it was quite apparent how she felt about him now. Good for you, Otto, he thought.

Finally she nodded at him. "He told me about you, and a little about what's going on."

"You didn't know Rolland, you said. How do you know Otto?"

Her gaze slid away from Marcus and she smiled warmly at her sleeping charge. There was true affection in that look.

"I knew him before he graduated from high school," she told him. "He was a few grades older than me. We didn't really know each other very well, but were, you know, friendly to each other. I always thought he was cute, even though he wasn't the type of guy I usually went out with. They were usually, you know, the big, dumb jock types, and they only wanted one thing. Most of them were pigs." She rested her bandaged hand on his arm.

"But not Otto. He was always so nice to me, always talked to me. Then he came through the drive-through at work, and I remembered just how sweet he was, and I had just broken up with my boyfriend, another pig, you know, and I decided to give him my phone number, hoping he'd call me and ask me out."

Jenna set the heavy backpack down next to the bed. Her ponytail flopped in front of her and she flicked it back with a practiced move that ironically echoed Otto's own hair flip.

"And then I got off work and was driving home and I got a call from Otto, and he was screaming for help, that he was at the Party Barn." Her voice sounded strained, thick with emotion, and she was leaning toward Marcus to make her point. "He could have called anybody for help, even, you know, 911, but he called me. *Me!* I live out that way, and I was already so close I knew it was karma and I had to do something. I drove like crazy to the Party Barn and it was burning, I mean really burning, so bad that half of it was already gone and the flames were shooting up twenty, thirty feet high. I had never seen anything like it before! The smoke was awful.

"I didn't know what to do. I pulled up to the back, the only part not completely on fire, and I saw Otto trying to crawl out the door. But he couldn't, he was stuck, so I ran up and tried to pull him but he wouldn't budge. So I went farther inside, through all the smoke and fire and everything burning and tumbling down, and saw some heavy beams had fallen and pinned his legs, and they were burning, you know, and I knew I had to get them off…" Her voice drifted off for just a moment and she looked at her bandaged hands as if truly seeing what had happened for the first time. "…and somehow I managed to pick them up and throw them off. It's like they were twigs, you know, the way I tossed them. But they were so, so big and heavy, I still don't know how I did that."

"Adrenaline?" Marcus suggested. "Adrenaline and emotion can make you do amazing things."

Her one hand drifted back to Otto's arm. "Yes, that must have been it. Anyway, I got the beams off and then dragged him out and into my SUV and brought him here. He was such a mess…"

"You were very brave. Thank you for saving him."

"Oh. Well, you're welcome, but it was fate, I'm convinced of it."

"Fate," he repeated.

"Yes," Jenna stated unequivocally. "Fate. And now that fate has brought us together, I'm going to make sure we stay together and nothing else happens to him. I'm going to protect him."

Marcus saw the determination in her brown eyes and her iron-clad will and knew without a doubt that she meant every bit of what she said. For some reason she had, for lack of a better word, *imprinted* herself on Otto, like a baby duckling might imprint itself onto the first living being it saw. She was now *with* Otto, completely and totally. Was it love? He didn't know and certainly couldn't say, especially with his own lousy track record in that department. But he could tell that this girl was not about to let him go, and he hoped that young Otto felt the same way. He wondered what would happen when they realized how little they had in common – she being the driven, athletic type, and Otto being, well, the polar opposite. Time would tell.

"What about your hands?" he asked her, motioning to her bandages. "What's your prognosis?"

"Oh, they'll be fine," she said dismissively, as if her wounds were of little or no concern. "Mainly second degree burns. I'll heal."

"That's great. By the way, just how old are you?"

"I'm eighteen, and a senior in high school. Why?"

"I was just curious why you weren't in school now, that's all."

She gently kicked the backpack at her feet. "I've got a 4.3 GPA, and my last bell is a study hall. Because of that, you know, I can leave early if I want to. And any homework I can get done in here while Otto sleeps. It's all right here in my back pack." She set aside the topic of school and turned to Otto, who was still dozing comfortably in his bed. Not looking at Marcus, she asked, "Has Dr. Wilson been in yet this afternoon on his rounds?"

"No, not yet. Just the nurse. Susan."

Jenna shook her head. "Susan's good, but she's not a doctor. What did she say?"

"She said he is doing well, and seems to be recovering. I've been here for over an hour and he's been asleep the entire time."

She stroked Otto's forehead with her hand and tried to smooth his hair down with limited success. The bandages that covered half his face kept getting in the way. She *tsk'd* and did more smoothing.

"Well that's good. He needs his sleep."

Marcus agreed, and just then Otto stirred a bit and opened his one good eye. He smiled broadly when he saw Jenna standing over him.

"Hi, you," she whispered.

He smiled more broadly. "Hi, you, too," he said, his voice still hoarse from the smoke and scorching heat of the fire.

Marcus walked closer into his limited field of vision and Otto's one eye widened in disbelief. He tried to sit up but couldn't quite manage it. Jenna worriedly, gently pushed his shoulders back down.

"Marcus, dude, you're back!"

"You bet. Otto, it's good to see you."

"Oh, man, it's good to see you, too. Hey, nice scar. Where'd you get that? Catfight down there in Mexico?" His voice sounded strained and scratchy.

Marcus traced the scar on his jaw line, feeling the ridge of new flesh already forming. He smiled at the young man who couldn't have looked much worse if he'd been hit by a train.

"I'll explain later," he replied warmly. "Cassie and I have been a little, ah, busy since you've been out of commission."

"So it's 'Cassie' now, eh? Not Cassandra?" the young man said with a crooked grin. "Making some progress there, are you? Good job."

They both laughed, Otto wincing in pain as it jarred his mending ribs. They spent the next few minutes catching up in general small talk, until a shadow passed over Otto's face. It was as if the lights in the room had dimmed. When he spoke his voice cracked.

“Marcus, man, I should’ve listened to you. I wasn’t careful and I wasn’t paying enough attention and those crazy bastards got me. If it hadn’t been for Jenna here,” he looked her way and she smiled tightly, “I doubt I would even be here now. I’m sure that fire would have cooked me. Really, dude, I was sure I was history.”

“No, Otto, it’s me who should be apologizing. I had no idea how badly these guys want Rolland. I never should’ve left you here without protection or making some arrangements. These guys are crazy and I underestimated their desire, and I’m sorry.”

“What? No, way, man. This is *not* your fault. Rolland is your brother but he’s my best friend. I’m glad I got in this thing with you, and I’m going to continue to do what I can to help.”

Marcus gripped the young man’s shoulder and thanked him, and in some way a nonverbal contract had been ratified between them, that they were still in this together. Then he looked toward Jenna. There were some things he didn’t want her to hear.

“Could you please give us a few minutes alone?”

She looked dubious for a moment until Otto assured her it was okay. She walked out saying she would get some fresh ice water in his pitcher. When she was gone and the door had closed behind her Marcus took a deep breath.

“Okay. First, I thought you should know. I’m pretty sure Hernandez is dead, down in Mexico. He won’t be bothering any of us anymore.”

Otto sucked in a deep breath. “What? How?”

Marcus told him about the note, the confrontation at the Sagrado Cenote, and what had happened after they both had fallen in. He absently scratched at his cheek as he relayed the events. Marcus also told him that apparently Hernandez had had no connection to the note. Someone else, he declared, must have sent it.

"First, can't say I'm sad that crazy little bastard is gone. In fact you just made my day. But if it wasn't him, then who was it?"

Marcus paused. "I have an idea, but it's just that – an idea. Some of the pieces of the puzzle are coming together, but I'm not ready to accuse anyone just yet."

Otto's face clouded over again, and he looked away in guilt and confusion.

"Some of this is my fault," he admitted, his heart a lump of steel in his chest. He had been dreading the time when he had to admit this to Marcus. "When they had me in that barn and were doing…stuff to me, I told them you and Cassie had gone to Mexico to do some more digging. I knew they wanted you, and I still told them. None of the shit that happened to you would have if I hadn't said anything. I'm sorry, man."

Marcus squeezed his shoulder again in reassurance. "Don't worry about it. Believe me, I'm pretty sure they would've known soon enough anyway."

Otto started to ask how, but before he could Marcus dug in his pocket and pulled out the orange key. He held it out and Otto took it in his good hand, looking it over carefully.

"Ever seen one of these before?"

The young man shook his head as he continued to inspect the little key. "No. Why? Where did you find it?"

Marcus smiled. "I found it because of you. Following your lead I looked in Sam's doghouse and it was stashed in there. Rolland hid it. It must be very important to him."

"Number 45? It looks like a key to one of those lockers at the airport, or something like that. What's it go to?"

He hid his disappointment. "I don't know. I was hoping you could tell me. No pun intended, but I'm sure it's key to this whole mess. It looks like I'm going to have to travel all over the county checking every lockbox and storage facility I can find. It's going to be a bitch, I'm sure, but it's got to be done. Think hard. Where would Rolland have hidden something?"

Otto closed his eyes in thought but came up blank. His expression was full of regret. "Sorry, man, I don't know. Nothing's coming to mind."

They talked a minute more. He wanted to quiz Otto about the events at the Party Barn and to fill him in on everything else that had happened in Mexico, but just then Jenna came back in with a fresh pitcher of water. She looked squarely at them both, as if to dare them to kick her out again. She poured a fresh glass for Otto and held it for him as he took a long drink through a straw. When he spoke again his voice sounded better.

"Thanks, hon. So, dude, what's next?"

He sighed and took the key back from Otto, pocketing it. "I'm not sure. I need to find out about this key before I can do anything. Guess I'll start making some calls and checking out different places around here, like the airport and bus terminals. If I can't find anything I'll have to widen my search. I can't think of anything else we can do until I can figure out what this key goes to."

Jenna cocked her head to one side. "Key? What key?"

Marcus hesitated, then figured *why not?* He pulled it back out and placed it in her open palm.

She looked at. "I've seen these before. They go to lockers at the YMCA here in town. I use them all the time when I work out."

Marcus was gone and out the door in a flash, barely taking the time to say goodbye. He ignored nurse Millie as he rushed out the automatic doors to the rental car. Several people walking in to the hospital gave him a wide berth as he sprinted through the parking lot. He knew the Wayne County YMCA was only about ten minutes away on the outskirts of town. His heart was beating fast and hard in his chest. Finally, was this the break he had been looking for? He almost couldn't believe it.

The traffic lights were in a benevolent and cooperative state of mind and he hit four greens in a row. Less than his projected ten minutes later he pulled up to the low, squat brick building that was the YMCA, quickly found a parking spot, and hustled to the front door. The building had been erected in the early 60s and was a sprawling, flat-roofed edifice that looked like several huge, interconnected shoeboxes joined randomly. Its gun-slit windows must have been architecturally popular years ago, but now they came across as dark and impersonal, soulless eyes in an aging beast. As he entered he saw that the interior had been painted in bright yellows, blues, and whites in an attempt to brighten the place up, but it only succeeded in pointing out how dreary it truly was. The narrow windows permitted a meager amount of natural light to enter, and humming fluorescents were employed to pick up the slack. Their white, impersonal light tended to wash out everything, making people and objects appear flat and two dimensional.

An older, matronly woman in her 70s was seated at a desk near the entrance. She had a kind round face and tightly curled gray hair. Her thick arms were straining the sleeves of a thin brown turtleneck sweater. Every Christmas she was certain to be tapped to be Mrs. Claus in some community production. There was a celebrity crossword puzzle book on the desk in front of her. She looked up and smiled as he rushed in.

"ID, please?" she asked in a pleasant voice.

"Um, I don't have one. Would it be okay if I just looked around for a few minutes? I need to check something out."

She paused to think and then waved him on ahead. "I guess that'd be okay. Just for a few minutes, hon."

He smiled at her and the minimal security. "Thanks. Oh, can you tell me where the lockers are? Where a key like this would fit?"

She looked at him and the key in his hand in mild bewilderment, her lips pursed, but pointed down the hall. "Down there, hon, near the weight room."

“Thanks.” He went in her offered direction and through a set of double doors. Ahead of him was a long hallway with several doorways leading to different locker rooms evenly spaced along the right-hand side. Near the end of the hall was a weight room, and outside of that was a bank of floor-to-ceiling lockers, most with orange keys still inserted in their appropriate slots. Marcus spotted the lockers and involuntarily sucked in a sharp breath. He slowed his pace and walked deliberately toward them. There was a smell of chlorine in the hallway that reminded him of a commercial Laundromat, and the back of his mind registered that the pool was to his right somewhere. He was so focused on the lockers staring at him that he didn’t notice the clanking weights, grunts, and muted music from the weight room just next door.

The lockers themselves were nothing spectacular, just beige metal trimmed in blue. They were numbered sequentially from one to one hundred and were a foot and a half square, stacked four high. Most were not being used at this time of day so the keys were still in place. The lockers themselves were a convenience for people working out who didn’t want or need to completely change outfits, for those who simply wanted a secure place to put wallets, purses, or other valuables. It was a quarter to rent one. There was a sign above them that read: *Members ONLY Please!*

Marcus stood frozen in front of number 45. The key in his hand might have weighed a thousand pounds, five thousand pounds. Just like his arrival at the Dayton Airport where he couldn’t take that next step to find Rolland he was having a terrible time forcing himself to look inside that locker. To him it was a terrifying Jack in the Box, its sealed contents to be shockingly, suddenly displayed by the twist of a key instead of a diminutive hand crank. He had no idea what he would find but inside was likely a side of Rolland he didn’t know if he could face. No, scratch that - not that he *couldn’t* face, but didn’t *want* to face. He was keenly aware that once he learned something about a someone, it was impossible to un-learn it. He also understood that whatever was inside that locker, whatever his brother had been involved in, Marcus himself was partially to blame. He stared at number 45 as deliberately as a demolitions expert would study a suspected explosive device. It wasn't warm in the hallway but a drop of sweat like a cold steel ball-bearing chilled his temple as it rolled down.

Suddenly out of the weight room burst three older women, laughing and chatting gaily and sounding like giddy teenage girls. They were tamping their foreheads and necks with white towels supplied by the Y. When they saw him standing there they hushed in amused embarrassment, twittered, and scurried on. Once they were out of sight around the corner he squared his broad shoulders and inserted the key, turning it. He heard the tiniest *snick*, and the door swung open.

Chapter 24

Three minutes later Marcus was back in his car and pulling out of the YMCA parking lot. On the passenger seat next to him was a cardboard box about twice the size of a shoebox. The four flaps of the lid were tucked in to each other to keep it closed. There was a mailing label on the front addressed to Rolland at his rental house. There was no return address on the box that he could see, but it looked like it had originally been shipped by FedEx. An abundance of clear packing tape had at one time kept it securely closed.

He was driving out of town, not certain of a destination. He knew he didn't want to go back to Rolland's house or anywhere he had frequented before for that matter - he was still too irrationally worried that Gonzalez could pop out of the woodwork at any minute. He just wanted someplace safe where he could open it without fear of anyone following or bothering him, but since he had no clue where that might be he was simply driving carefully, blindly. He passed the car wash where Otto had been kidnapped, not even noticing exactly where he was. He pointed the nose of the car out of town and accelerated.

As he was nearing the border of Wayne his cell phone rang and he jerked in his seat, his nerves on edge. He saw that it was Cassie and he quickly answered it.

"Cassie," he said, a little breathlessly. "I've got it."

He heard some dishes tinkling in the background as she said, "Got it? Got what?"

Marcus quickly relayed everything that had happened in the last twenty-four hours: finding the key, visiting Otto in the hospital, his trip to the YMCA. He could tell she was miffed at not being kept informed.

"Sorry, but it all happened so fast. Whatever Gonzalez and Hernandez were looking for I'm sure it's right here in this box."

"Wait a minute," she said, and a moment later there was a muffled thud and the kitchen sounds disappeared. Her voice echoed slightly when she spoke again. "There, I'm in the bathroom and can talk. So where are you going? What are you going to do?"

"I'm just driving out into the country and making sure no one is following me. I want to find a somewhere to open it without anyone around. These guys have shown before how badly they want whatever is in here. No sense just handing it over to them now."

"Well come by and pick me up!" she replied with unrestrained excitement. "My shift just ended and we can go somewhere together."

In his mind he vacillated about her request: he knew deep down that picking her up was not a great idea and may even put her in additional danger - but he acquiesced anyway. He hadn't seen her since their return and the lure of having her next to him in the car was too strong, his heart trumping common sense. He agreed and less than ten minutes later he pulled up to Foley's Diner. Still in her white waitress uniform replete with several food stains on her blouse, she hustled out and slid in the passenger seat next to him, the box in-between them on the bench seat. Her large almond eyes were bright as he locked the doors and they sped out of town. She smelled of breakfast, bacon and syrup.

Looking at the box that separated them, she said, her voice hushed, "So this is it? This is what everything is about?"

He nodded. "I think so." His palms were sweaty on the steering wheel.

"Should I open it?"

Perhaps irrationally he checked all his mirrors to make sure they weren't being followed: if nothing else he had learned the value of caution over the last few weeks. The road was clear in all directions, and now that they had left the city limits they were the only car in sight. He was headed west on a state route. Barns and frame farmhouses blurred by, but only intermittently.

"Yes, go ahead." He was both excited and fearful, his nerves jangling, on edge.

Cassie pulled open the flaps as he forced himself to keep his eyes on the road. She reached in and pulled out a bundle of what looked like business cards secured with a rubber band. But they were too thick, and he could see that they were plastic. Cassie held up the first bundle and inspected them.

"They're credit cards," she breathed, confirming what he had suspected. She dug in the box some more. "It's filled with credit cards. There must be hundreds of them. Thousands! It's full of them."

She pulled off the rubber band and fanned out the first group in her lap, across her apron. They were credit cards, new and fresh and branded with the names of banks from around the US. The first thirty or so were blue and emblazoned with the name and logo of the Bank of America, and the rest of the group were stamped with Chase Bank. Each card had a different individual's name on it, and every one looked clean and unused, as if they had just been pressed. She rummaged around more and pulled out several additional packs that were all neatly rubber-banded together. She counted out the number of cards in a pack.

"There are seventy-five cards or so in each, and it looks like there are about..." she tallied up the groups, counting under her breath as she did so, "...fifty bundles or so. Marcus," she whispered, "there are almost 4,000 credit cards in here! Good heavens!"

Still keeping his eyes resolutely trained on the road ahead, Marcus asked, "Is there anything else?"

"Oh, um, let me see." She stacked more cards on the seat next to her and pushed others around inside the box. "Yes, there's an envelope here." She fished out a folded manila envelope and gently extracted a wad of hand-written green ledger pages filled with tables of names and numbers, as well as several dozen pink and yellow pieces of paper fastened with a paperclip. She fingered through them and her eyes grew wide. The flimsy colored paper crinkled like dead leaves in her hands. She sucked in a breath and looked directly at Marcus.

"What?" he asked.

"They're receipts," she answered. "They're receipts for guns, all kinds of guns." She continued to stare at him, the unspoken question burning in both their minds:

What the hell was Rolland up to?

But Marcus had a feeling he knew, and it saddened him more than he thought possible.

They drove on deeper into the country, the occasional church steeple, grain elevator, or cell phone tower the only structures to break the monotony of the flat farm fields. He saw a sign declaring that Greenville, Ohio, was 15 miles straight ahead and he knew he had to turn around before then. He had no intention of going in to Greenville, Wayne or any other town now, not with the potentially explosive contents of the box spread out on the seat between them. He could think of no way in the world to explain this to anyone in law enforcement if he was stopped or pulled over, that was for damn sure. Cassie rooted around in the box some more and found a yellow flyer for something called Big Bob's Gun and Knife show at a Dayton convention hall. The flyer was several months out of date and highlighted several different weekends the show had been in town. It was similar to the one he had seen in his brother's mailbox.

"Looks like this gun show is a pretty regular thing around here," she said flatly, disapproval thick in her voice. "Why in the world would anyone need to have a gun show so often?"

Marcus shook his head. "People love their guns. I've never been a big fan but I know plenty of people who are. Some people are just nuts for them."

She continued to pore over the brochure. The longer she perused it the more irate she became. "Look at this. I've never even heard or seen guns like these before outside of war movies. They're nasty. Evil." She shuddered and stuffed the flyer and the receipts into the manila envelope before gathering up all the credit card bundles and packing them back in the box. She kept the green ledgers out and looked them up and down.

"What are those?" Marcus asked, snatching a look at her and the contents.

She squinted and looked through them. "I don't know, really," she said finally. "Just pages and pages of names, with some weird names and numbers in columns to the right of each one. Some of them could be dates, I guess, but there are lots of other numbers, too. Maybe you can make heads or tails of them." She folded the pages over and put them in the box, then closed the lid and pushed it away from her as if it were contagious.

"Do you know what all this is about?" she asked. "You're awfully quiet."

Marcus kept his eyes locked on the road ahead. What could he say? That his brother had most likely broken not only state but federal firearms laws as well? Not to mention the counterfeit credit cards and whatever was rolled into those potential crimes. That the brother he had abandoned, that had once been a sweet and carefree kid, was now looking at jail time that could wrap up when he'd be eligible for Social Security?

"I have an idea, yes," he said instead. "But it's just that. I don't have enough information quite yet. But I'm getting closer."

He could tell she was dying to push him for more, to know all that he knew. But he saw her catch herself and sit back, her eyes trained straight ahead, working to keep a neutral expression and not quite accomplishing it. He knew he was much more secretive than Rolland ever was and could see that it aggravated her, but she was learning to deal with it. Good for her.

"You say you're getting closer," she finally said. "I know this is hard for you, learning about Rolland like this."

He nodded, his lips a tight line.

"I just want you to know that I'll do whatever I can to help. You know that."

He finally looked her way and a sketchy smile moved across his face. "Thanks. And I haven't forgotten my promise to you – I will bring an end to this and I *will* figure out a way to make sure your parents are safe, too."

After a few seconds she nodded back at him, the warmth in her eyes calm and trusting. They cruised down the road in silence until they could see some of the industrial structures on the outskirts of Greenville. He ducked down a side road named, oddly enough, Hogpath Road, and did a precise three-point turn. He put his blinker on, eased back onto the country highway and headed back toward Wayne. The silence stretched out between them, but it was easy and relaxed, more like two people that had lived as a couple for years. They could have been out for a pleasant Sunday afternoon drive. Before either of them knew it the brown smudge of Wayne began to coalesce in front of them and traffic started to increase. A red Ford pickup just like Otto's passed them, but it wasn't his: the license plate wasn't DRIVER 8. They continued on into town.

"What are you going to do with the box?" Cassie asked.

Well that was a damn good question, Marcus thought. He had been so intent on finding out what was inside that he hadn't given any consideration to its safekeeping after the fact. It was certainly not secure back at Rolland's house, but he didn't want to put Cassie or her brothers in any danger, either. He thought for a moment more and then drove back to the YMCA. With the engine still running he parked outside the front door and took the manila folder, ledger papers, and a several bundles of the credit cards from the box and handed them to Cassie. He took the box inside, telling her to lock the rental car's doors and wait for him. He was only gone a minute. When he came back he had a grin on his face, hopping in the driver's seat and holding out a small key with an orange body.

"Number 45 again?" she inquired with a raised eyebrow. "Really?"

"Sure, why not? It's been safe and sound there all this time. No sense changing our luck now. Of course I had to promise the lady at the front desk that I was going to join the YMCA before she'd let me pass again, but that's a small price to pay for all this top-notch security." He slid the gear selector into Drive and pulled out.

"Yes, I can picture you doing water aerobics and square dancing once you've got your membership," she added.

They both chuckled as he merged into traffic and headed toward her house, the key gripped tightly in his hand. In his mind he was busy calculating his next step, certain that it involved a visit to that bastion of support for outdoor sportsmen, the National Rifle Association, and the 2nd Amendment. Big Bob's Gun and Knife show.

Marcus asked Cassie to check online after he dropped her off at home and they found that the gun show wasn't scheduled to be back in Dayton for another month. As unflappable as he was by nature this date so distant threatened to push him over the edge: he somehow *knew* in his gut that he needed to attend this particular gun show. He was certain that some answers would be forthcoming if he could just be there. Big Bob's show was important enough that Rolland had kept the flyer in the box, and for some reason gun advertisements and gun references had been popping up since Marcus had arrived in Wayne. To his relief Cassie saw that the itinerant show was slated to be in Cincinnati this coming weekend, both Saturday and Sunday, from nine in the morning until five at night, admission seven dollars, two dollars for kids under twelve. Popcorn and hotdogs available at the concession stand.

"Fantastic," he told her over the phone. "I've got the date locked and loaded."

"Oh, you are quite the comedian," she admonished playfully.

He spent the next few days visiting Otto at the hospital where Jenna grudgingly, slowly began to trust him. During his waking moments Marcus and the young man never discussed the events that had landed him in the hospital, mainly chatting about music and sports. These conversations confirmed his earlier assumption that Otto was a huge soccer fan, which necessitated that the young man spend a tremendous amount of time regaling Marcus with news and information about his favorite British and American teams, trying to convince him it was the best damn sport in the world. Marcus really didn't care for soccer that much but listened attentively and just tried to keep up.

One afternoon while he and Jenna were there and Otto was napping Lt. Doncaster strutted into the room. He froze when he spotted Marcus. His thick face clouded, his neck turning a mottled red as if he were holding his breath much longer than was healthy. He was in full blue uniform, replete with holstered pistol, shoulder mount radio, and foot-long black flashlight. He clanked like the Tin Man when he walked. The ornate gold buttons running up and down his shirt strained mightily against his thick bulk. Marcus may have been taller but Doncaster massed more, and worse, it was *angry* mass.

"What the fuck are you doing here," he growled, taking several menacing steps into the room.

Marcus stood, not backing down, his dislike of the man visibly radiating from him. He towered over the stocky cop. Jenna looked back and forth between them as if she were watching a game of ping pong, concern blossoming on her young face as her mouth formed an O.

"I'm visiting Otto," he replied evenly.

"You and your damn brother are the reason he's here in the first place." His voice was loud in the small room, thick with threat and menace.

Marcus had no comeback for that. He knew Otto's condition was a direct result of his involvement in their affairs. Voluntary or not, he wouldn't be in here if it weren't for them. He didn't need to be reminded of that fact.

"I'm just visiting. I want him better and out of here as badly as you do."

"The hell with that," Doncaster snapped. "Get the fuck out of here!" He moved toward Marcus, violent intent clear in the clenching of his hands, the way his shoulders hunched, the flaring of his nostrils. His breath hissed through tightly clenched teeth.

Jenna perceived the threat and jumped quickly to interpose herself between them. Her one hundred and thirty pounds were woefully inadequate against the combined mass of the two men, but she resolutely stood her ground.

"Stop it, you two!" she snapped, trying to keep her voice down. "Stop it right now! Otto needs his rest and he doesn't need you two in here being all macho and stupid."

Doncaster stuttered to a halt, not at all accustomed to being ordered around by anyone, much less some high school girl. Marcus smothered a smile at her bravado but appreciated it nonetheless. He had no desire to get into an altercation with Doncaster. That was a lose-lose proposition for him. In his bed Otto stirred but didn't awaken. A little moan escaped his lips as he shifted position in his sleep, trying to get comfortable.

"Do you want to wake him up? Do you? And what would he think about the two men he admires most in here fighting? Did you think about that?"

The cop's hands unclenched and he took several deep breaths, some of the fight evaporating. He shook his head silently, like a bull shooing flies. Marcus took a step back and lifted his own hands chest-high in capitulation. Jenna looked back and forth at each of them in turn, her arms still outstretched, until she was certain they would behave.

"Any more silly outbursts like that and I'll have Millie in here. She'll kick both of you out of here in a second, I mean it!"

The tension in the room eased, now simmering coals where there had been a raging firestorm. There would never be love between the two of them but they could at least operate under a tacit truce on Otto's behalf. Jenna lowered her arms and went back to Otto's side. She placed a tender hand on his shoulder.

"Good. Now instead of fighting with each other perhaps you can actually work together to find who did this to him and, you know, arrest them or something."

Marcus nodded his agreement, although he doubted Doncaster would ever share information with him. The cop crossed his arms and stared silently at him. The flesh around his neck subsided to a more natural color. Marcus decided to toss out the first friendly volley.

"Don't bother looking for the little guy, Hernandez, the one that did all the damage," he told him. "He's gone, out of the country, and I don't think he'll ever be back."

Doncaster cocked his head sideways, his eyes still suspicious. He took his little pad of paper from his shirt pocket then plucked out his Bic pen. He clicked it several times. *Click-click-click.*

"Why do you say that?"

Marcus ran several answers through his mind before he settled on one.

"Trust me. He won't ever be back."

Their eyes locked and the cop gathered this deeper meaning. He grunted once and jotted down a simple note. He closed the notebook and slid it back into his pocket. Both men looked at Jenna but she either wasn't listening or wasn't concerned. She was still stroking Otto's arm as he dozed peacefully once more.

Marcus decided it was time to go. He left the two of them at Otto's side, not really caring but knowing that he had possibly redeemed himself in Doncaster's eyes to a small degree. That could come in handy later.

The rest of his free time he spent catching up on his running and having as many meals at Foley's as he could without being labeled a stalker. The staff had since been assured by Cassie that he was okay so they no longer freaked out when he came in. He soon discovered that their panic at his first visit had stemmed from Cassie's original fear that any dealings with Rolland might further endanger her parents. She had told them all in no uncertain terms to stay away from him. So of course Marcus, looking so much like his brother, was enough to confuse and shock them all. Relationships were now to the point where even the original blond waitress that he had met weeks ago, Alice, could talk and smile at him without treating him like robber holding her at gunpoint.

He became a regular at Mrs. Kerr's house as well. She always had a honey-do list of chores for him to tackle and he did so with gusto. One day it might be as simple as raking leaves or sticks, and other times something more complex, like unjamming the disposal in her kitchen sink. She repaid him as she had done with Rolland, with home-cooked meals, and her Salisbury steak really was quite good. They were becoming fast friends and enjoyed their time together. Mrs. Kerr remarked several times that he reminded her of her husband.

He also spent time poring over the various documents that had been left in locker number forty-five. There were pages and pages of hand-written spreadsheets on green ledger paper, all in the same format: Column A was a single number or letter, usually a P or a D, that meant nothing to him; Column B was a first initial then a last name, and in many cases the same name cropped up over and over; Column C was always a number that may have been a price or dollar amount as they ranged from 800 to upwards of 2500; D was most certainly a date from mid-summer to January of this year; E was obviously a phone number with area code, and F seemed to be some sort of descriptor, like

DPMS AP4 308. Marcus spent some time in the Wayne Library on the public computers and Googled the descriptor field for each line. What he found didn't surprise him at all: every single entry from Column F was the description of a gun, always a rifle, and nearly always a semi-automatic assault rifle at that. When he searched for DPMS AP4 308 he found this:

Again listening to the demands of the customer, DPMS unveiled the LR-308 AP4. Featuring a standard A3 height receiver rail, with forward assist and dust cover, standard A2 front fixed sight, detachable rear sight, and a collapsible stock, the AP4 caught the attention of recreational and competition shooters, as well as the law enforcement and military community.

Its popularity as one of the most compact, light, and yet effective 308 carbines on the market earned it the title of NRA rifle of the year.

He researched many others and to some extent they all read similarly, a technical and impersonal narrative on grisly machines designed to kill and maim. He sat back in his chair in the booth at the library, running his hands over his face, despondent over the crash-course he was getting in personal firepower. He leafed through the spreadsheet and looked over the Name category next. As he had noted earlier most names were repeated at least two or three times, but someone named F. Lucas showed up twelve times, and R. Sandoval ten. Did that mean they had purchased twelve and ten weapons? What where they doing, planning on starting a war? Who in the world would need that many damn assault rifles? Unless…

Unless they weren't the end user.

He could almost see the light bulb shining over his head as this revelation hit him. If F. Lucas and R. Sandoval were buying these guns for someone else, if they were straw purchases, then that would make a whole lot more sense. If everyone on this spreadsheet had purchased a weapon – he roughly tallied up the total number of names – that would mean an astonishing five hundred straw sales of high-powered weapons in a very short period of time. That wasn't the number of weapons that could win or even tilt a conventional war one way or the other, but he figured it would certainly be enough to give an upper hand to an *unconventional* one. If there were more sales that he didn't know about, if these sheets didn't encompass all the activity, then who knew how many straw purchases had actually taken place? It gave him the shivers. This was bad, very bad, and his brother had been in the thick of it.

Saturday morning arrived and Marcus was driving down I-75 through Dayton toward Cincinnati, the skies low and heavy, the occasional drizzle and mist making windshield wipers necessary but annoying. In Mexico the locals had called rain like this *chipi chipi,* pronounced *cheepee cheepee*, a light mist that confounded and defied umbrellas, rendering them virtually useless. The day was gray and flat, little more than a washed out watercolor landscape.

As he continued through downtown Dayton he was not surprised that the highway crews were at work again. He remembered a joke about Ohio – the four seasons in Ohio were actually spring, summer, fall, and orange barrels. Some stretch of road always seemed to be under construction between Dayton and Cincinnati, and the traffic patterns meandered and snaked this way and that so often it felt like a different road each time, to the point where some GPS navigation systems mistakenly thought drivers were headed in the wrong direction on the highway and wouldn't stop barking frantic orders to make a U-turn.

Marcus looked at the empty seat next to him. Cassie had intended to go along on the short day-trip but had been called in to work at the last minute due to two of the Saturday girls calling in sick. She had not been pleased and he knew that Sal, the owner of Foley's, would certainly hear about it all morning. Poor Sal, Marcus smiled to himself, you're in for a rough day. While he missed her company he knew in his heart that having her attend a gun show would be akin to tossing bloody chum in a shark tank before diving in. Her hatred of guns would certainly drive her to the point where she'd cause a scene, which was not what he wanted or needed. No, it was best that she was not here, although doing what was best didn't always fill the growing hole he felt when she was not around.

Just under two hours after he left Wayne he pulled into the parking lot of the suburban Convention Center outside of Cincinnati. He expected to see a mass mob of pickup trucks with gun racks, and for the most part he wasn't disappointed. However there were also quite a few mini-vans, SUVs, and the occasional high end German luxury sedan scattered around. He parked next to a gaudy, bright yellow Hummer that dwarfed his rental before making his way to the main entrance.

As he began to merge with the small crowd of people standing in line to buy a ticket, something grabbed his attention that he had not expected: at least one out of each three attendees was carrying one or more guns into the hall. Most were looking to swap or sell, although he later found out that many attended for accessories such as additional clips or scopes. The practice he found most bizarre and intriguing were the individual sellers who had rifles slung across their backs with little flags stuck in the barrels, touting a brief description of the weapon and a selling price, like *AK-47, great condition, $1,200 or swap.* These hopefuls wandered the aisles up and down, over and over, hoping to make a deal. *AK-15, like new, make offer!*

He bought his ticket and lined up at the entrance where an off-duty cop asked him if he had any guns to declare. He shook his head no and was indifferently waved in. He followed the crowd and entered the main hall, still not fully aware what to expect next.

The first thing he noticed was the smell, an odd mixture of hot dogs and machine oil. The setup itself was fairly austere – no music, a few banners, people talking in low voices. Each booth was very basic, some looking homemade, most housed by bored, overweight people in ratty lawn chairs. Several of the booths were more professional-looking, and a few of these were manned by rather attractive young ladies displaying enhanced cleavage and bright, alluring smiles. These booths were busier than most, he noted with amusement, with a large contingent of men hanging around trying not to look too interested. Surprisingly several booths weren't selling guns at all, but exhibited a variety of knives, clips, stickers, NRA patches, and bumper stickers railing against Islamic extremist groups like Al-Qaeda. Actually, some of the most vitriolic slogans were against the US Government itself, which he hadn't expected. Two groups were pushing conceal and carry classes for $199.00. As he moved with the crowd, which naturally bore to the right, he was bumped by two young boys, no more than seven or eight years old, as they surged ahead of their harried, weary father who was pushing a stroller with an infant daughter. To Marcus the operation felt like a low-rent flea market, albeit a very well-armed one.

He really didn't know what to do next so he continued to be carried along by the colorful and diverse crowd, like a woodchip caught in a gentle river current. He knew he didn't belong there and felt ill at ease and self-conscious, as if he were sneaking around some hallowed ground where bold signs flat-out declared NO TRESPASSING. However not a single soul paid him any attention or challenged him. He was perhaps more clean-cut than most but he saw several very well-dressed men and couples wandering the aisles as well. His trepidation eased so he continued on. He made it a point to look at every booth and make eye contact with each vendor, no matter what they were selling. About a third of the attendees wore some type of camouflaged apparel, and more often than not each person wore a ball cap, most emblazoned with a gun manufacturer or farm equipment slogan. Had smoking been permitted in the hall he had a feeling the vast majority of the shoppers and vendors would have been happily puffing away. Tattoos were all the rage.

Several feet away an individual seller with a rifle strapped to his back, a crudely written For Sale sign stuck in the barrel, stared at him curiously. When Marcus made eye contact he quickly looked away. The abnormally skinny man had long, stringy dark hair tied back in a ponytail and was in his early fifties and looked like a lost, aging biker. Several dark, smudged tattoos of eagles adorned his scrawny arms. His eyes were abnormally bright, like glass marbles under a spotlight. The man glanced quickly back over his shoulder then walked stiffly away, quickly losing himself in the crowd. Marcus craned his neck and tried to follow him but was balked by a half dozen burly men who had just entered the hall. They were laughing and carrying on, slapping each other's backs and thoroughly clogging the walkway. By the time he got through them the aging biker was gone. He cursed and hoped he'd soon cross paths with him again.

Marcus was beginning to feel less uncomfortable as he realized no one but the aging biker cared or even noticed he was there. He moved on and was idly checking out a rack of hunting knives with tremendous, serrated blades when he heard a voice calling from down the aisle to his left.

"Yo, Rolland! Hey, Schmidt!"

He almost dropped the huge knife as his heart skipped a beat. Fortunately he was taller than most of his fellow shoppers so could easily crane his neck to scan the crowd. At the end of the aisle he spotted a booth with a banner across the top that read *Ohio Gun & Knife Swap Shop* in red and black letters. Inside it a man was waving at him. Marcus dropped the knife and politely but firmly pushed his way through the other attendees to the booth, never losing sight of the man.

He was short with a sturdy build. He had thinning blond hair that clung to his scalp like a cap, the light-colored hair in stark contrast to a round face that was red and rough from excessive sun and exposure to the elements. He sported a blond, three-inch long King Tut goatee that bobbed when he talked, like something on a ventriloquist's dummy. A glistening gold chain that was nearly as thick as an index finger adorned his neck like a trophy, and two gold signet rings gleamed on each ring finger. His arms and chest were thick through his shirt, a sure sign that he spent his fair share of time in the weight room, probably on the bench press. When he smiled he showed small, even teeth, no larger than baby teeth, tiny and undersized in his mouth. His hips were narrow and his stomach hung over his belt, but he wasn't fat. As Marcus stepped up to the booth the man's small-toothed smile faltered and slipped for just a moment, his face momentarily scrunched up in confusion as if he'd perhaps swallowed something unexpected, like an insect.

"Well I'll be dipped in shit," he said in a deep, husky voice. His accent was thick and southern. "Hot damn, I thought you were someone else."

"You called me Rolland," Marcus stated. "That's my brother."

"Yeah I did at that," the man admitted with his unnerving smile. His teeth were kernels of baby white corn. "From twenty feet away I couldn't tell the difference. Damn, ya'll could be twins."

"We get that a lot. If you don't mind me asking, how do you know my brother?"

The man paused and thought, looking away. He pursed his lips and sucked air through them in a hollow, toneless whistle. It was clear he was thinking hard.

"Well, I'm pretty busy here and really don't have time to shoot the shit. Got a business to run, you see."

Confused, Marcus looked around. The Ohio Gun and Knife Swap Shop booth had been relegated to a fairly low-rent spot in the convention hall. It was tucked back in a corner and enjoyed very little natural foot traffic. He was the only customer there right now. In fact, he was the only one within fifteen feet.

"What do you mean? You don't have any other customers."

"Sure, but if people see me talking to you then they won't come up and buy nothing. This is my livelihood, you know."

Oh, so that was how it was, Marcus realized.

"So you'd like me to buy something, I take it."

The man's face brightened. "I think that would be right businesslike of you."

"Fine." Marcus looked over his inventory. The table top that made up the booth was filled with knives of all kinds, from small pocket versions to huge hunting knives and old, nicked up bayonets. There was a section devoted to new and used pistols by makers such as Sig Sauer and Glock. A separate rack off to the side displayed rifles and shotguns and were locked together with a long rubber-coated cable. A dog-eared sign asking potential buyers not to handle the merchandise was propped in a corner. Marcus decided quickly and pointed to a three inch Swiss Army knife with a red handle.

"How much is that?"

"A fine choice. That little sticker is only two hundred dollars."

"What? That can't be worth more than twenty or thirty bucks!"

The man smiled. "Twenty bucks, two hundred bucks? What's a little money here? Remember, I'm trying to make a living, ya' know. Tell you what – in ten seconds I feel a price increase coming on, and that little baby will run you two hundred and fifty bucks. Want it now, or would ya' rather wait? Tick, tock, tick, tock. Time's a runnin' out."

Marcus felt his temper flare but the man's intentions were clear: there was a price for a conversation, and it was two hundred dollars. In angry resignation he pulled out his wallet.

"Fine. I don't have that much cash on me. Do you take credit cards?"

He laughed, but his eyes bored into Marcus. "Ha! Now you sound like your brother, too. No, we only take cash here. You'll have to hit up the ATM machine. There's one right over there."

Marcus stalked over to the small ATM, stabbed in his PIN, and withdrew the money. Tight-lipped he walked back to the booth and laid down the cash. The man deftly pocketed the money and handed over the knife and a receipt for twenty dollars. Marcus growled under his breath.

"A pleasure doing business with ya'." He turned and said to a heavy-set lady sharing the booth with him, "Denise, I'm taking a break. Watch the shop." Then to Marcus, "Come on, let's get a bite to eat and park it for a minute."

Together they threaded their way through the crowd to the concession stand where he proceeded to order three hot dogs and a large Coke from an exhausted-looking lady in a hairnet. She handed over the food and held out her hand, intoning in a bored voice that it would be eight dollars. He gave a head nod toward Marcus, who handed her a twenty. He got his change and they sat at a table in the back of the dining area, away from the crowd. The small table wobbled and was covered in the detritus of earlier diners, smeared mustard, a splatter of relish, and an empty Coke cup. He had regained his composure and again had a cocky air about him. He unwrapped the foil from the first sad little hot dog and loaded it up with ketchup.

"You a cop? Or a Fed?"

"Me? No, I'm a teacher. A professor."

He took a bite and talked around his food. "My name's Andy, and that's all you need to know about me, perfessor." Away from the crowd and his co-worker his southern drawl sloughed away and he sounded much more mainstream Midwestern, like someone from Michigan.

"Okay, Andy, what can you tell me about my brother. How do you know him?"

Andy chewed for a moment and washed it down with a swig of his Coke. A small glob of ketchup was in the corner of his mouth and hung there, defying gravity.

"Why are you looking for Rolland? Where'd he go? What's up?" Andy asked, ignoring Marcus' question.

"He's been missing for nearly four months," Marcus replied, drumming his fingers on the table. "I don't know what happened to him. I think he was involved in something…less than legal."

Andy snorted as he polished off the first hot dog. He carefully removed the foil from the second one. The glob of ketchup obstinately refused to budge from the corner of his mouth. Marcus had to concentrate on not staring at it.

"Well now, I can't say one way or the other about the legal thing, of course. I'm a federal firearms dealer with a Class 3 license, and I could get in big trouble for any illegal gun dealing. But," he took another bite and chewed carefully, "I can't say I didn't see something suspicious with your brother."

"What do you mean? What was suspicious about him?"

"Shit, everybody here saw it. He and his buddies were seriously into buying guns. I know that sounds stupid coming from someone like me, since it's my business, but it was different for him. He bought a shitload of stuff. Lots of long rifle guns, AKs, shotguns, some sniper rifles. He and a bunch of other guys came in to the gun show in Dayton a couple of times. They tried to look like they weren't together, but you could tell they were pretty much virgins at this shit. They got some from dealers, but mostly they bought from those individual sellers you see walking around, the guys with the for sale signs stuck in the barrels. From what I could tell the guns were always high caliber stuff, semi-automatics, usually. Each guy'd buy three, four, ten, twelve at a pop, load up on ammo, then head out. They didn't dilly dally around. In and out in a flash, they were."

"Okay, that certainly sounds suspicious, I'll give you that. But what about that was illegal?"

Andy made short work of the second hot dog and tucked into the third. He slurped his Coke noisily and kept chewing. He thumped his chest and released a deep belch.

"Oh, that's better. Need to make some room, you know." He patted his chest again. "Nothing on the face of it," he finally admitted after a moment's thought. "But anyone buying that many guns is up to something, or doing straw buys for someone else. I don't know. Reselling or gifting ain't wrong, but straw buys sure as hell are."

Marcus already knew what a straw buy was: purchasing firearms for someone else who for one reason or another wasn't able to do so themselves, like a convicted felon. It was a federal offense for the straw buyer, and for the seller, too, if it was intentional. Straw purchases were not illegal when a gun was bought from an individual, only from a federal firearms licensed dealer, or FFL. He had already given serious consideration to the possibility that these buys were straw purchases, back when he had first looked over the spreadsheet he and Cassie had found in the cardboard box containing the credit cards. He didn't feel any vindication or victory over this, just mute resignation.

"Your brother bought some merchandise from me, too," Andy admitted. "Couple of AKs and a few handguns. People want to buy stuff, I'll sell it to them, him included. I don't give a shit. I did everything I was supposed to do, including the NICS background check. He was clean."

"NICS? What's that?"

Andy stared at him over the rim of his Coke. He sucked the last of his drink with a slurping noise, and he kept at it for several seconds, efficiently vacuuming up the last few drops.

"Well you *are* a virgin at this shit, too, ain't ya'? Listen, NICS is the National Instant Criminal background check System, and it's what lets me sell any kind of gun to any eligible customer on the spot. Any Federal Firearms Licensed dealer runs an NICS on a buyer and it looks for things like felony convictions, crazies, illegals, crap like that. Used to be we had to wait seven days before we could sell a handgun to someone, but the NICS lets us check 'em out right now, and if they pass then we got us a sale. Easy as pie."

Marcus had a dozen questions careening through his mind, but before he could ask Andy wiped his mouth with a napkin and stuffed it and the hot dog foil wrappers in his empty Coke cup. He stood up and shot it into an open trashcan about ten feet away. He looked pleased with himself.

"Did ya' see that? Two points. The crowd goes wild!" He brushed crumbs from his shirt and smiled at Marcus. The ketchup was finally gone but bits of hotdog and bun were now stuck in his tiny teeth. "Perfesser, I don't know what your brother and his pals were up to, honest, but I just had this niggling feeling it wasn't good. I got no other info for you, and besides, I gotta get back to work and make some real money. Thanks for lunch, it was tasty." He sketched a casual salute. "Adios."

That random "adios" was odd coming from him. Andy was clearly done talking and headed back to his booth, his broad shoulders and thick body moving easily and smoothly through the crowd. The interview was over, and Marcus' two hundred dollars' worth of time was up.

Annoyed at Andy's abrupt exit, Marcus stood and stalked around the convention center for another thirty minutes, continuing to make eye contact with a number of vendors and private sellers. None paid him any undue attention. A few of the well-endowed female salespeople smiled at him coyly, and one went so far as to stroke the barrel of a pistol in a very suggestive manner, but he wasn't interested. He wanted to locate the aging, tattooed biker that had stared him down earlier, but wasn't having any luck. Tired of being bumped around and resolved that there was nothing left to glean here he finally decided it was time to go, disgruntled at not finding out more than he had.

Rain was coming down in earnest as he left the hall, a solid, steady downpour that fell straight down and pelted the parking lot with a sound like radio static. There was a large covered area just outside the door and a dozen people stood there smoking, each occupying his or her own tiny personal space and either concentrating on their cigarettes or with faraway looks on their faces, as if they were strangers packed in a crowded elevator. Marcus stopped while still under the overhang and considered whether he should wait until it slowed or make a break for it. Just then he felt a tap on his shoulder. He turned and to his surprise there was the aging biker, the man's bright eyes unnerving this close up. His thinning hair was peppered with the beginnings of gray and silver, and his lips and the skin around his mouth were creased with a hundred thin, spidery wrinkles, the sign of a lifelong smoker. In fact he reeked of cigarette smoke, and when he spoke Marcus saw that his teeth were stained an unhealthy tan, the color of a banana going bad.

"You. I thought I knew you, man. But you're not him," he said, an accusation that bordered on belligerence.

"No, I don't think I am. But I bet you know my brother, Rolland."

The biker stared over Marcus' shoulder in concentration, as if it took a minute for his thoughts to catch up. Finally he snapped his fingers so loudly that several people spun around, shocked, thinking someone had fired off a small caliber weapon. A few sighs and a nervous chuckle or two later and they all went back to puffing their cigarettes.

"Rolland, yeah, man," he said, both relieved and pissed that he hadn't recalled the name on his own. "That was him. Rolland. You two look a shitload alike, man."

Marcus was so accustomed to that remark that he automatically replied with his stock answer, "Yeah, we get that a lot. So how'd you know Rolland? Did he buy guns off you too?"

"You a cop? Or a Fed? You're not a FIBBIE or AT fucking F, are you?"

ATF, Marcus knew, stood for Alcohol, Tobacco, and Firearms, the Federal law enforcement organization within the U.S. Justice Department with the mandate to prevent and investigate any unlawful use, possession, or manufacture of firearms. They were not, it appeared, popular with the gun crowd.

"No, I'm not. I'm not even close. I'm a teacher on the west coast."

The man grunted and looked Marcus up and down. "Guess you don't look like no fucking ATF agent, but then that's sort of the point, ain't it? To not look like one. Not that I've done anything wrong, but you always gotta look out for the Feds."

Marcus agreed that yes, you probably didn't want to look like one if you were one. He assured him again that he wasn't anything but a teacher.

"I'm just trying to find my brother. He's been missing for months. Can you tell me anything about him? Whatever you know doesn't go beyond me. Honest."

The man pulled a battered Marlboro from a pack in his pocket and lit it with a cheap butane lighter. He took a deep drag and let the smoke trickle from his mouth and nose simultaneously. It hung in front of his face in the still air and partially obscured his features, except for those unnaturally bright eyes.

"Oh I remember. Your brother was kind of a dumb ass," he finally declared with a snort. "He and that group of guys with him was buying whatever they could from whoever they could. They weren't even haggling. What kind of guy doesn't haggle at a gun show? Damn." He looked disgusted, as if an unwritten Man Law had been violated. "He got a few pieces from me and bought a shitload from some other guys. I remember asking him what he planned to do with all this stuff, start some war in South America? Know what he said to me?"

Marcus shook his head.

"He said, 'How'd you know?' That's what he said, 'How'd you know?' I laughed at him, man, thinking he was making a joke, but he just stared at me, all serious-like."

"Really? That's what he said?"

"Yeah, and when I asked him if he was shittin' me, still, you know, keeping it light, he said, 'No joke.' And he was serious. There were three or four of them, a couple of Latinos and a couple of white guys, and then they packed all their shit into a van and took off. I never saw him again. People think I'm crazy, man, but your brother was fuckin' nuts with this South America thing. He really meant what he said."

The more Marcus heard and learned, the more he thought Rolland had meant what he said, too.

"I'm sorry, but I never caught your name."

The biker grinned his yellowish grin. "That's 'cause I never threw it at you. Everybody calls me Taz, you know, like the Tasmanian Devil."

"Taz?"

"Yeah, Taz, 'cause most folks think I'm nuts, psycho. Guy's a little quirky and everyone thinks he's a nut-job. Whatever." He spun his finger in tight circles next to his temple. "I'll tell you what's crazy – all these morons in here buying from dealers and getting run through the NICS. The Feds will watch you like a fuckin' hawk, man, as soon as you show up in that Skynet mainframe. You get in that system and that's it, they've got you. Me, I'd rather stay off the grid as much as I can."

"Off the grid?"

"Sure, man, off the grid. You know, no credit cards, no loans, no permanent address, no way to keep tabs on you. Anybody tells you this is a free country hasn't got a fuckin' clue, man. Guys like me, we're off the grid and we're free. Hell," he laughed, "I can't even tell you what my Social Security number is."

Marcus wondered, then, if that was what Rolland had done. Had he gone off the grid? Was he just laying low somewhere, keeping his head down? He hoped so, but if that was the case why did he have that empty feeling in his gut, like a deep, hollow pit?

"So, Taz, why'd you stop me? Just because you thought I was Rolland?"

Taz took another drag from his Marlboro. As he talked smoke puffed out from his mouth and nose in uneven clouds, still hanging low under the canopy. Outside the rain began to slow to a light drizzle, which was apparently the cue for several of the smokers to crush out their smoldering butts and trot to their cars. More people that had been dallying in the lobby peered out and decided it was safe to exit. The parking lot began to fill up cars moving toward the exits.

"Sure, man. I wanted to see how that whole South American war thing had turned out. Plus, if the Feds keep turnin' up the heat here in the lower forty-eight I may have to head down there. Can't have guns, which would suck, but talk about staying off the grid! Course I'd have to learn Spanish, but what the hell. *Cerveza, por favor*. That would get me started!"

Marcus chuckled at his horrible Spanish. "You know, it's funny, but you're the second person at the show today to mistake me for Rolland."

"Yeah? Who was the other guy?"

Marcus jabbed a thumb toward the arena. "A guy named Andy at one of the booths inside."

Taz scrunched his face up in thought for a second. "Andy? I know all these guys, and there's no Andy working in there. Sure you got it right?"

"Yes, I'm sure. He worked for the Ohio Gun and Knife Swap Shop."

"Well, shit, that's not Andy. His name's Saunders, or AJ, at least that's what we've always called him. And if you met AJ you know he's a son of a bitch. I wouldn't trust him as far as I could throw him, which ain't too far 'cause he's a solid sumbitch."

"Why not? I mean, why wouldn't you trust him?"

"Shit, Saunders is greedy and more than a little dirty, man, which is a bad combination in my book. Just watch yourself and keep your wallet in your front pocket if you plan on dealing with him, that's all. Plus he's a little creepy – got a smile like a piranha, with those tiny little teeth. He smiles at me I get a little nervous."

The longer they talked the more Marcus was starting to like this eccentric, odd man. Sure, the guy was a little left of center, but that was what made him interesting. He was clearly quite paranoid but he was straightforward and honest, which was refreshing.

Taz extinguished his cigarette in a large stone ashtray next to the trash can. He looked out and saw the rain had ended, at least for now.

"Time to go. Good luck finding your bro, man."

"Thanks, I appreciate it. Can I give you my number in case you remember anything else that I might find helpful? No strings attached. Honest."

"S'okay, I guess," the old biker muttered. "Yeah, I'll take your number, but don't count on me for anything. You need me, sorry, 'cause you can't find me, man. But I usually hang out at these gun shows, selling stuff. That's how I make my living. Buy from whoever out in the great big world and resell at these shows. I made almost five hundred bucks today. That's gas and groceries for three weeks, the way I live. Only thing I'm missing is a 401k."

Marcus scribbled his name and number on the back of his ticket and handed it over. Taz looked at it and took note of the 619 area code for San Diego. Satisfied he dipped his head and moved away, sticking the number in the cellophane of his cigarette pack.

"Let me tell ya' something before we split – ninety-nine percent of gun guys and dealers are straight up good people, law-abiding and God-fearing, 2nd Amendment lovers till the end and all that shit. But that one percent left over can be mean and nasty, more than you'll ever know, and this business'll bring out the worst of even them. If your brother was messed up with folks like that, well, then anything could've happened to him. See ya', man."

He walked over and hopped on a huge Harley Davidson motorcycle, black with a lot of gleaming chrome and now dripping wet from the downpour. Light winked off the drops like liquid diamonds. On the gas tank was a painting of the classic Looney Tunes Tasmanian Devil, all teeth and no brains, arms raised akimbo. It was an older bike but still worth a great deal of money. Marcus wondered how many guns the man had to peddle to buy transportation like that, and what he rode or drove when the snow started flying around Ohio in November. Taz hit the electric starter and the black bike barked once and burbled to life, its exhaust note deep and thrumming like the rumble of a distant, impending thunderstorm. He gunned the bike and it skidded perilously through the wet parking lot, forcing several angry pedestrians to quickly jump to safety. Marcus watched him go and decided to do the same, easily locating his rental car next to the bright yellow and rather ostentatious Hummer.

He merged on to I-75 north. The roads were wet although no new rain was falling. The sky was still flat and gray and it melded into the faded blacktop of the highway until they became a single, uniform gray on the horizon. He drove with the radio off, the only sounds the rumble of the tires on the road and the intermittent swish of the windshield wipers as they scraped away the water spattered up by passing cars. He was deep in thought, barely cognizant of the act of driving, and if asked later he wouldn't recall any specifics of the trip back to Wayne. In his own methodical way Marcus was reliving and categorizing everything he had learned since his arrival so many weeks ago: his encounter with Gonzalez and Hernandez in Rolland's house, the first time he saw Cassie at Foley's Diner, their trip to Mexico and the shootout in the market, the mysterious note and his visit to the Sagrado Cenote. He clearly recalled the short time spent with El Señor and his two interactions with Agent Cruzado, and how poorly the last interaction outside the bus had ended. Then of course there was the gun show, so fresh in his mind that he could still smell machine oil on his clothes and skin, to the point where he actually imagined he could taste a thin sheen of it on his tongue. The gun show, where it appeared conclusive and without doubt that his little brother had been involved not only with counterfeit credit cards but with illegal gun sales of some sort, too.

His grip on the steering wheel tightened, his knuckles white. This was *his* fault! He was the big brother and it was supposed to be his job to watch over his younger sibling and take care of him, to keep him out of trouble. But he hadn't, had he? No, he had taken off and left him alone in that crappy town. He knew Rolland could make lousy choices and he had left anyway. Sure, he had come back that one time three years ago, but the first time his brother screwed up Marcus had been in his car and gone, out the door...almost as if he had been looking for a reason to leave him behind.

Had he? Had he really been looking for a reason? Had he been so sick and tired of taking care of the family that he would have looked for any excuse to run away?

Looking into the mirror of his soul he found he didn't like what he saw in that stark reflection. He saw a solitary person, a lonely man, someone whose guilt at abandoning his own blood was now pushing him forward and would never give him peace, would never permit his soul to rest. He could never give up looking, he knew, or this guilt would eventually crush him completely.

That was when he understood that the time spent reacting to events was over. He could continue beating the bushes and hope to flush out answers - or he could make the answers come to him. It was time to go on the offensive. He knew just where to start.

Chapter 25

"You want what?!" Cassie exclaimed loudly. Her voice held a hysterical edge to it. She couldn't have been more shocked if he had demanded one of her kidneys.

They were sitting across from each other in Foley's. The spotty late afternoon sun was slanting in the large front windows and Marcus had only recently arrived back from his trip to the gun show. They were at a table in a far corner of the dining area, well away from the few late afternoon lunch or very early dinner customers that were scattered thinly about. Marcus had an untouched cup of coffee parked in front of him. They were both leaning forward intently, their forearms resting on the table, foreheads nearly touching. Cassie's cheeks were flushed pink with outraged emotion. Several of the patrons looked their way curiously, their forks stalled in mid-bite like a freeze-frame.

Marcus kept his voice low and calm as he stared at her. He had known what to expect before he arrived, even as his plan had coalesced in his mind on the drive here. There were many moving parts, many puzzle pieces that had to come together before this could possibly work. But everything started right here, right now.

"I need the phone number of whoever has been texting and calling you," he said evenly, his voice low. "Do you still have it?"

"Of course I still have it," she almost hissed. "But what in the world do you want it for? How can that possibly do any good?"

"I need it to flush out whoever is after us and threatening your parents. I need it to hopefully help find my brother."

She tried to pull back away from him. He grasped her hands in his and held them tight. She was shaking her head. Now some of the staff in Foley's were looking their way in mounting interest and concern as well. Everyone was staring at them.

"No, you can't have it. My parents! Whoever it is has already threatened my parents if I do anything. I can't put them in danger."

Marcus gripped her hands more tightly in an attempt to reassure her. "I won't let anything happen to them, I promise you. I can protect them. In fact, if I can bring this to an end they will be safe forever and you won't have to worry about them any longer. That's what you really want, isn't it?"

Of course it was what she wanted, and he knew that. She thought deeply for a moment, looking away from him over his left shoulder, biting her lip in concentration. She was in her white waitress uniform but the ribbon that held her hair back was green, the exact same green as the ribbon tied to his suitcase. Tiny lines, so thin they appeared drawn on with a pencil, appeared across the width of her forehead as she contemplated this outrageous request. Finally her head drooped slightly. She nodded.

"Yes, dammit, that's what I want," she said, her voice quiet.

He smiled at her, and eventually she smiled back, although it was clearly forced. The worry lines were not completely erased. She looked older, as if these responsibilities were weighing too heavily on her mind, but divesting herself of them was an even heavier burden. Now that their voices had lowered everyone in Foley's went back to the business of serving or eating, the potential show a bust.

"I've asked you to trust me before, right?"

She nodded again.

"So now I'm asking one more time. Do you trust me?"

"I do," she replied softly after a second's hesitation.

"Good. Would it help if I told you what I have planned? How I am going to end this?"

She didn't say no, so he told her, generally, what he was going to do, when he was going to do it, and who would be involved. When it was all boiled down to its essential elements there really weren't that many steps involved. He was very thorough, which Cassie expected out of him. She asked several questions along the way, and at one point he had to convince her of one vital thing she needed to do, something he had already laid the groundwork for. She resisted at first, mainly just a knee-jerk reaction, but in the end understood and agreed with his call. Despite her acute initial reservations she became more intrigued and interested as he went. After several minutes she stared at him mutely and the worry lines had almost vanished. Eventually Cassie took a deep breath and plucked a paper napkin from the silver dispenser. She wrote a telephone number on it with the pen from her apron, then folded it in half and placed it in his hand.

"Do it," she said.

Marcus sat at the table after Cassie had gone back to waiting on customers, alone again. He was tired of being alone. He realized again that he was by himself more often than not, even in San Diego where he was surrounded by thousands of students and hundreds of faculty members. On those rare occasions when he had a date or an evening out he always ended up keeping the woman at arm's length, never permitting himself to get too close. This was no way to go through life. As much as he despised this town, despite how torn up he was at his brother's disappearance, at least he had learned that much about himself.

He stared at the napkin. When explaining everything to Cassie he had made it sound so easy and straightforward, like a simple matter of one plus two equals three. He had intentionally oozed confidence. However deep down he knew how risky all this actually was. The problem of course was people. People were not static pieces from a Christmas puzzle that could be moved or manipulated at will, they weren't chess pieces with known capabilities and limitations. No, people were quirky and subjective, often unfathomable, and nearly always irrational. For Cassie's sake he had by necessity sounded certain of the outcome. However, truth be told, he was anything but that. He sighed and took a cautious sip of his coffee. It was now cold and bitter. He made a face and set the cup down, pushing it away in distaste.

Marcus had a very important phone call and one stop to make, so he bade farewell to Cassie. She was busy chatting with several customers at the breakfast bar but broke away long enough to wish him a sincere, albeit nervous, good luck. He smiled at her gamely then left. The earlier storm clouds had moved on and the late afternoon sun was eclipsed by the top of the courthouse, throwing most of the downtown in heavy shadow. With the sun directly behind the clock tower it looked as if the top few floors of the old stone courthouse were on fire. Several cars drove by slowly, one filled with teenage kids who had the radio booming a deep bass through their closed windows. He couldn't make out the song but the thumping was so strong it vibrated the storefront windows next to him like the head of a drum. He walked on past his rental car and crossed the street, aiming for the courthouse. The bright sun now behind it made the old edifice dark and foreboding, a cold, black silhouette, all details lost in the contrast between the glare and deep shadows. As distasteful as it was, everything had to begin here. He steeled himself, walked down the steps and went inside.

Twenty minutes later he was back in the rental car and accelerating toward Rolland's house, glad that this first part was over and done. The barely healed scar on his cheek was itching, which he supposed was a good thing. He ignored the distraction, thinking instead about step two, the phone call he had to make. He glanced down and saw Cassie's napkin in his lap. The phone number began with the area code 305 which he thought was from somewhere in Florida, maybe even Miami. He made a mental note to verify that, although at this point the Miami connection didn't surprise him.

When he arrived at Rolland's he performed his usual security check of the property, making sure no one was lying in wait for him. The house still radiated that feeling of a tired college rental, but oddly he was feeling more at home there each day, even more so than his apartment back in San Diego. He got a bottled water out of the refrigerator and sat at the heavy kitchen table, the same one Gonzalez and Hernandez had tied him to weeks earlier. It felt like a lifetime ago, almost as if it had happened to someone else entirely. Sipping his water he spread Cassie's napkin out on the table in front of him, studying the phone number. Her writing was large and curvy, not script but a bold combination of cursive and block lettering that mirrored her personality. The 305 area code haunted him. He did not want to make this call yet knew he had to. He was also keenly aware that once he dialed the number there was no turning back, that once he set these wheels in motion he could no more stop future events than his mere flesh and bone body could hold back a freight train. His mouth was dry so he took another sip of his water and dug his cell phone from his pocket. Almost angrily he punched in the number and waited for it to connect. After six rings a standard voice mail system kicked in with a pleasant, generic female voice asking him to leave a message at the beep. He would have been extremely surprised had someone answered it.

Beep.

"This is Marcus Schmidt. I have what you want – the credit cards and the ledger with the names and other information. This Thursday at noon you will show up at Rolland's house," he gave the address, even though he doubted it was necessary, "alone, with no one else. None of your hired muscle, just you. I am willing to make a deal, a very simple deal.

"However, if you don't do exactly as I say you will never get the cards or the ledger. I will destroy them all and you will have nothing. I hope I am making myself clear. This Thursday, at noon, at Rolland's house. If there is any variation from these instructions I will destroy the cards and the ledger."

He ended the call and tossed his phone on the table as if it had shocked him, his hands raised, palms out. He stared at the phone and wiped a thin sheen of sweat from his forehead, but was surprised to find that his hands were steady. He was...not calm, that wasn't it at all, but relieved that the call was done. He felt lighter, clear-headed, like he had just passed a difficult test that he had been convinced he would fail. There was indeed no turning back now.

Marcus finished off his water and changed into his running gear. He didn't know when he might get the time or opportunity to work out again in the coming days so didn't want to squander this chance. Outside the late afternoon Ohio sun was warm and a stiff breeze was blowing in from the southwest, promising yet another change in the weather. Spring in the Midwest could be all over the map, and he remembered the old saying: *If you don't like the weather in Ohio now, just wait a few minutes and it'll change.* In fact looking west he could see a thick, menacing storm front moving across the sky. He hustled outside, locking the door behind him. Across the street Mrs. Kerr was stationed at her spot in the yellow chair behind the picture window, the heavy curtain pulled back for once. She waved enthusiastically at him and he smiled, waving back. He had to talk to her about upcoming events, explain to her what was likely to happen and try to enlist her aid. Marcus was pretty certain he could count on her: she was tough and, well, plucky. Yes, *plucky* was the best word he could think of to describe her. She had a part to play, a small but potentially crucial part.

Clicking the timer on his watch he set off down the country road with the wind to his back. Errant gusts hit him hard enough that he could feel his shoes almost leave the ground, as if he were the god Mercury and had wings on his feet. Sweat ran into his eyes since he was running with the wind and there was no breeze drying his face. The steady *slap, slap, slap* of his shoes on the hot asphalt was the only noise on the quiet road. Rolland's house quickly disappeared from view behind him.

His mind clearing, he stepped through the mental bullet points he needed to check off in preparation for what was to come in three days. He had another call to make, and of course he needed to talk with Mrs. Kerr. He had to go back to the YMCA locker number 45, too. There was also an issue with Cassie, since the people behind this had clearly demonstrated that they wouldn't hesitate to injure or even kill to obtain the cards and information. He had to make sure she was safe, which had been the brief argument they'd just had at Foley's. Marcus had insisted that she leave work right away and not go home again, not until he'd given her the all clear. He had already talked to the owner of Foley's, Sal Black, and he had been happy to help, insisting she could stay with him and his wife. Cassie had resisted at first until he had reminded her about Otto and the young man's nearly fatal encounter. That had sobered her up and she had agreed. He rubbed a hand over his face to clear it of sweat. She had to remain safe. He would *not* let anyone else suffer, especially not her.

Damn there was a lot to do.

After fifteen minutes of running he reversed course. The stiff wind smacked into his face and nearly pushed him backwards. He lowered his head and muscled through the intermittent gusts that had to be approaching thirty or more miles per hour. His pace slowed and his planned thirty minute workout was certainly going to be extended. He hated running in wind. Hills were one thing, they came and went and he could at least adjust his steps and pace accordingly, could see the approaching apex and know the worst was nearly over. But wind like this just battered at him relentlessly, sapping his strength. He continued fighting as he knew this was what separated one runner from another, the leader of the pack from the pack itself, the determination and force of will necessary to power through obstacles. He cleared his mind and focused resolutely on keeping his pace strong. On the plus side, he mused between gusts, there was no issue of sweat running into his eyes now.

As he neared the house he felt his pace begin to slacken in the face of the strong wind. Falling back on an old runner's trick he looked ahead and saw a telephone pole about a hundred feet ahead. *I'll run to the phone pole,* he told himself. *I'll push hard till I get there, then I'll slow down and rest.* He reached his mark then picked an overhanging branch up ahead. He convinced himself he could keep up his pace that long, certainly, anyone could do that, and then he would call it quits.

He did that three more times before finally easing up as Rolland's house hove into view, very near to the ditch where he had spotted the lone credit card stuck in the dried mud weeks ago. His breathing was hard, bordering on gasping, but he smiled inwardly that he could still trick himself like that. His heart was banging against his sternum as if it were striving to break free of his body. Looking up he saw that the storm front was nearly on top of him, barreling toward him and now filling more than half the sky. The thick haze beneath it was the promise of heavy rain. He checked his watch and was pleased that he had kept a steady pace throughout regardless of the wind. His vitals were calming quickly, which was another good sign, one that meant his physical condition was still sound. The run had taken a little more out of him than he liked but some workouts were like that. The first spattering drops pelted him in the face as he unlocked the door and hustled in. Distant thunder rumbled. A saying from his mother popped into his mind and he grinned warmly: *God is bowling.* He and Rolland had always laughed whenever she had said that, back when they were little.

After a hot shower Marcus needlessly tidied up around the neat house and packed several days' worth of clothing and toiletries. Like Cassie he planned on leaving his usual haunts behind for the next few days, and that certainly included Rolland's place. He had no intention of making himself an easy target again for Gonzalez or anyone else. His plan was to hole up elsewhere, perhaps at a hotel in Greenville, and lay low until the three days were up and his meeting was due to take place. As he filled the suitcase in his typical, orderly fashion rain battered the western side of the house with the sound of gravel striking glass. He was happy he'd gotten out when he did. Running into the wind was one thing, but being out in that mess would have been miserable. He finished packing then walked around and made sure the doors and windows were locked even though he knew they were. He glanced out the kitchen window but couldn't see Sam's doghouse through the downpour. He knew the mound marking the grave would flatten out even more, and before long grass and weeds would cover it completely. The thought that it would soon disappear somehow saddened him, like one more vestige of his brother was disappearing as well. He flicked off the light in the kitchen and exited to the living room where he grabbed his suitcase and stood at the front door, staring outside, thinking, waiting for the rain to diminish. He fervently hoped it wasn't going to rain like this on Thursday. That would screw with his plans.

Then just like that it was over with the sun suddenly peeking out from the bottom edge of the clouds. Water still cascaded down the roof and overflowed the gutters, but it had slowed enough to make a dry exit to his car possible. He locked the door behind him, tossed the suitcase in the back seat, and then trotted across the street to Mrs. Kerr's house. She had been monitoring his progress and opened the door even before he stepped on her property. She was smiling as he walked up.

"Hello, dear. Nice to see you again. Care for some coffee and a Twinkie?"

He happily accepted the coffee but passed on the snack cake again. Her bright blue eyes sparkled as he came in and she patted his arm warmly saying, as she usually did, that it was so nice to have a man around the house again. When the coffee was ready they both sat on the couch and he doctored it under her amused gaze. Over his last few visits they had come to a tacit agreement where she didn't chastise him on how he took his coffee, assuming he didn't go to extremes. They made idle talk and he offered to knock a few items off their honey-do list, but she shooed that off with a flutter of her boney, knobby hand. She sat on her end near the concealed pistol and looked him up and down. Her makeup had been applied a little more carefully today and her wig was perfectly positioned. Nevertheless she still looked tiny and frail tucked into her corner of the couch.

"I see you're packed up and going somewhere."

He nodded as he sipped the coffee. It was still brutally strong and he wistfully eyed the sugar bowl. He considered adding more but stayed his hand with a resigned sigh.

"Yes, I need to be away from the house for a few days."

She nodded in return. She drank hers straight black, of course. Four Twinkies sat like a small pile of cord wood on the tray, their cellophane reflecting light unnaturally. He could not convince himself to eat one.

She raised a thin, penciled eyebrow. "Mind telling me why?"

It was time she knew. For the next fifteen minutes Marcus gave her the shortened version. He could tell he lost her when talking about the counterfeit credit cards, but she sat there raptly throughout. She patted at her chest and worried at the fabric of her robe when he talked about Rolland, and it warmed him to see how much his brother had meant to her. He needed her to understand enough of what had gone on before because he was going to ask a favor of her. From this point on, if she agreed, she would become a part of this. He had no intention of putting her into any danger but even being peripherally involved would carry some level of risk. After all, he hadn't thought Otto had been in harm's way, and look what had happened to him. Marcus couldn't take that chance again. He did, however, need her to perform one simple task.

When he had finished explaining everything to her she sat there, mute. He wasn't sure if she was confused, terrified, excited, or perhaps a combination of all three. He thought she might ask questions, or maybe berate him for abandoning Rolland like he had, which in his mind had likely been the catalyst for all of this. Instead she took another drink of her coffee then calmly set the cup down. She set her shoulders and stared at the fading picture of Mr. Kerr standing at the grill for a full minute, as if they were in silent communication with each other. Then she looked directly at Marcus with those sparkling blue eyes.

"What can I do to help?" she said, her voice stronger than he had yet heard.

He grinned in warm admiration and told her.

The trip to Greenville took no time at all. As he drove over the damp highway he kept the radio off, so the only sounds were the hum of the engine and the steady *whap, whap* of the tires as they struck the tar strips on the road. The wet green fields around him glistened brightly in the setting sun, as if they were in fact massive fields of jade. The cruise control was set at a steady fifty-five miles per hour. He pulled a business card from his pocket and carefully dialed a long number, uncomfortable with operating the phone while driving. After several clicks a voice answered. Marcus identified himself and for the next ten minutes he talked almost uninterrupted. A few times the conversation went back and forth and grew quite heated, but in the end it sounded as if cooler heads prevailed and some sort of agreement was reached. Had anyone been there to hear him they would have wondered what was going on, since the entire conversation had taken place in Spanish.

He hung up the phone and continued driving, the skyline of Greenville firming up ahead of him. Yes, things were falling into place.

For Marcus the next two days were a blurred combination of utter boredom punctuated by spikes of worry and anxiety. He was holed up in a small motel on the northern outskirts of Greenville, a town he now knew was also called the Treaty City. He knew that chiefly because the motel was called the Treaty City Motel and the elderly male owner was more than pleased to explain at length how the small city had gotten its name, that it was where General Mad Anthony Wayne had signed a treaty with the Indians several hundred years earlier and thereby opened up the west for further exploration and settlement. Marcus figured the Indians had again gotten a raw deal out of all that, but didn't argue that point with the proud proprietor.

The Treaty City Motel was comprised of ten small cottages. His tiny bungalow had a twin sized bed, a dresser and an aging tube television that got five channels, six if you counted the local access channel. It had a closet-sized bathroom and a window air conditioner that asthmatically blew out air only a degree or two cooler than outside. The upside was the cottage itself was clean, the sheets were white and crisp, and most importantly the hotel owner accepted cash and was flexible on what identification he required by his guests, which in this case was none. That suited Marcus just fine.

For those two days Marcus had plenty of time to think about what was likely to come, and to wonder if he had covered all his bases. He felt he had, but then out of the blue a bout of anxiety would strike if he mentally stumbled across unconsidered outcomes or other variables popped into his mind. Cassie may have thought the world of his ability to methodically plan, but he was replete with self-doubt.

The only real relief from the boredom and nervousness came when he would don a hat and spend some time at the Greenville Library where he could surf the Web. The free Internet service was a tremendous boon as he researched the security issues credit card issuers and consumers faced. He found that years earlier, at the onset of high-quality home printers, check fraud losses at banks and credit unions had skyrocketed nationwide. With a few minutes of study and some basic graphic arts skills it seemed anyone could make a bogus check that was nearly impossible for the average teller to detect. Longer check holds and stricter verifications finally trimmed those losses. This didn't stop the crooks, it merely shifted their focus in a different direction - towards credit and debit cards.

He was astounded at the massive amounts of money lost each year. What started as a cottage business where simply a card here or there would be counterfeited was now a worldwide criminal network where billions were stolen annually. The greatest threats came from the common compromises his contact at the credit bureau had talked about. These thefts would typically impact tens or hundreds of thousands of people each time, and weren't necessarily restricted to credit cards. Universities, public utilities, big box retail stores, travel rewards programs, the federal government – no personal or important information was safe, he determined. He was beginning to understand why Taz, the aging biker from the gun show, was so passionate about staying off the grid. These threats to his personal security were starting to make him paranoid as well.

The other diversion he looked forward to each day was when Cassie would call. She had followed his directions and was laying low at the home of Sal Black, the owner of Foley's Diner. They had a spare bedroom and Sal's young Mexican wife and Cassie were very close in age. Carmen spoke English well but delighted in slipping back into her native tongue and chatting gaily and at length with her guest. Marcus secretly wished they would chat just a little less since the more time the two girls spent together meant less time Cassie could talk to him. But she seemed happy there, professing to miss her brothers and her own home and work, but grudgingly understanding why she needed to stay out of sight. Also, it didn't hurt from Marcus' point of view that Sal had been in the Army and knew how to take care of himself and the others in his house. They would talk once or twice a day, but he looked forward to much more.

Then suddenly it was as if he had been caught dozing and an alarm was buzzing in his ear to wake up, proclaiming it was Thursday morning. Marcus paid the bill and loaded his few belongings into the car. He felt both nervous and apprehensive, like a high school senior athlete on the day of his final football game. The morning was cool and overcast with heavy gray clouds hanging so low in the sky they seemed to brush the top of the grain silos. Once back in Wayne he made a quick stop at the Ace Hardware store for several items, the disinterested youth behind the counter finally nodding at him in recognition. His next destination was the YMCA where he once again successfully negotiated the distaff gauntlet at the admissions desk to retrieve the cardboard box from number 45. He called Cassie's cell phone and she answered on the first ring, sounding a little breathless, as if she had pounced on the phone.

"Today's the big day," he said, fairly confident that his voice was steady. "How are you? How's everything at Sal's house."

"I'm fine, we're fine, and everything's good here, thanks. Carmen is great fun to hang around with," she replied, talking a little too quickly. She was trying to sound confident but wasn't very convincing. "It's just that I...well, today is the day. It's Thursday."

"I know, believe me," he replied as evenly as he could. He wanted to talk more, just to hear her voice and for a moment pretend nothing was wrong, that they had no worries at all, that this was just a casual conversation between two people that were more than friends. But that wasn't the case and he knew it. It was Thursday, the Big Day, and he just had to make sure she was safe throughout this. Only then could he even begin to relax. He was stern when he said, "This is all going down today. I need you to promise me that you'll stay holed up at Sal's until I give you the all clear, okay?"

"I know, I know," she snapped. "You don't have to remind me! No, no, I'm sorry," she amended quickly before he could say anything. She couldn't hide the quivering edge her voice held. "I'm just a nervous wreck. I won't be able to settle down until all this is over. I'm going to be sitting here pacing and worrying until you call to tell me this is done and you and my parents are all safe."

"Hopefully I'll be calling you by one or two o'clock. And don't worry – your parents are safe, okay?"

She shakily agreed, so they talked for another few minutes while she worked on calming down. He stayed away from what was going to happen in mere hours, instead chatting her up about other topics like the diner, Carmen, and the odd little proprietor at the Treaty City Motel. In the end he could tell she was more at ease but he knew it wouldn't take much to wind her up again. It was time to go.

"Cassie, I need to get back to Rolland's and get ready. I only have a few hours."

She sucked in air as if in shock. "I know. Just promise me one thing."

"Sure. Anything."

"Promise me you won't get hurt or...well, that you won't get hurt. I couldn't stand it if anything happened to you, too."

He smiled and knew she could sense it on the other end. "I promise."

They hung up. He felt a pang of guilt because he always kept his promises, but wasn't certain he would be able to this time.

Chapter 26

When he arrived at his brother's house Marcus performed his cursory security check of the area and found it clear. He quickly trotted over to Mrs. Kerr's to make sure she was all set and ready to go. She smiled warmly, happy to see him. Inside, by the window, the yellow chair was in place and the touch-tone phone was sitting on the end table near at hand.

"You remember what you need to do?" he asked her patiently.

"Of course. Don't you worry, I'm ready," she said, patting his arm. She was more animated than he had seen her before, her bright blue eyes alight.

He nodded, trying to hide his nervousness. "It's just after nine o'clock now. Pretty soon you should close your curtain and stay out of sight. Just to be sure."

She assured him that she would, and in fact went to the window and did just that. The gray daylight that had dimly illuminated the living room was gone, plunging everything into a deep velvet gloom. Just like that the furniture became nothing more than dark amorphous shapes barely seen. There was a thin, vertical shaft of light where the curtains met, as if he were backstage at a play and the house lights on the other side were up. He and Mrs. Kerr were two of the many actors in this production.

She again assured him she was all set before kindly shooing him out of the house. He looked back from Rolland's and the curtains were closed, no sign of life coming from her home at all. She was one of the puzzle pieces he couldn't control, but felt reasonably sure she would play her part successfully. He hoped. If she didn't this might end messily almost before it began.

Marcus opened the rental's trunk and pulled out a machete and a small saw he had purchased that morning at the Ace Hardware store. He made his way to the woods at the edge of the property and found what he thought was the trail, still overgrown with dense brush and weeds. He experimented with the long blade and quickly cleared a ragged opening large enough to enter, then kept swinging and hacking his way further into the woods. He soon found what he needed, a huge sycamore that had come down several years earlier, the same one Rolland had hurdled months before. It was long dead, which meant he could harvest plenty of aged wood from its boughs and the surrounding area with ease. He ferried a dozen armloads of the dry branches back to the gravel driveway and made an impressive pyre right there, about twenty feet from the house. The stacked wood was about four feet square and at least that tall, open in the middle. Most of the branches were cured enough to be easily broken but some had to be sawed to fit. After an hour he wiped sweat from his forehead and surveyed his work, satisfied that it would do just fine. He made two more trips into the woods and stacked the extra firewood nearby, just in case. Marcus went to the trunk a final time and pulled out a small butane torch and some starter logs. He wedged each of the starter logs at the four corners of the pyre, then stood back and inspected the results. Happy with his handiwork he went inside and got cleaned up.

After a change of clothes he got a bottled water from the fridge, grabbed a kitchen chair, and went back outside. The day was still overcast but the clouds were more white than gray, and he could even see several patches of blue sky here and there. He breathed a silent sigh of relief that the weather would cooperate. His watch told him it was just after eleven o'clock so he sat outside and tried not to fidget as time slowly crept by. Several random cars drove past him, their drivers staring in curiosity at the large man sitting in the kitchen chair by the impressive pile of wood.

Thirty minutes later he deemed it was time. Using the butane torch he lit each of the four starter logs, the hissing blue flame immediately catching the paper of each one. A breeze from the west fanned the nascent blaze and in no time the bonfire was crackling and popping, flames leaping seven feet into the air. Sparks danced and spun upwards and thick gray smoke roiled upwards where it was carried up and over the house. The smell reminded him of fall days growing up, back to a time when people burned piles of raked leaves. The fire was so hot he had to move the kitchen chair back several feet, but even so he tossed several more logs on where they quickly caught. So far so good.

He unlocked the rental and pulled out the box of credit cards, then went back and sat down on the chair and placed the box at his feet. He looked at his watch: eleven forty-two. Nothing to do now but wait and hope they showed. He had planned for just about everything except nobody showing up. He wiped his hands on his pants, put his foot on the box, and waited.

Noon came and nothing happened. His nerves jangled and he had to force his hands to sit still in his lap. What if they weren't coming? What if all his preparations were for nothing and all this was a waste? What would he tell Cassie? He had been so sure this would work. What would he do if they didn't show? His stomach churned and he felt flushed, as if he had a sudden case of the flu. Damn – where were they?

At 12:17 he heard another car and he sat up straighter, his senses straining. He had expected someone to arrive from the direction of town, but that wasn't the case. Down the road he spotted a huge black Cadillac Escalade SUV inching towards the house. Its headlights were on. What was the deal with bad guys and black SUVs? The Caddy's windows were tinted so dark they matched the exterior paint. It stopped about a hundred feet away and simply sat there, idling. Exhaust oozed from the tailpipe before drifting ephemerally up where it was shredded by the breeze. Marcus would not permit himself even a glance toward Mrs. Kerr's house although he felt a terrific urge to do so. He took the opportunity to stoke up the fire with several more logs. It was burning hot now.

For a full five minutes that felt like five days the SUV remained stationary, engine running, headlights on. To Marcus it looked like a massive metal shark with its shiny black skin, chrome grill teeth, and glaring headlight eyes, a predator through and through.

Suddenly the engine revved and it shot forward, coming in fast and hard, its prey located. It careened into the driveway so fast it first skidded and drifted a few feet on the street. Gravel popped under its heavy treads like gunshots as it roared into the driveway. It came to a jarring stop and threw more gravel, a few pieces of which pelted Marcus' feet and ankles. He could see that even the windshield was tinted black, so dark he couldn't tell who was inside or how many there were. The Caddy was facing the fire about twenty feet away. If whoever was driving was trying to ratchet up the tension they were doing a fine job of it. Regardless, throughout all this Marcus stayed seated on the wooden kitchen chair, a picture of stoicism. His short blond hair ruffled gently in the light wind.

The tense stare-down continued for several minutes. Marcus held his ground and remained seated, the box still at his feet. The Escalade continued to idle, a soft growl that was punctuated by the air conditioning compressor kicking on and off every ten or fifteen seconds. The huge SUV tilted side to side an inch as if someone inside were moving around. Then the engine was killed and the only sounds emanating from under the hood was a gentle pinging noise of the motor cooling. Still Marcus waited.

Suddenly there was a loud click and the driver's door swung open. A huge boot snaked out and planted itself firmly on the ground, followed by a massive hand with fingers like bratwursts that gripped the window frame.

Slowly, so slowly, a tremendous head eased out of the vehicle and the figure stood up and appeared to keep standing. He was incredibly tall and imposing.

Gonzalez stepped from the SUV and glared down at Marcus, his eyes black and dead.

"I told you we would meet again," he rumbled.

Marcus stood up as well. His guts churned as if he'd swallowed a blender. Belying his inner panic he calmly put one foot on the chair and tied his shoe, then reached down and picked up the box. He held it protectively in his arms, as tightly as he might hold a squirming infant. He stared at Gonzalez and slowly opened the flaps on the box. He pulled the ledger papers and a handful of credit cards from inside the box and held them in front of him. The light wind fluttered the loose pages of the ledger, but any noise they made couldn't be heard over the crackling of the fire.

"This is what you've been looking for, I take it?" he said flatly.

Gonzalez nodded, his giant lion's head moving up and down as if on a hinge. He made no move toward Marcus but stood planted next to the SUV.

"I thought so. Now we're going to talk, you and I," Marcus declared.

Safely ensconced in her house Mrs. Kerr was intently watching the baffling events unfold with a practiced eye. Through the narrow slit in the curtains she could see everything clearly across the street. Her hearing may have been fading, her skin was thinning, and her real hair might be brittle with age, but her vision was excellent. She found her heart racing in excitement. Things had been so very dreadfully boring and lonely for so long, but this – *this!* – was anything but boring! This was better than any of her afternoon stories on TV, no question about it! This was real life, like one of those cop shows she treated herself to once in a while on Friday nights, the ones with the real criminals being chased by police in a big city like Dayton or Memphis. She had to take several deep steadying breaths to help maintain her composure, keeping in mind all the while that dear Marcus could really be in danger here. She couldn't allow herself to get so caught up in what was happening that she forgot that she had a job to do. He was such a nice boy. He looked like his brother, whom she adored, but he reminded her of her late husband so much, back when they were both young. She sighed, the memory of Hank, Mr. Kerr, still etched so deeply in her mind, as if in granite. She loved him still and missed him terribly, even after all these years. When she thought of him she still saw the strong arms, wide smile, and dancing eyes. She could almost feel him standing behind her, his hands resting lightly on her shoulders, his breath on her neck.

As she watched she saw the big black vehicle wheel pell-mell into the driveway. Her breath caught in her chest, her hand fluttering about the robe. She never understood why anyone would want to drive a vehicle that large, really. It was a stupid waste unless you needed it for hauling or farming or something. But just to drive it around was too showy and wasteful for her liking. She could hear the muffled roar of its engine and the muted popping of gravel as it skidded to a halt not too far from Marcus and that huge fire he had going in the driveway. Truth be told she wasn't too clear what this was all about, although she hadn't wanted to admit that to him. She did know that Marcus was counting on her, and that was enough. She could be strong. Hank would have wanted her to be strong. That was one of the reasons they had gotten married – she looked frail and small, but she could be tough when she had to be. Hank had known that from the start and had loved her for it. It had let him travel for work without constantly worrying about her at home.

She continued watching anxiously as the black Cadillac sat there, then gasped when the huge Mexican lumbered out of the driver's door. My! Her initial impression of the hulking brute came to her from one of her favorite childhood books, Tom Sawyer. The Mexican looked just like she thought Injun Joe would have appeared in person. Good heavens! Even from across the street the man made her heart race in terror. He was a monster, the dark skin, black lanky hair, and hands as big as baseball gloves. My, oh my! She couldn't see his face from her angle but she just knew he had black, soulless eyes, like eyes on a dead deer sprawled and mangled on the side of the road. Her neck prickled in fear. Gooseflesh bumped up and down her arms. She hugged herself as if a chill wind had blown through the very walls of her living room.

She was so intent on watching Injun Joe that she almost missed it when Marcus stood and tied his shoe. Oh, Lord, that was the signal! He had told her he had hoped the ringleader would appear, but was afraid someone else might. If anyone else came he would tie his shoe, and that was her cue. She fumbled with the telephone and dialed the phone number Marcus had written out for her. She was so jumpy she misdialed and cursed under her breath, hung up and tried again. After four seconds a voice answered, a man's voice.

"Yeah."

"This is Mrs. Kerr. Marcus told me to call. He needs you."

There was a grunt on the other end and a click. That was it? My, she thought, I hope I did that right. She nervously dialed again but it rang six times then went to that pesky voicemail thing that always annoyed her so. She stood and stared at the phone, uncertainty and anxiety battling for attention. She prayed that she had done that right, but what if she hadn't? She couldn't let Marcus face that immense Injun Joe by himself. But what could she do? Her head swiveled back and forth around the dark living room until her eyes latched onto a shape by the front door. Oh, no, could she? She hesitated but swore she could feel Hank nudging her toward it, could feel his strong hands gently moving her. Yes, she could, she decided. If she had to, for Rolland and Marcus. And for Hank.

Marcus might have been amused had he known Mrs. Kerr's description of Gonzalez as Injun Joe, amused because he hadn't thought of the description himself. He had read Tom Sawyer and Huck Finn as a child, before his mother had died, and had adored them both. The thought of Injun Joe standing across from him somehow would have seemed quite apt: the character had terrified him as a kid, the same way the sight of the giant terrified him now. However, no matter how he felt, no matter how high his fear ratcheted up, outwardly he was determined to remain stoic. He would not show emotion. He stood there calmly, only fifteen feet and the roaring fire separating the two men.

The huge Mexican stared at him in that considered, thoughtful way he had. The door to the SUV was still open and he had one hand resting casually on the open door. He cocked his head to one side.

"You want to talk?" he asked. Marcus tried to place his Spanish accent but couldn't. It may have been Mexican, but was more likely from Central America. He again noticed that the man's speech was smooth and almost eloquent, not at all what he would've expected by looking at him. "I'm not here to talk."

Marcus took a handful of the credit cards and tossed them into the heart of the fire. The plastic quickly curled and turned black, the cards shriveling into useless plastic slag within seconds. Gonzalez hissed and took a step forward. Marcus snatched another handful of cards and held them toward the blaze like a weapon.

"Stay right there or the whole box and the ledgers go in, too," Marcus barked, his voice loud and imperious. "We're going to do this my way, understand?"

Gonzalez didn't answer directly but took a measured step backwards. His black eyes narrowed to no more than two small tar balls in his rough, asphalt face. The scar along his cheek throbbed an angry purple.

"Good," Marcus said. "I don't think your boss would be happy if anything happened to this stuff now, not when you're so close to getting your hands on it. Am I right?" Gonzalez didn't reply. "Now, like I said, you and I are going to talk. I want to know everything. What Rolland was doing, what the cards were for, why you were buying so many guns. I want to know it all."

"Really? Is that all?"

"For starters, yes. Then we're going to make a deal. Your boss is already treading on thin ice – I told him to come alone and not bring anyone else with him. I should just toss this whole lot into the fire and be done with it right now."

The corners of Gonzalez's lips turned up into what may have been a smile. He crossed his thick, muscled arms, arms thicker than a normal man's legs.

"Then there would be nothing to stop me from coming for you."

Marcus forced his own smile. "There is that, yes. So let's talk."

Gonzalez was subtly impressed at Marcus' cool resolve. "Go."

Marcus abstained from taking a deep breath. He had gotten past the first hurdle. "Let's talk about the cards first. Where did you get them?"

"You realize, of course, that I'm simply an employee? I'm not privy to all the ins and outs of the operation. However, this much I can tell you. The cards were purchased from an individual in Eastern Europe, someone who had hacked into one of your American financial databases, the tax department in your state of South Carolina, I believe. It is amazingly simple to secure cards such as these, and the cost is very reasonable. From what I understand this happens quite often, especially since your security is so outdated and ineffective. It makes you an easy global target. Counterfeiting of this type can't be done anywhere else in the world, but your VISA and MasterCard companies don't want to spend the money to upgrade their systems since they themselves suffer no monetary losses. It's child's play for a professional hacker, or so I'm told. You really should demand that they update their technology."

From his research Marcus had learned as much. Much of the security contained on each card could be traced to the 1970s. There were newer safeguards in place but not all financial institutions utilized them. He motioned Gonzalez to continue.

"But what we really needed was someone here in the States to manage all this, someone with no connection to us, someone low-profile. That person was your brother. We shipped the cards to him in many small quantities using your own US Mail service, UPS, and FedEx, over the course of several weeks. All the boxes got through, which shows another lapse in your security."

"But why Rolland? Why did you involve my brother?"

Gonzalez continued as if he hadn't heard. "Once he had the cards we instructed many dozens of our people to contact him to obtain the cards and begin making weapons purchases. Sadly we never had a way of knowing how much each card could purchase. In many cases we ended up going to stores like Wal-Mart and buying gift cards until each card was maxed out, then used the gift cards to make the buys. If there were balances left over we received the remainder of the money in cash. Other times we simply purchased guns from dealers who accepted credit cards or gift cards. Dealers are hungry for sales and will do anything. Your brother also bought guns for us on occasion. That ledger in your hands," he motioned to the papers Marcus was holding, "was used to track all the purchases. Who made them, how much they paid, where they got them, and so on. This was done in your States of Ohio, Kentucky, and Indiana. It was all done by hand and kept away from computers and the Internet, just in case we were being monitored. Each person was legally able to make the buys, so there were no problems with the ATF. Other times we simply gave gift cards to other people who bought guns directly. It's so simple to purchase weapons of any kind in your country."

"They're called 'straw-sales'. People buying guns for others who can't. What are all the guns for?" Marcus asked.

Gonzalez still ignored Marcus' questions, slightly annoyed at the interruption. His face clouded as he continued. "Then something happened.

About six months ago your brother tried to back out of our arrangement. He was getting, how do you say it? Cold feet?"

"Why? What changed?"

"I don't know. Something did, whether it was simply a change of heart or his conscience stepping in. It didn't matter. Hernandez had to have a face to face session with him to help him reconsider his rash decision. After that he was back on board, as you can imagine."

Wait, six months ago? That coincided with the time Doncaster's men had found Rolland beaten up and hiding in the bushes. They had locked him up for the night for his own protection. The timeline continued to become clearer.

"But then it happened again. Something happened and your brother changed his mind again, this time for good. He suddenly refused to cooperate any longer, and as you know he went so far as to hide the ledger and the rest of the cards. Since we don't place any faith in computer security the ledger was the only record we had, and without that we had little idea who had purchased what weapon or how many they had in their possession. His refusal to cooperate put the entire operation in jeopardy, which we couldn't tolerate. Where did you find them, by the way? Since we're sharing information, I mean."

"There was a key hidden in the doghouse. It went to a locker elsewhere," he explained quickly. "Why did Rolland do that? What changed his mind?"

"In the doghouse behind the house here? Really? We were so close and never knew it. I honestly have no idea what changed. Perhaps he realized what we were doing and what the guns were for? Whatever the reason, we could not stand for his mutinous behavior. We needed the cards and ledger so we could continue, but he refused us. We could not tolerate that, so we...came for him."

Marcus was almost shaking in anger, hearing him talk about his brother and his involvement. "What happened?"

"We came for him, to get the cards, but still he refused."

"Was that the day of the storm? The thunderstorm?"

Gonzalez's eyebrows raised in surprise. "Yes, that was it. How did you know? No matter. We came for him and he ran, into the woods. We looked for him but he was gone. Hernandez took several random shots into the woods to scare him but it didn't succeed, either. We have not been able to find him since."

"And that's when you shot his dog?"

"Yes. Unfortunately Hernandez took great pleasure in that, but that's his way. He enjoys harming both animals *and* people, I'm afraid. He is not a nice man, which you know."

Marcus took a slow, shaky breath. "Sam never did anything to you. And by the way, his name wasn't Hernandez, it was Calderon. I wouldn't count on his help any more. I don't think he'll be back anytime soon. Or ever."

"Well, you are a wealth of information, and apparently quite resourceful, too. Yes, his name is Calderon, and perhaps you can tell me what happened to him?"

Now it was Marcus' turn to ignore a question. "He was a crazy little shit and he won't be missed by anyone."

"Perhaps. Sometimes he was more trouble than he was worth, granted, but we need people like him at times. Now I shall have to find another one. They can be most useful. You continue to cause problems for us, much like your brother did."

Marcus was certain he was about out of time, so he hurried on. "The guns. What do you want the guns for?"

Gonzalez leaned up against the car door, almost casually. "Do you know how simple it is to smuggle guns into Mexico? There is only one gun dealer in the entire country, you know, in Mexico City, and guns are illegal for nearly all citizens there. Your government spends billions of your dollars each year making sure drugs and people aren't smuggled into your precious country, yet you do almost nothing to make sure nothing crosses the border in the other direction. We have shipped hundreds, thousands of guns into Mexico, with only a small handful of them being caught at the border. It's a crime, really, and so easy anyone can do it. Once they're in Mexico they are moved around in a matter of days."

"Yes, I know that. But why? Why are you shipping them into Mexico?"

The huge Mexican straightened up and Marcus could tell he was considering how much more to reveal. He took another handful of cards and tossed them into the center of the fire where they quickly melted like hot taffy. The fire had burned down a little but was still large enough and hot enough for his purposes. Gonzalez growled and bounced upright, off the SUV. Marcus thought he heard a car in the distance.

"That was not wise. Once those cards are gone there is nothing to keep me from you. You will not enjoy what I have in mind, trust me. I am not a violent man by nature, but you should not push me. I am not like Calderon but don't test my patience."

"Answer my question. Why are you shipping them to Mexico?"

"There is more going on than you know, and the weapons are needed. And it is necessary to be very…unobtrusive, very discreet. You see the news about drug cartels and what is going on, the fighting and the killing. My employer needs them to turn the tide, to help maintain the status quo. But he needs to do so with a very low profile."

And now came the big question. "Who is your employer?"

For the first time Gonzalez truly grinned, a large smile void of humor that made his face more hideous than ever. It was the look of a lion about to devour its prey.

"No, that I will not answer. That is for someone else to tell. Now give me the cards and the ledger. We are done talking, you and I."

Marcus took one sheet of the ledger, balled it up then pitched it into the fire. It burst into blue flames before its edges blackened, glowed red, and was gone. Its black ash mixed with the destroyed credit cards. Gonzalez clenched his massive fists and stalked toward him, death written across his mien. Marcus prepared to heave the entire contents of the box into the blaze and run when a huge red Dodge pickup truck flew up the road and came to a screeching halt directly behind the SUV, effectively blocking it in. The big Mexican whirled around to face this new threat, his great shaggy head snapping from Marcus, to the truck, and back again. His long black hair whipped across his face.

"What is this?" he growled.

"The cavalry," Marcus said with both relief and satisfaction.

The driver's door flew open and Donald Doncaster jumped out. Marcus was surprised that he wasn't driving his police car or in uniform, but instead was dressed in jeans and a T-shirt. He wasn't wearing his service revolver either, which was another surprise. Doncaster's thick neck was red and puffy, stretching the neck of his T-shirt to the breaking point. His thick, fireplug body was tense but he bounced on the balls of his feet like a fighter anxious for the bell to ring.

"So you got the call?" Marcus said loudly enough for the new arrival to hear. "Good. Glad you could make it." He inclined his head toward Gonzalez. "There's your man. Take him away."

Doncaster didn't acknowledge him. He reached back and knocked on the body of the pickup truck with a big, meaty fist. The pickup itself was a large four door diesel model, as big as Marcus had ever seen. At Doncaster's bidding all the doors burst open and six other men piled out. They assembled in a ragged line on either side of the policeman. They were all related, most likely brothers, that much was easy to tell. Marcus was astounded – as solid and stocky as Doncaster was, he was by far the smallest of this mob. Two of the men were the size of professional football players, topping six feet seven inches, although the older of the two was out of shape, a hefty gut protruding over his belt. Three of them cracked their knuckles. They all stared death at Gonzalez. Donald pointed at the Mexican.

“We’re going to roll you, fucker! No one messes with our brother.”

“What?” Marcus yelled. “Hold on! What are you talking about?”

That was when Marcus remembered: Otto was Driver 8, the youngest of eight boys. Otto’s seven older brothers were here to exact vengeance against one of the men responsible for so grievously injuring their youngest sibling. *An eye for an eye, a tooth for a tooth.* As if choreographed they moved as one toward the huge Mexican, stalking confidently forward, strength and courage in numbers. Marcus was ignored by everyone as Gonzalez stepped toward them, equally confident. A low, guttural, feral growl rumbled through the huge Mexican’s gritted teeth, rising in volume until it became a menacing howl filled with power and arrogance. Marcus remembered the story of how the huge Mexican had lifted a man over his head and had broken his back. Gonzalez clenched his fists and raised his arms in the air as if to declare his dominance over the entire world. Then the seven men were on him, fists swinging, yelling, shouting in pain and anger. Bodies flew away, bloodied, broken.

Shit, Marcus swore to himself. This was *not* part of his plan.

Marcus could do nothing but watch helplessly as the battled raged before him. Donald was the first man in, but with the back of his massive hand Gonzalez swatted him aside so hard that the cop did a cartwheel, blood exploding from his nose like a pane from a graphic novel. The big Mexican, either wisely or by accident, kept his back to the fire so he couldn’t be rushed from behind. Three brothers jumped on him but he shrugged them off before they could drag him down. One man flipped into the fire screaming, his hair and shirt catching before he could roll out. Sparks danced upward like a thousand fireflies as that half of the carefully constructed bonfire imploded under his weight. He was swatting madly at his head and face to put out the blaze, screeching like a little girl. The smell of charred meat and burnt hair almost overwhelmed him. Donald slowly levered himself to his feet and wiped blood from his eyes and face with the back of his hand. Enraged, not thinking clearly, he screamed as he charged Gonzalez and hit him with a shoulder, squarely in the big man's midsection. The Mexican staggered backwards a step, grabbed the cop around the waist, and flipped him over his back: Doncaster flew seven or eight feet and with a tremendous grunt landed hard on his head and neck, then lay still.

The five brothers that were still standing regrouped and advanced together then, more wary and respectful of the immense size and strength of the man before them. A few of them were already out of breath, huffing and puffing. They circled like cautious coyotes, slowly, their eyes never leaving Gonzalez. Suddenly the biggest and the oldest of the five yelled "Now!" and they swarmed over him, two hitting him low around the knees and the other three taking him high at his chest and waist. They drove him backwards several feet like a tackling dummy. His legs were entwined and he was unable to maintain his balance. Roaring he toppled slowly, like a demolished skyscraper coming to ground. His shouts of rage were cut off as his head hit the driveway and gravel exploded out in all directions.

Once on the ground his long reach and tremendous strength were blunted. The two brothers at his legs held tight while the other three began leveling hard punches and kicks at his face, his midsection, anywhere they could find an opening to inflict damage. Their fists were not just hitting him, they were trying to punch completely through him. They were swearing and cursing as they pummeled his face and body, their knuckles bruised and bloodied. It was clear that none of these men were strangers to violence. Gonzalez had the largest brother around the neck with his huge fingers, squeezing so hard the man's eyes rolled back in his head before he shuddered then fell limply on top of him. With his free arm he was flailing madly back and forth, making random contact with the other two brothers. But while he concentrated on one the other was busy pounding away at his face and leveling great kicks at his sides. There were several snapping sounds, loud cracks like branches breaking. Marcus couldn't tell if they were from the Mexican or one of the Doncaster brothers.

Just when it looked like he was out and done Gonzalez got a leg free, heaving one man off with tremendous force. The brother staggered backwards, off balance, and smacked his head on the fender of the red pickup truck. He slumped to the ground, dazed and out of the fight. Buoyed by his success the big Mexican rolled several times and broke free. He levered one knee under him and was about to stand when the remaining brothers tackled him one final time. He went down under a fierce barrage of kicks and fists. He was weakening rapidly, his breath coming in ragged gasps. The brothers sensed his declining strength so they ramped up their onslaught. They scattered gravel as they moved and their breathing was loud in the otherwise still afternoon as they continued pummeling him.

Finally the huge Mexican shuddered and lay still. His already mottled face was a mass of blood and swelling to the point where Marcus could barely make out his features. His nose was mashed flat like a bloody pancake, his eyes swollen shut under the huge brow, his left cheek ripped open and revealing bloodied bone. One arm was bent at a completely illogical angle, either broken or severely dislocated. The four brothers still standing did not look much better off. Each now sported bruises and gashes of their own and there was no telling what damage they had suffered out of sight under their tattered clothing. The biggest brother, the one with the overhanging gut, was bent over with his hands squarely on his knees, unable to catch his breath, his face pale. They all stared at the prostrate form at their feet, no sign of victory evident on their faces. Three of their number had been grievously injured. They knew the battle had been won, but the cost had been dear.

Slowly then, as if drunk, they staggered dumbly around to check on the condition of their fallen siblings. The burned brother was moaning and holding his arm delicately. The visible flesh under his shirt was raw and scorched, like meat left too long on the grill. His face was burned splotchy black and red in places and his brown hair was singed to the scalp on the right side. He winced as he stood. They spoke in low voices and gathered up the man who had collided with the pickup truck. He muttered that he was okay, dammit, he was fine, although he swayed as he leaned against the truck, almost falling over. He was pale, trembling. He bent over and vomited in the gravel.

Their biggest concern was Donald himself. They hovered over his unconscious, crumpled form, unsure what to do. Finally after some quiet discussion four of them gently lifted him up and placed him gingerly into the bed of the pickup. He moaned once but then quickly fell silent again. Anxiety was clear in their faces. Marcus finally set the box on the kitchen chair and jogged to the pickup truck. As tall as he was he had to look up to talk to the eldest brother. He pointed to Gonzalez.

"What about him?" he asked, motioning toward the mangled form on the ground. He was barely holding his temper in check. This had *not* gone as planned. "What are you going to do with him? You just can't leave him here."

The four brothers stared at the fallen Mexican. The one brother nodded.

"We'll take him, too."

"Take him where?"

"To the hospital. Donald will know what to do with him."

"Donald?" Marcus snapped. "In case you didn't notice he's in no shape to do much of anything, thanks to you guys and that little stunt you just pulled."

The biggest brother's face was covered with so much blood he could have just finished gutting a deer. He tried to wipe some away but only succeeded in smearing it around. He repeated his statement. "Donald will know what to do with him. We're going to the hospital."

Marcus stood by helplessly as the four brothers grunted and lifted Gonzalez with considerable difficulty into the pickup bed. With a lot less compassion than they had shown Donald they tossed him next to their brother but couldn't shut the gate due to the Mexican's size. Marcus saw that the big man was still breathing but it was shallow and thin. All six remaining brothers trudged and limped to the pickup and slowly climbed inside. With much less bravado than when they had arrived, the men started up the truck and slowly pulled away. It weaved down the road, around a bend and was out of sight. Shaking, Marcus could do nothing else but watch it go.

That had not gone well, but he could still salvage this. The second half of his plan was still viable.

Then the back door of the black Escalade opened and Andy Saunders, AJ, from Big Bob's Gun Show stepped out. In his hand he held a nasty looking black pistol. In his other hand he was holding the arm of Cassie. Her brown eyes were huge and terrified.

Shit. This really wasn't working out well at all.

Mrs. Kerr was confused and frightened but still resolute. She had witnessed the brutal beating of Injun Joe by the policeman from town and his clan. She recognized most of the boys from when they were younger and played football for Wayne High School. They had been a rough and tumble bunch back then, a bunch of hoodlums. Who in their right mind would have eight children? And all boys, to boot! Some damn-fool people were just crazy.

After the pickup truck had pulled away she had relaxed just a little, thinking that the worst was over and Marcus would signal the all clear, flashing her the okay sign with both hands. But that wasn't happening. Now there was some rough looking man with a strange blond beard. He had a gun and he was holding onto that nice girl Marcus was so fond of. She glanced briefly at the phone but knew that avenue was hopeless – no one could get out to their houses in time to do anything, especially since the policeman was obviously in no shape to help. Again she almost felt Hank's hands on her shoulders, directing her toward the door.

"Yes, dearest," she said in a firm voice. "I know what I have to do."

She swore she could feel her husband smiling at her. It warmed her inside.

"Well, hey there, perfessor, fancy meeting you here," Andy said, his voice confident and cocky. He had a tight grip on Cassie's forearm. Marcus saw that her wrists were bound with a thick plastic zip-tie. He looked her over quickly, inspecting her for any kind of abuse. He didn't immediately spot anything but his scan was purely superficial.

"You okay?" he asked her softly.

"Sure she's okay, perfessor. She's awfully pretty, I'll give you that. But she's just fine and dandy. Can't say as much for the poor devil you had watching her."

Marcus' heart sank. Oh my God, he thought, not another one!

"What did you bastards do to Sal?"

Andy waved the gun casually in the air. The large signet ring on his hand glinted and sparkled brightly. One of Marcus' co-workers in San Diego had been on a championship football team in college and had a ring just like that one, big and gaudy, with the university's initials surrounded by diamonds.

"Oh, he'll be fine. Probably. Our large friend gave him a little shove and he cracked his head on the wall. Poor bastard fell like a ton of bricks." He smiled, his tiny white teeth small and insignificant in his mouth. "Just remember – when you're trying to hide someone, make sure they stay away from windows and doors. We were hoping she was still in town, and when we saw your friend taking food from the restaurant several times we figured he was feeding someone else. We finally spotted her through the windows. Sloppy, really. Tsk, tsk."

Marcus took a step toward them and Andy stiffened up, lightning fast. The gun snapped to her temple and stayed there. "Not so fast, perfessor. You and me have some business to attend to and we don't have much time. I figure the rest of the cops in town will hear about their poor fallen comrade pretty soon, so let's finish this up."

"You want the cards."

He pulled the gun away from Cassie's head and used it as a pointer, aiming it at the box near the chair. "See? You are smart. Yes, I want the cards and what's left of the ledger, and then this little lady and I are going to leave together. We'll have her as an insurance policy against you doing anything, and we still have her family being watched in Mexico. Anybody does anything wrong and, well, let's just say you could be without a girlfriend or she could be without her folks. How's that strike you?"

Marcus' mind was racing. He needed those cards, but even more he needed to get Cassie away from this maniac. But how? He was about ten feet from the two of them and knew any move from either him or Cassie would be trouble, but he couldn't let her go with him, he couldn't! He could do nothing else but stall and hope for an opening of some type.

"Tell me, AJ, what are you getting out of this? How are you involved?"

Saunders laughed, still confident in his superior position. "You know, how much do you think an honest gun dealer makes, eh? Not enough, I'll tell you. I had the chance to make some extra jack on the side and I took it. Losers sit on the sidelines, perfessor. I'm no loser. Now quit fucking around and put the cards and ledger in the Caddy. We're done talking."

Marcus growled under his breath and slowly picked up the box. It felt heavy in his hands. The cards slid to one side with a thump. He stopped.

"What if I toss them all in the fire right now? What happens then?"

AJ made a face. "Well that wouldn't be too smart. I'd have to shoot you both. I like you, perfessor, and I really don't want to do that."

Marcus believed him. He nodded and walked slowly towards Saunders.

"Not so fast, hot shot." He stepped toward the back of the SUV, still dragging Cassie. She squirmed and moved to AJ's side. He had to stretch out his arm to hold her, but his focus was firmly on Marcus. "Now put them slowly on the floor in the backseat. Nothing stupid now."

Suddenly Cassie screamed and kicked out at her captor. She meant to hit him in the groin but missed and caught him on the thigh instead. He snarled and spun her around, shoving her brutally to the ground where she sprawled with a cry. Marcus started to lunge at him but the gun was up and pointed at his face before he could move. At that precise moment neither Marcus nor Cassie was close to him.

"No more fucking around!" he shouted. "Put the shit in the car! Now!"

Then a loud boom echoed from somewhere and the side of the black SUV erupted in a wide pattern of gray pea-sized dents. The back rear window shattered inward and bits of tempered glass showered down like a thousand diamonds, much of which settled on AJ's shoulders and head. He flinched as the glass rained down on him. Marcus dove for the ground and Cassie yelled and covered her head with her hands. AJ spun side to side wildly, looking for the assailant.

"What the fuck!" he screamed, just as another boom sounded. AJ screamed again although this time it was in pain, not just surprise. The pistol dropped from his hands and he grabbed at his thighs, blood welling between his fingers. Marcus lunged forward and kicked at the fallen gun. It spun away into the yard and vanished in the tall grass.

AJ held his hands up in disbelief, staring in shock at his blood-soaked hands. His mouth was open, his voice high and strained, cracking. "I've been shot! Me! I've been shot!"

Blood oozed from a dozen wounds to his thighs and knees. He wiped at his legs in a blind panic as if he could brush away the injuries. His jeans were slowly turning black from the thighs down as they became blood-soaked. He stumbled back and leaned against the SUV, oblivious to the glass shards that covered him like sparkling confetti. His face was pale and he began to shake, whimpering as he unsuccessfully tried to staunch the flow of blood: there were simply too many wounds, they were too spread out, and his hands weren't large enough. Marcus ignored him and hustled over to Cassie's side.

"Are you okay?" he asked her. She was sitting up on the driveway. Her hands were still bound by the plastic zip-tie and she mutely held them out to him. Marcus dug in his pocket and pulled out the two hundred dollar knife he had purchased from Saunders at Big Bob's Gun and Knife Show. A quick slice and her hands were free. She rubbed her wrists and stared at him.

"I'm pretty sure this wasn't part of your plan, was it?" she asked, deadpan. "Or did I miss something?"

His relief was so great he couldn't hold back a smile. He gave her a quick hug, then released it but still held on to her shoulders. He helped her to her feet. She brushed herself off and looked around, unsure what had just happened.

"No," he admitted, "this was not entirely planned."

"Entirely?"

"Okay, not at all, not like this. But the final outcome," he motioned around him, "is pretty much what I expected. I still have the cards and ledger, Gonzalez is out of the picture, and you're safe and sound."

At the words "safe and sound" she sucked in a quick breath. "My parents! You heard what he said about my parents. They're still in danger!"

"No, they're not. I've got that taken care of. A friend down in Merida contacted them three days ago and moved them out, into a safe hiding place. They are in no danger, I promise."

She stopped. "A friend? What friend? You're sure about that? They're okay?"

"Absolutely. I got a voicemail this morning confirming that. They're fine."

She exhaled and rubbed a trembling hand over her face. She reached for her silver cross but came up empty. She patted her neck and groped behind to see if it had flipped around but there was nothing there. She looked crestfallen.

"What's wrong?" Marcus asked.

She continued grabbing at her neck with both hands, searching. "My cross. It's gone. It must have broken loose sometime between Sal's and here. Oh, no – that was given to me by my mother at confirmation. I can't believe I lost it."

Marcus tried to console her but was interrupted by AJ behind them. He was still whimpering and clutching at his legs. He had slid down the side of the SUV and was on the driveway. His face was ash white which made his King Tut beard stand out starkly. Sticky thick blood began to cover the gravel beneath him. His legs twitched and he was sweating, huge drops covering his forehead.

"Dammit, I've been shot," he hissed. "I'm bleeding to death here. Help me!"

Marcus knelt beside him, gravel crunching under his shoes, and casually brushed some glass off the man's shoulders. He said nothing for a minute that felt like an hour, AJ staring at him, his tiny white teeth clenched tight, his breathing heavy and fast. Marcus' expression was devoid of sympathy or compassion. Finally he turned to Cassie.

"Would you please go into the house and grab some towels from the bathroom?"

Cassie nodded and trotted into Rolland's. She was still absently rubbing her sore wrists. Marcus watched her go before he spoke again.

"You're not bleeding to death. You've just got some shot in you, although I bet it hurts like hell, eh?"

AJ nodded in quick jerks. "Uh, yeah."

He smiled thinly at Saunders. "You know that old saying? 'Those who live by the sword die by the sword.' Of course in your case that would be 'gun'.

Anyway, here's what we're going to do. I'm going to fix you up a bit and then you're going to leave. I'd highly recommend finding an urgent care or a doctor, but I'm not sure how you're going to explain what happened. Doctors have to report all gunshot wounds to the police, and it won't be too hard to put one and one together with Gonzalez and Doncaster. I'll leave that up to you.

"Then you're going to contact your boss and tell him that you guys screwed up massively, and that I'm so pissed I may just burn everything. Unless," he held up a finger, "unless he shows up here, by himself, on Sunday at noon. If he doesn't come here alone at noon on Sunday it's all gone and he can kiss it goodbye. Do you understand? Am I perfectly clear?"

All the cockiness had drained out of AJ. He nodded fast, maybe a dozen times, like a manic bobble-head. "I understand. I'll tell him."

"I don't suppose you know who he is, do you?"

AJ shook his head rapidly. "No, I don't. I worked with Gonzalez directly. I never met whoever is doing all this. I got a phone number, but that's it. Shit, this is killing me. Give me something for the pain, would you?" His southern accent had vanished again.

"And I don't suppose you know how my brother got tapped to be involved in this, do you? No, I suspected as much."

Cassie came back out of the house with several towels and handed them to Marcus. He held up the knife to Saunders, smiled, then began using it to cut the towels into strips.

"It really is a nice knife," he commented, "although I don't think it was worth two hundred dollars. I'm thinking of asking for my money back."

AJ smiled shakily. He looked like he was trying to think of something to say but thought better of it and kept his mouth shut. Marcus began wrapping the freshly cut strips around his thighs and tying the ends tightly. Blood seeped into the cotton terrycloth, but the flow had already diminished.

“So, why’d you even talk to me at the gun show?” he asked. “Why didn’t you just ignore me? I never would have known a thing.”

AJ winced as Marcus synched up the wrappings. “Man, I thought you were Rolland and I about shit when I saw you. I knew these guys were looking for him. I thought you were him and I got so excited – ouch, do you have to do that so tight? – I got so excited that I yelled before I knew better. Then when you walked over and I realized it wasn’t him I had to say something, didn’t I? I didn’t know what to do, so I just said pretty much what anyone around the show knew, that he was around and buying shit up. I just wanted to get you out of there, man.”

Marcus pulled the last cotton strip tight, probably too tight, and AJ jerked and hissed in pain. He surveyed his handiwork and grunted.

“That should do it. Now get in the vehicle and get the hell out of here. You know what to do?” The injured man nodded. Marcus roughly helped him to his feet and steered him toward the driver’s door. AJ cursed and gingerly got in, blood staining the leather seats and interior door handle. He left a bright red handprint on the center armrest.

“Sunday, at noon. Got it?”

AJ grimaced and nodded. He pulled the door shut, started the engine, and roughly drove away. Less than a minute later the two of them were the only ones there, with the fire behind them finally burning down to black and red embers, smoke barely visible in the afternoon sunlight. She kept unconsciously reaching for the silver cross that was no longer there, a slightly bemused look on her face as if she had forgotten something.

“So what now?” she asked, peering down the road where the SUV had gone, as if she half-expected it to return. “What’s next?”

“What’s next,” he replied, “is to thank our unseen sharpshooter, the woman who just saved our lives. Bless her heart, I knew she was a gutsy girl with plenty of pluck.”

Inside Mrs. Kerr's dimly lit living room Marcus was busy giving their benefactor a huge hug. She was so tiny against his size XL frame that she looked no older than twelve or thirteen years old. The thick, heavy smell of cordite hung in the room and the old, tarnished .20 gauge shotgun was propped up against the wall next to the window. The breach was open and two spent shells were lined up on the windowsill, their yellow open ends burnt black.

"I can't believe you actually did that," Marcus told her, still in shock.

"Did I do that right?" she asked hopefully. "I called the number like you asked. That was for the policeman, Donacaster, wasn't it?"

"You bet. He was waiting several miles away, on a side road, out of sight. I talked to him earlier in the week and told him what I thought was going to happen and that I needed his help. He was, shall we say, reluctant at first, until I told him I thought it would be Gonzalez that showed up. He agreed pretty fast then, which should've been a dead giveaway that he had something up his sleeve. Anyway," he concluded, "I should give you grief for that stunt with the shotgun, but I don't know what we would've done without you. You likely saved our lives, I hope you know. That's two times for me."

Her smile was wide and happy, although her right arm hung loosely at her side. The .20 gauge had minimal kick but it was enough to bruise her aging muscles and bones. There was no serious damage, but it would be several weeks and many aspirins before it felt right again. Both Cassie and Marcus fussed at her about the arm, but she would listen to none of it. Instead she tottered off to the kitchen and made a pot of coffee. When it was ready he carried the tray in for her, replete with cream, sugar, and several Twinkies. He prepped his coffee under her watchful gaze, and to her delight opened one of the snack cakes and took a big bite, washing it down with the hot coffee. It was pretty much as bad as he thought it would be.

"Mrs. Kerr," Cassie said warmly, "thank you so very much. That was very brave, you know. Where did you learn to shoot like that? Your aim was amazing."

The older woman waved her off. "You're welcome, dear. My dear husband taught me. He insisted I know how to take care of myself."

"Mr. Kerr would have been proud," Marcus commented as he chewed.

Her old, red-rimmed eyes welled up and she smiled again. "Hank. His name was Hank. Yes, I believe he would have. Should we call the police and tell them what happened? Or will that policeman take care of that?"

Marcus shook his head. "I don't think we have to worry. Doncaster won't report any of this, I'm sure. He was taking care of some personal business, off the clock, so to speak. We won't have to concern ourselves about the police."

She accepted this and drank her coffee. Her hand shook, adrenaline still coursing through her for perhaps the first time in years. Cassie took her coffee black which pleased their host to no end. She nodded in appreciation at the younger woman.

"I like her. She knows how to drink coffee."

At this they both laughed, which did wonders to lift the anxiety left over from the earlier fight, although Cassie looked a little miffed that she didn't get their inside joke about the coffee. They sat and relaxed some more while most of the residual tension gradually melted away. Marcus noticed that the dim living room, which he had once thought of as dingy and old, now felt warm and comfortable to him. The worn furniture and fading wallpaper did wonders to ease his mind and body. He was mildly surprised to find that, like Rolland's house across the street, this place was growing on him.

They soon said their goodbyes. Marcus made sure she had his cell phone number in case she needed to get in touch with him for whatever reason. He also gave her Cassie's. Marcus enveloped the older woman in a final hug, made sure she would lock up the house, and they left. Mr. Whiskers was on the porch as they walked out so he gave him an affectionate head rub as he passed. The cat purred loudly and scampered off into the yews, intent on a mission of its own.

Together they walked across the street, both keenly aware of the other's physical presence, their personal bond closer after having gone through their most recent ordeal. This latest shared experience was still keen in their minds. Cassie rubbed at her neck as she reached for the missing cross. It took some effort but she forced her hand to her side.

"What are you going to do with the cards?" she asked. "Back to locker number forty five?"

"I may as well," he said, picking up the box and peering at the contents inside. There weren't as many cards inside as there should have been since as a precaution he'd left the majority of them in the locker before this even began. He had needed insurance of his own and had never had any intention of handing them all over to Gonzalez or anyone else.

She sighed deeply, troubled. "And now you have to leave? That's the second part of your plan, right?"

He went to the front door and stepped inside Rolland's, grabbing a suitcase he had packed earlier. He checked the front pocket and was reassured that his passport was still there although he had known it would be.

"Yes, it is. I have to go."

She looked away from him, staring at nothing but perhaps the woods next to the house. Her eyes were unfocused as she thought what to say and how to say it. She wrapped her arms around her chest, hugging herself. She looked like a little girl herself just then, he thought, young and uncertain, vulnerable. Finally she turned to him. Her eyes were huge and pleading.

"Promise me you will be careful. These people are crazy and they will be so mad at you, I'm afraid what could happen."

He slung the suitcase into the back seat and the box of cards on the floor of the passenger side where he could keep an eye on them. The key to locker forty-five was in his pocket. Emotions were raging inside of him. He wanted with all his heart to simply grab her around the waist and draw her to him, kissing her long and hard, so happy she was safe after the close call. But he restrained himself from that as difficult as it was, as much as he desired it. It was all he could to not tell her how he truly felt. He was afraid if he opened his mouth he would say too much, so he said nothing at all.

"Promise me!" she demanded. "I…I don't want to lose you, too."

"I will," he finally answered. "I'll be careful. But I have to do this. If we don't put an end to this they'll always be able to manipulate us through your parents, or just like they did now, by holding you. I can't allow that. Hernandez and Gonzalez might be out of the picture but there are always more thugs waiting in the wings. We have to end this now."

They both knew he was right. They stared silently for another few seconds until the moment for speaking their hearts was gone. Marcus walked away from her then, around the house, making sure it was locked up tight. He patted the doghouse as he went by it. The mound of dirt was dotted with new shoots of grass and several dandelions. In silence they got into the rental car and he drove her back home. When they got there she mutely gripped his hand once and went inside without glancing back. He very nearly called after her, but by that time she was inside with the door closed firmly behind her.

He drove in dark silence first to the YMCA where he deposited the box, then to the Dayton Airport, his thoughts twisting like a whirlwind inside his head and heart.

Chapter 27

His flight to Merida was without incident. In fact much like his drive to the gun show the prior week, had anyone asked him for details of his trip he would have been unable to recount any meaningful events. He spent the time deep in thought mentally covering his bases and reliving the past month, searching his memory for anything he may have missed, any incident that might sway him from his current path. He found none. Marcus knew what had to be done, but he also knew what the consequences would be. They would be terrible, but doing nothing would be more terrible still. He could see no outcome where people he loved wouldn't be significantly impacted for the worse. He almost wished he had never come to Ohio, that he had never taken the call from Rolland's landlady. That was the coward's way out, he knew, but that didn't make it any less inviting.

At the Merida airport nothing had changed. It was still loud and crowded, a polyglot of languages and cultures. The pastel blues and greens were muted today, flat, victims of an overcast day outside. Marcus made it through customs without incident and retrieved his suitcase from the baggage claim area. He donned a black Cincinnati Reds baseball cap to conceal as much of his blond hair as possible, then slid on a pair of sunglasses. There was nothing he could do about his height, but he kept near the walls and out of the way to draw as little attention to himself as he could. He was acutely aware of his size and skin color here. Near the front doors he pulled out his cell phone and dialed a long number. After several rings he heard a click, and a voice said, "Bueno?"

"Estoy aqui," he said. *I'm here.*

Their conversation continued for just over a minute. Finally Marcus sighed deeply. He nodded his head, the phone still to his ear.

"Verdad? Mañana, a las dos?" he asked. *Really? Tomorrow at two o'clock?*

The voice on the other end repeated the information. Marcus sighed again, wiping his hand over his face. His stomach felt like a huge sucking hole where all his emotions were draining out. Again he nearly wished he had never heard from Rolland's landlady.

"Bien. Estaré aqui antes de uno." *Fine. I'll be here before one o'clock.*

The voice said goodbye and the phone went dead. He stared at it accusingly, as if the phone itself were to blame for his problems. He jammed it into his pocket and walked out into the stifling, humid air. The smells of Merida washed over him but this time he was unaware of them. He hailed a taxi. The driver of the green and white Nissan grunted at him, requesting a destination.

"I'm looking for a hotel that's out of the way, not frequented by tourists," he said in Spanish.

If the driver was surprised at the gringo's mastery of the language he didn't show it. The man nodded, mumbling that he knew just the place. His tires chirped as he jetted away from the curb, narrowly missing several pedestrians and an angry policeman who'd been attempting to direct traffic. The driver chuckled as the cop yelled indistinct threats at the back of his speeding car.

The taxi driver had a local news talk show on, and between loud commercials the major topic of the day was the discovery of a score of men found in a deserted warehouse outside of town. Each had been systematically shot in the back of the head. Half of them had been decapitated as well to further strike fear into their enemies. Locals calling into the radio station were incensed at the escalating violence, and equally furious at local law enforcement for its inability to curb it. Tourism, one of the most lucrative sources of revenue for many in the city, was starting to be impacted. People could tolerate liberal amounts of violence and injustice to their fellow man, but should their collective wallets be impacted then outrage would quickly follow. Tourism in the city was already down over ten percent from the year before. If it continued to falter then the local and federal governments would certainly come under even more fire. The taxi driver grunted and changed the dial on the radio until he found a current pop hit.

The Federal Agent that Marcus had met on several occasions, Cruzado, had pleaded with him to help stop this madness. The man knew his city was being torn apart but felt virtually powerless to do anything about it. Marcus sympathized with him.

The Nissan taxi jerked to a halt outside an older part of town, near the *zócalo*, or local square. There was an aging fountain in the middle of the square that was now dry and littered with leaves and trash. Around the fountain was a block of scruffy grass and dirt where kids played. Outside of that area there were shops and outdoor cafes with faded awnings protecting diners from the elements. There were several old two and three story hotels there as well, past their prime and falling into disrepair. Street vendors had staked their claims on the crowded sidewalks, selling everything from slices of mango to deep fried tacos and enchiladas wrapped in banana leaves. This was old Mexico, off the normal tourist route except for traveling college students exploring the world on a budget. It was a perfect place for him to lay low for the night.

He paid the taxi driver and thanked him, tipping him well. He checked out his lodging options and chose one at random, a three story stucco building named Hotel Carmen. As he went inside the dim lobby at the front desk sat a small, very dark clerk who looked him over briefly and sold him a room for the night, no questions or identification asked. The price was a mere fifteen dollars which garnered him a single room on the second floor overlooking the square. There was no bathroom in the room, only a bed and a huge dresser with the finish worn off to the bare wood. Blackened marks all along the edge of the dresser were mute declarations of many a forgotten cigarette left burning. The shared bathroom was down the hall. He smiled at the toilet's pull chain leading up to an elevated tank, like something out of the distant U.S. past.

In his room he flopped down on the bed. The bedspread was ancient and worn, but at least seemed clean. The bowed floorboards creaked under his weight. There was no air conditioning, only a tired ceiling fan that spun in lazy circles, just enough to keep the heavy air moving in sluggish waves. He shrugged. Fifteen dollars seemed just about right for the room. *Caveat emptor* and all that.

Since he wasn't planning on staying but the one night he didn't feel the need to unpack. Instead he locked the room with the heavy brass key and made his way outside. The first street vendor he found was selling bottled water, tacos, and some random candy bars. He bought several waters, three tacos wrapped in newsprint, and treated himself to a Mexican chocolate bar. He took his dinner back up to his room and quickly ate it all. The bottled water was cold and tasted wonderful. There were sinks in the common bathroom, but not even the locals liked to drink the water. In fact, much of the upper crust in Mexico wouldn't have dared to eat from the street vendors for fear of stomach problems, but Marcus didn't have much choice. He could only cross his fingers and hope that however the tacos had been prepared it wouldn't cause him any gut issues in the next twenty four hours, or at least until he was back in the States. His meal completed, he reclined on the bed and dozed off and on the rest of the night, true sleep eluding him even though he was physically tired from the day's travel and emotionally spent with the knowledge of what was to come. When he did finally manage to sleep his dreams were punctuated with visions of him tumbling into the green waters of the Sagrado Cenote. But instead of clawing to the surface he kept sinking deeper and deeper, the dim glow above growing faint and finally vanishing altogether.

The next day dawned dark and overcast, the sun completely shrouded in heavy gray clouds. It had rained in the night and the cracked sidewalks below him were filled with black puddles where trash and litter had collected. Young children, boys in heavy dark pants and little girls in cotton sundresses, ran around splashing in the puddles, oblivious to the trash. The vendor from the night before was setting up shop and snapped at the kids as they bumped into him. One very small boy with a round face and huge brown eyes, wearing a battered New York Yankees hat, said something, probably an apology from the looks of it, and then scampered off. He had a string of colorful yarn bracelets in his hand that he no doubt planned to sell to the few tourists that ventured into this part of town. He was thin and undernourished but happy nonetheless. Marcus smiled at his youthful innocence. The boy skipped around a corner and was gone from sight.

Marcus went down the hall to the communal bathroom and freshened up, shaving and brushing his teeth. Several other men, all native Mexicans, came and went during that time, and while none said anything to him besides the obligatory "Buenos días", each was evidently shocked at the sight of the large blond foreigner sharing their facilities. He patted his face dry and didn't hang around any longer than necessary.

Back in his room he packed his few belongings and went downstairs for a copy of the local paper and something to eat. Reading it reclined in his bed he found the story of the murdered men he had heard about on the radio. To his surprise it had been relegated to a brief single paragraph on the last page with nothing but an antiseptic description of the events, positioned right before the sports section. It gave no details of the grisly crime, no names of the dead, no discussion of next steps by the authorities. There was some reference to a possible drug connection but little else of substance, and there were certainly no cartels mentioned. It was as if even the newspapers had been cowed by the drug gangs. He leafed through the rest of the paper but found no additional references to the murders. He tossed the flimsy newspaper onto his bed, upset. He slowly munched on a handful of tortillas and salsa and watched the time tick away on his watch.

At eleven o'clock he roused himself, grabbed his suitcase, and checked out. The same dark skinned man at the front desk accepted the key, barely giving Marcus a second glance. A small television was on behind the counter. On its fuzzy screen was an American sitcom dubbed into Spanish, the voices not at all matching what he remembered. He left, the laugh-track roaring hilariously, mindlessly, behind him.

About halfway to the airport there was some commotion on the road ahead and his taxi stuttered to a halt. There was a large delivery truck directly in front of them, the colorful logo for Pan Bimbo, a popular white bread brand, bright on the white of the truck. They sat there for nearly a minute while the exhaust from the truck drifted back into the taxi. Marcus was already feeling slightly anxious and this unscheduled stop did nothing to calm his jittery nerves. He asked the driver what was wrong.

The driver shrugged. "No sé," he said. "No puedo ver nada." *I don't know. I can't see anything.*

Marcus sat back with a huff and tried to relax. He looked at his watch. Eleven thirty, plenty of time before he promised he'd be at the airport. The driver murmured into his radio and asked about the hold up, but the nasal dispatcher at the other end had no idea either. He caught Marcus' eye in the rearview mirror and raised his hands, palms up, and said, "Que será será." *Whatever will be will be.*

Que será será. Marcus almost laughed, the irony of those three simple words not lost on him. That saying had been made popular from a 1956 movie from the famous director Alfred Hitchcock, *The Man Who Knew Too Much*. It was the story of an American doctor who had become embroiled in an assassination attempt on a European head of State. He had been totally out of his element while trying to stop the murder, but of course in the end had prevailed. It was a typical Hitchcock tale of an Everyman caught up in events outside his control. Marcus felt like that Everyman, unsure of himself and full of doubt, wondering feverishly if what he was doing was the right thing. He could not see himself as a hero like Jimmy Stewart and wished he could be as confident as the tall, lanky character the actor portrayed in the movie. He hoped he was doing the right thing, hoped he was wrong in what he believed.

Ten minutes passed painfully slowly as they idled in traffic. Marcus kept glancing at his watch and noted with rising impatience that it was eleven forty-five. The airport was still at least fifteen minutes away. He had planned on being there well ahead of time but that cushion was quickly vanishing. He briefly considered walking the rest of the way but couldn't afford being spotted out on the streets: a tall, blond gringo carrying a suitcase would not go unnoticed, especially in this part of town. He exhaled loudly through his nose and made himself relax in the back seat. He didn't do a particularly good job of it. It was hot in the taxi and he felt sweat running down his back. His stomach was tight and a little queasy.

Finally the Pan Bimbo truck ahead of them jerked and began to move. He sighed with relief as the taxi gathered speed and was traveling at a decent clip again. Several local policemen were there with a young man on a motorcycle, a red milk crate lashed to the back of the bike. The motorcycle had slammed into the side of a taxi and people were shouting and gesturing wildly at one another, blame being tossed around grandly in typical Mexican fashion. One of the policeman directed traffic around the accident and soon they were on their way again, the pastel colored stores and houses rushing by on either side of them in a colorful, rainbow blur. Merida's smells wafted through the taxi as they drove on, tortillas, snatches of fruit, tobacco, and the ever-present exhaust of a million vehicles.

At twelve o'clock on the nose the taxi skidded around a corner and up the drive to the airports' passenger drop off area. Marcus sighed in relief as he gathered up his bag and tipped the driver. He finally saw the man for the first time. He was tiny, barely five feet tall, with a tight, wrinkled little face and tired eyes that couldn't see beyond tomorrow. He may have been thirty or as much as fifty, it was impossible to tell. Marcus tossed a handful of extra pesos his way. The driver grinned briefly, his white teeth in bright contrast to his dark skin, pocketed the tip, and said a warm thank you before driving off in a cloud of blue smoke.

Marcus briefly looked around at the milling passengers and quickly entered the terminal, eager to be less conspicuous. As he went over and stood in the thin shadows against a wall his cell phone rang.

"Yes," he said, his free hand covering his open ear to muffle the crowd noise. He listened for a moment and nodded. "Está bien. Entiendo." *That's fine. I understand.* He hung up the phone and stuffed it back in his pocket. He thought he would be more nervous, that he would be a jittery wreck, but that seemed to have passed and now he found he was oddly calm. He inspected his palms and found they were dry, his hands steady. He walked down the terminal hallway and found a bank of lockers much like the ones in the Wayne YMCA. He almost chuckled when he saw that number 45 was available. He stuffed his suitcase into the dirty locker and locked it tight, pocketing the key, happy not to be lugging his baggage around. He pulled his ball cap down low and continued back to the entrance of the terminal where he stood to the side of the main bank of doors, next to a large tinted window. He had a perfect view of people pulling up and dropping off their charges. He leaned against a pillar and waited, watching. Outside he could see several dozen green and white taxis coming and going, like large insects dutifully completing unknown, specific tasks. One nondescript Volkswagen taxi near the head of the line was pulled up onto the curb, its overhead light out, with a sign in the window that read *No Servício*. He stared at it for a moment before glancing at his watch. He saw it was nearly twelve-thirty. A cute little girl of no more than five years old boldly walked up to him.

"Chícle, Señor?" she asked, holding out a selection of American gum.

He knelt down and selected a pack, paying her the asking price, which was more than he could have purchased it at a stand or in the gift shop. She barely nodded at him before scampering off to hit up another mark. He popped a piece of peppermint gum in his mouth and chewed, waiting. People flowed past him, most too intent on making their flight or looking for loved ones to even notice him. A uniformed policeman sauntered by, swinging his Billy club from a leather thong in a timeless fashion. Neither man paid any attention to the other. Still he waited.

Ten more minutes passed before he saw a large black SUV pull up. He stood at attention, his heart suddenly pounding. Despite himself he stood up tall. The calmness he had been feeling fled instantly, like a switch being flipped. The SUV's windows were tinted black, effectively barring prying eyes from seeing inside. Several taxis must have seen it arrive as well as they quickly moved out of the way to make room for the large, ominous vehicle. They knew someone important had arrived and were more concerned with accommodating the SUV than earning a quick fare. This was it, he was certain. Now his palms were damp and he ineffectively wiped them over and over on his shirt, like Lady Macbeth trying to wash the stain from her hands. The hair on the back of his neck prickled. Marcus leaned back against the post to keep out of sight although he was sure he couldn't be seen through the tinted glass of the terminal.

The driver parked in a no parking zone and hopped out of the car, looking around without appearing to look around at all. He had a dark, Mediterranean complexion and features, olive skin with black hair combed back over a young, thin, face. His black sunglasses were huge on his face. He wore a black suit and tie and a white shirt over a trim, athletic build, and he moved with cautious grace. There was a bulge under his jacket that had to be a holstered pistol. The cop in the terminal that had been swinging his Billy club was quickly walking in the other direction. The driver trotted around to the back of the SUV and opened the rear hatch, pulling out a single hard-shell suitcase. He went to the back passenger door and opened it wide, still carefully taking in the surroundings. He spoke to someone inside, nodded, then held the door open wider. A man slowly eased out. Marcus' heart sank.

It was El Señor. Damn. Of course it was.

He was as handsome as ever, his black hair artfully brushed back, his widow's peak prominent. The anchorman features were perfect, the black suit wonderfully tailored to highlight his frame. His eyes were hidden behind expensive Prada sunglasses, but Marcus could sense a hint of nervousness in his movements, some anxiety in his actions that he wasn't used to seeing. He spoke to his driver and both men walked toward the terminal door, the SUV left running in the no parking zone.

The double doors swished open and they entered the air-conditioned terminal, still talking quietly to each other. Marcus quickly threw away his gum and fell into step behind them, watching from a few feet back as they walked toward the security checkpoint. All noise around him seemed to fade to a dim rumble as he concentrated on their backs. El Señor, Javier, was several inches taller than the driver, who himself seemed to be agitated as well. He was doing most of the talking and gesturing, almost seemed to be pleading with his boss about something, pointing back toward the exit. It was clear he didn't want him to go. Finally Javier held up an imperious hand and the driver stopped talking, cowed. Marcus took three large strides and placed a hand on his uncle's shoulder.

"El Señor? Necesitamos hablar." *Sir, we need to talk.*

His uncle jerked at the touch and the driver whipped around, his hand diving into his jacket. Marcus snatched his wrist and held it in a crushing grip. The driver was wiry strong and took a half-step back to give himself room to move. Marcus held firm, his other hand clenched in a fist at his side, ready to lash out if necessary. El Señor quickly looked at both men and made an executive decision. He held up his left hand.

"Alto!" he commanded, his voice cutting through the crowd noise. Marcus and the driver froze, still staring daggers at each other. "Está bien. El es mi sobrino." *It's okay. He's my nephew.*

The driver stood frozen in place, his hand still within his jacket. Finally he nodded once, a single, subtle movement of his head. He slowly withdrew his hand. As he did so Marcus released his grip and the three men stood there as the rest of the milling crowd unconsciously gave them a wide berth. The driver slowly rubbed his wrist where Marcus had squeezed it. El Señor turned to his nephew and spoke to him, oddly enough, in English. His accent was nearly perfect, and Marcus found himself thinking that the man really could be an American anchorman on some nightly news show.

"Marcus, how nice to see you, although I must say I'm surprised. What in the world are you doing here?"

He looked at his uncle and inclined his head toward the driver. "We need to talk. Just the two of us."

Javier looked at his watch, a large silver Rolex, and shook his head. "I'm afraid that's not possible. I have a plane to catch."

Marcus nodded, his eyes never leaving his uncle's face. "I know. You're flying to Ohio. That's why we need to talk."

El Señor sucked in air through his teeth, just a half breath, but Marcus was certain that behind the sunglasses his eyes had gone momentarily wide in shock. He looked side to side quickly but no one was paying them any overt attention. He leaned in to Marcus.

"How do you know that? What is this all about?"

"As I said, we need to talk. But not here. Outside."

He looked at his watch again but made no move. Marcus gently placed a hand on his shoulder and gave a minute tug. "Come on, please. Just a quick taxi drive. We won't be gone long."

El Señor made no move. The driver evidently didn't speak English and was vainly trying to follow the conversation. Marcus gave another gentle tug.

"Come on. You don't have to do it for me, or for Rolland. Do it for Mary."

At the sound of his wife's name he jerked as if he'd been hit with an electrical charge. He rose to his full height but still had to look up to stare hard into Marcus' face.

"What about Mary?" he hissed. "She is not involved in any of this!"

His voice still even and smooth, Marcus said, "I know. Let's keep it that way. Just come with me for a few minutes and we'll take a short taxi drive and talk, away from everyone."

Javier's solid jaw worked back and forth as he thought hard. Finally he nodded once and commanded his driver to stay here and wait for him. The driver protested but his desires held no sway. El Señor ignored him and walked toward the door, back the way they had come, leaving the driver guarding nothing but his single suitcase and a bruised ego. Marcus fell into step beside him and together they exited the terminal into the scorching outside heat. The sun hit them both hard, almost as if it were a physical thing. Marcus fleetingly was thankful that he was still wearing the ball cap.

Outside he pointed to the lead taxi in line, the VW Bug that earlier had had the No Servício sign in the window. He pointed at it.

"There, that one. That'll do."

The two men climbed into the back seat with some difficulty since neither was particularly small. The driver didn't turn around but looked at them in the rearview mirror. He was thin with black hair and sported a red and green ball cap of the Mexican National soccer team on his round head. He wore a typical white campesino cotton shirt, the back stained with sweat. The inside of the cab smelled of cigarette smoke. A tiny representation of the crucified Jesus Christ was mounted on the narrow dashboard.

"A donde va?" he asked in a muffled voice.

Marcus told him to just drive so the man shrugged and turned on the meter. The peso count began running up slowly and smoothly. With a clumsy jerk the taxi pulled out, quickly merging into traffic. In less than a minute they were on the road and moving slowly away from the airport, towards downtown. Neither man in the backseat had spoken yet, as if it were a contest and the first to say a word would be the loser. The taxi driver honked at an unwary pedestrian and drove on. The inside of the taxi was eerily quiet, so quiet they could almost hear themselves breathing. Finally Marcus turned to his uncle.

"I know what you are doing, but I don't know why. Tell me. Tell me why you're doing this."

Marcus hoped for some reaction from the man but no emotion passed across Javier's distinguished face - no surprise, no shock, no outrage. His stony gaze didn't waver. Anything he was thinking was effectively hidden behind the dark sunglasses. His hands were folded comfortably in his lap, the brilliant diamond ring on his right hand flashing in the sunlight brighter than a mirror ball in a dance hall.

Marcus pressed ahead. "You hired Rolland to be a middle-man for you. Let's call him a straw man. You bought hundreds of inexpensive counterfeit credit cards from Eastern Europe and you were using Rolland and others to buy guns through straw sales, which you shipped back to Mexico." He paused. "Tell me if I'm wrong so far."

Javier kept his eyes locked straight ahead. His hands in his lap may have twitched, but if so that was the only reaction.

“Once in Mexico you were using those guns to wage a war here with the drug cartels. It’s easy to get guns into the country, I’ve learned. So you hired my brother to help, and he did. He never could pass up what looked like an easy buck. You also had help from Ramón Calderon, Gonzalez, as well as people in the U.S. like Andy Saunders, among others. You also found out Cassandra was romantically involved with Rolland and knew you could force her to help you by threatening her parents. Am I still on track?” He shifted in his seat so he could see his uncle’s strong profile.

“But something went wrong. Something happened and my brother decided he either didn’t want to or couldn’t do it anymore. I think he finally found out what you were doing with the guns and couldn’t stand it any longer. He was a good kid at heart and finally had enough. He took the credit cards and hid them, but you sent your guys after him. Then something else went wrong and you lost both Rolland and the credit cards, and you couldn’t buy any more guns.” Frustrated by his silence, he grabbed the man’s shoulder and tried to force him look at him. He felt his anger rising, a strong tide that couldn’t be stopped. The driver briefly glanced at them in the rearview mirror but kept motoring down the highway. “Talk to me, dammit! Why were you doing all this?”

El Señor ripped off his sunglasses and stared daggers at Marcus, his eyes void of kindness or warmth. His lips were tight lines, almost invisible. When he finally spoke his voice was hard and condescending, as if talking in this fashion were beneath him.

“Don’t speak to me like that! And keep your hands off me!” he snapped in English, certain that the lowly taxi driver couldn’t understand them. “You have no idea what you’re meddling with here. Yes, I hired your idiot brother, damn him. I needed someone in the States with no business connection to me at all, someone stupid enough to do what we needed and not ask questions. Your brother was perfect, or so I thought. No one would suspect him, especially no one in Mexico. I hired him as a buyer, what you just called a straw man, someone who could track and distribute the credit cards and make weapons purchases as well."

"Why? Why did you need so many guns?"

"To survive, that's why!" he barked. "To survive!"

Marcus sat back. "What do you mean?"

"You don't get it, do you?" he snapped. "We've been working in Merida and the Yucatan for years, decades! And then all of a sudden Los Hermanos get it in their heads that they can take over our territory and steal our business. And what do we do about it? Nothing! Our leadership is so entrenched and old school that the fire has gone out of their bellies. They're nothing but a bunch of scared old men who can barely decide what to have for dinner, much less what we should do about young, aggressive bastards like Los Hermanos. They do nothing but argue and fight amongst themselves like terrified children, and while we sit on our asses Los Hermanos are taking over! We're losing everything, and still we can't act!"

Marcus was confused. "But if you can't act then why the guns?"

"Idiot," he sneered. "I said we can't act, I didn't say I couldn't. All that has taken place, buying the credit cards, employing your brother and the others, importing the guns, all this has been done by me. Me, and no one else! My money! My planning! All without anyone else knowing about it or suspecting. If my terrified, gridlocked, so-called leaders can't do anything, then I will. I will *not* sit back and watch Los Hermanos take over."

It finally clicked for Marcus. He leaned back against the side of the taxi and stared at El Señor. He had feared all along that this might be the case. No, not just feared it, but deep down he had known it and had forcefully pushed away the possibility, just as his Aunt Mary had no doubt been doing this whole time.

"You're with El Grúpo, and El Grúpo can't or won't take action – so you did it on your own."

"Of course I'm with El Grúpo! I've worked for them for decades, but not for much longer. I've almost got enough guns and men in place to take it to Los Hermanos once and for all. I've been setting this up for nearly a year! All I need are a several hundred more guns for my men. Merida's streets will run with blood, but I will win. I will win and Los Hermanos will never set foot in my town or this part of the Yucatan again." He stared hard at Marcus, daring him to disagree.

"But for that I need those credit cards and fine US citizens like your AJ Saunders to set up the gun sales for me. I no longer have enough cash on hand to fund this on my own. I already spent huge sums of my own money just to buy the credit cards and to bankroll the men I'll need. All along I've been doing this without anyone in El Grúpo knowing what's going on, and I intend to keep it that way. The idiots can't even see what's happening right under their noses. But if they found out what I had planned, what I've done, well, I doubt even the scared, doddering old fools would hesitate to act." He glanced at his surroundings for a moment, then in Spanish snapped at the taxi driver, "Back to the airport. Now!"

Marcus did not countermand the order. The driver muttered something but performed a clumsy, illegal U-turn and began heading back the way they'd come. Half a dozen angry honks trailed in their wake, along with the screeching of tires as someone braked hard to miss their taxi. With several jerks their car got under way again.

"So where's my brother? What happened to Rolland?"

"How should I know? Calerdon and Gonzalez chased him into some woods by his house and we never saw him again. The idiot is probably still running or hiding somewhere. I don't know, and I don't care. You, on the other hand, are important to me. You have the credit cards. I will have those credit cards."

Marcus felt his temper flaring again. It was all he could do not to tear into the man. El Señor either didn't notice or didn't care that Marcus was barely able to control himself. Perhaps he still thought of his nephew as the quiet young man who had come to live with him years earlier, Marcus decided, or he felt so superior that he simply wasn't concerned. Regardless, he showed no outward sign of fear or anxiety.

"And what," Marcus said softly, evenly, though it took every ounce of will to do so, "will you do if I won't give them to you?"

Javier smiled thinly, never showing his even teeth but only using his lips. He tapped his temple with his index finger once, twice. When he spoke it was if he were having difficulty remembering something.

"Ah, let's see. There is a certain someone that you care about, am I right?"

Marcus shifted uncomfortably in his seat. His fists were clenched.

"What was her name again? Oh, yes, Cassandra," he finished with a smile. "Quite a pretty girl, I must say. I sincerely doubt that you want anything to happen to her, or her parents for that matter. I can promise you that if I don't have those cards in my possession within the next three days grave harm will come to all of them. You somehow took care of both Calderon and Gonzalez but I have other resources at my disposal still. Trust me," he promised, his voice flinty and cold, "I will take them, and I will hurt them. Oh, and if you so much as touch me again I will take her myself and I will scar her pretty face beyond recognition. Is that understood?"

Marcus was shaking in anger, his face red. His breathing was coming fast and loud in his ears, like the bellows of a kiln pushed beyond its limits.

Javier sat back, secure in the safety of his threat. He relaxed in the cramped backseat of the taxi and casually put the sunglasses back on, in control of himself and the situation. He looked around and saw they were nearing the airport again. He checked his watched and nodded to himself.

"I'm glad we understand each other. You may not feel it now, but I've always been fond of you, you know. And you certainly have a knack for staying alive in circumstances that would have killed others. That said, you could prove helpful to me in the future."

"What? What are you talking about?"

"You went up against two of my best several times, and you won each time. Well done. Not to mention that unfortunate incident in the market. I still don't understand how you survived that one. Very nicely done, I must say."

"Unfortunate incident in the market? Wait. Are you saying you didn't have anything to do with that?"

He laughed. "Me? No, you were just unlucky. Wrong place at the wrong time, as they say. It almost killed Santiago that he took you there in the first place, even though he talked you into going there just to keep the two of us apart. He knew something was going on, figured that I was involved with all this, but he didn't know how. He is also the one who slipped that note to the child in the street to give to Naibi, the note that sent you to the ruins."

"I don't understand."

"He was desperately trying his best to keep us apart so we wouldn't talk, so you wouldn't suspect me and wouldn't put two and two together. It was just damn bad luck for you that Calderon went above and beyond the call of duty and followed you all the way to the ruins to find the credit cards. Or," he admitted, "it was apparently his bad luck in the end. You really need to tell me how you took care of him. I honestly never thought he could be killed. He was a terrific pain but he could also be very helpful at times. Now I shall have to find his replacement somehow. Good, dependable muscle is very hard to come by."

Marcus was relieved that his cousin was not directly involved. It took some of the sting out of all this. But while these details all helped to put the final puzzle pieces in place, he really wasn't surprised. Deep down he had suspected his uncle all along, he supposed, but had been unwilling to admit that to himself. More important yet, if Santiago was innocent then it meant his Aunt was in the clear as well. His uncle had said as much, thank God.

The taxi pulled up to the airport and stuttered clumsily to a halt. Javier brushed non-existent lint from his sleeves and shot his cuffs in his practiced, unconscious manner. He adjusted the sunglasses and ran his fingers through already perfect black hair.

"What were you talking about, that I could prove helpful in the future?" Marcus asked. The taxi idled and the driver sat patiently, the meter still racking up the peso count.

"Well, now that this is out in the open between us I see no reason to fly to America. All this time I have taken great pains to keep everything secret, since I know how much you mean to Mary. But that's over now. Now you'll go back home and get the credit cards. I will send someone to your brother's house and you will assist him in whatever he asks. You will certainly help in purchasing more weapons and bringing them back across the border into Mexico. You will do this, and you will tell no one. You, Marcus, will be my new Straw Man. If you tell anyone, if anything happens to my operation, I will follow through on my promise to take both the girl and her parents, and I will have them hurt. Terribly. Do you understand?"

Marcus didn't move. "And then what?"

El Señor shrugged. "And then I may have other tasks for you in the future. Once I take over El Grúpo here I will need other 'favors' in the States and you will be happy to do them for me. In fact," he smiled, a tightening of the muscles around his mouth, "you may even become my replacement Calderon there in the U.S. Yes, I think that would be quite fitting, don't you?"

"You're fucking crazy."

His uncle stiffened at the slur, then shrugged and in Spanish told the driver he wanted out. The man reached over and opened the passenger door and both men climbed laboriously from the small back seat. They were next to the black SUV and the young driver with the Mediterranean complexion was standing there with the suitcase, the rest of the milling passengers and visitors studiously ignoring them, keeping their distance as if they were unclean.

His uncle turned to him and said in English, "Three days, the cards, at your brother's house. Be ready, or else. Oh, and if Mary should find out about this, about my involvement and what I do for a living, then I will kill you myself."

He ordered his driver to place the suitcase in the SUV before climbing into the back without so much as a glance at Marcus. The young driver nimbly jumped into the front seat and they pulled away, heedless of traffic. Marcus stood in the road and patiently watched them go until the vehicle was nothing but a black speck that merged into more traffic and was gone. Slowly then he got into the taxi and collapsed in the back seat, both mental and physical exhaustion threatening to claim him. Finally he sighed and leaned forward.

"Please tell me you got all that?" he asked in Spanish.

The taxi driver took off his red and green ball cap and turned around, his young face and round head now obvious. He pointed to a tiny, nearly invisible video camera lens above his visor.

"Yes, I got it all," Agent Cruzado said, smiling. "Now we have him."

Chapter 28

Marcus arrived back in the States the next night on the red-eye from Merida. The Dayton Airport, while never a bustling place, was almost completely deserted at this hour. As he and his bleary-eyed fellow passengers shuffled like zombies toward the baggage claim area he noticed that the newsstands and restaurants were closed and dark, each one with a security gate pulled down and locked tight. They were strangely reminiscent of the stores all up and down Merida's streets in the early morning. The only sound came from the several dozen feet on the worn carpet, an occasional yawn, or hushed conversation on a cell phone. The pleasant bass male voice intoned over the speakers, "The current threat level, as determined by the office of Homeland Security, is Orange." Marcus grinned to himself, thinking that perhaps someone really should make those threat levels more intuitive after all…

He gathered his lone suitcase from the conveyor belt while stifling his own yawn. It was nearly midnight, after all. Marcus had called Cassie from Merida to let her know that he was okay, that it was over, and most importantly that her parents were safe once and for all. He had wanted to talk more, to say so much more, but hadn't had the time or the opportunity. Now he was dying to see her in person and to explain everything that had taken place, but the flight had gotten in late and he still needed to drive all the way to Wayne. Then of course he would need to do the same with Otto, and since his young friend was still laid up in the hospital and there was no way he could bypass the gauntlet at the Nurse's Station at this hour, that wasn't going to happen. It was frustrating but it would all have to wait until morning. He climbed into his rental car and drove sleepily back to Rolland's where he collapsed into bed, clothes and all, a blanket loosely tossed over him.

The next morning at first light he got cleaned up and immediately went to see Mrs. Kerr across the street. She was overjoyed to see him safe and sound and back home again. She clapped her hands with dainty little claps, beaming with happiness.

"Dear," she said warmly, a hand placed on his forearm, "thank heavens you're home. How did everything go down in Mexico?"

He drank his coffee and ate a Twinkie, the sponge cake and filling not exactly his idea of breakfast. Marcus didn't go into great detail since she wouldn't understand all the complexities of the situation, but he explained enough that he could tell she was satisfied. She was overjoyed to know that both he and Cassie wouldn't be in danger any longer.

"But what about Rolland?" she asked. "What did you find out about your brother?"

He shook his head sadly. "I don't know. Nobody does. The last known contact seems to have been right here as they chased him into the woods. Nobody's seen him since as far as I can tell."

"Oh, dear."

She made warm, sympathetic noises as they drank their coffee quietly on the worn davenport, peaceful and secure with each other. He was eager to get to the hospital but he owed her such an incredible debt that keeping her company for a little while was the least he could do. They sat together for over an hour, three cups of coffee, and one more Twinkie. She was so pleased he seemed to be enjoying the snack cakes that he couldn't stand to tell her that he could barely stomach them. Finally she patted his knee and told him she was tired and wanted to lay down for a spell.

"Just a little nap, dear. This getting old business is for the birds, really."

He smiled. "I'll come back later and help out around the house. Have a few things lined up for me to do, okay?"

"Oh, yes, that would be wonderful."

She was pleased to no end and promised she would get to work on a honey-do list for him right after her nap. He kissed her on the cheek as he left and was certain she actually blushed under her make-up. She shooed him out, waving goodbye to him from the doorway. He was amazed yet again at how tiny and frail she looked physically. He knew better, so much better.

He called Cassie and told her to meet him at the hospital. She was dying to ask a million questions but he held her off, much to her dismay. He laughed, almost able to visualize her impatient, irritated expression. She heard the laugh, something she had rarely heard from Marcus before, and knew that the worst must be over. That laugh warmed her to the point where she couldn't maintain her ire. She chided him playfully but agreed to meet him at Otto's room, all traces of anger dissipating like fog hit by bright sunlight.

Thirty minutes later Marcus met her in the parking lot. They hugged as if they had been separated by months instead of just days. Several people walking by nudged each other and smiled, and one young man about Otto's age playfully suggested they get a room. They reluctantly broke their embrace but he held her at arm's length, staring into her dark brown eyes.

"It's over," he stated confidently.

"You're sure?"

"Yes, I'm sure. And your parents are safe. Come on, let's get inside and I'll explain everything. I want to tell Otto, too."

They breezed past the nurse's station and eased into Otto's room. For some reason Marcus always expected people in the hospital to be napping, perhaps with the lights down low, but Otto was sitting up and flipping impatiently through his limited channel selection on the television. He didn't see them at first so this gave Marcus a chance to look him over. His hand was still wrapped up, as was his one eye, but the visible bruising seemed to have vanished. It was amazing how good he looked, Marcus thought, marveling at the healing power of youth. He was still connected to a saline drip although the rest of the monitors were pulled back and disconnected, dark and unplugged, sentinels no longer on duty. His long brown hair still stuck up at odd angles from the gauze around his head, almost like a punk rocker's carefully tended hairdo. But he seemed alert and lively and looked ready to be discharged. Marcus was very pleasantly surprised at how much he had improved in such a short time.

Cassie elbowed past him and burst into the room. "Otto! You look wonderful!"

An unabashed smile lit up his face. "Cassie? Marcus? Guys, hey, this is great!"

Marcus moved to the side of his bed and stared down at him warmly. Cassie gave him a huge hug, which he didn't seem to mind in the least. He winked at Marcus.

"I like this kind of reunion," he said, smiling.

They asked him about his condition and he filled them in. He was healing nicely, he admitted, and was due to be discharged any day now, the sooner the better. He was sick to death of hospital food. Worse, if he had to listen to much more Muzak from the nurse's station he was going to jump out of the window. He didn't care that his room was on the first floor. They all laughed, Marcus in relief and Otto with genuine humor, seemingly his old self again. They passed some more small talk before Otto finally broached the subject of Rolland and the credit cards and what had happened in Mexico.

Marcus sighed. It was still painful to talk about it, but he owed him this much at least. "It was my uncle, it was El Señor. He was behind the entire operation."

"Oh, damn, dude," Otto whispered.

"Yeah, damn." For the next several minutes he recounted the facts about his uncle and his involvement in El Grúpo and the war they were unsuccessfully waging with the aggressive Los Hermanos cartel. He couldn't give too many details about the war itself because he didn't know all that much, at least not yet. But he told them all he knew and they sat there, spellbound, while he relayed the facts. A nurse came in to check on Otto once, briefly, and after she left he continued.

"Let me back up a little first and fill you in. When I left you at Foley's, Cassie, after I talked you into giving me that phone number, I went ahead and called it. Turns out that phone was the one my uncle had picked up on a trip to Miami he and my aunt Mary had taken not too long ago. It was one of those pay as you go phones, you know, with no contract and no way to trace it. I got a generic voicemail but told whoever was listening to be in Ohio, here, in three days or I would destroy all the cards and ledgers. I needed the ringleader behind this, not another thug or flunky. Unfortunately Gonzalez and AJ Saunders showed the first time, which I figured might happen. That's why I had your brother ready just in case, Otto. I wanted him waiting in the wings to grab Gonzalez. That didn't work out exactly as I had planned."

Cassie rolled her eyes at this. "You could say that."

Marcus grinned at her. "But after Mrs. Kerr saved both our skins I told AJ in no uncertain terms that I needed whoever was behind this to be on a plane within the next three days. Then I made another call, this time to Agent Cruzado in Merida. I told Cruzado I had a pretty good idea what was going on, that I might be able to help him stop some of the current violence, and could definitely help stop more that was brewing. He was all ears, as you can imagine."

"I would think so," Otto said.

"But I needed him to do something for me first."

His young friend leaned forward, mute testimony that his ribs were well-healed already. "What? What'd you ask him to do?"

"I made him promise that he'd take Cassie's parents under protective custody, for one thing. After some convincing he agreed. I also told him he had to talk the airlines into telling him if someone made a sudden reservation to Ohio, likely Dayton, leaving within the next few days. It would also very likely be someone we knew, and I gave him a short list of names to watch for. He had no problem with that – seems he has enough contacts to pull that sort of thing off. When I got to Merida I called him and he confirmed it. El Señor had made a reservation that morning, flying out the next day." When he'd gotten that news from the Federal Agent it had just about killed him. And his Aunt Mary, he thought, this is going to destroy her.

"Ouch," Otto said. "Busted."

"Busted is right. I waited for him at the airport. I had to get him into a special taxi that Cruzado had waiting. Once I got him in there I needed him to start talking, to admit to his part in all this. Thankfully, with some goading, he did that, and we had him."

"What was so special about the taxi?" Cassie asked.

Marcus grinned tightly. "It was bugged. Video and audio. Pretty high tech stuff, I guess. I insisted that Cruzado be the taxi driver, and with a little more convincing he was okay with that, too. Although," he added, "he's a lousy driver, barely knew how to operate a damn stick shift. His driving was so bad I thought he was going to give the whole thing away. He almost stalled it several times and he practically ran over a few people."

"Wow. Well, what about your uncle now? Where is he?" Cassie wanted to know.

"I haven't a clue. Cruzado's men picked him up about ten minutes later. The driver of the SUV thought about putting up a fight but was outmanned and outgunned, and in the end he surrendered without any problem. Good thing, too, since they were near downtown and a lot of innocent people could have been hurt. The Federales took both of them away somewhere. I have no idea where, and I probably never will."

"What's going to happen to him?" Otto asked, not concerned for the man but still curious.

Marcus shrugged. "I don't know that either. I imagine they'll be interrogating him for information about El Grúpo and what he knows. I don't know how high up in the organization he was, but I'm sure his part in all this is over."

Cassie placed a tender hand on his forearm. He looked her way, concern clearly evident in her brown eyes. "But what about your Aunt Mary? What about her? What will happen to her and Santiago?"

Marcus felt his heart sink in his chest. He exhaled nosily through pursed lips. "I don't know, honestly, but I suspect their easy life is crashing to a halt now, too."

Cassie sucked in a quick breath. "She's not going to be happy about that."

He nodded, fully aware what his beloved aunt, his mother's sister, would be going through. She would certainly blame Marcus for this, for taking away the love of her life and her easy life itself. That was a bridge he would've done anything not to cross, regardless that his uncle had forced his hand. Certainly the last remaining people he called family would no longer have anything to do with him, would despise and blame him forever. He felt terribly, completely alone. He had understood the consequences of his actions going in to this but had been compelled to follow through with everything regardless. He almost felt sick to his stomach. Marcus caught a sympathetic look from Cassie. She knew, he realized. She understood what he had sacrificed, and he loved her for it.

Otto looked at both of them, back and forth, not fully comprehending the impact this was having on Marcus. His expression mirrored that of someone who didn't quite get the punch-line.

"But this means it's all over, right?" he asked finally, always looking for the bright side, a glass half-full person to the end.

"Almost," Marcus replied. "Cruzado has been in touch with the ATF here in the States and he said they're going after Andy Saunders, AJ, the guy Mrs. Kerr wounded. He has a lot of explaining to do and I'm sure they'll pin something on him. He's dirty through and through."

Cassie was ticking off names on her fingers. "So that just leaves Gonzalez, right?" she asked.

It was Otto's turn to fill them in. "Oh, I got this one. Don-Don told me he's still here at the hospital. He's in bad shape, I guess, and under 24 hour surveillance. They're not even sure he's going to make it. Too bad for him," he added sarcastically, glancing with his good eye at the bandages around his hand. "Serves him right, the crazy bastard."

They talked for a bit longer, the mood in the room easing as it rang home that the threats to them, the threats that had been hovering over them so long like a curse, were over. Marcus' mood slowly lifted as he saw how happy and relieved his friends were. It really was as if heavy, thick clouds had parted and they could feel the sun for the first time, its warming rays finally on their upturned faces. Both Cassie and Otto were smiling and laughing, almost giddy with joy and released tension. Despite the impact his actions had had on his remaining family Marcus found himself nominally caught up in the celebration. Cassie caught his grin and smiled back at him, warming him more than any sun could. Maybe, just maybe, this had been worth it after all. Only time would tell.

They stayed another thirty minutes until the nurse came back and told them it was time to go, much to their displeasure. They promised Otto they would be back soon for another visit, maybe even to bring him home. That cheered the young man up more than anything, to the point that he in mock-seriousness swore that even the Muzak wasn't so bad after all. He picked up the TV remote control and started cycling through the channels again.

"Now if only I could find a soccer game. Would it hurt to at least give me some sports channels?" he yelled out the door to nobody in particular.

Marcus and Cassie laughed and said their goodbyes, promising again to be back soon. Once in the hall Cassie smiled hugely, her brown eyes alight with happiness.

"I feel so, I don't know, relieved," she said "Is this truly over? My parents are safe, all of us are safe, Otto is mending well and should be able to go home soon. And the bad guys are no longer a threat. Is it really over, Marcus? Really?"

He allowed himself a smile as well. "Yes, I think it really is."

She clapped her hands together. "I almost feel like skipping or something!"

"Then by all means skip," he joked.

Much to his surprise, as well as the surprise of two candy-stripers that she almost collided with, Cassie did start skipping. She was tentative at first but her speed and skill quickly improved as her confidence increased. Marcus had to jog to keep up with her, but he finally caught her from behind just as she was leaving the building. They fell against a car in the parking lot laughing and out of breath, the many-colored cars around them gleaming in the sunshine. An older couple walking by smiled kindly at them as if they too could remember those early days of romance. The man grasped his wife's hand warmly and they continued on their way.

It took Cassie and Marcus a few minutes to stop laughing and catch their breath. Suddenly it dawned on her that it wasn't over, that there were still loose ends. One loose end, really. She sobered immediately and stared at him.

"Rolland," she said flatly. "It's not over yet, not until we find Rolland, is it?"

Marcus sighed and looked away, out over the tops of the parked cars and SUVs. Someone at the other end of the parking lot honked their horn, the sound echoing around them. Overhead the summer sky was beginning to darken with the thick heavy clouds of a pop-up thunderstorm, the type that was so common on hot days in Ohio. Storms like this tended to roll in and out quickly, leaving the asphalt steaming and the humidity bumping up against the one hundred percent mark. These storms were rash, unpredictable and could ruin a planned summer outing in a matter of minutes. He had hoped to let Cassie revel in her relief for a while at least, but that question had dampened her spirits just as quickly as this storm would ruin a day at the community pool or a picnic in the park.

"No, it's not completely over yet. I can't move on, *we* can't move on, until I find my brother or what happened to him." They both understood what he meant with the emphasis on "we".

Cassie crossed her arms and looked away as well, her face suddenly flushed. He knew she was doing all she could to hold her temper in check. They had been over this time and time again, his unwillingness or inability to take their relationship to the next level without some kind of sign-off from Rolland. On the surface she understood his guilt and the reasons behind it, he knew, but that didn't mean she accepted it. She involuntarily reached for the non-existent silver cross at her neck but clenched her fist and swore under her breath when it came up empty. Frustration was clear on her face and in her stance, her back rigid, her arms crossed.

"We've talked about this," he began.

"I know!" she snapped. "I know we've been over this before. I've told you Rolland and I were through before he disappeared, that we didn't have any real feelings for each other any longer. You've got this deep-seated guilt about the way you abandoned him. I guess I can understand that, but it doesn't make this any easier." She mellowed slightly and took a step toward him. "You and I can have something special, Marcus Schmidt. I know we can. Don't screw it up." She turned and began walking away then, toward her car.

"Cassie, wait," Marcus said.

She stopped and turned around, looking a stern, impatient question at him. He paused before pulling a tiny wax paper bag out the pocket of his pants. He drew out a long silver chain, but whatever was at the end of the chain was concealed in his closed hand. She was looking at him curiously, still angry but obviously intrigued. He slowly opened his fingers, one by one, until he revealed the silver cross he had purchased at the ruins. The silver glittered even in the dimming sunlight and the black obsidian and blue turquoise visually popped as if lit internally.

"Here," he said. "I know your old cross was special to you and was a gift from your mom, so I can't hope to replace that. But I saw this and thought, well..."

She placed one hand to her chest and with the other slowly reached out toward it as if she were a surgeon performing a delicate operation. She tenderly picked it up and held it in her palm, gazing at it in amazement. He breathed a sigh of relief then, knowing that she found it as beautiful as he did. Marcus gently plucked it from her hand and motioned for her to turn around. He fastened the thin chain around her neck. She turned back to him, gratitude written in her eyes, the curve of her mouth. She was breathing faster.

"Thank you," she said softly. "It's gorgeous." Her hand drifted to her chest in the practiced, habitual motion, locating the cross perfectly the very first time.

"You're welcome. I saw this when..."

He never finished the sentence. In a sudden movement she pulled his face down to hers and kissed him, holding it for several long seconds. Thunder rumbled behind them as the summer storm moved closer. Several fat drops hit the tops of their heads and the cars around them, making a light tapping noise each time one impacted a hood or roof.

"Wow. Uh, what was that for?"

Cassie took a step back, her one hand still rubbing the new cross between her fingers. She shook her head and stared up at him, her expression softening.

"Damn you, Marcus," she said, all anger washed from her voice and replaced with warm exasperation. She saw the storm moving closer, now almost on top of them. "Here I am all pissed off and ready to make you commit one way or the other, to give you an ultimatum, and you go and do this. How the hell am I supposed to stay mad at you now? Damn."

He took a step toward her but she backed away, keeping her distance. Behind them she could see a wall of water moving their way, the storm coming in hard and fast.

"Cassie."

She began weaving between parked cars, their colors now muted as the storm blotted out the sun. She lithely trotted toward the old powder blue Pontiac Sportwagon she owned with her brothers, the car he had seen in her garage.

"Cassie!"

He watched her deftly navigate the maze of sedans and mini-vans until she found hers, about fifteen spaces from his own. She turned to him.

"You just bought yourself a little more time, Marcus Schmidt," she said, her voice carrying across the parking lot. "But this doesn't give you an open ticket. You need to figure out our next step sooner than later. I won't wait forever."

As had happened so many times in the past, he wanted to talk more, to explain himself again, but there really was nothing more to say that hadn't already been said. She was in the car and backing out before he could do anything. He watched the light blue station wagon pull away and out of the parking lot before he realized the storm was upon him in earnest. He cursed and ran for the rental but was totally drenched by the time he tumbled inside.

When he was back at Rolland's and had changed into dry clothing he saw he had missed a call from his friend and fellow professor in Latin American Studies, Anthony Barasalo, the other half of the Axis Powers. As always Tony started off the message with his familiar salutation.

"Hey, Dr. Schmidt," the deep voice rumbled in the message, "hope you're coming home soon. People are starting to wonder if you still work here or not. Call me."

Marcus called and they had a few minutes to chat before Tony needed to get back to class. The summer session was in full swing, and while both of their schedules were lighter than during the normal school year Marcus could tell that having Tony cover all their classes was beginning to wear on him. Against his friend's protestations Marcus promised to be back soon, as soon as he wrapped up a few more loose ends.

"So what about your brother?" Tony asked cautiously. "Any word?"

Marcus didn't feel he could do justice to the story over the phone, so promised a full recounting over some beers when he got back. Tony accepted that and swore he'd have a few cold ones waiting.

"That'll work. See you when you get back."

"Thanks, Tony," he said, grateful as ever. "I'll be there soon."

"No worries."

They hung up after some more small talk. Marcus stood in the living room of his brother's house and mentally began a checklist of what he needed to do. The fact that he was being forced to leave before finding out what happened to Rolland gnawed at him. Regardless, he knew pragmatically and in his heart that he could no longer delay his return, and that he had done all he could. Rolland was missing and it was possible he would stay missing. He swore and kicked at a chair, sending it spinning to the floor. It wasn't fair, he thought darkly. He had come so close, had uncovered so much, only to fail. He was right here where he had started so many weeks ago. *Shit!*

He took a long, slow breath and picked up the fallen chair. Outside the rain was still coming down, but more gently now, and a stray beam of sunlight glimmered through the window and momentarily lit up the cramped, spare living room. He felt in his top pocket and pulled out the picture he had salvaged from the broken frame, the photo of him and Rolland sitting on the edge of the fountain at Balboa Park. The happy, smiling face of his brother looked at him without accusation or blame, simply a young man content with life and his place in it. Marcus felt his eyes tear and he stared at the picture as the two of them blurred and became indistinct, completely unrecognizable. He blinked and slid the snapshot back into his pocket.

He slowly, with little direction, began walking around the house, gathering up his few belongings and putting them haphazardly into the suitcase. He didn't even fold his clothing, just balled it up and tossed it in. He found he didn't care now and that his almost obsessive desire for neatness and order had vacated him. He threw his running shoes on top of the mess along with everything else he could find.

In his pants pocket he pulled out the wax paper bag that had contained Cassie's cross. Fingering the slick paper he slumped into a chair and ran it through his fingers, the wax covering almost completely worn off. What was he going to do about Cassie? He knew he could never be with her, not in good conscience, not the way it was. He crumpled up the bag and threw it angrily into the trash can. This was all too fucking difficult!

Nearly thirty minutes passed as he sat morosely in the chair, thoughts tumbling through his mind in an endless, fruitless attempt at finding answers where he knew there were none. When his cell phone rang it took him several seconds before he realized what it was. He didn't recognize the number, just that the area code was from somewhere in Cincinnati.

"Hello?" he said.

"Dr. Marcus Schmidt?"

"Yes. Who's this?"

"This is Special Agent Samuel Moses with the Bureau of Alcohol, Tobacco, and Firearms. I'm following up on a rather confusing report of allegedly illegal arms sales that made its way to my desk through the office of Homeland Security. It's got something to do with information passed back to that office through the Mexican government. I'd like to talk with you right away. Could we meet tomorrow morning?"

He couldn't say he hadn't seen this coming. "Sure, no problem," Marcus agreed, giving him the address.

Agent Moses was at his front door bright and early the next morning. He was a clean-cut African American man in his mid-thirties, with a round face and short black hair. He smiled at Marcus, revealing a large gap in his two front teeth that could have been easily rectified with braces. It was already warm outside and the agent's ample forehead was beaded with sweat. He blotted at his brow with a white handkerchief. Under his dark sport coat was a bulge that was certainly a holstered pistol. He showed his badge and politely asked to come in. Once inside Marcus offered him the last bottle of water from the fridge, which he declined. The two men said down opposite each other.

The discussion over the next hour was nothing like Marcus had imagined. It was perfunctory at best, almost superficial, bordering on routine. Agent Moses took limited notes in a small spiral notebook similar to the one Lt. Doncaster used. As he mopped again at his forehead and face he opened up the questions, first asking about Rolland and moving on from there. A sports analogy came to mind then: the agent was pitching him softballs, underhand and slow, never throwing the heater at him. Marcus gave short, truthful answers to everything without going in to too much detail and the agent never pressed for more, keeping their conversation very high-level. Oddly, Marcus found he wasn't nervous in the least even though he was aware that his involvement in the affair had certainly crossed over many legal lines. The realization hit him then, dully, that right then he didn't much care what happened to him.

When the hour was up and the agent had filled a few pages in large, tidy print, the man leaned back in his chair and stared hard at Marcus. He tamped at his face again with the white handkerchief which was now visibly wet through and through. The questions had continued to be simple and never once had the Agent dug or probed to the point where Marcus had to give more than cursory answers. They had to do almost entirely with Andy Saunders from the gun show, his brother's part in the operation, and what had happened to Otto and Cassie. Rarely did they focus on Marcus and his role or anything to do with Gonzalez or Hernandez. Not one word was mentioned about his uncle. It was as if the agent had been instructed to keep him out of it altogether.

As he relaxed in the chair Marcus noticed for the first time that agent Moses' gaze was one of astute and penetrating intelligence. The man across from him was probably very bright, more so than he had given him credit for at first. He felt a sudden twinge of nervousness then, as if he were in junior high school again, parked in the principal's office waiting for punishment. But without warning the agent closed his notebook and pocketed it. The interview, such as it was, was over.

"Dr. Schmidt," he began, motioning to the suitcase with the damp handkerchief. "From the looks of this room you are getting ready to leave. Right?"

Marcus nodded. "Yes. I have to get back to school. I have classes waiting for me. My co-worker has been covering for me these last few weeks."

"I see. Normally we would ask you to remain in the area as our investigation continues, especially with a case such as this. However," he added, "for some reason we have been asked by our friends in the Mexican government to keep your involvement in this out of the spotlight, and at their significant urging we have agreed to do so. They have promised us additional help in investigating and prosecuting this case, so we plan on honoring their request. You've got some friends in high places, I'm guessing."

Shocked, Marcus could only stare at him. *Agent Cruzado*, he thought.

"That doesn't mean you are off the hook. We ask that you not leave the country, and that you make yourself available for further questions should the need arise. Are you agreeable to this?"

"Yes, that's fine. No problem."

"Good. I'll probably have to contact you again later, but unless we find reasons to the contrary you are free to go right now. Just make yourself available should we need to talk again. Deal?"

Mutely, he agreed.

The agent stood and extended his hand. "Off the record, I believe we owe you a debt of thanks for your help. From what we've been told you were instrumental in breaking up a complex and illegal arms scam. However, in the future please don't take measures like this into your own hands. These are dangerous criminals and this is a very dangerous business. These people are brutal killers, and one more dead body, American or not, isn't going to bother them in the least. From now on please let the ATF handle it."

Marcus shook his outstretched hand and mumbled thanks. The agent handed him a business card with a toll free number and an address in downtown Cincinnati. He thanked him again, flashing a final gap-toothed smile. He went to the door and stepped outside, looking at the sky and wiping the sweat away from his face again.

"Going to be a hot one today," he commented aloud, walking to his government-issued, non-descript Chevrolet.

Marcus pocketed the business card and watched him go, then finished packing.

He waited around the rest of the day and took care of final loose ends. He called the landlady and cancelled the lease. She was vocal about terminating the contract early, but lightened considerably when he agreed to pay another month's rent for her trouble. She was mollified even more when she realized she would be keeping the security deposit too. He also called the water and power companies and cancelled service effective immediately. His final call was to make a reservation at the Dayton Airport for a flight back to San Diego that evening. Every call he made jabbed at him cruelly, reminding him that his brother was still missing and he had failed to discover his whereabouts. All the good that he had done seemed insignificant, trivial, although he knew deep down that wasn't the case. He had directly or indirectly saved dozens, perhaps hundreds or maybe thousands of lives, but all that paled in significance when held up to the light of his failure. He had, to him, let his brother down again. He felt as thoroughly helpless as he had so long ago when his father had forced him and Rolland onto the plane to Merida. He angrily threw his suitcase into the rental car and went to say goodbye to Mrs. Kerr.

She was waiting for him at the door, holding Mr. Whiskers and scratching him gently between his ears. The tiny woman was still dressed in a long, buttoned down bathrobe, but today her hair and makeup were perfect. She smiled sorrowfully at him.

"So you're leaving?"

"Yes, I've got to get back home. I've been gone too long."

"I thought as much, dear. Would you like a final cup of coffee?"

He knew he should indulge her, but his mood was too foul and he wouldn't be much company. He politely declined and she shook her head, as if she had anticipated that.

"You've done good work, dear, you should be proud."

He turned away and looked at Rolland's white frame house. It was still run-down and tired, forever destined to be a rental. It felt odd that he would miss the place.

"I guess."

"You can't blame yourself, you know. Whatever Rolland was doing was his choice and not your fault. We all make choices, dear, and we must live with them. Before Hank passed he used to kick himself for being gone so much of the time for work. He was angry with himself for being away from me so often, even though I told him over and over that it was okay. He did what he had to do, and so did you. Please don't beat yourself up over it. We do the best we can, and that's the best we can do."

Marcus turned back and gave her a final hug. Mr. Whiskers gave a growl at being caught in the middle of their embrace and squirmed away, scampering into the yews next to the house. They heard him roaming through the bushes and around the house, intent on his own business.

"I've asked Otto to come by and help out once he's feeling better, and I'm going to talk to Doncaster and make sure he keeps his eye on the place, too."

"Thank you, dear," she said.

"And I want you to write or call once in a while and let me know how you're doing."

"Of course."

"I can't thank you enough for your help. You saved our lives."

She smiled brightly and placed a hand on his shoulder. "I wouldn't have missed it for the world, dear."

There was nothing left to say so he kissed her on the cheek and left. As he pulled away she was still on the porch, thc bronze eagle door knocker shining like a protective talisman behind her. She waved as he drove off, a tiny, petite figure standing there, all alone.

He parked in front of Foley's Diner. The lunchtime crowd was in full swing and nearly all the tables were occupied. Back in the kitchen he could see Sal helping out with orders, a single bandage affixed to his left temple. He saw Marcus and sketched him a smile and a quick thumbs up. The waitress who had waited on him during his first visit, Alice, grinned at him and ushered him to a table in the back, near the kitchen door.

"Hi, Alice."

"Hi," she said brightly. "Cassie will be with you in a minute."

He sipped his water for a bit and saw Cassie moving lithely around the crowded tables. For a brief second their eyes met as she unloaded a platter full of food to four Latino men, conversing with them in Spanish. She chatted with them for a second then came and slid into the seat opposite him.

"Busy?" he asked.

"We're getting slammed," she said tiredly, pushing a wisp of hair from her face. Marcus saw the cross around her neck. "Got a bunch of new migrant workers in town working on the farms and I think they all came here for lunch at the same time."

"Good tips then."

"Well, we'll see. Most probably haven't been paid yet."

"Just smile pretty and they won't be able to resist."

They made small talk for several minutes, Marcus reliving his morning and what he had done with the house, his meeting with Agent Moses, and his goodbye to Mrs. Kerr. They were both avoiding the elephant in the diner, the subject of their relationship and what was to come next. Neither was comfortable broaching the topic since both were painfully aware how that conversation would end. Finally Marcus could hold back no longer.

"I made my flight reservation. I'm going back to San Diego this afternoon. I've got to get back."

Cassie's hand started to move to the cross but she forced it back. She had difficulty looking at him. The din in the dining area faded to a muted rumble of indistinct sounds, as if there were only the two of them in the room. Her expression was strangely composed. He reached for her and she didn't pull away. He rested his hand on her forearm.

"So that's it then," she said flatly.

Marcus didn't reply. He had nothing to say. The silence between them said it all.

"You're going back to your job, your school, and everything we've been through, everything between us, is over. Is that it?" Her eyes began to well with tears but she made no move to wipe them clear.

It took Marcus a few moments to answer. "No, it's not over. It can't be."

She finally wiped at her eyes. "Whatever. Have a nice life, Dr. Schmidt."

She stood, not in anger but in disappointment. Her motions were tired and slow, as if even these small movements were too much for her. As he watched her his heart felt close to bursting, like a balloon filled to the breaking point. He saw a red stain, ketchup or salsa, on her left breast near her nameplate. It looked like an oozing wound.

"Cassie, I'll...call you when I get home." Even to him it sounded lame.

She waved him away and almost stumbled back to the kitchen, her gait clumsy. He waited at his table for a while but she never came back. He finally left, his water untouched.

Outside on the sidewalk Lt. Doncaster was leaning against his police car. His left arm was in a sling and he had a thick white foam brace straining around his oversized neck. His face was red and bruised, dark sunglasses hiding his expression and some black eyes. With a grunt he heaved himself off the car and stood straight.

"You leaving town?" he said without preamble. His words were thick, the neck brace not permitting full movement of his jaw. Marcus could tell he was in pain but the cop was intent on not showing any. He was in full uniform even on a day as hot as this and a single thread of sweat trickled down his temple. Three Bic pens were lined up perfectly in his breast pocket like orderly soldiers.

"Uh, huh. Flying out later today."

"Good. You know I've had nothing but trouble since you showed up."

Marcus said nothing. He made to move past him to his car but Doncaster held up his good hand to stop him.

"Wait," he commanded, then took a deep breath and with difficulty softened his tone. "Uh, thanks for your help the other day. At your brother's house."

Marcus nodded. Then he turned and faced him directly.

"Keep an eye on her, okay?" He didn't need to clarify who "she" was. "And your brother and Mrs. Kerr, too."

The cop nodded back at him. "I will. Don't worry."

Without another word Marcus stepped around him and got in his car. He pulled out into the street and looked back but Doncaster was already gone. Silently he drove away from Foley's Diner and headed out of town. In a matter of minutes he was on the county roads, the City of Wayne nothing more than that familiar brown smear in his rearview mirror.

Chapter 29

Two months later Marcus was teaching an undergraduate class the basics of the Spanish language in Spanish 101 at San Diego State University. He was in front of the auditorium of seventy-five students covering the differences between the verb "to be". He could easily see in the one-hundred and fifty eyes trained on him that only a handful had any clue what he was actually talking about. Okay, he admitted to himself, there were only about one hundred eyes that were honestly paying any attention to his lecture. The other fifty were checking their phones, texting, or just napping. He sighed. Undergrad classes were really not his favorite. If the parents of those not paying attention actually knew what they were getting for their tuition dollars they'd probably have a righteous fit.

As had been his habit forever he had his lesson plan all worked out ahead of time. He had prepared it weeks before and was a stickler for following his plan each and every day. However this time he sat on the edge of his desk and surveyed the class. Those same one hundred eyes remained trained on him, wondering what was going on. Let's mix this up, he decided suddenly.

"Okay," he said loudly, so loudly that several of the texters lifted their eyes from their phones. "Let's do something a little different today, what do you say?"

Several other sets of eyes stared at him. Two students in the back that had been dozing picked up their heads in mild curiosity. He hoped they hadn't drooled on the desks.

"Let's have a little fun, okay? Instead of learning the differences between *ser* and *estar*, let's try this. You, in the front row. What's your name?" He pointed at a twenty-year old with long brown hair and a T-shirt that said *Pledge Delta. It's good for your wood.*

"Uh, Steve."

"Okay, Uh-Steve," he said, causing several students to chuckle. "What would you like to know how to say in Spanish? Anything? Take your pick."

Steve was momentarily nonplussed at being the focus of the class. He sat up straight in his seat and looked around. "Uh, how about, 'I want a beer?'"

Marcus nodded and turned to the white board behind him. In block letters he wrote *Quiero cerveza.* Out loud he repeated what he had written, then looked at Steve.

"Now it's your turn. Quiero cerveza. Say it."

Steve gamely tried his hand, coming close but mispronouncing the "r" in *quiero*.

"Spanish pronunciation is extremely easy and consistent, unlike our own fine English language," he stated. "An 'r' is always pronounced like a 'd'. Now try it again. Quiero cerveza."

Steve gave it another shot and did amazingly well, almost nailing it.

"Very good. Much better. Now the rest of you try it."

The rest of the class time was spent on learning fun and interesting phrases like "Where's the bathroom", "This music sucks", and "You're a moron". By the end of the fifty minutes all seventy-five students were laughing and actively participating, joking around but perhaps actually learning something. When the buzzer rang signaling the end of class fully half of the students were still there, some even coming up and asking more questions.

Finally they had all filed out and only Marcus remained, tidying up his desk and preparing for his next class that afternoon. He was smiling to himself when he heard a noise and looked up. Tony Barsalo, his one true friend at the school, was standing there clapping softly.

"Interesting teaching method, Dr. Schmidt," he remarked wryly. Tony was dressed in black slacks and a white short-sleeved shirt, his olive skin and black hair in stark contrast to the white.

Marcus chuckled. "Yeah, well, I wasn't doing any good with *ser* and *estar*, so I figured I'd mix things up a little today."

"*You* changed things up? Dr. Marcus Schmidt? Mr. Straight and Narrow? Man, I don't even know who you are any more."

Marcus laughed again. "Maybe I've learned some new things lately."

Tony motioned toward the hall, suddenly serious. "You've got a call in the office."

He didn't stop gathering his papers. "Yeah? What about?"

"I think you'd better take it. I'll finish up in here."

The tone of Tony's voice immediately caught his attention and he stopped. "What is it? What's going on?"

He shook his head. "Go take the call. I'll finish up here," he repeated.

Marcus didn't press for more details but hustled three doors down to the office. Marilyn, the thin secretary who was a staple in the department, held the phone out to him as he walked in. Her face was serious.

"It's somebody from Ohio," she whispered in her reedy voice, phone extended towards him. "Something about your brother."

Tentatively, as if the receiver might be blazing hot, he took it from her and slowly pressed it to his ear.

"This is Marcus Schmidt. Who's this?"

The voice from over two thousand miles away was clear. "Schmidt? This is Lt. Doncaster in Wayne. We found your brother."

Nearly a week earlier two brothers named Steven and Tyler had been sitting in their dark basement playing video games. The home was about a half mile down the street from Rolland's old house in Wayne. The boys' father, a huge fan of the American rock band Aerosmith, had named the boys after the lead singer of the band, Steven Tyler. Steven, the seven year old, after having lost to his older brother seven times in a row at the game, tossed his controller down in disgust.

"This sucks," he crabbed. His lower lip stuck out. "I'm tired of playing. Let's do something else."

Tyler, who was so close to being ten that he could taste it, never broke stride in the game he was playing. He gunned down a Nazi soldier who had been trying to flank his position. His pale face was blank, his eyes staring at the television screen almost without blinking. Colors from the game flickered across his face like a kaleidoscope.

"Quit being a pussy," he mumbled. "You're just tired of losing."

"Am not!" Steven snapped, although he most certainly was. He didn't share his brother's love of video carnage and would rather play outside. He would never say anything to Tyler but he didn't like the blood and guts of the newer games, either. It sometimes made him sick to his stomach, like when he'd eaten all those jelly beans last Halloween. Plus this was a Sunday afternoon and school was tomorrow. He hated sitting in the dark basement all day, especially on a Sunday, with the thought of school hanging over his head like one of those guillotine-things he'd seen on the History Channel.

"Come on, Ty," he pleaded, "let's go fishing. You promised last week you'd go fishing with me. Let's go down to the river. I'll even carry the poles and tackle box."

Tyler executed a very complicated jump, spin, and shoot maneuver, managing to pick off two Nazis in as many seconds. His younger brother was impressed, although he would never think to admit that out loud.

"Sorry, loser," his older brother said. "That's not going to happen. I'm not going anywhere."

"But you promised!"

"Fuck off," Tyler snapped. With no parents or adults around the forbidden expletive rolled off his tongue as easily as if he had said "pass the salt". He liked the sound of the word and said it as often as he could. It made him feel older and more mature.

"Ah! You said the F-word," Steven yelled. "I'll tell mom. Go fishing with me or I'll tell mom you said the F-word!"

Tyler looked away from his game for one second. "Tell mom and I'll beat the shit out of you. Now get outta here, pussy."

"I hate you!" Steven snapped. He stomped up the steps. In an act of defiant retribution he flicked on the lights in the basement as he left, knowing it would piss off his brother to no end.

"Hey, turn those lights off!" his older brother screamed, but Steven was already out of the house and in the garage.

Once there he found his old Wal-Mart fishing pole then located and grabbed the small plastic tool box that held all his tackle. In the garage refrigerator was a Styrofoam cup with nightcrawlers and dirt and he snatched that, too. He kept up a steady stream of foul names for his brother, muttering under his breath and kicking anything that got in his way.

"I know what he is," he concluded morosely, "he's a dildo, that's what he is."

Honestly, Steven had no idea what a dildo was but had heard Tyler use the rather exotic sounding word last week. He had committed it to memory immediately. He liked the hard sounding Ds in it, and thought it sounded a lot like "dodo", a word he knew.

"Dildo, dildo, dildo," he repeated. When he had his gear together he stuck his head back in the door and yelled to his mom. "Mom, I'm going fishing down at the fishing spot at the river!"

A muffled voice from upstairs drifted down, "Okay, but be home in two hours for dinner."

"Okay!"

He let the screen door slam behind him and trotted through his back yard, past the old wooden swing set and into the woods on the familiar path. The well-worn trail snaked through the woods around stumps and fallen trees, the ground beaten down to hard-packed dirt from thousands of Nike and Adidas sneakers. The woods themselves were bright and airy this time of the afternoon, with plenty of sunlight streaming through the leaves far overhead. Steven thought it looked like some natural chapel, like at that church camp he went to for a week each summer, what with the branches high overhead making a kind of vaulted ceiling. A few birds flew from branch to branch and a startled squirrel corkscrewed up a nearby tree. He loved spending time in here, and wished his dildo brother would hang out here with him instead of living in the basement playing those stupid games.

It was a short walk, and when he arrived he had to carefully navigate down the steep, crumbly bank to the river's edge. The Stillwater was low this time of year so he was able to stand quite comfortably on the five foot spit of dried mud that jutted out like a natural pier. Thirty feet to his left, down river, were the skeletal remains of a huge oak tree that had come crashing down during some storm a few years back. Its leaves and most of its bark were long gone, the wood bleached a bright white by the sun and elements. Only the larger branches remained. Steven opened his tackle box, grabbed a random hook, and fumbled a bit tying it on the line. He only stabbed himself once.

"Ouch!" he hissed, sucking on the wounded finger.

He plucked a nightcrawler from the Styrofoam bait container and stuck the hook through it three times, like his dad had shown him. He felt bad for the worm as it writhed on the hook, but he tried to ignore that and slid a bobber on the line. Ready to go he cast out into the river, the worm and bobber spinning crazily in opposite directions. It plopped into the brown water about fifteen feet in front of him, the river's current steadily pushing the red and white bobber to his left. Steven wanted to get it close to the downed oak tree since he knew from experience that small-mouth bass liked to hang around down there. How cool would it be to catch a great big bass by himself! Yeah, Tyler'd be pissed he wasn't here then, he groused. Serve that dildo right…

The bobber drifted towards the tree and Steven let out more line, his eyes locked on the red top of the plastic globe. The Stillwater was living up to its name today, the current smooth and even, moving lazily along as if it had nowhere to be and was content with this gentle pace. Steven had been to the top of the bank before when the river was mad, after a storm or during a thaw, and knew how big and strong it could be. He respected it during those times, was scared of it, actually. He remembered hearing a story of a little kid that fell in a long time ago, and before anyone could figure out what to do he was half a mile away and drowned, dead as a doornail. But that was an angry river that killed that kid, not this peaceful one.

Just then, when his thoughts were elsewhere, the bobber jumped once, twice. Steven was so shocked he reflexively jerked the pole upwards hard. Had he not hooked something the worm would have flown back over his head like a whip. But he did have something, something large.

"Oh, man, it's a big one!" His heart was pounding in his chest.

He tried to reel whatever it was toward him. At first it didn't move and he was certain he'd simply snagged an underwater branch or something. Determined, he pulled harder, the little Wal-Mart pole bending almost in a U.

Then he stumbled backwards as whatever it was came loose and inched toward him. He frantically wound the reel to take up the slack, then bent the pole again and wound in some more line. He did this half a dozen times until the bobber was near the water's edge. He grabbed his little net and splashed into the river to collect his prize, only to see that it wasn't a fish at all.

"Oh, man, it's just some skanky old boot. Dang it."

He reached down and picked up his catch. The boot was covered in algae and filled with foul-smelling mud. The nylon shoestrings were still tied in a bow. The leather and rubber sole were starting to separate. In disgust he tried to get his hook out of the rotting leather. He tipped it upside down. Water and some oddly-shaped gray sticks or rocks tumbled out in a sloppy pile at his feet. Curious, he looked closely at the objects, picking up several larger ones. He peered at them from different angles, holding them up to his eyes. Suddenly he realized they weren't sticks at all. They were bones, little bones, some with bits of what looked like rotten meat still attached in places. He didn't know it, but the ones he held happened to be a first metatarsal and a talus.

Steven threw it all down as if they were electrified. He wiped his hands on his pants frantically and stumbled backwards. When it came, his scream, high-pitched and piercing, flushed out birds all up and down the river. The original Steven Tyler would have been proud of that scream. He scrambled madly up the bank and sprinted home, still wiping his hands on his pants as he ran.

Marcus' heart leapt. He couldn't believe it! This was wonderful news.

"Are you sure? How is he? Where is he?" The words tumbled from his mouth in a single run-on sentence. Marcus didn't realize it but he had begun pacing back and forth nervously, only the short telephone line holding him back like a leash.

"Schmidt, hold on. It's not like that," Doncaster warned. The tone of his voice made Marcus stop so fast his shoe squeaked on the tile floor. The hair on the back of his neck bristled.

"What? What do you mean? Where's Rolland?"

The cop told him then. He told him about the young boy who had found the boot, and how on a hunch he had had the DNA analyzed and compared to tissue samples taken from one of the times his brother had been jailed in Wayne. They had no crime lab but he had sent the samples off to Cincinnati to be tested. The match had been perfect and conclusive. He and a forensic team from Dayton had gone to the fishing spot and had retrieved more human remains from around the fallen oak tree. The remains included a pelvis, a partial ribcage, and a skull, minus the lower jawbone. All the DNA matched.

"I'm sorry, Schmidt," he said, and actually sounded sorry. "I'm afraid your brother is dead."

Marcus barely heard that last sentence. The phone slipped numbly from his limp hand and banged loudly on the tile floor.

"Dr. Schmidt?" Marilyn asked. "What's wrong?"

Marcus waved her off and walked out of the office, past his classroom and out of the building. He was oblivious to pedestrians and traffic as he stumbled down the sidewalk in a daze. He bumped into several people as he walked. After he had wandered blindly for a block a hand settled on his shoulder. It was Tony Barsalo.

"Hey, what's going on? You're pale as a ghost, man," his friend said.

Marcus turned to him, his face blank, empty. "Rolland's dead. My brother is dead."

Tony's square face sank at the news. "Oh, man, I'm so sorry."

They started walking again, mainly because Marcus felt that he had to be doing something, anything, and walking was the least objectionable action. Tony only came up to his shoulder and had to press himself to keep up with

Marcus' longer legs. They continued on in silence, the seemingly eternally bright San Diego sun hot on their necks. After they had gone on two more blocks Tony broke the heavy silence.

"What happened?"

After several minutes Marcus relayed the information Doncaster had given him. He said it in a flat monotone, as if he were describing something mundane, a weather forecast or assembly instructions for a bicycle. Tony listened without interruption until Marcus was done.

"It's not your fault, man," he said softly. "I know you think it is, but it's not. Rolland knew what he was getting into."

Marcus shook his head. "No, that's the thing. He probably didn't, not really. He wouldn't have looked at the big picture, wouldn't have realized how this could have gone down. He was too trusting, too naïve. I guess in the end he finally figured out how bad it all was and tried to get away, but by then it was too late." He sighed, a shaky sound. They were passing a metal newspaper box on the corner and Marcus suddenly lashed out with his fist. A huge dent appeared in the box and several people on the sidewalk jumped at the noise, staring at him in shock. "I should have been there! I should have been there and I wasn't!"

Tears started flowing down Marcus' face, huge tears, running freely and soaking his suddenly red cheeks and staining his shirt. More people were staring at them now but Marcus didn't notice. For all he knew or cared he was alone in the world, isolated, cut off from everyone. He leaned back against the wall of a college bookstore and sobbed, Tony standing next to him. Tears continued to flow. His chest heaved as his guilt threatened to flatten him completely.

Several minutes passed before Marcus began to regain his normal composure. He remained leaning against the wall until his breathing evened out. He wiped at his face and exhaled deeply. His breath rattled in his chest like a machine gun.

"I guess," he began, "I guess I knew all along that he was dead. I mean, he's been missing for what, five or six months now? If he was still alive there would have been some news, some contact. I guess I knew and just didn't want to admit it."

He pushed himself off the wall and looked up, momentarily uncertain where he was. He glanced at his hand curiously and saw his knuckles were scraped and bloody. When he spoke again his voice was detached.

"Guess I need to make some arrangements, don't I?" he asked. "I'm supposed to be the responsible one. That's what a responsible brother would do, isn't it?"

Tony nodded gently. "Yeah, you do. Come on, let's go back to your office and make some phone calls. I'll tell Marilyn to get someone to cover your classes for a while, okay?"

In Marcus' tiny office he sat heavily in his chair, the one covered with a Mexican *sarape*, a present from a student who had traveled to South America a few years back. On the walls were posters of ruins from around Central and South America. His desk was organized and neat, much tidier than those of his colleagues. An obsidian jaguar, its shiny black surface reflecting the fluorescent overhead light like a dark gem, sat on the corner of his desk, forever poised to attack. Marcus took out a small pad of paper and began making notes, people to call, next steps to take. Suddenly his hand froze. He stared wide-eyed at Tony.

"I just thought of something. Now I have to call my father. Ah, shit."

Chapter 30

The funeral service at the cemetery outside of Wayne was a small, private affair. The twenty or so mourners in attendance gathered under a green and white striped canopy. The weather was dank and misty, suitable for a funeral service, with heavy, low clouds that were tangled in the tree tops. The thin rain hung suspended in the air like a transparent fog that left a thick layer of dewy mist over everything, including the black metal and brass casket containing Rolland's remains. The striped canopy itself collected enough water that periodically a heavy trickle ran down and puddled on the trampled grass. The casket was suspended by thick nylon straps over a neat, sharp-edged six foot deep hole. A bouquet of red and white flowers adorned the lid. Wooden folding chairs were lined up, four rows of five chairs.

Marcus sat in the front row, at the far right, Cassie immediately next to him on the left. There were two empty seats separating them and the one at the end. That was occupied by a square, older man with thick gray hair. His cheeks were run through with spider webs of blue and red veins and his nose was thick with skin that was rough and bumpy, like cooked bacon. He had been a large, powerful man at one time, that much was easy to see, but now he appeared small and defeated, his shoulders worn down and slumped. He wouldn't or couldn't meet anyone's gaze. He held a rumpled black felt hat in his hands and kneaded it mercilessly, as if he were wringing every last drop of water out of a washcloth.

It was the first time in years that Marcus had seen his father. Time and the man's own guilt had not been kind to him.

Behind Marcus sat Otto and Jenna along with Santiago and his Aunt Mary. His cousin had been warm and welcoming with both Marcus and Cassie, much to Marcus' relief, hugging them and passing along his heartfelt condolences. Mary looked stunning in an obviously expensive black dress and veil. But the veil was a barrier between them and she maintained a distinct distance at all times, refusing to look his way, staring instead at the casket. Santiago insisted that she would come around in time, but Marcus wasn't so sure.

In the third row were seated other friends of his brother, plus one very unexpected guest. Agent Roberto Cruzado, his young round face full of sympathy for their loss, sat quietly with his hands in his lap. His black hair, glistening with mist, was as shiny as the obsidian jaguar on Marcus' desk. Just before the service he had motioned Marcus aside to pass along more information, his eyes darting to both Santiago and Mary as they had taken their seats. Even this far away from Mexico he was uncomfortable showing his face in public. He pulled Marcus slightly away from the crowd.

"It turns out your Uncle," he had begun saying quietly, other mourners milling around out of earshot, "was really little more than a mid-level bureaucrat in El Grúpo. That's why he always managed to, as you say, fly beneath our radar. He had access to a significant amount of information and data but he himself had little to do with actual day to day dealings. I guess you could call him a regional manager of sorts. Perhaps a glorified paper shuffler?"

"That's it?"

Cruzado nodded, still staring hard at Santiago. "Well, a paper shuffler with high aspirations. As he told you he saw the leadership of El Grúpo unable to effectively move against Los Hermanos. He had access to records showing past and present employees, routes, growers, everything he needed to be able to make a move himself. But he had to continue to do his job so no one would suspect him. He was playing a very dangerous game, my friend, one that would have meant the death of many people, innocent or not, had he been successful."

"Where is he now?"

Cruzado tilted his head in thought before answering. "Let's just say he is safe in our custody as we continue to gather additional information. We've already made dozens of arrests and have some very influential people under lock and key, some from within our government. Your uncle will likely do time in jail but the more he cooperates the less time he'll spend there. Also, Los Hermanos don't know exactly what is happening, so for the moment they have backed off, too. Merida and the rest of the Yucatan are uncharacteristically quiet right now. It is a wonderful, delightful change of pace. Thank you for your help. The country and I am in your debt."

Marcus looked toward Mary and Santiago. "What about them? What's going to happen to them?"

Cruzado followed his gaze. "I can't say. Your aunt is not under suspicion, but your cousin is a different matter. I'm not completely certain he is innocent in this. We will continue keeping a keen eye on him."

"He's not involved in any of this," Marcus insisted. "He worked to save me several times. Please leave him alone."

Cruzado grunted. "I can't promise that."

"Then do me a favor and move him to the bottom of your list, okay?"

The agent grunted again, but after several seconds nodded his assent.

"Thanks."

Back in the present the minister came to stand in front of the casket. He began the service but Marcus wasn't listening, tuning him out. He was still shocked to see his father, to see the shrunken, contrite man he had become. The weight of his own guilt must be nothing compared to what was crushing his father. The man had abandoned everything and everyone, had put in motion a series of events that had ultimately led to the death of his youngest son. A parent should never, ever outlive a child. He wanted to feel sorry for him, to feel anything but disdain for the man, but he couldn't. Cassie rested her hand on his arm. They had talked on the phone a lot in the last few days as she helped him through all this. He would never forget that. Marcus turned his attention back to the casket, water now running freely from its shiny flanks like tears.

The presiding minister was from the local Lutheran church in town and hadn't known Rolland. Of necessity the eulogy was generic, commonplace. He spoke for several minutes and quoted two or three standard scriptures. The final quote was the popular *Ashes to ashes, dust to dust*, a verse loosely based on Genesis 3:19. There followed a brief benediction and suddenly the service was over. It couldn't have lasted ten minutes.

Wham, bam, thank you, ma'am, Marcus thought in honor of his brother. The lyrics from the David Bowie song seemed appropriate.

The mourners stood and filed past the casket, paying their final respects to the dead and passing their sorrows on to the family. Marcus almost envied his brother then, thinking that perhaps the dead had it much easier than the living. Rolland's part in this life was over but now the survivors had to figure out how to continue, slogging through with the knowledge of what they had done, or worse, had not done. His guilt continued to drag him down like an anchor, but time does heal most wounds, albeit slowly, so very slowly. Perhaps that anchor wouldn't weigh so heavily on him later on. He desperately hoped so.

He was still in his seat as his aunt and cousin stepped in front of the casket. She placed her hand on the shiny wet metal and murmured a silent prayer. She was sobbing softly as she walked away, her hand print clearly visible on the casket's damp flank.

When the last of the mourners had gone only Marcus, Cassie and his father were left under the canopy. The three stood there in silence, the sound of the rain tapping on the canvas top broken by the murmured conversations as the rest of the mourners slowly made their way back to their cars and their lives. Cassie caught Marcus' eye and not so discreetly motioned to where his father stood, still working his hat in his hands. She gave his arm a firm tug.

"Family's important," she reminded him. "No matter who they are or what they've done."

He resisted still, the memory of his father's actions forever bright in his mind. She gave another tug, this time so strong it almost made him stumble. After a moment of stubborn refusal he stepped toward his father.

"Dad," he said.

As his father lifted his head Marcus felt an involuntary wave of pity wash over him. The man's eyes were red and watery, his cheeks sunken. He had an air of defeat and despair about him. His face was white and heavily wrinkled, like an alabaster bust struck with a hammer and marred with thick, jagged cracks. He tried to talk but no words came out, his mouth opening and closing silently. He held his hands out toward the casket and started to cry, wracking sobs that shook his once-broad and powerful shoulders. Slowly Marcus took three steps toward him and gave him a brief hug, then released him and walked away, not looking back, leaving him to his despair. Cassie walked next to Marcus.

"It's a start," she whispered.

On the way to the parking lot Doncaster stood in full dress uniform, waiting for them. The neck brace was off but he still held his one arm at an odd angle as if it bothered him. It would never be the same and would always cause him problems, especially as he got older. Wintertime would be the worst.

"Sorry about your brother," he said, intentionally not making eye contact with Cassie.

"Thanks. And thanks for your help, such as it was."

Doncaster nodded. "Yeah, such as it was. Just doing my job. By the way, your big Mexican, Gonzalez? He apparently recovered enough to get up and slip past his guard. He's nowhere to be found. The ATF is still looking for Andy

Saunders. They are very interested in talking to him." He handed him an envelope. "Don't forget this." He turned and walked stiffly to his parked cruiser, the thick neck still flushed red. In the parking lot Marcus could see Otto and Jenna walking arm in arm toward her old Ford Explorer. It warmed him to see the two of them together, so innocent and obviously in love. They would make it work, he thought. Somehow, even as different as they were, they would make it work. Mrs. Kerr was slowly tottering along next to them. She was finally out of the robe and into a black dress that hadn't seen daylight since her husband's death. Jenna and Otto were set to drive her back home. He could tell that, despite the circumstances, she was happy to be outside with other people for once.

Marcus opened the envelope and took out a red piece of paper. He read it over and his hands dropped to his sides in disgust.

"I don't believe it. That son of a bitch still wants me to pay that parking ticket," he growled. "The one I got my first week here. I'll be damned."

Despite herself Cassie smothered a small laugh. Marcus stuffed the parking ticket in his pocket and tossed the crumpled envelope in the trash. He shook his head in dismay, starting to laugh as well.

"I'll be damned," he repeated.

They began walking back towards her old station wagon. Rolland was gone forever, but somehow Marcus knew that he and Cassie were okay, that Rolland would give them his blessing. They both keenly felt his brother's silent approval.

"You okay with us?" she asked.

He nodded, looking down at her. "Yeah, I guess I am. Even more important I think Rolland's okay with us. Just a feeling that I have. I don't know how to explain it."

"Then don't," she said softly. "Just accept it."

They continued walking. Halfway to the parking lot they slowly, tentatively, found each other's hands. They fit together perfectly, as they had always known they would. They walked hand in hand to the car and drove slowly away, the cemetery behind them.

A preview of **Fever**, the new novel from **David Kettlehake**, due in 2014

Alyssa Morris had been a flight attendant for so long she still thought of herself as a stewardess. She was old enough that she could retire reasonably well on the balance of her pension and Social Security, but she was one of those rare individuals that truly liked what she did for a living. While for the most part Alyssa enjoyed the people she met, she deeply loved the opportunities she'd had to travel around the world. Had she chosen to cover her suitcase with stickers from all the cities and countries she'd visited, like they once did to steamer trunks in days gone by, it would've been plastered over a score of times. She took the St. Augustine quote about travel very seriously: *The world is a book, and those that do not travel read only one page.* Alyssa Morris had read volumes.

Delta Airlines flight number 1032 had originated in Brasilia, Brazil, refueled in Atlanta, and was now on its final approach into Louisville International Airport. The Boeing 737-NG already had its gear locked and she could sense the big bird hunkering down for a landing. She took her seat outside the cockpit near the galley and strapped herself in. As she did so she peered down the aisle, through first class and into coach. *Tsk, tsk.* The grumpy business passenger in C-13 still had his tray down, a definite no-no. Alyssa picked up the handset and thumbed the PA.

"Please remember, as we begin our final descent into Louisville all tray tables must be locked and all seatbacks should be in their upright positions." She intentionally stared at the passenger in C-13. He must have felt her eyes boring holes into him because with a huff he acquiesced and latched the tray. Good.

She leaned back and relaxed. It had been a long day. She had deadheaded from Brazil to Atlanta due to a scheduling snafu, and after they landed and refueled in Louisville she would be flying right back to Atlanta. That was fine. Her granddaughter's first birthday was tomorrow and she wouldn't miss that for the world.

As she felt the even thrumming of the engines and the wind whipping past the fuselage she noticed a slight tremor rumble through the plane. It wasn't much, just a shudder that she wrote off as turbulence and so was insignificant the passengers didn't even notice. Then it happened again, only this time it was more sustained and followed by a very unexpected, jerky banking to port of several degrees. She frowned, staring at the locked and reinforced cockpit door. To be honest she had never liked having the cockpit secured from the inside, since in the past she could have simply slid the curtain aside and asked the pilot if everything was okay. Now she was as blind as the passengers and at the mercy of her only connection to the captain and first officer, the intercom. She hated bothering them during takeoff and landing since that was the most difficult and dangerous part of the flight, so she put her hands in her lap and resisted this time, too. She told herself everything was fine. The corduroy-like fabric of the wall behind her snagged at her short blond hair as she leaned against it.

Then suddenly the plane lurched, that was the only way she could describe it. It lurched then banked even harder to port and the nose tipped down so quickly she felt her stomach flip-flop at the abrupt loss of altitude. Okay, *that* was wrong. This should not be happening at this stage of the landing. She grabbed the intercom and rang the cockpit.

"Guys, everything okay up there?" she asked in a strained voice, her right hand shielding her mouth from view. Several peoplc in first class were craning their necks to look at her. Alyssa's years of training forced her to keep a calm exterior in front of the passengers, but inside her heart was thumping in her chest like she'd just narrowly avoided a car accident. "Talk to me, sirs. Passengers are getting nervous out here." She waited several seconds for a reply but heard nothing. The big bird shuddered again, this time so violently she cracked the back of her head on the bulkhead hard enough to make her wince. One of her co-workers, Lucy, was strapped in at the tail end of the plane. The intercom next to her chimed.

"Lyssa, what's going on?" Lucy asked in a tight, strained voice. She was quite a bit younger and obviously terrified. "What's happening?"

"I don't know. I'm trying to ring the cockpit but no one is answering. Stay strapped in," she ordered. Alyssa hung up and frantically tried to contact the pilot or first officer again but neither would answer. She clicked on the PA system.

"Ladies and gentlemen, please remain buckled in. There's nothing to worry about, we're just encountering some turbulence. Everything is under control." That was a big fat lie and she knew it. Something was most definitely wrong. She decided to screw standard landing protocol and tried to unbuckle her seatbelt. Her hands were shaking so hard she couldn't grasp the latch, the irony not lost on her that she'd demonstrated this simple act about a million times before. Finally the buckle popped open and she stumbled to the locked door. The plane was listing far enough to port that standing was difficult even for someone with as many air miles logged as her. She knocked hard on the door with an open palm. Her traditionally calm composure was slipping away as if on ice.

"Sirs? Everything alright in there? Sirs?"

Suddenly the door crashed open. She jumped back in surprise and nearly tripped over her own feet. Jack Galardi, the first officer, was on his hands and knees between the two seats. His face and bald head were as bright red as a stop light and he was swaying back and forth like a toddler. His hand fell from the doorknob and he tumbled over onto his side in the cramped space, shaking violently, shivering as if he'd just been pulled from freezing water. Alyssa's eyes jumped to the pilot, Eric Handler. His round face was bright red, too, but his hands were on the yoke and they quivered as if he were trying to lift the plane barehanded. She caught a brief glimpse of his face, a profile only. The one eye she could see was huge and his teeth were gritted, spittle running down his chin. He looked paralyzed and unable to control himself. Then she stole a glance out the windshield and gasped.

Oh my God. All she could see was green, the green of grass. The ground was coming toward them, incredibly fast. *Shit!*

She turned and sprinted toward the back of the plane as if she could run away from the impending impact. She bounced between the seats and horrified passengers, frantic to put distance between herself and the nose of the plane.

"Crash positions!" she yelled so loudly it ripped at her throat. "Assume crash positions! Heads down, between your knees! *Now!*"

The passenger compartment erupted in panicked, horrified screams. Alyssa stumbled once and fell but shot to her feet without slowing. The passenger in C-13 grabbed at her but she knocked his hands away as she continued her manic, uphill sprint. If she could just get to the back of the plane! The instinct to flee was overwhelming, blinding. The 737 was shaking like it was caught in a mixer and worse yet it was still listing farther to port. The terrified passengers on the starboard side were actually looking down at the people at the other end of their row. The engines were beginning to scream. There were only seconds left...

She breathlessly arrived at the stern and realized with a bemused start that there was nowhere else to go. Alyssa spun around like a cornered cat, then without hesitation jumped into the open door of the restroom. She twisted around and slammed the lock home then fell to her knees and wrapped her arms over her head in a position she remembered practicing in elementary school, back when she was just a young girl and they'd had bomb drills as often as fire drills. Alyssa had never been very devout but now seemed like an excellent time to convert.

"Oh God oh God oh God…"

When the big 737 hit it felt like God Himself had punched her in retribution. She slammed face-first into the wall of the bathroom and felt something in her cheek crunch. Tumbling out of control she smacked the back of her head on something while several bones in her arm snapped like deadwood as she tried to protect herself. For a moment she found herself oddly weightless, floating, all sounds muted and distant, as if the horrifying tableau had been captured in a high-definition photograph, and Alyssa scrunched up her face and began to mouth a scream. Then reality rushed back and she was upside down and twisting, banging into the ceiling, the air knocked forcefully from her lungs as several ribs broke. She crashed limply back to the floor as the plane continued to roll. As she thudded to a landing she cracked her head on the stainless steel toilet and saw an explosion of stars and white light. Blood, unnaturally bright in the flickering lights of the tiny compartment, spattered against the gray walls like a glass of port wine recklessly flung around. She heard a tremendous roaring boom and the horrid sound of tortured metal shredding as if the plane were being flown into a garbage disposal.

Then the outside bulkhead imploded and smashed into her and everything went as black as if the sun itself had been snuffed out.

Fever

CPSIA information can be obtained at www.ICGtesting.com
Printed in the USA
BVOW05s1523150416

R6929500001B/R69295PG443601BVX16B/7/P

9 781494 860080